INTO THE
MUMMY'S TOMB

INTO THE MUMMY'S TOMB

EDITED BY

JOHN RICHARD STEPHENS

BERKLEY BOOKS, NEW YORK

B

A Berkley Book
Published by The Berkley Publishing Group
A division of Penguin Putnam Inc.
375 Hudson Street
New York, New York 10014

Copyright © 2001 by John Richard Stephens
Text design by Tiffany Kukec
Cover design by Judith Murello
Cover art by Danilo Ducak

A full acknowledgments of credits and permissions can be found on pages 351–52.

PRINTING HISTORY
Berkley trade paperback edition / April 2001

The Penguin Putnam Inc. World Wide Web site address is
http://www.penguinputnam.com

Library of Congress Cataloging-in-Publication Data
Into the mummy's tomb / edited by John Richard Stephens.—Berkley trade pbk. ed.
        p.   cm.
ISBN 0-425-17664-9
1. Horror tales, English.   2. Horror tales, American.   3. Archaeologists—Fiction.
4. Mummies—Fiction.   5. Egypt—Fiction.   I. Stephens, John Richard.

PR1309.H6 I58   2001
823'.0873808—dc21   00-065128

PRINTED IN THE UNITED STATES OF AMERICA

10   9   8   7   6   5   4   3   2   1

John Richard Stephens would like to thank Theresa Quintanilla; Martha and Jim Goodwin; Scott Stephens; Marty Goeller; Joyce Whiteaker; Terity, Natasha, and Debbie Burbach; Branden, Alisha, and Kathy Hill; Jeff and Carol Whiteaker; Doug, Michelle, and Christopher Whiteaker; Bill and Norene Hilden; Monte and Joanne Goeller; Doug and Shirley Strong; Frank, Marybeth, Leah, and Clare DiVito; Dr. Beth Hart; Stan and Barbara Main; Tim Cissna; Cheryl Cohen; Joe and Irma Rodriguez; Beth Bailey; Les Benedict; Sarah Collins; Dr. Rich Sutton; Kim Smith; Kim Walker; Gary Bain and Frances Lanier; Carl Chafin; Arthur Tress; Janet Bord; Trudy Lynn; Christine Randall; and his agent, Charlotte Cecil Raymond.

CONTENTS

INTO THE
MUMMY'S TOMB

Introduction

THE TRUTH OF THE MUMMY'S CURSE

John Richard Stephens

WHY MAKE MUMMIES?

Perhaps no other people have devoted as much time and attention to the funereal arts as the Ancient Egyptians. Their care and attention to detail in preparing a corpse for mummification seems strange to us. Today we either quickly cremate a body or go through the motions of trying to preserve it with the use of embalming fluids, but the result is a pale imitation of what the Ancient Egyptians accomplished. They wanted the body to last for eternity, and often, for those who could afford to pay for the more expensive treatment, the mummification process took upward of three months. The result was that some mummies appear much the same today as they did when they were interred three or four thousand years ago. While today we do have the knowledge to preserve a body in its lifelike state, this is generally only used in special cases—like Lenin, Mao, Ferdinand Marcos, and Evita Perón.

The Egyptians had a profound fear of decomposition after death because they believed there could be no afterlife without the body. The process of mummification was actually supposed to raise the person from the dead, just as it supposedly had for Osiris, the ruler of the dead and one of the most important Ancient Egyptian gods. Part of the resurrection process consisted of a ceremony called "Opening of the Mouth," which was performed at the end of the mummification process. This was supposed to restore the body's ability to see, hear, eat, speak, and walk. The Egyptians used a similar magical ceremony to animate the statues of their gods. Amulets were used to stimulate the functions of the spine, heart, and blood.

This practice lasted for almost three and a half millennia—from about 3000 B.C. to A.D. 500. Literally millions of people were made into mummies. Some historians estimate that 730 million corpses were mummified during that time period. Tombs and caves were so packed with mummies that the Egyptians ran out of places to put them. Many bodies were just taken to the desert and buried in the sand. Because of the dry climate, virtually every body was preserved, whether it was embalmed or not.

OKAY, SO WHAT ARE THEY GOOD FOR?

The Egyptians would have been horrified if they knew what eventually happened to most of the mummies. Many were ground up for medicine, and for centuries mummy powder was one of the most popular remedies in Europe—even more so than aspirin is today. It was smeared on as an ingredient in ointments, or mixed into food and tea and eaten. Other mummies were ground up for fertilizer. Still more were used as locomotive fuel during the late nineteenth century, since mummies were then more common in Egypt than wood or coal. On his trip through Egypt, Mark Twain said he heard an engineer call out, "Damn these plebeians, they don't burn worth a cent! Pass out a king!"

Mummies were once so plentiful they were sold by the ton or by the graveyard. The Egyptians even used them to thatch the roofs of their houses. The wood from the coffins was used as firewood to cook on, and some Italian homes are paneled with such coffin wood. Renaissance painters sometimes mixed mummy powder into their paints, believing it would help keep their colors bright. And then during the 1860s, American and Canadian companies bought shiploads of mummies and used their linen wrappings to make wrapping paper. Bits of mummy were even used as fish bait.

Hundreds of thousands more mummies were lost underwater when the Aswan Dam was built. And the mummies were not only people; the Ancient Egyptians of the later periods also mummified all sorts of animals—from cows and crocodiles to scorpions and insects.

CURSES!

When most people think of mummies, one of the first things that comes to mind is the mummy's curse. It's said the belief in the curse dates back to when the Arabs invaded Egypt in A.D. 641. Even though they couldn't read the hieroglyphics in the tombs and on the ancient monuments, they were convinced the Ancient Egyptians had strong magical powers and they concluded that such people would not leave their treasure-filled tombs unprotected. The Arabs were sure the dead would do everything in their power to seek revenge on those who violated their eternal resting places. Reinforcing this belief were the paintings on the walls showing the mummies being resurrected by the Opening of the Mouth ceremony. Finding pictures of a reanimated mummy can be rather unnerving when you're violating its tomb.

The earliest known fictional short story about a mummy's curse was published in 1699, and they have continued to appear ever since. The first major news story about the curse hit the papers sometime around the turn of the century. As the story goes, one day in the 1880s, as a form of amusement, a young gentleman of means named Douglas Murray went to a well-known palm reader and mystic called Cheiro, whose real name was Louis Hamon. Cheiro was shocked when he saw the young man's hand, and told him a gun would explode and cause his arm to have to be amputated. He said, "Your hand, sir, seems to be calling to me to try and save it from this impending disaster." He also said that Murray would win an Egyptian mummy case in a lottery and that this would be followed by a series of misfortunes, both to him and anyone else who had anything to do with the case. Murray laughed it off and departed, forgetting all about the incident, though Cheiro didn't.

A year or so later, Murray went to Egypt. While in Cairo, his dragoman—or guide—told him of a beautiful mummy case that was for sale which had belonged to a priestess of the Temple of Amen-Ra who had died in Thebes in about 1600 B.C. The mummy was gone, but her beautiful image was painted on the lid. Even though he had a strong aversion to it, Murray decided to buy the case anyway. It was taken back to his hotel, where two of his friends greatly admired it. Eventually they decided to draw lots for it and Murray won three out of three, so he packed it up and shipped it off to England.

A few days later he was up the Nile shooting when a gun exploded in his hand. By the time he got back to Cairo, gangrene had set in and the arm was amputated just above the elbow. Then on the voyage back to England, both of his friends got sick and died.

When he arrived home, he found the unpacked mummy case in his hallway. Later he said, "If such a thing could be, as I looked at the carved face of the priestess on the outside of the mummy case her eyes seemed to come to life, and I saw such a look of hate in them that my very blood seemed to turn to ice."

Convinced that this was the cause of his troubles, he allowed a well-known literary woman to talk him into giving the mummy case to her. After she brought it to her home, her mother fell down a flight of stairs and eventually died, her fiancé broke off their engagement, all her pets became ill and had to be put down, and she herself became seriously ill. The case was returned to Murray.

He decided to sell the thing, so he sent it to a photography studio to have a picture taken for the advertisements. The following week the photographer told him that one of the pictures strangely showed the malevolent face of a real Egyptian woman. The photographer died soon after that from an overdose of sleeping medication and apparently he had destroyed the picture. Anyone who later tried to draw or photograph the case also suffered serious injuries or committed suicide.

After deciding that selling the case would just endanger someone else, Murray donated it to the British Museum. This was followed by several more deaths—bringing the total to thirteen—and odd things began to happen in the museum's Egyptian section. One night the doorman said he saw a figure suddenly sit up in the bottom half of the case and glide toward him. He said it had a glowing, wrinkled, yellowish green face that resembled a sheep's bladder. He fled but it chased him, and when he thought it was about to push him through a trapdoor, he lunged at it in an attempt to push it out of the way, but it vanished just before he touched it.

The museum withdrew the case from exhibition. Rumor had it that it was quietly sold to a museum in New York and was being shipped there on the *Titanic* when it sank, but the British Museum eventually put it back on display and strange things began to happen again.

That is, until two psychics named Wyeth and Neal performed something of an exorcism in 1921. They claimed the priestess was a "Looking Maid," which meant she could see what was happening far away by looking into a silver cup, and that she lived during an evil period when dead bodies were used in the temples for black magic rites. When she, the priest of Amen-Ra, and his assistant died, their bodies were protected by very powerful curses that involved enslaving the spirit of someone as each of them died, such as a tortured slave, and attaching it to the lid of the mummy case. They said this "thing" would blindly strike out when any violation of the tomb was threatened.

There were no more problems following the exorcism, though Douglas Murray died at about that same time.

That's the story anyway. I'll discuss it more in a bit. But first, let's look at the other famous mummy curse story.

THE EVIL CURSE OF KING TUT

The pharaohs' curse made international headlines again in 1923, less than six months after the opening of Tutankhamen's tomb. Lord Carnarvon, who financed the excavation, had died suddenly after being bitten by a mosquito. Some papers reported that all the lights in Cairo went out at the moment he passed away, while back in England his favorite fox terrier, Susie, began to howl inconsolably. It's said the dog then sat up and fell over dead.

Legend also has it that when Lord Carnarvon first entered the tomb a worker was overheard stating "He will be dead in six weeks," which turned out to be true. (Actually it was closer to seven weeks, but let's not get picky here.)

Oddly enough, when Tutankhamen's coffin was opened and the mummy unwrapped, it was discovered that the boy king had a depression on his left cheek and that there was a corresponding irregularity on the famous gold mask that had covered the mummy's head, both of which were in the same spot where Lord Carnarvon was bitten by the mosquito. A few people insisted that it wasn't a mosquito bite that had done him in, but rather pricking his finger on a spear in the tomb.

Carnarvon was just the first to go. Here is an unconfirmed list of the other victims:

2. Lord Carnarvon's wife, Lady Elizabeth, allegedly also died from an insect bite in 1929.

3. Colonel Aubrey Herbert, who was Lord Carnarvon's younger half-brother, died in 1923 during a fit of temporary insanity following a visit to the tomb.

4. Archaeologist Arthur C. Mace, of the Metropolitan Museum of Art in New York, who helped open the tomb's entrance, complained of exhaustion and fell into a coma before dying in 1928.

5. Egyptologist Herbert E. Winlock, also of the Met, took part in the opening of the tomb's entrance and the burial chamber. He died in 1950.

6. Dr. Albert M. Lythgoe, curator of Egyptian antiquities for the Met, died of a mysterious ailment in 1934. He was present at the opening of the tomb's entrance.

7. Professor Foucrat also took part in the opening of the burial chamber.

8. Archaeologist Dr. Douglas Derry of the Egyptian Museum helped unwrap the mummy.

9. Garry Davies, an archaeologist with the Tut excavation.

10. Archaeologist Harkness, also with the Tut excavation.

11. Assistant Astor, who was present when the tomb's entrance was opened.

12. Dr. Jonathan W. Carver, who was an assistant to Howard Carter—the man who discovered King Tut's tomb—and was present when the entrance was opened.

13. A. R. Callender, who was Carter's right-hand man.

14. Sir Archibald Douglas Reid, an X-ray specialist, died shortly after signing an agreement to examine the mummy. Some say he was the first to cut the mummy's wrappings.

15. Frederick Raleigh, another X-ray specialist, died before reaching the tomb.

16. George Jay Gould, the son of an American financier, died in 1924 of pneumonia (or bubonic plague) after visiting the tomb.

17. British industrialist Joel Wool (or Woolf Joel) died after visiting the tomb. While sailing his yacht up the Nile, he was swept overboard and drowned in 1924.

18. Prince Ali Kemel Fahmy Bey was shot in London after visiting the tomb.

19. Georges Bénédite, director of Egyptian antiquities at the Louvre, died after a fall while visiting the tomb. (Some say he died two years later.)

20. M. Laffleur of McGill University in Canada died the day after visiting the tomb. He was a houseguest of Carter's.

21. Evelyn Greely, an American, committed suicide in Chicago after visiting the tomb.

22. Carter's secretary Richard Bethell was found dead of unknown causes slumped over a chair at the Mayfair Club in London in November 1929 (or was found in bed of circulatory collapse).

23. Lord Westbury, who was Richard Bethell's father, committed suicide by jumping off a building in February 1930. His son was his only connection with the tomb, but according to a Universal News Service report, he had been frequently heard muttering, "the curse of the pharaohs."

24. An anonymous eight-year-old boy was struck and killed by Lord Westbury's hearse on its way to the crematorium.

25. M. Cassanova of the Collège de France had excavated in the Valley of the Tombs and ended up dead.

26. Edgar Steel, a custodian from the British Museum's Egyptian antiquities department, died while being operated on in a London hospital.

27. H. G. Evelyn White, an Egyptologist at Leeds University, committed suicide in 1924 after discovering a secret room full of manuscripts in a Coptic monastery. In his suicide note he wrote, "I knew there was a curse on me, though I had leave to take those manuscripts to Cairo. The monks told me the curse would work all the same."

28. The daughter of the Egyptian director of antiquities Mohammed Ibrahim was critically injured in an auto accident a few days after he failed to block the first exhibition of Tutankhamen's treasures outside of Egypt, in 1966, even though he had strongly objected to it.

29. Mohammed Ibrahim then dreamt he would have a serious accident if he didn't block the exhibition in France, but French officials convinced him he was being superstitious so he backed down. He was struck by a car as he left his meeting with them and died two days later of a fractured skull—the same thing Tutankhamen is believed to have died from.

30. An anonymous person connected with an X-ray team circa 1968 died while they were X-raying the mummy; and the lights of Cairo went out, as they did when Lord Carnarvon died.

31. In 1969 the sole surviving member of the 1923 expedition, Richard Adamson—who had been a security guard for Lord Carnarvon—spoke out against the curse and within twenty-four hours his wife died.

32. Then in 1972, Mohammed Ibrahim's successor, Dr. Gamal Mehrez, died of circulatory collapse on the day Tut's golden mask and some of his treasures were packed up and flown to London for the fiftieth anniversary of the tomb's discovery.

It's said that thirteen of the twenty-six people involved in opening the tomb died prematurely. The number of deaths reported by 1929 ranges from eleven to twenty-two people, depending on who you believe, and some insist the total eventually went over three dozen. People involved with shipping the treasures to various exhibitions were still being added to the list as recently as the late 1970s. The number grows much larger if you include as part of the curse the claim that there was a severe outburst of the plague in Upper Egypt in 1924.

BUT THIS IS WHAT REALLY HAPPENED

Okay, back to the deadly mummy case. There are many versions of this tale and I have given just a very brief outline of one of the most elaborate ones. The stories vary considerably and often are full of historical errors and impossibilities. For example, some tell of how the famous spiritualist Madame Helena Blavatsky visited the mummy case after it was donated to the museum in the late 1890s, which would have been rather spectacular since she died in 1891. Others say the mummy was of a princess of the temple, but princesses aren't associated with temples in that way—priestesses are. Then there are those that describe Amen-Ra (or Amun-Ra or Ammon-Ra) as being a place associated with the "Cult of the Dead," when actually Amen-Ra is a god who is not associated with death. And some say Douglas Murray was with the British Foreign Office in Egypt and bought the case from an Egyptian in 1881, while others say he was an Egyptologist who bought it from an American in 1910, but none of this is correct.

In reality, the case was given to the British Museum by A. F. Wheeler in 1899. Actually, the case is not really a case at all; it's not even a lid—it's a wooden cover that was placed over the mummy and never had a bottom to it, though it is shaped like a lid. Apparently it dates from 1050 B.C., and according to the famous Egyptologist and keeper of the British Museum Sir E. A. Wallis Budge, it was made for the mummy of "a great lady, who was a Priestess of Amen, and was a member of the College of Amen-Ra at Thebes."

According to legend, the mummy (or cover) caused so much trouble that the museum pulled it from display and quietly sold it to a New York museum, which is how it ended up on the *Titanic*. In a 1934 article in the *London Sunday Times,* Sir Wallis Budge insisted that the only time the cover had been moved to the museum basement was during the air raids of World War I and that neither he, nor the trustees, could sell or give away anything in the museum—even duplicates—without a special act of Parliament.

The British Museum has repeatedly denied that anything unusual has happened concerning any of its mummies, and this cover in particular. Sir Wallis Budge said, "As a matter of fact, no mummy which did things of this kind was ever in the British Museum, and there is none of its kind in it at the present time. The whole story, or let us say 'cycle of stories,' rests on a series of misunderstandings by the late Mr. Douglas Murray and the late Mr. W. T. Stead."

Little is known of Murray, but William Thomas Stead was a very well-known journalist who gained notoriety by writing about white slavery. Later he was known as a psychic and founded a journal on psychic studies called *Borderland*. He was also the author of such books as *Real Ghost Stories* and *How I Know That the Dead Return,* and was also involved with Christian organizations like the Salvation Army.

Sir Wallis Budge explained that Murray and Stead told him they knew of a mummy that had been brought to England by a lady who put it in her drawing room. The next morning it was found that everything breakable in the room had been smashed. The same thing then happened when it was moved to another room. It was then locked in a cupboard, and all sorts of racket ensued, sounding like troops of entities marching about smashing stuff and shaking the staircase, and strange lights were seen. The next day all the servants resigned.

It was about this time that Wheeler presented the mummy cover to the museum. After it was placed on exhibition, Murray, Stead, and some others looked it over and declared that "the expression on the face was that of a living soul in torment" and they wanted to hold a séance to see if they could remove "the anguish and misery from the eyes of the coffin-lid."

When all this landed in the press, people from as far away as Algiers and New Zealand began sending money to the museum requesting flowers be placed in front of the cover. The museum didn't do it.

Then the S.S. *Titanic* sank in 1912 and one of those who happened to go down with it was none other than William Stead.

THE MUMMY ON THE *TITANIC*

Apparently the *Titanic* entered the story when Jay Henry Mowbray interviewed survivor Fred Seward for his book *The Sinking of the* Titanic (1912). In this book, he wrote:

Frederic K. Seward, who sat next to W. T. Stead at the *Titanic*'s saloon table, told of the veteran English journalist's plans for his American visit.

His immediate purpose was to aid in the New York campaign of the Men and Religion Forward Movement.

"Mr. Stead talked much of spiritualism, thought transference and the occult," said Seward. "He told a story of a mummy case in the British Museum which, he said, had had amazing adventures, but which punished with great calamities any person who wrote its story. He told of one person after another who, he said, had come to grief after writing the story, and added that, although he knew it, he would never write it. He did not say whether ill-luck attached to the mere telling of it."

Seward later told a reporter that he would never repeat Stead's story, implying that Stead's telling of it might have been responsible for this disaster which claimed between 1,490 and 1,517 lives. From this, the story evolved into a myth that the ship sank because of the curse and that there was actually a king's mummy somewhere on board.

Most variants of the Murray/Stead story end with the mummy or mummy case going down on the *Titanic*. A thorough search of the ship's manifest and cargo hold diagrams shows that there was no mummy or mummy case on the ship. Still, some believers insist that it was placed in a storage room directly behind the ship's command bridge so the captain could keep a close eye on it, since it was very valuable, and others have said it was hidden under the body of a new Renault automobile.

A few stories go on to say that the mummy's owner, Lord Canterville,[1] bribed a bunch of people and rescued the mummy on one of the lifeboats. It then made it to America, where it continued to wreak havoc, so it was sold to a millionaire in Montreal, Canada, with the same result. The millionaire then decided to ship it back to England in 1914 onboard the *Empress of Ireland,* which collided with a Norwegian ship on the St. Lawrence River, causing 1,029 people to drown. Deciding it best to send the mummy back to Egypt, the millionaire then shipped it on the *Lusitania,* which was sunk by a German torpedo in 1915, taking 1,198 people with it. Of course, all this is getting pretty far-fetched.

So a story that began with a mummy smashing up stuff in a room eventually evolved into the myth of a pharaoh's mummy that sank four ships and

---

[1] Some say William Stead was the owner.

killed thousands of people. It seems people just can't resist embellishing a good story.

Now, let's go back to Pharaoh Tutankhamen's curse, which the newspapers initially called "the Curse of Osiris."

KING TUT EXPOSED

This time the story began shortly before Lord Carnarvon's death, with a letter written by the then-popular Gothic novelist Marie Corelli to the *New York Times,* which was also reprinted by the London newspapers. In the letter she said:

> I cannot but think some risks are run by breaking into the last rest of a king in Egypt whose tomb is specially and solemnly guarded, and robbing him of his possessions. According to a rare book I possess . . . entitled *The Egyptian History of the Pyramids* [an ancient Arabic text], the most dire punishment follows any rash intruder into a sealed tomb. The book . . . names "secret poisons enclosed in boxes in such wise that those who touch them shall not know how they come to suffer." That is why I ask, Was it a mosquito bite that has so seriously infected Lord Carnarvon?

She also claimed the book said, "Death comes on wings to he who enters the tomb of the Pharaoh."

A few days later Lord Carnarvon died. When his death was announced, a reporter for the *London Times* asked Sir Arthur Conan Doyle— the creator of Sherlock Holmes and a believer in spiritualism—what he thought of this and Corelli's letter. Doyle was very impressed and declared that he believed the pharaoh was responsible. Suddenly the story shot around the world. The day after Carnarvon died, the front page of the *New York Times* had the headline "Carnarvon's death spreads theories about vengeance." And on page three was "Death by evil spirit possible, says Doyle."

Soon newspapers were mistakenly reporting that two curses had been found *inside* Tutankhamen's tomb—one almost identical to Corelli's. The first, which they claimed was found on a clay tablet, said, "Death will slay with his wings whoever disturbs the peace of the pharaoh." The second was supposedly found on the back of a statue, reading, "It is I who drive back the robbers of the tomb with the flames of the desert. I am the protector of Tutankhamen's grave." Some said that written over the door to the burial chamber was "Death shall come on swift wings to him that toucheth the tomb of the Pharaoh." None of this is true, but even today books are being published that report it as fact.[2]

Actually, Lord Carnarvon had been ill for years—ever since he'd had a near-fatal auto accident. That was the reason he first went to Egypt. The official explanation of his death was that an insect bite he received became infected after he cut the wound while shaving.[3] He then developed a fever, which turned into pneumonia. His death certificate says it was pneumonia that killed him.

Arthur C. Mace (victim number 4) and some of the others were also not in the best of health. Many of them originally went to Egypt because of their poor health. It's not unusual for people to suffer untimely deaths, and it should be noted that thousands of people visited the tomb during this period, and millions have since then. According to Egyptologist Herbert E. Winlock, who looked into this in the mid-1930s and is said himself to be among the curse's victims (victim number 5), of the twenty-six people who were present when the burial chamber was opened, only six died within the next ten years. Of the twenty-six, twenty-two were present when the actual sarcophagus was opened, but only two of these died within the next ten years. And only ten of the original twenty-six were present when the mummy was unwrapped, and none of these died in the next ten years. So those with the most contact with the mummy had a better survival rate than those whose contact was slight. In addition, many of those involved in opening the tomb, including Howard Carter, lived into their sixties, and several lived into their eighties and nineties. Of the ten principal diggers, two were still alive forty years later.

---

[2] Another curse is said to have been found on a tablet near the Meidum pyramid, which is five miles south of Saqqara, inscribed, "The spirit of the dead will wring the neck of a grave robber as if it were that of a goose." And next to it was supposedly the body of a grave robber who had been killed by a fallen stone.

[3] It's said that Egyptian tomb workers today do not shave because shaving was connected with Lord Carnarvon's death.

THE DEADLY FUNGUS

Many explanations for the curse have been proposed, including radiation from rare elements in the tomb, unknown poisons, long-lived bacteria or viruses, a strange black fungus, and the effects of superstition and fear. Some of these explanations are pretty far-fetched and have been disproven, but not all of them.

When the burial chamber was opened, five samples were taken from the walls and floor at the far end of the mummy chamber and were found to be virtually sterile. Fungus growths were seen on the walls, but they were "apparently dead," yet some insist that the mummy wrappings and the floor were heavily infested with *Actinomyces,* which are organisms that fall somewhere between a true bacteria and mold fungi[4] and play an important role in decomposition. They can be spread by spores and are one of the causes of what is commonly called "farmer's lung."

One symptom of exposure to this fungus can be a swelling of the jaw called "lumpy jaw," which can also develop into pneumonia and can be fatal, although usually only people with a sensitivity to the fungus become ill. In Lord Carnarvon's case, he had a history of lung ailments. It's interesting that he and Carter entered Tutankhamen's burial chamber on February 17. It was a little over two weeks later, on or about March 6th, that Lord Carnarvon got his mosquito bite and died on April 5, but all this was in 1923, and the mummy itself wasn't unwrapped until 1925.

While the fungus might account for Lord Carnarvon's death, and maybe a couple others, it certainly doesn't account for all the people said to have been done in by the curse. Of course, the official explanation for Lord Carnarvon's death is just as viable. With either cause, the end result is the same—Carnarvon died from pneumonia.

It's doubtful anything was put in the tomb on purpose to infect tomb robbers, as some have suggested, especially since tombs occasionally had to be reopened by the priests. Also, it wasn't the Ancient Egyptians' style. They generally left punishment to the gods and pharaohs.

As for the lights going out at the time of Carnarvon's death, this wasn't

---

[4] *Actinomyces* are referred to as either a bacteria or a fungus, depending on what book you're reading at the time.

confirmed, but it also wasn't unusual—the power was always going out in Cairo, and it still does. Some say it was only the lights in the hospital that went out, for about five minutes, and this happened sometime around the time he died, rather than at the exact moment of his death.

Whether his dog actually dropped dead at the same time he did is unclear, but it seems unlikely. Most versions of the legend say they both died about 2 A.M., which doesn't take into account that they were in different time zones. Philipp Vandenberg, in his book *The Curse of the Pharaohs* (1975), says Lord Carnarvon's son told him that the dog died "shortly before 4 A.M. London time." While this does attempt to take into account the time difference, the compensation is in the wrong direction. Lord Carnarvon died just before twelve midnight London time.

Curses were actually very rare in Ancient Egypt, and generally they were directed at people who entered a tomb without being purified, or people who had grudges against the deceased. More often the inscriptions in tombs welcomed the living since the immortality of those entombed was linked with people remembering their names and making proper offerings. For the most part, the paintings and inscriptions were blessings of the deceased and magical spells to ensure a good afterlife.

The purpose of the tomb was to provide a permanent house to protect the mummy. Obviously this didn't work, since most of the mummies have now been destroyed; but then, perhaps that's the true curse. Perhaps it's the mummies who are the true victims here. At least museums now protect the few remaining mummies from the depredations of the living.

THE MALEVOLENCE OF ANCIENT EGYPTIAN SPIRITS

Arthur Weigall

Arthur Weigall was an expert Egyptologist and the author of about thirty-five books—most of them historical, and many on Egypt and its antiquities. For many years, he was the chief inspector of antiquities for the Egyptian government and head of the Cairo Museum. He also worked closely with Lord Carnarvon and Howard Carter, who discovered the tomb of Pharaoh Tutankhamen. While we may not believe in magic, the Ancient Egyptians sure did. We may dismiss all this talk of curses as superstition or just journalists creating a good story, but see if you can read these accounts without wondering if there might be something mysterious going on.

During the recent excavations which led to the discovery of the tomb of Tutankhamen, Mr. Howard Carter had in his house a canary which daily regaled him with its happy song. On the day, however, on which the entrance to the tomb was laid bare, a cobra entered the house, pounced on the bird, and swallowed it. Now, cobras are rare in Egypt, and are seldom seen in winter; but in ancient times they were regarded as the symbol of royalty, and each Pharaoh wore this symbol upon his forehead, as though to signify his power to strike and sting his enemies. Those who believed in omens, therefore, interpreted this incident as meaning that the spirit of the newly-found Pharaoh, in its correct form of a royal cobra, had killed the excavator's happiness symbolized by this song-bird so typical of the peace of an English home.

At the end of the season's work, Lord Carnarvon was stung mysteriously upon the face, and died.

Millions of people throughout the world have asked themselves whether the death of the excavator of this tomb was due to some malevolent influence which came from it, and the story has been spread that there was a specific curse written upon a wall of the royal sepulchre. This, however, is not the case.

There are very few such curses known during the Eighteenth and Nineteenth Dynasties in ancient Egypt, that is to say, during the century or two before and after the time of Tutankhamen, and they are not at all common at any Pharaonic period.

Whenever they do appear, their object is simply to terrify the would-be tomb-robbers of their own epoch, who might smash up the mummy in their search for jewelry, or damage the tomb, thereby causing that loss of the dead man's identity which the Egyptians thought would injure the welfare of his spirit in the Underworld. The mummy and the tomb were the earthly home of the disembodied spirit, and to wreck either was to render the spirit homeless and nameless. On the other hand, to enter a tomb for the purpose of renewing the dead man's memory was always considered by the Egyptians to be a most praiseworthy proceeding; and inscriptions are often found on the wall of a sepulchre stating that some friendly hand had been at work there, setting things to rights after a lapse of many years.

As an example of one of these curses, I will give here the translation of an inscription which is written upon a mortuary-statue of a certain Ursu, a mining engineer who lived less than a hundred years before the time of Tutankhamen. "He who trespasses upon my property," he says, "or who shall injure my tomb or drag out my mummy, the Sun-god shall punish him. He shall not bequeath his goods to his children; his heart shall not have pleasure in life; he shall not receive water (for his spirit to drink) in the tomb; and his soul shall be destroyed for ever." On the wall of the tomb of Harkhuf, at Aswân, dating from the Sixth Dynasty, these words are written: "As for any man who shall enter into this tomb . . . I will pounce upon him as on a bird; he shall be judged for it by the great god."

The fear is that the tomb or the body will be broken up; and thus the scientific modern excavators, whose object is to rescue the dead from that oblivion which the years have produced, might be expected to be blessed rather than cursed for what they do. Only the robber would come under the scope of the curse. If we are to treat these questions seriously at all, it may be said that in general no harm has come to those who have entered these ancient tombs with reverence, and with the sole aim of saving the dead from native pillage and their identity from the obliterating hand of time.

The large number of visitors to Egypt and persons interested in Egyptian antiquities who believe in the malevolence of the spirits of the Pharaohs and their dead subjects, is always a matter of astonishment to me, in view of the fact that of all ancient people the Egyptians were the most kindly and, to me, the most lovable. Sober and thoughtful men, and matter-of-fact matrons, seem to vie with the lighter-minded members of society in recording the misfortunes which have befallen themselves or their friends as a consequence of their meddling with the property of the dead. On all sides one hears tales of the trials which have come upon those who, owing to their possession of some antiquity or ancient relic, have given offense to the spirits of the old inhabitants of the Nile valley. These stories are generally open to some natural explanation, and those tales which I can relate at first hand are not necessarily to be connected with black magic. I will therefore leave it to the reader's taste to find an explanation for the incidents which I will here relate.

In the year 1909 Lord Carnarvon, who was then conducting excavations in the necropolis of the nobles of Thebes, discovered a hollow wooden figure of a large black cat, which we recognized, from other examples in the Cairo Museum, to be the shell in which a real embalmed cat was confined. The figure looked more like a small tiger as it sat in the sunlight at the end of the pit in which it had been discovered, glaring at us with its yellow painted eyes and bristling its yellow whiskers. Its body was covered all over with a thick coating of smooth, shining pitch, and we could not at first detect the line along which the shell had been closed after it had received the mortal remains of the sacred animal within; but we knew from experience that the joint passed completely round the figure—from the nose, over the top of the head, down the back, and along the breast—so that, when opened, the two sides would fall apart in equal halves.

The somber figure was carried down to the Nile and across the river to my house, where, by mistake on the part of my Egyptian servant, it was deposited in my bedroom. Returning home at dead of night, I here found it seated in the middle of the floor directly in my path from the door to the matches; and for some moments I was constrained to sit beside it, rubbing my shins and my head.

I rang the bell, but receiving no answer, I walked to the kitchen, where I found the servants grouped distractedly around the butler, who had been stung by a scorpion and was in the throes of that short but intense agony. Soon he passed into a state of delirium and believed himself to be pursued by a large gray cat, a fancy which did not surprise me since he had so lately assisted in carrying the figure to its ill-chosen resting-place in my bedroom.

At length I retired to bed, but the moonlight which now entered the room through the open French windows fell full upon the black figure of the cat; and for some time I lay awake watching the peculiarly weird creature as it stared past me at the wall. I estimated its age to be considerably more than three thousand years, and I tried to picture to myself the strange people who, in those distant times, had fashioned this curious coffin for a cat which had been to them half pet and half household god. A branch of a tree was swaying in the night breeze outside, and its shadow danced to and fro over the face of the cat, causing the yellow eyes to open and shut, as it were, and the mouth to grin. Once, as I was dropping off to sleep, I could have sworn that it had turned its head to look at me; and I could see the sullen expression of feline anger gathering upon its black visage as it did so. In the distance I could hear the melancholy wails of the unfortunate butler imploring those around him to keep the cat away from him, and it seemed to me that there came a glitter into the eyes of the figure as the low cries echoed down the passage.

At last I fell asleep, and for about an hour all was still. Then, suddenly, a report like that of a pistol rang through the room. I started up, and as I did so a large gray cat sprang either from or on to the bed, leapt across my knees, dug its claws into my hand, and dashed through the window into the garden. At the same moment I saw by the light of the moon that the two sides of the wooden figure had fallen apart and were rocking themselves to a standstill upon the floor, like two great empty shells. Between them sat the mummified figure of a cat, the bandages which swathed it round being ripped open at the neck, as though they had been burst outward.

I sprang out of bed and rapidly examined the divided shell; and it seemed to me that the humidity in the air here on the bank of the Nile had expanded the wood which had rested in the dry desert so long, and had caused the two halves to burst apart with the loud noise which I had heard. Then, going to the window, I scanned the moonlit garden; and there in the middle of the pathway I saw, not the gray cat which had scratched me, but my own pet tabby, standing with arched back and bristling fur, glaring into the bushes, as though she saw ten feline devils therein.

I will leave the reader to decide whether the gray cat was the malevolent spirit which, after causing me to break my shins and my butler to be stung by a scorpion, had burst its way through the bandages and woodwork and had fled into the darkness; or whether the torn embalming cloths represented the natural destructive work of Time, and the gray cat was a night-wanderer which had strayed into my room and had been frightened by the easily-explained bursting apart of the two sides of the ancient Egyptian figure. Coincidence is a factor in life not always sufficiently considered; and the events I have related can be explained in a perfectly natural manner, if one be inclined to do so.

My next story tells how a little earthenware lamp once in my possession brought misfortune upon at least two persons.

It sometimes happens that people who have visited Egypt and have there purchased a few trifling antiquities are suddenly seized with the fear that these relics are bringing them bad luck; and, in a moment of frenzy, they pack up their Egyptian purchases, and post them back to the Nile. When I was Inspector-General of Antiquities they not infrequently used to address these parcels to me or to my office at Luxor; and without further consideration the objects were laid away on the shelves of the store-room, where soon the dust gathered upon them and they were forgotten.

Now it chanced that a little earthenware lamp was once returned to me in this manner; and, happening to mention the fact to some friends, I learnt that it had been returned by a lady who declared herself dogged with misfortune ever since it came into her possession, and who had often stated that she intended to get rid of it by sending it back to the unoffending official in charge of antiquities. I cannot now recall the series of misfortunes which had occurred to the owner of the lamp, but I remember that they included little incidents such as the spilling of a bottle of ink over her dress. I paid, of course, small attention to the matter, and the lamp lay unnoticed on the shelf for a year or more.

One day, a certain royal lady who was travelling in Egypt asked me to give her some trifle as a souvenir of her visit; and, without recalling its history to my mind, I gave her the unlucky lamp, which, so far as I know, did not bring any particular ill-fortune to its owner. There the matter would have tamely ended, had it not been for a chance conversation on the subject of unlucky antiquities, which occurred one night at a dinner-party in London. One of the ladies present told me a long story of the ill-luck from which she had suffered during the whole time in which she was the owner of a little earthenware lamp which came from Egypt. To such a state of apprehension had she been brought, she said, by the intuitive feeling that this little antiquity was the cause of her troubles, that at last she went down to the Embankment and hurled it into the Thames.

Vague recollections of the story of the unlucky lamp which I had given to our illustrious visitor began to stir in my mind, and I asked with some interest how she came into possession of the malevolent object. Her reply confirmed my suspicions. The lamp had been given to her by the royal lady to whom I had presented it as a souvenir!

Most people have heard the story of the malevolent "mummy" in the British Museum. As a matter of fact, it is not a mummy at all, but simply a portion of the lid of a coffin. It was bequeathed to the museum after it had wrought havoc wherever it went, but now it is said to confine its dangerous attentions to those visitors who are disrespectful to it. A lady of my acquaintance told me that she had "been rude" to it, with the startling result that she fell headlong down the great staircase and sprained her ankle. There is also the well-known case of a journalist who wrote about it in jest, and was dead in a few days.

The originator of the whole affair was the late Mr. Douglas Murray, who told me the following facts. He purchased the coffin some time in the sixties, and no sooner had he done so than he lost his arm, owing to the explosion of his gun. The ship in which the coffin was sent home was wrecked, as also was the cab in which it was driven from the docks; the house in which it was deposited was burnt down; and the photographer who made a picture of it shot himself. A lady who had some connection with it suffered great family losses, and was wrecked at sea shortly afterwards, her life being saved, so she told me, only by the fact that she clung to a rock for the greater part of a night. The list of accidents and misfortunes charged to the spirit which is connected with this coffin is now of enormous length, a fact which is not surprising, since persons who have seen the coffin attribute all their subsequent troubles to its baneful influence, and misfortunes in this life are not so rare that they can be counted on the five fingers. Personally, I think that, if these matters are to be considered at all, we should attempt rather to incur this restless spirit's benediction by refusing to credit it with an evil purpose.

The veracity of the next story cannot be questioned. A photograph in my possession, about which there is no fake, tells the tale more accurately than could any words of mine; and there can be no getting away from the fact that a shadowy human face has come between the camera and the object which was being photographed. The facts are as follows.

Some years ago we were making excavations in the tomb of a Great Vizir of about B.C. 1350, when we came upon a highly decorated coffin of a certain priest, which, by the style of the workmanship, appeared to date from some two hundred years later, and evidently must have been buried there by unscrupulous undertakers who opened up the original tomb for its reception in order to save themselves the trouble of making a new sepulchre. Now this act of desecration might be thought to have called down upon the intruding mummy the wrath of the Vizir's spirit, whose body was probably ousted to make room for the newcomer; but, whether this be so or not, those who believe in these powers might have reason to suppose that the priestly usurper lay restlessly in his coffin, retaining, in place of the usual quiescence of the dead, a continued activity which caused an atmosphere of malignity to linger around his mortal remains.

As soon as the coffin and mummy were deposited in my store-room, I began to feel an unaccountable sense of apprehension whenever I stood in its presence; and every time I opened the door of the room to enter its dark recesses I glanced uneasily at the embalmed figure which lay in the now lidless coffin, as though expecting it to do me some injury. This appeared to me to be remarkable, for I had long been accustomed to the presence all around me of the embalmed dead. I had slept night after night in the tombs, sharing their comfortable shelter with the human remains which still lay therein; I had, during a *dahabiyeh* trip in the south, filled the cabin bunkers with the skulls and bones of the dead and had worked and slept contentedly in their company; I had eaten many a luncheon on the lid of a not empty coffin. But this particular mummy seemed to draw my eyes towards it, so that when I was at work in the room in which it lay, I caught myself glancing over my shoulder in its direction.

At length I decided to unwrap the bandages in which the mummy was rolled, and to look upon the face of the dead man who had now begun to haunt my thoughts, after which I proposed to send both it and the coffin down to the Cairo Museum. The process of unwrapping was lengthy, for of course many notes had to be taken and photographs made at the different stages of the proceedings; but at last it was completed, and the body was placed in the packing-case in which it was to travel. Some of the linen cloths which had covered the face were of such beautifully fine texture that I took them into the house to show them to the friends who were staying with me at the time; and one of the servants, shortly afterwards, placed them upon a shelf in a bedroom wardrobe.

Now it happened that this room was occupied by a lady and her little girl, and a day or two later, while the body still lay in the portico outside the house, and the ancient linen still rested upon the shelf inside the room, the child was seized with violent illness. There followed some days of anxiety, and at length one morning, when the doctor's visit had left us distraught with anxiety, the mother of the invalid came to me with a haggard face, holding in her hands the embalmer's linen. "Here," she cried, with an intensity which I shall not soon forget, "take this horrible stuff and burn it; and for goodness' sake send that mummy away, or the child will die."

The mummy and its linen went down to Cairo that night, and the little girl in due course recovered; but when, a month or two later, I developed the photographs which I had taken of the unwrapped body, there, between it and my camera, stared a shadowy face. It is possible that I took two photographs upon one plate; I do not remember, but that, and the state of my nerves, due to overwork, may account for all that happened.

I am minded now to relate an experience which befell me when I was conducting excavations in the desert behind the ancient city of Abydos. The tale does not deal with any very particular malevolence of any spirit of the past, but it bears sufficiently closely upon that subject to be recorded here. We were engaged in clearing out a vertical tomb-shaft which had been cut through the rock underlying the sandy surface of the desert. The shaft was about ten foot square; and by the end of the second day's work we had cleared out the sand and stones, wherewith it was filled, to the depth of some twenty feet. At sunset I gave the order to stop work for the night, and

I was about to set out on my walk back to the camp when the foreman came to tell me that, with the last strokes of the pick, a mummied hand had been laid bare, and it was evident that we were about to come upon an interred body.

By lamplight, therefore, the work was continued; and presently we had uncovered the sand-dried body of an old woman, who by her posture appeared to have met with a violent death. It was evident that this did not represent the original burial in the tomb, the bottom of the shaft not yet having been reached; and I conjectured that the corpse before us had been thrown from above at some more recent date—perhaps in Roman times—when the shaft was but half full of debris, and in course of time had become buried by blown sand and natural falls of rock.

The workmen were now waiting for their evening meal, but I, on the other hand, was anxious to examine the body and its surroundings carefully, in order to see whether any objects of interest were to be found. I therefore sent all but one of the men back to the camp, and descended into the shaft by means of a rope ladder, carrying with me a hurricane lamp to light my search. In the flickering rays of the lamp the body looked particularly gruesome. The old woman lay upon her back, her arms outstretched upwards, as though they had stiffened thus in some convulsion, the fingers being locked together. Her legs were thrust outwards rigidly, and the toes were cramped and bent. The features of the face were well preserved, as was the whole body; and long black hair descended to her bony shoulders in a tangled mass. Her mouth was wide open, the two rows of teeth gleaming savagely in the uncertain light, and the hollow eye-sockets seemed to stare upwards, as though fixed upon some object of horror. I do not suppose that it is often man's lot to gaze upon so ghastly a spectacle, and it was only the fact of the extreme antiquity of the body which made it possible for me to look with equanimity upon it; for the centuries that had passed since the occurrence of this woman's tragedy seemed to have removed the element of personal affinity which sets the living shuddering at the dead.

Just as I was completing my search I felt a few drops of rain fall, and at the same time realized wind was howling and whistling above me and that the stars were shut out by dense clouds. A rain storm in Upper Egypt is a very rare occurrence, and generally it is of a tropical character. If I left the body at the bottom of the shaft, I thought to myself, it would be soaked and destroyed; and since, as a specimen, it was well worth preserving, I decided to carry it to the surface, where there was a hut in which it could be sheltered. I lifted the body from the ground, and found it to be quite light, but at the same time not at all fragile. I called out to the man whom I had told to wait for me on the surface, but received no reply. Either he had misunderstood me and gone home, or else the noise of the wind prevented my voice from reaching him. Large spots of rain were now falling, and there was no time for hesitation. I therefore lifted the body on to my back, the two outstretched arms passing over my shoulders and the linked fingers clutching, as it were, at my chest. I then began to climb up the rope ladder, and as I did so I noticed with something of a qualm that the old woman's face was peeping at me over my right shoulder and her teeth seemed about to bite my right ear.

I had climbed about half the distance when my foot dislodged a fragment of rock from the side of the shaft, and, as luck would have it, the stone fell right upon the lamp, smashing the glass and putting the light out. The darkness in which I found myself was intense, and now the wind began to buffet me and to hurl the sand into my face. With my right hand I felt for the woman's head and shoulder, in order to hitch the body more firmly on to my back, but to my surprise my hand found nothing there. At the same moment I became conscious that the hideous face was grinning at me over my *left* shoulder, my movements, I suppose, having shifted it; and, without further delay, I blundered and scrambled to the top of the shaft in a kind of panic.

No sooner had I reached the surface than I attempted to relieve myself of my burden. The wind was now screaming past me and the rain was falling fast. I put my left hand up to catch hold of the corpse's shoulder, and to my dismay found that the head had slipped round once more to my right, and the face was peeping at me from that side. I tried to remove the arms from around my neck, but, with ever-increasing horror, I found that the fingers had caught in my coat and seemed to be holding on to me. A few moments of struggle ensued, and at last the fingers released their grip. Thereupon the body swung round so that we stood face to face, the withered arms still around my neck, and the teeth grinning at me through the darkness. A moment later I was free, and the body fell back from me, hovered a moment, as it were, in mid air, and suddenly disappeared from sight. It was then that I realized that we had been struggling at the very edge of the shaft, down which the old woman had now fallen, and near which some will say that she had been wildly detaining me.

Fortunately the rain soon cleared off, so there was no need to repeat the task of bringing the gruesome object to the surface. Upon the next morning we found the body quite uninjured, lying at the bottom of the shaft, in almost precisely the position in which we had discovered it; and it is now exhibited in the museum of one of the medical institutes of London.

Most people who have visited Upper Egypt will be familiar with the lioness-headed statue of Sekhmet which is to be seen in the small temple of Ptah, at Karnak. Tourists usually make a point of entering the sanctuary in which it stands by moonlight or starlight, for then the semi-darkness adds in an extraordinary manner to the dignity and mystery of the figure, and one feels disposed to believe the goddess not yet bereft of all power. Sekhmet was the agent employed by the sun-god, Ra, in the destruction of mankind; and she thus had a sinister reputation in olden times. This has clung to her in a most persistent manner, and to this day the natives say that she has the habit of killing little children. When the statue was discovered a few years ago, a fall of earth just in front of her terminated the lives of two of the small boys who were engaged in the work, a fact which, not surprisingly, has been quoted as an indication of the malevolence of the spirit which resides in this impressive figure of stone. One hears it now quite commonly said that those who offend the goddess when visiting her are pursued by ill-fortune for weeks afterwards.

It actually became the custom for English and American ladies to leave their hotels after dinner and to hasten into the presence of the goddess, there to supplicate her and to appease her with fair words. On one of these occasions, a few years ago, a well-known lady threw herself upon her knees before the statue, and rapturously holding her hands aloft, cried out, "I believe, I believe!" while a friend of hers passionately kissed the stone hand and patted the somewhat ungainly feet. On other occasions lamps were burnt before the goddess and a kind of ritual was mumbled by an enthusiastic gentleman; while a famous French lady of letters, who was a victim of the delusion that she possessed ventriloquial powers, made mewing noises, which were supposed to emanate from the statue, and which certainly added greatly to the barbaric nature of the scene. So frequent did these séances become that at last I had to put an official stop to them, and thereafter it was deemed an infringement of the rules to placate the malevolent goddess in this manner. There she stands alone, smiling mysteriously at her visitors, who are invariably careful not to arouse her anger by smiling back. A native, who probably believed himself to be under her ban, burgled his way, one summer's night, into the sanctuary and knocked her head and shoulders off; but the archeologist in charge cemented them on again, and thus she continues as before to dole out misfortune to those who credit her with that ill desire.

During the winter of 1908–9 the well-known Bostonian painter and pageant-master Joseph Lindon Smith, and his wife, were staying with my wife and myself in our house on the banks of the Nile, at Luxor, the modern town which has grown up on the site of the once mighty "hundred-gated Thebes," the old capital of Egypt. It was our custom to spend a great part of our time amongst the ruins on the western side of the Nile, for my work made it necessary for me to give constant attention to the excavations which were there being conducted, and to supervise the elaborate system of policing and safeguarding, which is nowadays in force for the protection of the many historical and artistic treasures there on view. Mr. Smith, also, had painting work to do amongst the tombs; while the ladies of our party amused themselves in the hundred different ways which are so readily suggested in these beautiful and romantic surroundings.

Sometimes we used to camp the night amongst the tombs, the tents pitched on the side of the hill of Shêkh abd'el Gurneh in the midst of the burial-place of the great nobles; and at sunset, after the tourists had all disappeared along the road back to Luxor, and our day's occupations were ended, we were wont to set out for long rambling walks in the desert ravines, over the rocky hills, and amongst the ruined temples; nor was it until the hour of dinner that we made our way back to the lights of the camp. The grandeur of the scenery when darkness had fallen is indescribable. In the dim light reflected from the brilliant stars, the cliffs and rocky gorges assumed the most wonderful aspect. Their shadows were full of mystery, and the broken pathways seemed to lead to hidden places barred to man's investigation. The hills, and the boulders at their feet, took fantastic shape; and one could not well avoid the thought that the spirits of Egypt's dead were at that hour roaming abroad, like us, amongst these illusory scenes.

It was during one of these evening walks that we found ourselves in the famous Valley of the Tombs of the Queens, a rock-strewn ravine in which some of Egypt's royal ladies were buried. At the end of this valley the cliffs close in, and an ancient torrent, long ago dried up, has scooped out a cavernous hollow in the face of the rock, into which, as into a cauldron, the waters must have poured as they rushed down from the hills at the back. The sides of the hollow form two-thirds of a circle, and overhead the rock somewhat overhangs. In front it is quite open to the valley, and as the floor is a level area of hard gravel, about twenty-five feet at its greatest breadth and depth, the hollow at once suggests to the mind a natural stage with the rocky valley which lies before it as the theatre. The place was well known to us, and in the darkness we now scrambled up into the deep shadows of the recess, and, sitting upon the gravel, stared out into the starlit valley, like ghostly actors playing to a deserted auditorium. The evening wind sighed quietly around us, and across the valley the dim forms of two jackals passed with hardly a sound. Far away over the Nile we could see, framed between the hills on either side of the mouth of the ravine, the brilliant lights of Luxor shining in the placid water; and these added the more to the sense of our remoteness from the world and our proximity to those things of the night which belong to the kingdom of dreams.

Presently I struck a match, in order to light my pipe, and immediately the rough face of the rocks around us was illuminated and made grotesque. As the flame flickered, the dark shadows fluttered like black hair in the wind, and the promontories jutted forward like great snouts and chins. An owl, startled by the light, half tumbled from its roost upon a deep ledge high above us and went floundering into the darkness, hooting like a lost soul. The match burnt out, and immediately blackness and silence closed once more about us.

"What a stage for a play!" exclaimed the amateur actor-manager; and a few moments later we were all eagerly discussing the possibility of performing a ghostly drama here amongst the desert rocks. By the time that we had reached our camp a plot had been evolved which was based on the historical fact that the spirit of the above-mentioned Pharaoh Akhnaton was, so to speak, excommunicated by the priests and was denied the usual prayers for the dead, being thus condemned to wander without home or resting-place throughout the years. Akhnaton, the son of the powerful and beautiful Queen Tiye, reigned from B.C. 1375 to 1358; and being disgusted with the barbarities perpetrated at Thebes in the name of the god Amon, and believing that the only true god was Aton, the life-giving "Energy of the Sun," overthrew the former religion and preached a wonderfully advanced doctrine of peace and love, which he associated with the worship of Aton. He removed his capital from Thebes to "The City of the Horizon of Aton," and there reigned with his wife and children, devoting his whole energy to his religion and to the demonstration of his lofty teaching. He died at the age of about thirty years; and thereupon the nation unanimously returned, under Tutankhamen, to the worship of Amon and the old gods, whose priests erased the dead king's name from the book of life.

Here, then, was a ghost ready to hand, and here was our stage. The part of the young Akhnaton should be assigned to my wife, for his gentle character and youthful voice could better be rendered by a woman than by a man. Then we must bring in the beautiful Queen Tiye, who could well be impersonated by Mrs. Lindon Smith. Mr. Smith could take the part of the messenger of the gods, sent from the Underworld to meet the royal ghost. And as for myself, I would be kept busy enough, managing the lights, prompting the actors, and doing the odd jobs. There would have to be some weird music at certain moments; and for this purpose our friend, Mr. F. F. Ogilvie, that painter of Anglo-Egyptian fame, might be commandeered together with his guitar.

On our return to Luxor we busied ourselves during all our spare hours in designing and making the costumes and properties; and it fell to me to write as fast as I could the lines of the play. They have no merit in themselves; but when a few days later they were read over in our desert theatre, beneath the starlit heavens, the quiet, earnest diction of the two ladies, and the strange, hawk-like tones of our celebrated amateur, caused them to sound very mysterious and full of meaning.

We now fixed the date for the performance and invited our friends to come by night to the Valley of the Tombs of the Queens to see the expected appearance of the ghost of the great Pharaoh, and a few days before that date we moved over once more to our desert camp.

We rehearsed the play a few nights later, but alas! hardly had Mrs. Smith finished her introductory lines, when she was struck down by agonizing pains in her eyes, and in less than two hours she had passed into a raving delirium. The story of how at midnight she was taken across the deserted fields and over the river to our house at Luxor, would read like the narration of a nightmare. Upon the next day it was decided that she must be sent down immediately to Cairo, for there was no doubt that she was suffering from ophthalmia in its most virulent form, and there were grave fears that she might lose her sight. On this same day my wife was smitten down with violent illness, she being ordered also to proceed to Cairo immediately. On the next morning, Mr. Smith developed a low fever, and shortly afterwards, I myself was laid low with influenza. Mr. Ogilvie, returning to his head-quarters by train, came in for a nasty accident in which his mother's leg was badly injured. And thus not one of us could have taken part in the production of the play on the date announced.

For the next two or three weeks Mrs. Smith's eyes and my wife's life hung in the balance and were often despaired of. Mercifully, however, they were both restored in due time to perfect health; but none of us entertained any desire to undertake the rehearsals a second time. Many of our friends were inclined to see in our misfortunes the punishing hand of the gods and spirits of ancient Egypt; but they must not forget that the play was to be given in all solemnity and without the smallest suggestion of burlesque. For my own part, as I have said, I do not think that the possibilities of that much under-rated factor in life's events, coincidence, have been exhausted in the search for an explanation of our tragedy; but far from me be it to offer an opinion upon the subject. I have heard the most absurd nonsense talked in Egypt by those who believe in the malevolence of the ancient dead; but at the same time, I try to keep an open mind on the subject.

Fiction

LOST IN A PYRAMID,
OR THE MUMMY'S CURSE

Louisa May Alcott

Louisa May Alcott spent most of her life in Concord and Boston, Massachusetts, where she grew up in poverty, with Ralph Waldo Emerson, Henry David Thoreau, and Nathaniel Hawthorne as friends and neighbors. At an early age she helped support her family by working as a servant and seamstress. During the Civil War she volunteered as a nurse, but she eventually contracted typhoid and never fully recovered. She wrote many novels and short stories, but she is best known for her classic autobiographical novel, Little Women. Today she is largely remembered for her children's literature, but she also wrote a string of stories on much more interesting topics, such as one on hashish eaters which ends with the line "'Heaven bless hashish, if its dreams end like this!'" Unfortunately these stories are extremely difficult to find today, but I have been able to locate the following story involving the mummy of an Ancient Egyptian sorceress.

I

"And what are these, Paul?" asked Evelyn, opening a tarnished gold box and examining its contents curiously.

"Seeds of some unknown Egyptian plant," replied Forsyth, with a sudden shadow on his dark face, as he looked down at the three scarlet grains lying in the white hand lifted to him.

"Where did you get them?" asked the girl.

"That is a weird story, which will only haunt you if I tell it," said Forsyth, with an absent expression that strongly excited the girl's curiosity.

"Please tell it, I like weird tales, and they never trouble me. Ah, do tell it; your stories are always so interesting," she cried, looking up with such a pretty blending of entreaty and command in her charming face, that refusal was impossible.

"You'll be sorry for it, and so shall I, perhaps; I warn you beforehand, that harm is foretold to the possessor of those mysterious seeds," said Forsyth, smiling, even while he knit his black brows, and regarded the blooming creature before him with a fond yet foreboding glance.

"Tell on, I'm not afraid of these pretty atoms," she answered, with an imperious nod.

"To hear is to obey. Let me read the facts, and then I will begin," returned Forsyth, pacing to and fro with the far-off look of one who turns the pages of the past.

Evelyn watched him a moment, and then returned to her work, or play, rather, for the task seemed well suited to the vivacious little creature, half-child, half-woman.

"While in Egypt," commenced Forsyth, slowly, "I went one day with my guide and Professor Niles, to explore the Cheops. Niles had a mania for antiquities of all sorts, and forgot time, danger and fatigue in the ardor of his pursuit. We rummaged up and down the narrow passages, half choked with dust and close air; reading inscriptions on the walls, stumbling over shattered mummy-cases, or coming face to face with some shriveled specimen perched like a hobgoblin on the little shelves where the dead used to be stowed away for ages. I was desperately tired after a few hours of it, and begged the professor to return. But he was bent on exploring certain places, and would not desist. We had but one guide, so I was forced to stay; but Jumal, my man, seeing how weary I was, proposed to us to rest in one of the larger passages, while he went to procure another guide for Niles. We consented, and assuring us that we were perfectly safe, if we did not quit the spot, Jumal left us, promising to return speedily. The professor sat down to take notes of his researches, and stretching my self on the soft sand, I fell asleep.

"I was roused by that indescribable thrill which instinctively warns us of danger, and springing up, I found myself alone. One torch burned faintly where Jumal had struck it, but Niles and the other light were gone. A dreadful sense of loneliness oppressed me for a moment; then I collected myself and looked well about me. A bit of paper was pinned to my hat, which lay near me, and on it, in the professor's writing were these words:

"'I've gone back a little to refresh my memory on certain points. Don't follow me till Jumal comes. I can find my way back to you, for I have a clue. Sleep well, and dream gloriously of the Pharaohs. N.N.'

"I laughed at first over the old enthusiast, then felt anxious then restless, and finally resolved to follow him, for I discovered a strong cord fastened to a fallen stone, and knew that this was the clue he spoke of. Leaving a line for Jumal, I took my torch and retraced my steps, following the cord along the winding ways. I often shouted, but received no reply, and pressed on, hoping at each turn to see the old man poring over some musty relic of antiquity. Suddenly the cord ended, and lowering my torch, I saw that the footsteps had gone on.

"'Rash fellow, he'll lose himself, to a certainty,' I thought, really alarmed now.

"As I paused, a faint call reached me, and I answered it, waited, shouted again, and a still fainter echo replied.

"Niles was evidently going on, misled by the reverberations of the low passages. No time was to be lost, and, forgetting myself, I stuck my torch in the deep sand to guide me back to the clue, and ran down the straight path before me, whooping like a madman as I went. I did not mean to lose sight of the light, but in my eagerness to find Niles I turned from the main passage, and, guided by his voice, hastened on. His torch soon gladdened my eyes, and the clutch of his trembling hands told me what agony he had suffered.

"'Let us get out of this horrible place at once,' he said, wiping the great drops off his forehead.

"'Come, we're not far from the clue. I can soon reach it, and then we are safe'; but as I spoke, a chill passed over me, for a perfect labyrinth of narrow paths lay before us.

"Trying to guide myself by such land-marks as I had observed in my hasty passage, I followed the tracks in the sand till I fancied we must be near my light. No glimmer appeared, however, and kneeling down to examine the footprints nearer, I discovered, to my dismay, that I had been following the wrong ones, for among those marked by a deep boot-heel, were prints of bare feet; we had had no guide there, and Jumal wore sandals.

"Rising, I confronted Niles, with the one despairing word, 'Lost!' as I pointed from the treacherous sand to the fast-waning light.

"I thought the old man would be overwhelmed but, to my surprise, he grew quite calm and steady, thought a moment, and then went on, saying, quietly:

"'Other men have passed here before us; let us follow their steps, for, if I do not greatly err, they lead toward great passages, where one's way is easily found.'

"On we went, bravely, till a misstep threw the professor violently to the ground with a broken leg, and nearly extinguished the torch. It was a horrible predicament, and I gave up all hope as I sat beside the poor fellow, who lay exhausted with fatigue, remorse and pain, for I would not leave him.

"'Paul,' he said suddenly, 'if you will not go on, there is one more effort we can make. I remember hearing that a party lost as we are, saved themselves by building a fire. The smoke penetrated further than sound or light, and the guide's quick wit understood the unusual mist; he followed it, and rescued the party. Make a fire and trust to Jumal.'

"'A fire without wood?' I began; but he pointed to a shelf behind me, which had escaped me in the gloom; and on it I saw a slender mummy-case. I understood him, for these dry cases, which lie about in hundreds, are freely used as firewood. Reaching up, I pulled it down, believing it to be empty, but as it fell, it burst open, and out rolled a mummy. Accustomed as I was to such sights, it startled me a little, for danger had unstrung my nerves. Laying the little brown chrysalis aside, I smashed the case, lit the pile with my torch, and soon a light cloud of smoke drifted down the three passages which diverged from the cell-like place where we had paused.

"While busied with the fire, Niles, forgetful of pain and peril, had dragged the mummy nearer, and was examining it with the interest of a man whose ruling passion was strong even in death.

"'Come and help me unroll this. I have always longed to be the first to see and secure the curious treasures put away among the folds of these uncanny winding-sheets. This is a woman, and we may find something rare and precious here,' he said, beginning to unfold the outer coverings, from which a strange aromatic odor came.

"Reluctantly I obeyed, for to me there was something sacred in the bones of this unknown woman. But to beguile the time and amuse the poor fellow, I lent a hand, wondering as I worked, if this dark, ugly thing had ever been a lovely, soft-eyed Egyptian girl.

"From the fibrous folds of the wrappings dropped precious gums and spices, which half intoxicated us with their potent breath, antique coins, and a curious jewel or two, which Niles eagerly examined.

"All the bandages but one were cut off at last, and a small head laid bare, round which still hung great plaits of what had once been luxuriant hair. The shriveled hands were folded on the breast, and clasped in them lay that gold box."

"Ah!" cried Evelyn, dropping it from her rosy palm with a shudder.

"Nay; don't reject the poor little mummy's treasure. I never have quite forgiven myself for stealing it, or for burning her," said Forsyth, painting rapidly, as if the recollection of that experience lent energy to his hand.

"Burning her! Oh, Paul, what do you mean?" asked the girl, sitting up with a face full of excitement.

"I'll tell you. While busied with Madame la Momie, our fire had burned low, for the dry case went like tinder. A faint, far-off sound made our hearts leap, and Niles cried out: 'Pile on the wood; Jumal is tracking us; don't let the smoke fail now or we are lost!'

"'There is no more wood; the case was very small, and is all gone,' I answered, tearing off such of my garments as would burn readily, and piling them upon the embers.

"Niles did the same, but the light fabrics were quickly consumed, and made no smoke.

"'Burn that!' commanded the professor, pointing to the mummy.

"I hesitated a moment. Again came the faint echo of a horn. Life was dear to me. A few dry bones might save us, and I obeyed him in silence.

"A dull blaze sprung up, and a heavy smoke rose from the burning mummy, rolling in volumes through the low passages, and threatening to suffocate us with its fragrant mist. My brain grew dizzy, the light danced before my eyes, strange phantoms seemed to people the air, and, in the act of asking Niles why he gasped and looked so pale, I lost consciousness."

Evelyn drew a long breath, and put away the scented toys from her lap as if their odor oppressed her.

Forsyth's swarthy face was all aglow with the excitement of his story, and his black eyes glittered as he added, with a quick laugh:

"That's all; Jumal found and got us out, and we both forswore pyramids for the rest of our days."

"But the box: how came you to keep it?" asked Evelyn, eyeing it askance as it lay gleaming in a streak of sunshine.

"Oh, I brought it away as a souvenir, and Niles kept the other trinkets."

"But you said harm was foretold to the possessor of those scarlet seeds," persisted the girl, whose fancy was excited by the tale, and who fancied all was not told.

"Among his spoils, Niles found a bit of parchment, which he deciphered, and this inscription said that the mummy we had so ungallantly burned was that of a famous sorceress who bequeathed her curse to whoever should disturb her rest. Of course I don't believe that curse has anything to do with it, but it's a fact that Niles never prospered from that day. He says it's because he has never recovered from the fall and fright and I dare say it is so; but I sometimes wonder if I am to share the curse, for I've a vein of superstition in me, and that poor little mummy haunts my dreams still."

A long silence followed these words. Paul painted mechanically and Evelyn lay regarding him with a thoughtful face. But gloomy fancies were as foreign to her nature as shadows are to noonday, and presently she laughed a cheery laugh, saying as she took up the box again:

"Why don't you plant them, and see what wondrous flower they will bear?"

"I doubt if they would bear anything after lying in a mummy's hand for centuries," replied Forsyth, gravely.

"Let me plant them and try. You know wheat has sprouted and grown that was taken from a mummy's coffin; why should not these pretty seeds? I should so like to watch them grow; may I, Paul?"

"No, I'd rather leave that experiment untried. I have a queer feeling about the matter, and don't want to meddle myself or let anyone I love meddle with these seeds. They may be some horrible poison, or possess some evil power, for the sorceress evidently valued them, since she clutched them fast even in her tomb."

"Now, you are foolishly superstitious, and I laugh at you. Be generous; give me one seed, just to learn if it will grow. See I'll pay for it," and Evelyn, who now stood beside him, dropped a kiss on his forehead as she made her request, with the most engaging air.

But Forsyth would not yield. He smiled and returned the embrace with lover-like warmth, then flung the seeds into the fire, and gave her back the golden box, saying, tenderly:

"My darling, I'll fill it with diamonds or bonbons, if you please, but I will not let you play with that witch's spells. You've enough of your own, so forget the 'pretty seeds' and see what a Light of the Harem I've made of you."

Evelyn frowned, and smiled, and presently the lovers were out in the spring sunshine reveling in their own happy hopes, untroubled by one foreboding fear.

II

"I have a little surprise for you, love," said Forsyth, as he greeted his cousin three months later on the morning of his wedding day.

"And I have one for you," she answered, smiling faintly.

"How pale you are, and how thin you grow! All this bridal bustle is too much for you, Evelyn," he said, with fond anxiety, as he watched the strange pallor of her face, and pressed the wasted little hand in his.

"I am so tired," she said, and leaned her head wearily on her lover's breast. "Neither sleep, food, nor air gives me strength, and a curious mist seems to cloud my mind at times. Mamma says it is the heat, but I shiver even in the sun, while at night I burn with fever. Paul, dear, I'm glad you are going to take me away to lead a quiet, happy life with you, but I'm afraid it will be a very short one."

"My fanciful little wife! You are tired and nervous with all this worry, but a few weeks of rest in the country will give us back our blooming Eve again. Have you no curiosity to learn my surprise?" he asked, to change her thoughts.

The vacant look stealing over the girl's face gave place to one of interest, but as she listened it seemed to require an effort to fix her mind on her lover's words.

"You remember the day we rummaged in the old cabinet?"

"Yes," and a smile touched her lips for a moment.

"And how you wanted to plant those queer red seeds I stole from the mummy?"

"I remember," and her eyes kindled with sudden fire.

"Well, I tossed them into the fire, as I thought, and gave you the box. But when I went back to cover up my picture, and found one of those seeds on the rug, a sudden fancy to gratify your whim led me to send it to Niles and ask him to plant and report on its progress. Today I hear from him for the first time, and he reports that the seed has grown marvelously, has budded, and that he intends to take the first flower, if it blooms in time, to a meeting of famous scientific men, after which he will send me its true name and the plant itself. From his description, it must be very curious, and I'm impatient to see it."

"You need not wait; I can show you the flower in its bloom," and Evelyn beckoned with the *mechante* smile so long a stranger to her lips.

Much amazed, Forsyth followed her to her own little boudoir, and there, standing in the sunshine, was the unknown plant. Almost rank in their luxuriance were the vivid green leaves on the slender purple stems, and rising from the midst, one ghostly-white flower, shaped like the head of a hooded snake, with scarlet stamens like forked tongues, and on the petals glittered spots like dew.

"A strange, uncanny flower! Has it any odor?" asked Forsyth, bending to examine it, and forgetting, in his interest, to ask how it came there.

"None, and that disappoints me, I am so fond of perfumes," answered the girl, caressing the green leaves which trembled at her touch, while the purple stems deepened their tint.

"Now tell me about it," said Forsyth, after standing silent for several minutes.

"I had been before you, and secured one of the seeds, for two fell on the rug. I planted it under a glass in the richest soil I could find, watered it faithfully, and was amazed at the rapidity with which it grew when once it appeared above the earth. I told no-one, for I meant to surprise you with it; but this bud has been so long in blooming, I have had to wait. It is a good omen that it blossoms today, and as it is nearly white, I mean to wear it, for I've learned to love it, having been my pet for so long."

"I would not wear it, for, in spite of its innocent color, it is an evil-looking plant, with its adder's tongue and unnatural dew. Wait till Niles tells us what it is, then pet it if it is harmless. Perhaps my sorceress cherished it for some symbolic beauty—those old Egyptians were full of fancies.

It was very sly of you to turn the tables on me in this way. But I forgive you, since in a few hours, I shall chain this mysterious hand forever. How cold it is! Come out into the garden and get some warmth and color for tonight, my love."

But when night came, no-one could reproach the girl with her pallor, for she glowed like a pomegranate-flower, her eyes were full of fire, her lips scarlet, and all her old vivacity seemed to have returned. A more brilliant bride never blushed under a misty veil, and when her lover saw her, he was absolutely startled by the almost unearthly beauty which transformed the pale, languid creature of the morning into this radiant woman.

They were married, and if love, many blessings, and all good gifts lavishly showered upon them could make them happy, then this young pair were truly blest. But even in the rapture of the moment that made her his, Forsyth observed how icy cold was the little hand he held, how feverish the deep color on the soft cheek he kissed, and what a strange fire burned in the tender eyes that looked so wistfully at him.

Blithe and beautiful as a spirit, the smiling bride played her part in all the festivities of that long evening, and when at last light, life and color began to fade, the loving eyes that watched her thought it but the natural weariness of the hour. As the last guest departed, Forsyth was met by a servant, who gave him a letter marked "Haste." Tearing it open, he read these lines, from a friend of the professor's:

"DEAR SIR—Poor Niles died suddenly two days ago, while at the Scientific Club, and his last words were: 'Tell Paul Forsyth to beware of the Mummy's Curse, for this fatal flower has killed me.' The circumstances of his death were so peculiar, that I add them as a sequel to this message. For several months, as he told us, he had been watching an unknown plant, and that evening he brought us the flower to examine. Other matters of interest absorbed us till a late hour, and the plant was forgotten. The professor wore it in his buttonhole—a strange white, serpent-headed blossom, with pale glittering spots, which slowly changed to a glittering scarlet, till the leaves looked as if sprinkled with blood. It was observed that instead of the pallor and feebleness which had recently come over him, that the professor was unusually animated, and seemed in an almost unnatural state of high spirits. Near the close of the meeting, in the midst of a lively discussion, he suddenly dropped, as if smitten with apoplexy. He was conveyed home insensible, and after one lucid interval, in which he gave me the message I have recorded above, he died in great agony, raving of mummies, pyramids, serpents, and some fatal curse which had fallen upon him.

"After his death, livid scarlet spots, like those on the flower, appeared upon his skin, and he shriveled like a withered leaf. At my desire, the mysterious plant was examined, and pronounced by the best authority one of the most deadly poisons known to the Egyptian sorceresses. The plant slowly absorbs the vitality of whoever cultivates it, and the blossom, worn for two or three hours, produces either madness or death."

Down dropped the paper from Forsyth's hand; he read no further, but hurried back into the room where he had left his young wife. As if worn out with fatigue, she had thrown herself upon a couch, and lay there motionless, her face half-hidden by the light folds of the veil, which had blown over it.

"Evelyn, my dearest! Wake up and answer me. Did you wear that strange flower today?" whispered Forsyth, putting the misty screen away.

There was no need for her to answer, for there, gleaming spectrally on her bosom, was the evil blossom, its white petals spotted now with flecks of scarlet, vivid as drops of newly spilt blood.

But the unhappy bridegroom scarcely saw it, for the face above it appalled him by its utter vacancy. Drawn and pallid, as if with some wasting malady, the young face, so lovely an hour ago, lay before him aged and blighted by the baleful influence of the plant which had drunk up her life. No recognition in the eyes, no word upon the lips, no motion of the hand— only the faint breath, the fluttering pulse, and wide-opened eyes, betrayed that she was alive.

Alas for the young wife! The superstitious fear at which she had smiled had proved true: the curse that had bided its time for ages was fulfilled at last, and her own hand wrecked her happiness for ever. Death in life was her doom, and for years Forsyth secluded himself to tend with pathetic devotion the pale ghost, who never, by word or look, could thank him for the love that outlived even such a fate as this.

Nonfiction

RAIDING MUMMIES' TOMBS

Amelia Edwards

Amelia Edwards was an English novelist who became fascinated by Ancient Egypt and became an Egyptologist. She helped found the Egypt Exploration Fund and devoted much of her time to promoting research and the preservation of antiquities. Here she describes a visit to Sakkara.

It is a long and shelterless ride from the palms to the desert; but we come to the end of it at last, mounting just such another sand-slope as that which leads up from the Giza road to the foot of the Great Pyramid. The edge of the plateau here rises abruptly from the plain in one long range of low perpendicular cliffs pierced with dark mouths of rock-cut sepulchres, while the sand-slope by which we are climbing pours down through a breach in the rock, as an Alpine snowdrift flows through a mountain gap from the ice-level above.

And now, having dismounted through compassion for our unfortunate little donkeys, the first thing we observe is the curious mixture of debris underfoot. At Giza one treads only sand and pebbles; but here at Sakkara the whole plateau is thickly strewn with scraps of broken pottery, limestone, marble, and alabaster; flakes of green and blue glaze; bleached bones; shreds of yellow linen; and lumps of some odd-looking dark brown substance, like dried-up sponge. Presently someone picks up a little noseless head of one of the common blue-ware funereal statuettes, and immediately we all fall to work, grubbing for treasure—a pure waste of precious time; for though the sand is full of debris, it has been sifted so often and so carefully by the Arabs that it no longer contains anything worth looking for. Meanwhile, one finds a fragment of iridescent glass—another, a morsel of shattered vase—a third, an opaque bead of some kind of yellow paste. And then, with a shock which the present writer, at all events, will not soon forget, we suddenly discover that these scattered bones are human—that those linen shreds are shreds of cerement cloths—that yonder odd-looking brown lumps are rent fragments of what once was living flesh! And now for the first time we realize that every inch of this ground on which we are standing, and all these hillocks and hollows and pits in the sand, are violated graves.

"Ce n'est que le premier pas que coûte." We soon became quite hardened to such sights, and learned to rummage among dusty sepulchres with no more compunction than would have befitted a gang of professional body-snatchers. These are experiences upon which one looks back afterwards with wonder, and something like remorse; but so infectious is the universal callousness, and so overmastering is the passion for relic-hunting, that I do not doubt we should again do the same things under the same circumstances. Most Egyptian travelers, if questioned, would have to make a similar confession. Shocked at first, they denounce with horror the whole system of sepulchral excavation, legal as well as predatory; acquiring, however, a taste for scarabs and funerary statuettes, they soon begin to buy with eagerness the spoils of the dead; finally they forget all their former scruples, and ask no better fortune, than to discover and confiscate a tomb for themselves. . . .

The thing that . . . caught the painter's eye . . . was a long crack running transversely down the face of the rock. It was such a crack as might have been caused, one would say, by blasting.

He stooped—cleared the sand away a little with his hand—observed that the crack widened—poked in the point of his stick; and found that it penetrated to a depth of two or three feet. Even then, it seemed to him to stop, not because it encountered any obstacle, but because the crack was not wide enough to admit the thick end of the stick.

This surprised him. No mere fault in the natural rock, he thought, would go so deep. He scooped away a little more sand; and still the cleft widened. He introduced the stick a second time. It was a long palm-stick like an alpenstock, and it measured about five feet in length. When he probed the cleft with it this second time, it went in freely up to where he held it in his hand—that is to say, to a depth of quite four feet.

Convinced now that there was some hidden cavity in the rock, he carefully examined the surface. There were yet visible a few hieroglyphic characters and part of two cartouches, as well as some battered outlines of what had once been figures. The heads of these figures were gone (the face of the rock, with whatever may have been sculptured upon it, having come away bodily at this point), while from the waist downwards they were hidden under the sand. Only some hands and arms, in short, could be made out.

They were the hands and arms, apparently, of four figures; two in the center of the composition, and two at the extremities. The two center ones, which seemed to be back to back, probably represented gods; the outer ones, worshippers.

All at once, it flashed upon the painter that he had seen this kind of group many a time before—*and generally over a doorway.*

Feeling sure now that he was on the brink of a discovery, he came back; fetched away Salame and Mehemet Ali; and, without saying a syllable to anyone, set to work with these two to scrape away the sand at the spot where the crack widened.

Meanwhile, the luncheon bell having rung thrice, we concluded that the painter had rambled off somewhere into the desert; and so sat down without him. Towards the close of the meal, however, came a penciled note, the contents of which ran as follows:

"Pray come immediately—I have found the entrance to a tomb. Please send some sandwiches—A. M'C."

To follow the messenger at once to the scene of action was the general impulse. In less than ten minutes we were there, asking breathless questions, peeping in through the fast-widening aperture, and helping to clear away the sand.

All that Sunday afternoon, heedless of possible sunstroke, unconscious of fatigue, we toiled upon our hands and knees, as for bare life, under the burning sun. We had all the crew up, working like tigers. Every one helped; even the dragoman and the two maids. More than once, when we paused for a moment's breathing space, we said to each other: "If those at home could see us, what would they say!"

And now, more than ever, we felt the need of implements. With a spade or two and a wheelbarrow, we could have done wonders; but with only one small fire-shovel, a birch broom, a couple of charcoal baskets, and about twenty pairs of hands, we were poor indeed. What was wanted in means, however, was made up in method. Some scraped away the sand; some gathered it into baskets; some carried the baskets to the edge of the cliff, and emptied them into the river. The Idle Man distinguished himself by scooping out a channel where the slope was steepest; which greatly facilitated the work. Emptied down this shoot and kept continually going, the sand poured off in a steady stream like water.

Meanwhile the opening grew rapidly larger. When we first came up—that is, when the painter and the two sailors had been working on it for about an hour—we found a hole scarcely as large as one's hand, through which it was just possible to catch a dim glimpse of painted walls within. By sunset, the top of the doorway was laid bare, and where the crack ended in a large triangular fracture, there was an aperture about a foot and a half square, into which Mehemet Ali was the first to squeeze his way. We passed him in a candle and a box of matches; but he came out again directly, saying that it was a most beautiful Birbeh, and quite light within.

The writer wriggled in next. She found herself looking down from the top of a sandslope into a small square chamber. This sand-drift, which here rose to within a foot and a half of the top of the doorway, was heaped to the ceiling in the corner behind the door, and thence sloped steeply down, completely covering the floor. There was light enough to see every detail distinctly—the painted frieze running round just under the ceiling; the bas-relief sculptures on the walls, gorgeous with unfaded color; the smooth sand, pitted near the top, where Mehemet Ali had trodden, but undisturbed elsewhere by human foot; the great gap in the middle of the ceiling, where the rock had given way; the fallen fragments on the floor, now almost buried in sand.

Satisfied that the place was absolutely fresh and untouched, the writer crawled out, and the others, one by one, crawled in. When each had seen it in turn, the opening was barricaded for the night; the sailors being forbidden to enter it, lest they should injure the decorations.

Theodore Davis

American millionaire Theodore Davis was the sponsor of many digs in Egypt. One of his greatest discoveries was the tomb of Yuya and Thuyu in the Valley of the Kings. Before entering this tomb, he summoned the director of antiquities for Egypt, Sir Gaston Maspero, and the chief inspector of antiquities, Arthur Weigall. The following day, the three of them entered the tomb.

The chamber was as dark as dark could be and extremely hot. Our first quest was the name of the owner of the tomb, as to which we had not the slightest knowledge or suspicion. We held up our candles, but they gave so little light and so dazzled our eyes that we could see nothing except the glitter of gold. In a moment or two, however, I made out a very large wooden coffin, known as a funeral sled, which was used to contain all the coffins of the dead person and his mummy and to convey them to his tomb. It was about six feet high and eight feet long, made of wood covered with bitumen, which was as bright as the day it was put on. Around the upper part of the coffin was a stripe of gold-foil, about six inches wide, covered with hieroglyphs. On calling Monsieur Maspero's attention to it, he immediately handed me his candle, which, together with my own, I held before my eyes, close to the inscriptions so that he could read them. In an instant he said, "Iouiya [a variant spelling of Yuya]." Naturally excited by the announcement, and blinded by the glare of the candles, I involuntarily advanced them very near the coffin; whereupon Monsieur Maspero cried out, "Be careful!" and pulled my hands back. In a moment we realized that, had my candles touched the bitumen, which I came dangerously near doing, the coffin would have been in a blaze. As the entire contents of the tomb were inflammable, and directly opposite the coffin was a corridor leading to the open air and making a draft, we undoubtedly should have lost our lives, as the only escape was by the corridor, which would have necessitated climbing over the stone wall barring the doorway. This would have retarded our exit for at least ten minutes.

As soon as we realized the danger we had escaped, we made our way out of the chamber and, seating ourselves in the corridor, sent for workmen, who took down the door blocking the doorway. Then the electricians brought down the wires with bulbs attached, and we made our second entry into the chamber, each of us furnished with electric lights which we held over our heads, and we saw that every foot of the chamber was filled with objects brilliant with gold. In a corner stood a chariot, the pole of which had been broken by the weight of a coffin lid that the robber had evidently deposited upon it. Within a foot or two of the chariot stood two alabaster vases of great beauty and in perfect condition.

From the neck of one of the vases hung shreds of mummy-cloth which had originally covered the mouth of the vase. Evidently the robber, expecting the contents to be valuable, tore off the cloth. Three thousand years thereafter I looked into the vase with like expectation; both of us were disappointed, for it contained only a liquid which was first thought to be honey, but which subsequently proved to be natron.

The mummies of Iouiya and Touiyou [a variant spelling of Thuyu] were lying in their coffins. Originally each mummy was enclosed in three coffins; the inner one holding the body. Evidently the robber had taken the inner coffins out and then had taken off their lids, though he did not take the bodies out of their coffins, but contented himself with stripping off the mummy-cloth in which they were wrapped. The stripping was done by scratching off the cloth with his nails, seeking only the gold ornaments or jewels. At least that seems to have been the manner of robbing the bodies, as we found in both coffins, on either side of the bodies, great quantities of mummy-cloth torn into small bits. Among the shreds were found numerous valuable religious symbols, several scarabs, and various objects of interest and beauty. In lifting the body of Iouiya from his coffin, we found a necklace of large beads made of gold and of lapis lazuli, strung on a strong thread, which the robber had evidently broken when scratching off the mummy-cloth, causing the beads to fall behind the mummy's neck.

The robber had also overlooked a gold plate about the size of the palm of a man's hand, which had been inserted by the embalmer to conceal the incision he had made in extracting the dead man's heart for special mummification.

When I first saw the mummy of Touiyou she was lying in her coffin, covered from her chin to her feet with very fine mummy-cloth arranged with care. Why this was done no one can positively state, but I am disposed to think that the robber was impressed by the dignity of the dead woman whose body he had desecrated. I had occasion to sit by her in the tomb for nearly an hour, and having nothing else to do or see, I studied her face and indulged in speculations germane to the situation, until her dignity and character so impressed me that I almost found it necessary to apologize for my presence.

From all the evidence furnished by the acts of the robber, it seems reasonable to conclude that the entry into the tomb was made within the lifetime of some person who had exact knowledge of its location. Evidently the robber had tunneled through the overlying debris which concealed the door of the tomb; otherwise he would have been compelled to remove a mass of rock and soil which would have required many days, and would also have exposed the robbery to the first passer-by. When the robber found the outer doorway barred by a wall, he took off enough of it to enable him to crawl through; and when he reached the second and last doorway, he found a corresponding wall, which he treated in the same manner. He seems to have had either a very dim light or none at all, for when he was in the burial chamber he selected a large stone scarab, the neck-yoke of the chariot, and a wooden staff of office, all of which were covered with thick gold foil, which evidently he thought to be solid gold: he carried them up the corridor until he came to a gleam of daylight, when he discovered his error and left them on the floor of the corridor, where I found them.

When the robber got out of the tomb, he carefully concealed the doorway and his tunnel with stones and debris, and did it so effectively, that it was not disturbed until its discovery three thousand years later.

Arthur Weigall

*Arthur Weigall had just been appointed chief inspector of antiquities un-
der Sir Gaston Maspero when Theodore Davis discovered the tomb of Yuya
and Thuyu. In the following excerpts from two of his letters, he describes
the first time he, Maspero, and Davis entered the tomb and what they
found.*

[W]e] slipped and slid down the long steep passage to the blocked
door, and with some difficulty we crawled into the inner chamber.
For some moments we couldn't see anything much, but as our eyes got used
to the candle light we saw a sight which I can safely say no living man has
ever seen. The chamber was pretty large—a rough hewn cavern of a place. In
the middle of the room were two enormous sarcophagi of wood inlaid with
gold. The lids had been wrenched off by the plunderers and the coffins inside had been tumbled about so that the two mummies were exposed. . . .
All round the sarcophagi—piled almost to the roof—were chairs, tables, beds,
vases, and so on—all in perfect condition. . . . In one corner a large chariot—
quite perfect—as clean as a London hansom—lay; and by it a huge bedstead
of inlaid wood something like Chippendale. Here, there was a group of lovely
painted vases—here, a pile of gold and silver figures. In one corner were some
jars of wine, the lids tied on with string, and among them was one huge alabaster jug full of honey[5] still liquid. When I saw this I really nearly
fainted. . . . The extraordinary sensation of finding oneself looking at a pot
of honey as liquid and sticky as the honey one eats at breakfast and yet three
thousand five hundred years old, was so dumfounding that one felt as
though one were mad or dreaming. The room looked just as a drawing room
would look in a London house shut up while the people were away for the
summer. But with this terrifying difference—that everything was in the
fashion of thirty-four centuries ago—in the fashion of a period hundreds of

---

[5] This was later found to be natron.

years before Moses and the Exodus. There were lovely gold and wood arm chairs with cane bottoms. There were cushions stuffed with feathers and down—as soft as though they were made yesterday.

Maspero, Davis and I stood there gaping and almost trembling for a time—and I think we all felt we were face to face with something which seemed to upset all human ideas of time and distance. Then we dashed for the inscribed objects and read out the names of Prince Auai and his wife Thuaie [variant spellings of Yuya and Thuyu]—the famous mother and father of Queen Tiye. They had been known so well and discussed so often that they seemed old friends. . . . But nobody had ever expected to see them, [and] as we looked at the mummies—Princess Thuaie with her hair still plaited and elaborately dressed, and Prince Auai with his eyes peacefully closed and his mouth a little open—an awful feeling came over me. All three of us very soon crawled out of the tomb into the sunlight—one step from the seventeenth century before Christ to the twentieth century after Him.

[*A few days later Weigall wrote of some items found in the tomb.*]

One piece was a little chest made entirely of inlaid wood, the inlay being jasper blue porcelain and gold, in beautiful patterns. It has a charming lid and inside were some jewels. It looked as though it had been made yesterday. The lady Thuai has a fine face, and we have been hunting about her body and have found some jolly scarabs and amulets. Her head is bound up in white linen, and all the features of the face are perfect. She must have been an old woman. Poor soul, how she must have hated having an electric lamp blazing in her eyes after thirty-four centuries of darkness. We have not yet examined her husband closely, but he stares solemnly at us all the time as we work and whistle and swear about the tomb.

Giovanni Belzoni

Italian-born Giovanni Belzoni had been an engineer and a circus strong-man (he was six-foot-seven) when he was hired by the British consul in Egypt to acquire ancient artifacts for the British Museum. At this he was very successful, though many criticized him for his methods. In one ten-day period alone he discovered six new tombs.

Taking Mrs. Belzoni with me, I visited Portugal, Spain and Malta, from which latter place we embarked for Egypt. . . . Here I had the good fortune to be the discoverer of many remains of antiquity of that primitive nation. I succeeded in opening one of the two famous Pyramids of Giza, as well as several of the Tombs of the Kings at Thebes. Among the latter, that which has been pronounced by one of the most distinguished scholars of the age to be the tomb of Psammuthis, is at this moment the principal, the most perfect and splendid monument in that country. The celebrated bust of young Memnon, which I brought from Thebes, is now in the British Museum; and the alabaster sarcophagus, found in the Tombs of the Kings, is on its way to England.

Near the second cataract of the Nile, I opened the temple of Ybsambul; then made a journey to the coast of the Red Sea, to the city of Berenice, and afterwards an excursion in the western Elloah, or Oasis. I now embarked for Europe, and after an absence of twenty years, returned to my native land, and to the bosom of my family; from whence I proceeded to England.

On my arrival in Europe I found so erroneous accounts had been given to the public of my operations and discoveries in Egypt, that it appeared to be my duty to publish a plain statement of facts; and should anyone call its correctness in question, I hope they will do it openly, that I may be able to prove the truth of my assertions.

Gournow is a tract of rocks, about two miles in length, at the foot of the Libyan mountains, on the west of Thebes, and was the burial place of the great city of a hundred gates. Every part of these rocks is cut out by art, in the form of large and small chambers, each of which has its separate entrance; and though they are very close to each other, it is seldom that there is any interior communication from one to the other. I can truly say, it is impossible to give any description sufficient to convey the smallest idea of those subterranean abodes, and their inhabitants. There are no sepulchres in any part of the world like them; there are no excavations or mines, that can be compared to these truly astonishing places; and no exact description can be given of their interior, owing to the difficulty of visiting these places. The inconvenience of entering into them is such, that it is not everyone who can support the exertion.

A traveler is generally satisfied when he has seen the large hall, the gallery, the staircase, and as far as he can conveniently go: besides, he is taken up with the strange works he observes cut in various places, and painted on each side of the walls: so that when he comes to a narrow and difficult passage, or to have to descend to the bottom of a well or cavity, he declines taking such trouble, naturally supposing that he cannot see in these abysses anything so magnificent as what he sees above, and consequently deeming it useless to proceed any farther. Of some of these tombs many persons could not stand the suffocating air, which often causes fainting. A vast quantity of dust rises, so fine that it enters into the throat and nostrils, and chokes the nose and mouth to such a degree, that it requires great power of lungs to resist it and the strong effluvia of the mummies. This is not all: the entry or passage where the bodies are is roughly cut in the rocks, and the falling of the sand from the upper part or ceiling of the passage causes it to be nearly filled up. In some places there is not more than the vacancy of a foot left, which you must contrive to pass through in a creeping posture like a snail, on pointed and keen stones, that cut like glass. After getting through these passages, some of them two or three hundred yards long, you generally find a more commodious place, perhaps high enough to sit. But what a place of rest! surrounded by bodies, by heaps of mummies in all directions; which, previous to my being accustomed to the sight, impressed me with horror. The blackness of the wall, the faint light given by the candles or torches for want of air, the different objects that surrounded me, seeming to converse with each other, and the Arabs with the candles or torches in their hands, naked and covered with dust, themselves resembling living mummies, absolutely formed a scene that cannot be described. In such a situation I found myself several times, and often returned exhausted and fainting, till at last I became inured to it, and indifferent to what I suffered, except from the dust, which never failed to choke my throat and nose; and though fortunately I am destitute of the sense of smelling, I could taste that the mummies were rather unpleasant to swallow. After the exertion of entering into such a place, through a passage of fifty, a hundred, three hundred, or perhaps six hundred yards, nearly overcome, I sought a resting place, found one, and contrived to sit; but when my weight bore on the body of an Egyptian, it crushed it like a bandbox. I naturally had recourse to my hands to sustain my weight, but they found no better support; so that I sunk altogether among the broken mummies, with a crash of bones, rags, and wooden cases, which raised such a dust as kept me motionless for a quarter of an hour, waiting till it subsided again. I could not remove from the place, however, without increasing it, and every step I took I crushed a mummy in some part or other. Once I was conducted from such a place to another resembling it, through a passage of about twenty feet in length, and no wider than that a body could be forced through. It was choked with mummies, and I could not pass without putting my face in contact with that of some decayed Egyptian; but as the passage inclined downwards, my own weight helped me on; however, I could not avoid being covered with bones, legs, arms and heads rolling from above. Thus I proceeded from one cave to another, all full of mummies piled up in various ways, some standing, some lying, and some on their heads. The purpose of my researches was to rob the Egyptians of their papyri; of which I found a few hidden in their breasts, under their arms, in the space above the knees, or on the legs, and covered by the numerous folds of cloth, that envelop the mummy. The people of Gournow, who made a trade of antiquities of this sort, are very jealous of strangers, and keep them as secret as possible, deceiving the travelers by pretending, that they have arrived at the end of the pits, when they are scarcely at the entrance. I could never prevail on them to conduct me into these places till my second voyage, when I succeeded in obtaining admission into any cave where mummies were to be seen.

My permanent residence in Thebes was the cause of my success. The Arabs saw that I paid particular attention to the situation of the entrance into the tombs, and that they could not avoid being seen by me when they were at work digging in search of a new tomb, though they are very cautious when any stranger is in Gournow not to let it be known where they go to open the earth; and as travelers generally remain in that place a few days only, they used to leave off digging during that time. If any traveler be curious enough to ask to examine the interior of a tomb, they are ready to show him one immediately, and conduct him to some of the old tombs, where he sees nothing but the grottoes in which mummies formerly had been deposited, or where there are but few, and these already plundered; so that he can form but a poor idea of the real tombs, where the remains were originally placed.

The people of Gournow live in the entrance of such caves as have already been opened, and by making partitions with earthen walls, they form habitations for themselves, as well as for their cows, camels, buffaloes, sheep, goats, dogs, etc. I do not know whether it is because they are so few in number, that the Government takes so little notice of what they do; but it is certain that they are the most unruly people in Egypt. At various times many of them have been destroyed, so that they are reduced from three thousand, the number they formerly reckoned, to three hundred, which form the population of the present day. They have no mosque, nor do they care for one; for though they have at their disposal a great quantity of all sorts of bricks, which abound in every part of Gournow, from the surrounding tombs, they have never built a single house. They are forced to cultivate a small tract of land, extending from the rocks to the Nile, about a mile in breadth, and two and a half in length; and even this is in part neglected; for if left to their own will, they would never take a spade in their hands, except when they go to dig for mummies; which they find to be more profitable employment than agriculture. This is the fault of travelers, who are so pleased the moment they are presented with any piece of antiquity, that, without thinking of the injury resulting from the example to their successors, they give a great deal more than the people really expect. Hence it has arisen, that they now set such an enormous price on antiquities, and in particular on papyri. Some of them have accumulated a considerable sum of money, and are become so indifferent, that they remain idle, unless whatever price they demand be given them; and it is to be observed, that it is a fixed point in their minds, that the Franks would not be so liberal, unless the articles were worth ten times as much as they pay for them. . . .

After having described the tombs, the mummies, the rocks and the rogues of Gournow, it is time to cross the Nile and return to Karnak. . . . My daily employment kept me in continual motion. In the morning I used to give my directions for the works at Karnak. The Arabs generally come to work at the rising of the sun, and leave off from noon till two or three o'clock. When I had many employed, I divided them into parties, and set an overseer over each, to see that they worked at the proper hours, and on the allotted spots of ground, which I had previously marked out; but generally some of our people were obliged to be there, for no trust is to be reposed in the Arabs, if they should find any small pieces of antiquity. Before noon I used to cross the river and inspect the works at Gournow. Having been there the year before, and had dealings with these people, I was at home in every part of Thebes, knew every Arab there, and they knew me as well. Mr. Beechy had taken possession of the temple at Luxor, without requesting permission from the gods, and we made a dwelling place of one of the chambers: I believe it must have been the *sekos*. By the help of some mats we procured a very tolerable accommodation, but could not prevent the dust from coming on our beds, and clothes to which for my part I had long before become indifferent. We could not sleep any longer in the boat; for in consequence of the provision we had on board, such quantities of large rats accompanied us all the way to Luxor, that we had no peace day or night, and at last they succeeded in fairly dislodging us. We thought to have been a match for them, however, for we caused all the provision to be taken out, and the boat to be sunk at Luxor, but as they were good swimmers, they saved their lives, and hid themselves in the holes of the pier; and when the provision had been put on board again, they all returned cheerfully, a few excepted, and were no doubt grateful to us for having given them a fresh appetite and a good bathing.

In Gournow our researches continued among the mummies. The Arabs had become quite unconcerned about the secret of the tombs; for they saw it was their interest to search, as they were rewarded for what they found, and those who were duly paid were indifferent whether we or their brethren found a tomb. The men were divided into two classes. The most knowing were making researches on their own account, employing eight or ten to assist them. They indicated the ground where they hoped to find a tomb, and sometimes were fortunate enough to hit on the entrance of a mummy pit in the first attempt. At other times after spending two or three days, they often found only a pit filled with mummies of the inferior class, which had nothing among them worthy of notice: so that, even to the most skilful explorer, it was a mere chance what he should find. On the other hand, in some of the tombs of the better class they found very good specimens of antiquity, of all sorts. I met with some difficulty at first in persuading these people to work in search of tombs, and receive a regular daily payment; for they conceived it to be against their interest, supposing I might obtain the antiquities at too cheap a rate: but when they saw, that sometimes they received their pay regularly, and I had nothing for it, they found it was rather in their favor, to secure twenty paras (three pence) a day, than run the risk of having nothing for their labor, which often happened with those who worked at adventure.

It was from these works that I became better acquainted with the manner in which the Egyptians regulated their burial places; and I plainly saw the various degrees and customs of the divers classes, from the peasant to the king. The Egyptians had three, different methods of embalming their dead bodies, which, Herodotus informs us, were according to the expense the persons who presented the dead bodies to the mummy-makers chose to incur. This father of history thus expresses himself on the subject:

Certain persons were appointed by the laws to the exercise of this profession. When a dead boy was brought to them, they exhibited to the friends of the deceased different models, highly finished in wood. The most perfect of these, they said, resembles one whom I do not think it religious to name on such an occasion; the second was of less price, and inferior in point of execution; the other was still more mean. They then inquired after which model the deceased should be represented. When the price was determined, the relations retired, and the embalmers proceeded in their work. In the most perfect specimens of their art, they extracted the brain through the nostrils, partly with a piece of iron, and partly by the infusion of drugs. They then, with an Ethiopian stone, made an incision in the side, through which they drew out the intestines. These they cleaned thoroughly, washing them in palm-wine, and afterwards covering them with pounded aromatics. They then filled the body with powder of pure myrrh, cassia, and other spices, without frankincense. Having sewn up the body, it was covered with nitre for the space of seventy days, which time they were not allowed to exceed. At the end of this period, being first washed, it was closely wrapped in bandages of cotton, dipped in gum, which the Egyptians use as a glue. It was then returned to the relations, who enclosed the body in a case of wood, made to resemble a human figure, and placed it against the wall in the repository of their dead. This was the most costly mode of embalming.

For those who wished to be at less expense, the following method was adopted. They neither drew out the intestines, nor made any incision in the dead body, but injected a liniment made from the cedar. After taking proper means to secure the injected oil within the body, it was covered with nitre for the time above specified. On the last day they withdrew the liquid before introduced, which brought with it all the intestines. The nitre dried up and hardened the flesh, so that the corpse appeared little but skin and bone. In this state the body was returned, and no further care taken concerning it.

There was a third mode of embalming, appropriated to the poor. A particular kind of lotion was made to pass through the body, which was afterwards merely left in nitre for the above space of seventy days and then returned.

Such is the account given us by Herodotus.

Nothing can more plainly distinguish the various classes of people, than the manner of their preservation: but there are many other remarks that may be made to the same effect. I shall describe how I found the mummies of the principal class untouched, and hence we may judge how they were prepared and deposited in their respective places. I am sorry that I am obliged to contradict my old guide, Herodotus; for in this point, and many others, he was not well informed by the Egyptians. In the first place, speaking of the mummies in their cases, he mentions them as erect: but it is somewhat singular, that in so many pits as I have opened, I never saw a single mummy standing. On the contrary, I found them lying regularly, in horizontal rows, and some were sunk into a cement, which must have been nearly fluid when the cases were placed on it. The lower classes were not buried in cases: they were dried up, as it appears, after the regular preparation of the seventy days. Mummies of this sort were in the proportion of about ten to one of the better class, as near as I could calculate by the quantity I have seen of both; and it appeared to me, that, after the operation of the nitre, adopted by the mummy-makers, these bodies may have been dried in the sun. Indeed for my own part, I am persuaded it was so; as there is not the smallest quantity of gum or anything else to be found on them. The linen in which they are folded is of a coarser sort, and less in quantity; they have no ornaments about them of any consequence, and they are piled up in layers so as to crowd several caves excavated for the purpose in a rude manner. In general these tombs are to be found in the lower grounds, at the foot of the mountains of Gournow; and some extend as far as the border to which the inundation reaches. They are to be entered by a small aperture, arched over, or by a shaft four or five feet square, at the bottom of which are entrances into various chambers, all choked up with mummies: and though there is scarcely anything to be found on them, many of these tombs have been rummaged, and left in the most confused state.

I must not omit that among these tombs we saw some which contained the mummies of animals intermixed with human bodies. There were bulls, cows, sheep, monkeys, foxes, bats, crocodiles, fishes and birds in them; idols often occur; and one tomb was filled with nothing but cats, carefully folded in red and white linen, the head covered by a mask representing the cat, and made of the same linen. I have opened all these sorts of animals. Of the bull, the calf and the sheep there is no part but the head which is covered with linen, and the horns projecting out of the cloth; the rest of the body being represented by two pieces of wood, eighteen inches wide and three feet long, in a horizontal direction, at the end of which was another, placed perpendicularly, two feet high, to form the breast of the animal. The calves and sheep are of the same structure, and large in proportion to the bulls. The monkey is in its full form, in a sitting posture. The fox is squeezed up by the bandages, but in some measure the shape of the head is kept perfect. The crocodile is left in its own shape, and after being well bound round with linen, the eyes and mouth are painted on this covering. The birds are squeezed together, and lose their shape, except the ibis, which is found like a fowl ready to be cooked, and bound round with linen like all the rest.

It is somewhat singular that such animals are not to be met within the tombs of the higher sort of people; while few or no papyri are to be found among the lower order, and if any occur they are only small pieces stuck upon the breast with a little gum or asphaltum, being probably all that the poor individual could afford to himself. In those of the better classes other objects are found. I think they ought to be divided into several classes, as I cannot confine myself to three. I do not mean to impute error to Herodotus when he speaks of the three modes of embalming; but I will venture to assert that the high, middling and poorer classes, all admit of farther distinction. In the same pit where I found mummies in cases, I found others without; and in these, papyri are most likely to be met with. I remarked, that the mummies in the cases have no papyri; at least I never observed any: on the contrary, in those without cases they are often obtained. It appears to me that such people as could afford it would have a case to be buried in, on which the history of their lives was painted; and those who could not afford a case, were contented to have their lives written on papyri, rolled up and placed above their knees. Even in the appearance of the cases there is a great difference: some are exceedingly plain, others more ornamented, and some very richly adorned with figures well painted. The cases are generally made of Egyptian sycamore: apparently this was the most plentiful wood in the country, as it is usually employed for the different utensils. All the cases have a human face, male or female. Some of the large cases contain others within them, either of wood or of plaster, painted. The inner cases are sometimes fitted to the body of the mummy: others are only covers to the body, in form of a man or woman, easily distinguishable by the beard and the breast, like that on the outside. Some of the mummies have garlands of flowers, and leaves of the acacia, or stunt tree, over their heads and breasts. This tree is often seen on the banks of the Nile, above Thebes, and particularly in Nubia. The flower when fresh is yellow, and of a very hard substance, appearing as if artificial. The leaves also are very strong, and though dried and turned brown, they still retain their firmness. In the inside of these mummies are found lumps of asphaltum, sometimes so large as to weigh two pounds. The entrails of these mummies are often found bound up in linen and asphaltum. What does not incorporate with the fleshy part, remains of the natural color of the pitch; but that which does incorporate becomes brown, and evidently mixed with the grease of the body, forming a mass, which on pressure crumbles into dust. The wooden case is first covered with a layer or two of cement, not unlike plaster of Paris; and on this are sometimes cast figures in *basso rilievo,* for which they make niches cut in stone. The whole case is painted; the ground generally yellow, the figures and hieroglyphics blue, green, red and black. The last is very seldom used. The whole of the painting is covered with a varnish, which preserves it very effectually. Some of the colors, in my humble opinion, were vegetable, for they are evidently transparent; besides, I conceive it was easier for the Egyptians to produce vegetable colors than mineral, from the great difficulty of grinding the latter to such perfection.

The next sort of mummy that drew my attention, I believe I may with reason conclude to have been appropriate to the priests. They are folded in a manner totally different from the others, and so carefully executed as to show the great respect paid to those personages. The bandages are strips of red and white linen intermixed, covering the whole body and forming a curious effect from the two colors. The arms and legs are not enclosed in the same envelope with the body, as in the common mode, but are bandaged separately, even the fingers and toes being preserved distinct. They have sandals of painted leather on their feet, and bracelets on their arms and wrists. They are always found with their arms across the breast, but not pressing it; and though the body is bound with such a quantity of linen, the shape of the person is carefully preserved in every limb. The cases in which mummies of this sort are found are somewhat better executed, and I have seen one, that had the eyes and eyebrows of enamel, beautifully executed in imitation of nature. . . .

The tombs containing the better classes of people are of course superior to the others. There are some more extensive than the rest, having various apartments, adorned with figures representing different actions of life. Funeral processions are generally predominant. Agricultural processes, religious ceremonies, and more ordinary occurrences such as feasting, etc. are to be seen everywhere. . . . It would be impossible to describe the numerous little articles found in them, which are well adapted to show the domestic habits of the ancient Egyptians. It is here the smaller idols are occasionally found, either lying on the ground, or in the cases of the mummies. Vases are sometimes found containing the embalmed entrails of the mummies. These are generally made of baked clay, and painted over; their sizes differ from eight inches to eighteen; their covers represent the head of some divinity, bearing either the human form, or that of a monkey, fox, cat, or some other animal. I met with a few of these vases of alabaster in the Tombs of the Kings, but unfortunately they were broken. A great quantity of pottery is found, and also wooden vessels in some of the tombs as if the deceased had resolved to have all he possessed deposited along with him. The most singular among these things are the ornaments, in particular the small works in clay and other composition. I have been fortunate to find many specimens of their manufactures, among which is leaf gold, beaten nearly as thin as ours. The gold appears to me extremely pure and of a finer color than is generally seen in our own.

Fiction

THE VENGEANCE
OF NITOCRIS

Tennessee Williams

Pulitzer Prize–winning playwright Thomas Lanier "Tennessee" Williams is considered to be one of America's greatest dramatists. He is known for such classics as A Streetcar Named Desire, Cat on a Hot Tin Roof *(both of which won Pulitzers),* The Night of the Iguana, *and* The Glass Menagerie. *In 1994 the U.S. Postal Service honored him by issuing a postage stamp with his picture on it. In general, his plays dealt sympathetically with such social outcasts as alcoholics, homosexuals, cripples, and the mentally disturbed. In spite of the dominance of tenderness and compassion in his plays, he was often criticized for the violence and sexuality in them. Besides plays, he also wrote poetry, short stories, and two novels—one of which is* The Roman Spring of Mrs. Stone. *A number of his works were made into movies. Williams wrote the following story when he was sixteen, and it was one of his first published works. It is based on a true story.*

Hushed were the streets of many-peopled Thebes. Those few who passed through them moved with the shadowy fleetness of bats near dawn, and bent their faces from the sky as if fearful of seeing what in their fancies might be hovering there. Weird, high-noted incantations of a wailing sound were audible through the barred doors. On corners groups of naked and bleeding priests cast themselves repeatedly and with loud cries upon the rough stones of the walks. Even dogs and cats and oxen seemed impressed by some strange menace and foreboding and cowered and slunk dejectedly. All Thebes was in dread. And indeed there was cause for their dread and for their wails of lamentation. A terrible sacrilege had been committed. In all the annals of Egypt none more monstrous was recorded.

Five days had the altar fires of the god of gods, Osiris, been left unburning. Even for one moment to allow darkness upon the altars of the god was considered by the priests to be a great offense against him. Whole years of dearth and famine had been known to result from such an offense. But now the altar fires had been deliberately extinguished, and left extinguished for five days. It was an unspeakable sacrilege.

Hourly there was expectancy of some great calamity to befall. Perhaps within the approaching night a mighty earthquake would shake the city to the ground, or a fire from heaven would sweep upon them, or some monster from the desert, where wild and terrible monsters were said to dwell, would rush upon them and Osiris himself would rise up, as he had done before, and swallow all Egypt in his wrath. Surely some such dread catastrophe would befall them ere the week had passed. Unless—unless the sacrilege were avenged.

But how might it be avenged? That was the question high lords and priests debated. Pharaoh alone had committed the sacrilege. It was he, angered because the bridge, which he had spent five years in constructing so that one day he might cross the Nile in his chariot as he had once boasted that he would do, had been swept away by the rising waters. Raging with anger, he had flogged the priests from the temple. He had barred the temple doors and with his own breath had blown out the sacred candles. He had defiled the hallowed altars with the carcasses of beasts. Even, it was said in low, shocked whispers, in a mock ceremony of worship he had burned the carrion of a hyena, most abhorrent of all beasts to Osiris, upon the holy altar of gold, which even the most high of priests forbore to lay naked hands upon!

Surely, even though he be pharaoh, ruler of all Egypt and holder of the golden eagle, he could not be permitted to commit such violent sacrileges without punishment from man. The god Osiris was waiting for them to inflict that punishment, and if they failed to do it, upon them would come a scourge from heaven.

Standing before the awed assembly of nobles, the high Kha Semblor made a gesture with his hands. A cry broke from those who watched. Sentence had been delivered. Death had been pronounced as doom for the pharaoh. The heavy, barred doors were shoved open. The crowd came out, and within an hour a well-organized mob passed through the streets of Thebes, directed for the palace of the pharaoh. Mob justice was to be done.

Within the resplendent portals of the palace the pharaoh, ruler of all Egypt, watched with tightened brow the orderly but menacing approach of the mob. He divined their intent. But was he not their pharaoh? He could contend with gods, so why should he fear mere dogs of men?

A woman clung to his stiffened arm. She was tall and as majestically handsome as he. A garb of linen, as brilliantly golden as the sun, entwined her body closely and bands of jet were around her throat and forehead. She was the fair and well-loved Nitocris, sister of the pharaoh.

"Brother, brother!" she cried. "Light the fires! Pacify the dogs! They come to kill you."

Only more stern grew the look of the pharaoh. He thrust aside his pleading sister, and beckoned to the attendants.

"Open the doors!"

Startled, trembling, the man obeyed.

The haughty lord of Egypt drew his sword from its sheath. He slashed the air with a stroke that would have severed stone. Out on the steep steps leading between tall, colored pillars to the doors of the palace he stepped. The people saw him. A howl rose from their lips.

"Light the fires!"

The figure of the pharaoh stood inflexible as rock. Superbly tall and muscular, his bare arms and limbs glittering like burnished copper in the light of the brilliant sun, his body erect and tense in his attitude of defiance, he looked indeed a mortal fit almost to challenge gods.

The mob, led by the black-robed priests and nobles who had arrived at the foot of the steps, now fell back before the stunning, magnificent defiance of their giant ruler. They felt like demons who had assailed the heavens and had been abashed and shamed by the mere sight of that which they had assailed. A hush fell over them. Their upraised arms faltered and sank down. A moment more and they would have fallen to their knees.

What happened then seemed nothing less than a miracle. In his triumph and exultation, the pharaoh had been careless of the crumbling edges of the steps. Centuries old, there were sections of these steps which were falling apart. Upon such a section had the gold-sandaled foot of the pharaoh descended, and it was not strong enough to sustain his great weight. With a scuttling sound it broke loose. A gasp came from the mob—the pharaoh was about to fall. He was palpitating, wavering in the air, fighting to retain his balance. He looked as if he were grappling with some monstrous, invisible snake, coiled about his gleaming body. A hoarse cry burst from his lips; his sword fell; and then his body thudded down the steps in a series of somersaults, and landed at the foot, sprawled out before the gasping mob. For a moment there was breathless silence. And then came the shout of a priest.

"A sign from the gods!"

That vibrant cry seemed to restore the mob to all of its wolflike rage. They surged forward. The struggling body of the pharaoh was lifted up and torn to pieces by their clawing hands and weapons. Thus was the god Osiris avenged.

A week later another large assembly of persons confronted the brilliant-pillared palace. This time they were there to acknowledge a ruler, not to slay one. The week before they had rended the pharaoh and now they were proclaiming his sister empress. Priests had declared that it was the will of the gods that she should succeed her brother. She was famously beautiful, pious, and wise. The people were not reluctant to accept her.

When she was borne down the steps of the palace in her rich litter, after the elaborate ceremony of the coronation had been concluded, she responded to the cheers of the multitude with a smile which could not have appeared more amicable and gracious. None might know from that smile upon her beautiful carmined lips that within her heart she was thinking, "These are the people who slew my brother. Ah, god Issus, grant me power to avenge his death upon them!"

Not long after the beauteous Nitocris mounted the golden throne of Egypt, rumors were whispered of some vast, mysterious enterprise being conducted in secret. A large number of slaves were observed each dawn to embark upon barges and to be carried down the river to some unknown point, where they labored through the day, returning after dark. The slaves were Ethiopians, neither able to speak nor to understand the Egyptian language, and therefore no information could be got from them by the curious as to the object of their mysterious daily excursions. The general opinion, though, was that the pious queen was having a great temple constructed to the gods and that when it was finished, enormous public banquets would be held within it before its dedication. She meant it to be a surprise gift to the priests who were ever desirous of some new place of worship and were dissatisfied with their old altars, which they said were defiled.

Throughout the winter the slaves repeated daily their excursions. Traffic of all kinds plying down the river was restricted for several miles to within forty yards of one shore. Any craft seen to disregard that restriction was set upon by a galley of armed men and pursued back into bounds. All that could be learned was that a prodigious temple or hall of some sort was in construction.

It was late in the spring when the excursions of the workmen were finally discontinued. Restrictions upon the river traffic were withdrawn. The men who went eagerly to investigate the mysterious construction returned with tales of a magnificent new temple, surrounded by rich, green, tropical verdure, situated near the bank of the river. It was a temple to the god Osiris. It had been built by the Queen probably that she might partly atone for the sacrilege of her brother and deliver him from some of the torture which he undoubtedly suffered. It was to be dedicated within the month by a great banquet. All the nobles and the high priests of Osiris, of which there were a tremendous number, were to be invited.

Never had the delighted priests been more extravagant in their praises of Queen Nitocris. When she passed through the streets in her open litter, bedazzling eyes by the glitter of her golden ornaments, the cries of the people were almost frantic in their exaltation of her.

True to the predictions of the gossipers, before the month had passed the banquet had been formally announced and to all the nobility and the priests of Osiris had been issued invitations to attend.

The day of the dedication, which was to be followed by the night of banqueting, was a gala holiday. At noon the guests of the empress formed a colorful assembly upon the bank of the river. Gaily draped barges floated at their moorings until preparations should be completed for the transportation of the guests to the temple. All anticipated a holiday of great merriment, and the lustful Epicureans were warmed by visualizations of the delightful banquet of copious meats, fruit, luscious delicacies and other less innocent indulgences.

When the Queen arrived, clamorous shouts rang deafeningly in her ears. She responded with charming smiles and gracious bows. The most discerning observer could not have detected anything but the greatest cordiality and kindliness reflected in her bearing towards those around her. No action, no fleeting expression upon her lovely face could have caused anyone to suspect anything except entire amicability in her feelings or her intentions. The rats, as they followed the Pied Piper of Hamelin through the streets, entranced by the notes of his magical pipe, could not have been less apprehensive of any great danger impending than were the guests of the empress as they followed her in gaily draped barges, singing and laughing down the sun-glowing waters of the Nile.

The most vivid descriptions of those who had already seen the temple did not prepare the others for the spectacle of beauty and grandeur which it presented. Gasps of delight came from the priests. What a place in which to conduct their ceremonies! They began to feel that the sacrilege of the dead pharaoh was not, after all, to be so greatly regretted, since it was responsible for the building of this glorious new temple.

The columns were massive and painted with the greatest artistry. The temple itself was proportionately large. The center of it was unroofed. Above the entrance were carved the various symbols of the god Osiris, with splendid workmanship. The building was immensely big, and against the background of green foliage it presented a picture of almost breathtaking beauty. Ethiopian attendants stood on each side of the doorway, their shining black bodies ornamented with bands of brilliant gold. On the interior the guests were inspired to even greater wonderment. The walls were hung with magnificent painted tapestries. The altars were more beautifully and elaborately carved than any seen before. Aromatic powders were burning upon them and sending up veils of scented smoke. The sacramental vessels were of the most exquisite and costly metals. Golden coffers and urns were piled high with perfect fruits of all kinds.

Ah, yes—a splendid place for the making of sacrifices, gloated the staring priests.

Ah, yes indeed, agreed the Queen Nitocris, smiling with half-closed eyes, it was a splendid place for sacrifices—especially for the human sacrifice that had been planned. But all who observed that guileful smile interpreted it as gratification over the pleasure which her creation in honor of their god had brought to the priests of Osiris. Not the slightest shadow of portent was upon the hearts of the joyous guests.

The ceremony of dedication occupied the whole of the afternoon. And when it drew to its impressive conclusion, the large assembly, their nostrils quivering from the savory odor of the roasting meats, were fully ready and impatient for the banquet that awaited them. They gazed about them, observing that the whole building composed an unpartitioned amphitheater and wondering where might be the room of the banquet. However, when the concluding processional chant had been completed, the Queen summoned a number of burly slaves, and by several iron rings attached to its outer edges they lifted up a large slab of flooring, disclosing to the astonished guests the fact that the scene of the banquet was to be an immense subterranean vault.

Such vaults were decidedly uncommon among the Egyptians. The idea of feasting in one was novel and appealing. Thrilled exclamations came from the eager, excited crowd and they pressed forward to gaze into the depths, now brightly illuminated. They saw a room beneath them almost as vast in size as the amphitheater in which they were standing. It was filled with banquet tables upon which were set the most delectable foods and rich, sparkling wines in an abundance that would satiate the banqueters of Bacchus. Luxurious, thick rugs covered the floors. Among the tables passed nymphlike maidens, and at one end of the room harpists and singers stood, making sublime music.

The air was cool with the dampness of under-earth, and it was delightfully fragrant by the perfumes of burning spices and the savory odors of the feast. If it had been heaven itself which the crowd of the Queen's guests now gazed down upon they would not have considered the vision disappointing. Perhaps even if they had known the hideous menace that lurked in those gay-draped walls beneath them, they would still have found the allurement of the banquet scene difficult to resist.

Decorum and reserve were almost completely forgotten in the swiftness of the guests' descent. The stairs were not wide enough to afford room for all those who rushed upon them, and some tumbled over, landing unhurt upon the thick carpets. The priests themselves forgot their customary dignity and aloofness when they looked upon the beauty of the maiden attendants.

Immediately all of the guests gathered around the banquet tables, and the next hour was occupied in gluttonous feasting. Wine was unlimited and so was the thirst of the guests. Goblets were refilled as quickly as they were emptied by the capacious mouths of the drinkers. The singing and the laughter, the dancing and the wild frolicking grew less and less restrained until the banquet became a delirious orgy.

The Queen alone, seated upon a cushioned dais from which she might overlook the whole room, remained aloof from the general hilarity. Her thick black brows twitched; her luminous black eyes shone strangely between their narrow painted lids. There was something peculiarly feline in the curl of her rich red lips. Now and again her eyes sought the section of wall to her left, where hung gorgeous braided tapestries from the East. But it seemed not the tapestries that she looked upon. Color would mount upon her brow and her slender fingers would dig still tighter into the cushions she reclined upon.

In her mind the Queen Nitocris was seeing a ghastly picture. It was the picture of a room of orgy and feasting suddenly converted into a room of terror and horror; human beings one moment drunken and lustful, the next screaming in the seizure of sudden and awful death. If any of those present had been empowered to see also that picture of dire horror, they would have clambered wildly to make their escape. But none was so empowered.

With increasing wildness the banquet continued into the middle of the night. Some of the banqueters, disgustingly gluttonous, still gorged themselves at the greasy tables. Others lay in drunken stupor, or lolled amorously with the slave girls. But most of them, formed in a great, irregular circle, skipped about the room in a barbaric, joy-mad dance, dragging and tripping each other in uncouth merriment and making the hall ring with their ceaseless shouts, laughter and hoarse song.

When the hour had approached near to midnight, the Queen, who had sat like one entranced, arose from the cushioned dais. One last intent survey she gave to the crowded room of banquet. It was a scene which she wished to imprint permanently upon her mind. Much pleasure might she derive in the future by recalling that picture, and the imagining what came afterwards— stark, searing terror rushing in upon barbaric joy!

She stepped down from the dais and walked swiftly to the steps. Her departure made no impression upon the revelers. When she arrived at the top of the stairs, she looked down and observed that no one had marked her exit.

Around the walls of the temple, dim-lit and fantastic-looking at night, with the cool wind from the river sweeping through and bending the flames of the tall candelabra, stalwart guardsmen were standing at their posts, and when the gold-cloaked figure of the Queen arose from the aperture, they advanced towards her hurriedly. With a motion, she directed them to place the slab of rock in its tight-fitting socket. With a swift, noiseless hoist and lowering, they obeyed the command. The Queen bent down. There was no change in the boisterous sounds from below. Nothing was yet suspected.

Drawing the soft and shimmering folds of her cloak about her with fingers that trembled with eagerness, excitement and the intense emotion which she felt, the Queen passed swiftly across the stone floor of the temple towards the open front through which the night wind swept, blowing her cloak in sheenful waves about her tall and graceful figure. The slaves followed after in silent file, well aware of the monstrous deed about to be executed and without reluctance to play their parts.

Down the steps of the palace into the moon-white night passed the weird procession. Their way led them down an obviously secreted path through thick ranks of murmuring palms which in their low voices seemed to be whispering shocked remonstrances against what was about to be done. But in her stern purpose the Queen was not susceptible to any discussion from god or man. Vengeance, strongest of passions, made her obdurate as stone.

Out upon a rough and apparently new-constructed stone pier the thin path led. Beneath, the cold, dark waters of the Nile surged silently by. Here the party came to a halt. Upon this stone pier would the object of their awful midnight errand be accomplished.

With a low-spoken word, the Queen commanded her followers to hold back. With her own hand she would perform the act of vengeance.

In the foreground of the pier a number of fantastic, wand-like levers extended upwards. Towards these the Queen advanced, slowly and stiffly as an executioner mounts the steps of the scaffold. When she had come beside them, she grasped one upthrust bar, fiercely, as if it had been the throat of a hated antagonist. Then she lifted her face with a quick intake of breath towards the moon-lighted sky. This was to her a moment of supreme ecstasy. Grasped in her hand was an instrument which could release awful death upon those against whom she wished vengeance. Their lives were as securely in her grasp as was this bar of iron.

Slowly, lusting upon every triumph-filled second of this time of ecstasy, she turned her face down again to the formidable bar in her hand. Deliberately she drew it back to its limit. This was the lever that opened the wall in the banquet vault. It gave entrance to death. Only the other bar now intervened between the banqueters, probably still reveling undisturbed, and the dreadful fate which she had prepared for them. Upon this bar now her jeweled fingers clutched. Savagely this time she pulled it; then with the litheness of a tiger she sprang to the edge of the pier. She leaned over it and stared down into the inky rush of the river. A new sound she heard above the steady flow. It was the sound of waters suddenly diverted into a new channel—an eager, plunging sound. Down to the hall of revelry they were rushing—these savage waters—bringing terror and sudden death.

A cry of triumph, wild and terrible enough to make even the hearts of the brutish slaves turn cold, now broke from the lips of the Queen. The pharaoh was avenged.

And even he must have considered his avenging adequate had he been able to witness it.

After the retiring of the Queen, the banquet had gone on without interruption of gaiety. None noticed her absence. None noticed the silent replacing of the stone in its socket. No premonition of disaster was felt. The musicians, having been informed beforehand of the intended event of the evening, had made their withdrawal before the Queen. The slaves, whose lives were of little value to the Queen, were as ignorant of what was to happen as were the guests themselves.

Not until the wall opened up with a loud and startling crunch did even those most inclined towards suspicion feel the slightest uneasiness. Then it was that a few noticed the slab to have been replaced, shutting them in. This discovery, communicated throughout the hall in a moment, seemed to instill a sudden fear in the hearts of all. Laughter did not cease, but the ring of dancers were distracted from their wild jubilee. They all turned towards the mysteriously opened wall and gazed into its black depths.

A hush fell over them. And then became audible the mounting sound of rushing water. A shriek rose from the throat of a woman. And then terror took possession of all within the room. Panic like the burst of flames flared into their hearts. Of one accord, they rushed upon the stair. And it, being purposely made frail, collapsed before the foremost of the wildly screaming mob had reached its summit. Turbulently they piled over the tables, filling the room with a hideous clamor. But rising above their screams was the shrill roar of the rushing water, and no sound could be more provoking of dread and terror. Somewhere in its circuitous route from the pier to the chamber of its reception it must have met with temporary blockade, for it was several minutes after the sound of it was first detected that the first spray of that death bringing water leapt into the faces of the doomed occupants of the room.

With the ferocity of a lion springing into the arena of a Roman amphitheater to devour the gladiators set there for its delectation, the black water plunged in. Furiously it surged over the floor of the room, sweeping tables before it and sending its victims, now face to face with their harrowing doom, into a hysteria of terror. In a moment that icy, black water had risen to their knees, although the room was vast. Some fell instantly dead from the shock, or were trampled upon by the desperate rushing of the mob. Tables were clambered upon. Lamps and candles were extinguished. Brilliant light rapidly faded to twilight, and a ghastly dimness fell over the room as only the suspended lanterns remained lit. And what a scene of chaotic and hideous horror might a spectator have beheld! The gorgeous trumpery of banquet invaded by howling waters of death! Gaily dressed merrymakers caught suddenly in the grip of terror! Gasps and screams of the dying amid tumult and thickening dark!

What more horrible vengeance could Queen Nitocris have conceived than this banquet of death? Not Diablo himself could be capable of anything more fiendishly artistic. Here in the temple of Osiris those nobles and priests who had slain the pharaoh in expiation of his sacrilege against Osiris had now met their deaths. And it was in the waters of the Nile, material symbol of the god Osiris, that they had died. It was magnificent in its irony!

I would be content to end this story here if it were but a story. However, it is not merely a story, as you will have discerned before now if you have been a student of the history of Egypt. Queen Nitocris is not a fictitious personage. In the annals of ancient Egypt she is no inconspicuous figure. Principally responsible for her prominence is her monstrous revenge upon the slayers of her brother, the narration of which I have just concluded. Glad would I be to end this story here; for surely anything following must be in the nature of an anticlimax. However, being not a mere storyteller here, but having upon me also the responsibility of a historian, I feel obligated to continue the account to the point where it was left off by Herodotus, the great Greek historian. And, therefore, I add this postscript, anticlimax though it be.

The morning of the day after the massacre in the temple, the guests of the Queen not having made their return, the citizens of Thebes began to glower with dark suspicions. Rumors came to them through divers channels that something of a most extraordinary and calamitous nature had occurred at the scene of the banquet during the night. Some had it that the temple had collapsed upon the revelers and all had been killed. However, this theory was speedily dispelled when a voyager from down the river reported having passed the temple in a perfectly firm condition but declared that he had seen no signs of life about the place—only the brightly canopied boats, drifting at their moorings.

Uneasiness steadily increased throughout the day. Sage persons recalled the great devotion of the Queen towards her dead brother, and noted that the guests at the banquet of last night had been composed almost entirely of those who had participated in his slaying.

When in the evening the Queen arrived in the city, pale, silent, and obviously nervous, threatening crowds blocked the path of her chariot, demanding roughly an explanation of the disappearance of her guests. Haughtily she ignored them and lashed forward the horses of her chariot, pushing aside the tight mass of people. Well she knew, however, that her life would be doomed as soon as they confirmed their suspicions. She resolved to meet her inevitable death in a way that befitted one of her rank, not at the filthy hands of a mob.

Therefore, upon her entrance into the palace she ordered her slaves to fill instantly her boudoir with hot and smoking ashes. When this has been done, she went to the room, entered it, closed the door and locked it securely, and then flung herself down upon a couch in the center of the room. In a short time the scorching heat and the suffocating thick fumes of the smoke overpowered her. Only her beautiful dead body remained for the hands of the mob.

Fiction

UNDER THE PYRAMIDS

H. P. Lovecraft
(WRITTEN FOR HARRY HOUDINI)

The works of Howard Philips Lovecraft originally appeared in pulp magazines or amateur presses, and he remained virtually unknown until well after his death. It was through the persistent efforts of his friends and
admirers that he finally received a wider, and ever-growing, audience. Two
fellow writers tried to convince publishers to reprint posthumous collections of Lovecraft's work. When their efforts failed, they formed Arkham
House Publishers and published the books themselves. Soon many major
publishers came out with collections of his stories. He is now one of the
best-known authors of horror and supernatural fiction. Lovecraft was the
creator of the Cthulhu Mythos, a collection of stories which are widely imitated and supplemented. His most famous stories are "The Call of
Cthulhu" and "The Dunwich Horror." Much of his work has been made into
movies, and even some fantasy role-playing and computer games are
based on his fiction. His stories are now continually in print and have been
anthologized countless times. "Under the Pyramids" is this story's original title, and the text presented here is from its first publication. It has
also been published under the title "Imprisoned with the Pharaohs." It
was ghostwritten for the famous magician and escape artist Harry Houdini. How much involvement Houdini had in the story is unknown. Reading
it gives the impression he must have at least told Lovecraft some of his
experiences of traveling through Egypt, though the second half of the tale
is definitely pure Lovecraft.

I

Mystery attracts mystery. Ever since the wide appearance of my name as a performer of unexplained feats, I have encountered strange narratives and events which my calling has led people to link with my interests and activities. Some of these have been trivial and irrelevant, some deeply dramatic and absorbing, some productive of weird and perilous experiences, and some involving me in extensive scientific and historical research. Many of these matters I have told and shall continue to tell very freely; but there is one of which I speak with great reluctance, and which I am now relating only after a session of grilling persuasion from the publishers of this magazine, who had heard vague rumours of it from other members of my family.

The hitherto guarded subject pertains to my non-professional visit to Egypt fourteen years ago, and has been avoided by me for several reasons. For one thing, I am averse to exploiting certain unmistakably actual facts and conditions obviously unknown to the myriad tourists who throng about the pyramids and apparently secreted with much diligence by the authorities at Cairo, who cannot be wholly ignorant of them. For another thing, I dislike to recount an incident in which my own fantastic imagination must have played so great a part. What I saw—or thought I saw—certainly did not take place; but is rather to be viewed as a result of my then recent readings in Egyptology, and of the speculations anent this theme which my environment naturally prompted. These imaginative stimuli, magnified by the excitement of an actual event terrible enough in itself, undoubtedly gave rise to the culminating horror of that grotesque night so long past.

In January, 1910, I had finished a professional engagement in England and signed a contract for a tour of Australian theatres. A liberal time being allowed for the trip, I determined to make the most of it in the sort of travel which chiefly interests me; so accompanied by my wife I drifted pleasantly down the Continent and embarked at Marseilles on the P. & O. Steamer *Malwa,* bound for Port Said. From that point I proposed to visit the principal historical localities of lower Egypt before leaving finally for Australia.

The voyage was an agreeable one, and enlivened by many of the amusing incidents which befall a magical performer apart from his work. I had intended, for the sake of quiet travel, to keep my name a secret; but was goaded into betraying myself by a fellow-magician whose anxiety to astound the passengers with ordinary tricks tempted me to duplicate and exceed his feats in a manner quite destructive of my incognito. I mention this because of its ultimate effect—an effect I should have foreseen before unmasking to a shipload of tourists about to scatter throughout the Nile Valley. What it did was to herald my identity wherever I subsequently went, and deprive my wife and me of all the placid inconspicuousness we had sought. Travelling to seek curiosities, I was often forced to stand inspection as a sort of curiosity myself!

We had come to Egypt in search of the picturesque and the mystically impressive, but found little enough when the ship edged up to Port Said and discharged its passengers in small boats. Low dunes of sand, bobbing buoys in shallow water, and a drearily European small town with nothing of interest save the great De Lesseps statue, made us anxious to get on to something more worth our while. After some discussion we decided to proceed at once to Cairo and the Pyramids, later going to Alexandria for the Australian boat and for whatever Greco-Roman sights that ancient metropolis might present.

The railway journey was tolerable enough, and consumed only four hours and a half. We saw much of the Suez Canal, whose route we followed as far as Ismailiya, and later had a taste of Old Egypt in our glimpse of the restored fresh-water canal of the Middle Empire. Then at last we saw Cairo glimmering through the growing dusk; a twinkling constellation which became a blaze as we halted at the great Gare Centrale.

But once more disappointment awaited us, for all that we beheld was European save the costumes and the crowds. A prosaic subway led to a square teeming with carriages, taxicabs, and trolley-cars, and gorgeous with electric lights shining on tall buildings; whilst the very theatre where I was vainly requested to play, and which I later attended as a spectator, had recently been renamed the "American Cosmograph." We stopped at Shepherd's Hotel, reached in a taxi that sped along broad, smartly built-up streets; and amidst the perfect service of its restaurant, elevators, and generally Anglo-American luxuries the mysterious East and immemorial past seemed very far away.

The next day, however, precipitated us delightfully into the heart of the Arabian Nights atmosphere; and in the winding ways and exotic skyline of Cairo, the Baghdad of Haroun-al-Raschid seemed to live again. Guided by our Baedeker, we had struck east past the Ezbekiyeh Gardens along the

Mouski in quest of the native quarter, and were soon in the hands of a clamorous cicerone who—notwithstanding later developments—was assuredly a master at his trade. Not until afterward did I see that I should have applied at the hotel for a licensed guide. This man, a shaven, peculiarly hollow-voiced, and relatively cleanly fellow who looked like a Pharaoh and called himself "Abdul Reis el Drogman," appeared to have much power over others of his kind; though subsequently the police professed not to know him, and to suggest that *reis* is merely a name for any person in authority, whilst "Drogman" is obviously no more than a clumsy modification of the word for a leader of tourist parties *dragoman*.

Abdul led us among such wonders as we had before only read and dreamed of. Old Cairo is itself a story-book and a dream—labyrinths of narrow alleys redolent of aromatic secrets; Arabesque balconies and oriels nearly meeting above the cobbled streets; maelstroms of Oriental traffic with strange cries, cracking whips, rattling carts, jingling money, and braying donkeys; kaleidoscopes of polychrome robes, veils, turbans, and tarbushes; water-carriers and dervishes, dogs and cats, soothsayers and barbers; and over all the whining of blind beggars crouched in alcoves, and the sonorous chanting of muezzins from minarets limned delicately against a sky of deep, unchanging blue.

The roofed, quieter bazaars were hardly less alluring. Spice, perfume, incense, beads, rugs, silks, and brass—old Mahmoud Suleiman squats cross-legged amidst his gummy bottles while chattering youths pulverise mustard in the hollowed-out capital of an ancient classic column—a Roman Corinthian, perhaps from neighbouring Heliopolis, where Augustus stationed one of his three Egyptian legions. Antiquity begins to mingle with exoticism. And then the mosques and the museum—we saw them all, and tried not to let our Arabian revel succumb to the darker charm of Pharaonic Egypt which the museum's priceless treasures offered. That was to be our climax, and for the present we concentrated on the medieval Saracenic glories of the Caliphs whose magnificent tomb-mosques form a glittering fairy necropolis on the edge of the Arabian Desert.

At length Abdul took us along the Sharia Mohammed Ali to the ancient mosque of Sultan Hassan, and the tower-flanked Bab-el-Azab, beyond which climbs the steep-walled pass to the mighty citadel that Saladin himself built with the stones of forgotten pyramids. It was sunset when we scaled that cliff, circled the modern mosque of Mohammed Ali, and looked down from the dizzy parapet over mystic Cairo—mystic Cairo all golden with its carven domes, its ethereal minarets, and its flaming gardens. Far over the city towered the great Roman dome of the new museum; and beyond it—across the cryptic yellow Nile that is the mother of aeons and dynasties—lurked the menacing sands of the Libyan Desert, undulant and iridescent and evil with older arcana. The red sun sank low, bringing the relentless chill of Egyptian dusk; and as it stood poised on the world's rim like that ancient god of Heliopolis—Re-Harakhte, the Horizon-Sun—we saw silhouetted against its vermeil holocaust the black outlines of the Pyramids of Gizeh—the palaeogean tombs there were hoary with a thousand years when Tut-Ankh-Amen mounted his golden throne in distant Thebes. Then we knew that we were done with Saracen Cairo, and that we must taste the deeper mysteries of primal Egypt—the black Khem of Re and Amen, Isis and Osiris.

The next morning we visited the pyramids, riding out in a Victoria across the great Nile bridge with its bronze lions, the island of Ghizereh with its massive lebbakh trees, and the smaller English bridge to the western shore. Down the shore road we drove, between great rows of lebbakhs and past the vast Zoölogical Gardens to the suburb of Gizeh, where a new bridge to Cairo proper has since been built. Then, turning inland along the Sharia-el-Haram, we crossed a region of glassy canals and shabby native villages till before us loomed the objects of our quest, cleaving the mists of dawn and forming inverted replicas in the roadside pools. Forty centuries, as Napoleon had told his campaigners there, indeed looked down upon us.

The road now rose abruptly, till we finally reached our place of transfer between the trolley station and the Mena House Hotel. Abdul Reis, who capably purchased our pyramid tickets, seemed to have an understanding with the crowding, yelling, and offensive Bedouins who inhabited a squalid mud village some distance away and pestiferously assailed every traveller; for he kept them very decently at bay and secured an excellent pair of camels for us, himself mounting a donkey and assigning the leadership of our animals to a group of men and boys more expensive than useful. The area to be traversed was so small that camels were hardly needed, but we did not regret adding to our experience this troublesome form of desert navigation.

The pyramids stand on a high rock plateau, this group forming next to the northernmost of the series of regal and aristocratic cemeteries built in the neighbourhood of the extinct capital Memphis, which lay on the same side of the Nile, somewhat south of Gizeh, and which flourished between 3400 and 2000 B.C. The greatest pyramid, which lies nearest the modern road, was built by King Cheops or Khufu about 2800 B.C., and stands more than 450 feet in perpendicular height. In a line southwest from this are successively the Second Pyramid, built a generation later by King Khephren, and though slightly smaller, looking even larger because set on higher ground, and the radically smaller Third Pyramid of King Mycerinus, built about 2700 B.C. Near the edge of the plateau and due east of the Second Pyramid, with a face probably altered to form a colossal portrait of Khephren, its royal restorer, stands the monstrous Sphinx—mute, sardonic, and wise beyond mankind and memory.

Minor pyramids and the traces of ruined minor pyramids are found in several places, and the whole plateau is pitted with the tombs of dignitaries of less than royal rank. These latter were originally marked by *mastabas,* or stone bench-like structures about the deep burial shafts, as found in other Memphian cemeteries and exemplified by Perneb's Tomb in the Metropolitan Museum of New York. At Gizeh, however, all such visible things have been swept away by time and pillage; and only the rock-hewn shafts, either sand-filled or cleared out by archaeologists, remain to attest their former existence. Connected with each tomb was a chapel in which priests and relatives offered food and prayer to the hovering *ka* or vital principle of the deceased. The small tombs have their chapels contained in their stone *mastabas* or superstructures, but the mortuary chapels of the pyramids, where regal Pharaohs lay, were separate temples, each to the east of its corresponding pyramid, and connected by a causeway to a massive gate-chapel or propylon at the edge of the rock plateau.

The gate-chapel leading to the Second Pyramid, nearly buried in the drifting sands, yawns subterraneously southeast of the Sphinx. Persistent tradition dubs it the "Temple of the Sphinx"; and it may perhaps be rightly called such if the Sphinx indeed represents the Second Pyramid's builder Khephren. There are unpleasant tales of the Sphinx before Khephren—but whatever its elder features were, the monarch replaced them with his own that men might look at the colossus without fear. It was in the great gateway-temple that the life-size diorite statue of Khephren now in the Cairo Museum was found; a statue before which I stood in awe when I beheld it. Whether the whole edifice is now excavated I am not certain, but in 1910 most of it was below ground, with the entrance heavily barred at night. Germans were in charge of the work, and the war or other things may have stopped them. I would give much, in view of my experience and of certain Bedouin whisperings discredited or unknown in Cairo, to know what has developed in connection with a certain well in a transverse gallery where statues of the Pharaoh were found in curious juxtaposition to the statues of baboons.

The road, as we traversed it on our camels that morning, curved sharply past the wooden police quarters, post-office, drug-store, and shops on the left, and plunged south and east in a complete bend that scaled the rock plateau and brought us face to face with the desert under the lee of the Great Pyramid. Past Cyclopean masonry we rode, rounding the eastern face and looking down ahead into a valley of minor pyramids beyond which the eternal Nile glistened to the east, and the eternal desert shimmered to the west. Very close loomed the three major pyramids, the greatest devoid of outer casing and showing its bulk of great stones, but the others retaining here and there the neatly fitted covering which had made them smooth and finished in their day.

Presently we descended toward the Sphinx, and sat silent beneath the spell of those terrible unseeing eyes. On the vast stone breast we faintly discerned the emblem of Rē-Harakhte, for whose image the Sphinx was mistaken in a late dynasty; and though sand covered the tablet between the great paws, we recalled what Thutmosis IV inscribed thereon, and the dream he had when a prince. It was then that the smile of the Sphinx vaguely displeased us, and made us wonder about the legends of subterranean passages beneath the monstrous creature, leading down, down, to depths none might dare hint at—depths connected with mysteries older than the dynastic Egypt we excavate, and having a sinister relation to the persistence of abnormal, animal-headed gods in the ancient Nilotic pantheon. Then, too, it was I asked myself an idle question whose hideous significance was not to appear for many an hour.

Other tourists now began to overtake us, and we moved on to the sand-choked Temple of the Sphinx, fifty yards to the southeast, which I have previously mentioned as the great gate of the causeway to the Second Pyramid's mortuary chapel on the plateau. Most of it was still underground, and although we dismounted and descended through a modern passageway to its alabaster corridor and pillared hall, I felt that Abdul and the local German attendant had not shown us all there was to see. After this we made the conventional circuit of the pyramid plateau, examining the Second Pyramid and the peculiar ruins of its mortuary chapel to the east, the Third Pyramid and its miniature southern satellites and ruined eastern chapel, the rock tombs and the honeycombings of the Fourth and Fifth Dynasties, and the famous Campbell's Tomb whose shadowy shaft sinks precipitously for fifty-three feet to a sinister sarcophagus which one of our camel-drivers divested of the cumbering sand after a vertiginous descent by rope.

Cries now assailed us from the Great Pyramid, where Bedouins were besieging a party of tourists with offers of guidance to the top, or of displays of speed in the performance of solitary trips up and down. Seven minutes is said to be the record for such an ascent and descent, but many lusty sheiks and sons of sheiks assured us they could cut it to five if given the requisite impetus of liberal *baksheesh*. They did not get this impetus, though we did let Abdul take us up, thus obtaining a view of unprecedented magnificence which included not only remote and glittering Cairo with its crowned citadel background of gold-violet hills, but all the pyramids of the Memphian district as well, from Abu Roash on the north to the Dashur on the south. The Sakkara step-pyramid, which marks the evolution of the low *mastaba* into the true pyramid, showed clearly and alluringly in the sandy distance. It is close to this transition-monument that the famed Tomb of Perneb was found—more than four hundred miles north of the Theban rock valley where Tut-Ankh-Amen sleeps. Again I was forced to silence through sheer awe. The prospect of such antiquity, and the secrets each hoary monument seemed to hold and brood over, filled me with a reverence and sense of immensity nothing else ever gave me.

Fatigued by our climb, and disgusted with the importunate Bedouins whose actions seemed to defy every rule of taste, we omitted the arduous detail of entering the cramped interior passages of any of the pyramids, though we saw several of the hardiest tourists preparing for the suffocating crawl through Cheops' mightiest memorial. As we dismissed and overpaid our local bodyguard and drove back to Cairo with Abdul Reis under the afternoon sun, we half regretted the omission we had made. Such fascinating things were whispered about lower pyramid passages not in the guide-books; passages whose entrances had been hastily blocked up and concealed by certain uncommunicative archaeologists who had found and begun to explore them. Of course, this whispering was largely baseless on the face of it; but it was curious to reflect how persistently visitors were forbidden to enter the pyramids at night, or to visit the lowest burrows and crypt of the Great Pyramid. Perhaps in the latter case it was the psychological effect which was feared—the effect on the visitor of feeling himself huddled down beneath a gigantic world of solid masonry; joined to the life he has known by the merest tube, in which he may only crawl, and which any accident or evil design might block. The whole subject seemed so weird and alluring that we resolved to pay the pyramid plateau another visit at the earliest possible opportunity. For me this opportunity came much earlier than I expected.

That evening, the members of our party feeling somewhat tired after the strenuous programme of the day, I went alone with Abdul Reis for a walk through the picturesque Arab quarter. Though I had seen it by day, I wished to study the alleys and bazaars in the dusk, when rich shadows and mellow gleams of light would add to their glamour and fantastic illusion. The native crowds were thinning, but were still very noisy and numerous when we came upon a knot of revelling Bedouins in the Suken-Nahhasin, or bazaar of the coppersmiths. Their apparent leader, an insolent youth with heavy features and saucily cocked tarbush, took some notice of us; and evidently recognised with no great friendliness my competent but admittedly supercilious and sneeringly disposed guide. Perhaps, I thought, he resented that odd reproduction of the Sphinx's half-smile which I had often remarked with amused irritation; or perhaps he did not like the hollow and sepulchral resonance of Abdul's voice. At any rate, the exchange of ancestrally opprobrious language became very brisk; and before long Ali Ziz, as I heard the stranger called when called by no worse name, began to pull violently at Abdul's robe, an action quickly reciprocated, and leading to a spirited scuffle in which both combatants lost their sacredly cherished headgear and would have reached an even direr condition had I not intervened and separated them by main force.

My interference, at first seemingly unwelcome on both sides, succeeded at last in effecting a truce. Sullenly each belligerent composed his wrath and his attire; and with an assumption of dignity as profound as it was sudden, the two formed a curious pact of honour which I soon learned is a custom of great antiquity in Cairo—a pact for the settlement of their difference by means of a nocturnal fist fight atop the Great Pyramid, long after the departure of the last moonlight sightseer. Each duellist was to assemble a party of seconds, and the affair was to begin at midnight, proceeding by rounds in the most civilised possible fashion. In all this planning there was much which excited my interest. The fight itself promised to be unique and spectacular, while the thought of the scene on that hoary pile overlooking the antediluvian plateau of Gizeh under the wan moon of the pallid small hours appealed to every fibre of imagination in me. A request found Abdul exceedingly willing to admit me to his party of seconds; so that all the rest of the early evening I accompanied him to various dens in the most lawless regions of the town—mostly northeast of the Ezbekiyeh—where he gathered one by one a select and formidable band of congenial cutthroats as his pugilistic background.

Shortly after nine our party, mounted on donkeys bearing such royal or tourist-reminiscent names as "Rameses," "Mark Twain," "J. P. Morgan," and "Minnehaha," edged through street labyrinths both Oriental and Occidental, crossed the muddy and mast-forested Nile by the bridge of the bronze lions, and cantered philosophically between the lebbakhs on the road to Gizeh. Slightly over two hours were consumed by the trip, toward the end of which we passed the last of the returning tourists, saluted the last in-bound trolley-car, and were alone with the night and the past and the spectral moon.

Then we saw the vast pyramids at the end of the avenue, ghoulish with a dim atavistical menace which I had not seemed to notice in the daytime. Even the smallest of them held a hint of the ghastly—for was it not in this that they had buried Queen Nitokris alive in the Sixth Dynasty; subtle Queen Nitokris, who once invited all her enemies to a feast in a temple below the Nile, and drowned them by opening the water-gates? I recalled that the Arabs whisper things about Nitokris, and shun the Third Pyramid at certain phases of the moon. It must have been over her that Thomas Moore was brooding when he wrote a thing muttered about by Memphian boatmen—

> *The subterranean nymph that dwells*
> *'Mid sunless gems and glories hid—*
> *The lady of the Pyramid!*

Early as we were, Ali Ziz and his party were ahead of us; for we saw their donkeys outlined against the desert plateau at Kaft-el-Haram; toward which squalid Arab settlement, close to the Sphinx, we had diverged instead of following the regular road to the Mena House, where some of the sleepy, inefficient police might have observed and halted us. Here, where filthy Bedouins stabled camels and donkeys in the rock tombs of Khephren's courtiers, we were led up the rocks and over the sand to the Great Pyramid, up whose time-worn sides the Arabs swarmed eagerly, Abdul Reis offering me the assistance I did not need.

As most travellers know, the actual apex of this structure has long been worn away, leaving a reasonably flat platform twelve yards square. On this eerie pinnacle a squared circle was formed, and in a few moments the sardonic desert moon leered down upon a battle which, but for the quality of the ringside cries, might well have occurred at some minor athletic club in America. As I watched it, I felt that some of our less desirable institutions were not lacking; for every blow, feint, and defence bespoke "stalling" to my not inexperienced eye. It was quickly over, and despite my misgivings as to methods I felt a sort of proprietary pride when Abdul Reis was adjudged the winner.

Reconciliation was phenomenally rapid, and amidst the singing, fraternising, and drinking which followed, I found it difficult to realise that a quarrel had ever occurred. Oddly enough, I myself seemed to be more of a centre of notice than the antagonists; and from my smattering of Arabic I judged that they were discussing my professional performances and escapes from every sort of manacle and confinement, in a manner which indicated not only a surprising knowledge of me, but a distinct hostility and scepticism concerning my feats of escape. It gradually dawned on me that the elder magic of Egypt did not depart without leaving traces, and that fragments of a strange secret lore and priestly cult-practices have survived surreptitiously amongst the fellaheen to such an extent that the prowess of a strange "hahwi" or magician is resented and disputed. I thought of how much my hollow-voiced guide Abdul Reis looked like an old Egyptian priest or Pharaoh or smiling Sphinx . . . and wondered.

Suddenly something happened which in a flash proved the correctness of my reflections and made me curse the denseness whereby I had accepted this night's events as other than the empty and malicious "frame-up" they now showed themselves to be. Without warning, and doubtless in answer to some subtle sign from Abdul, the entire band of Bedouins precipitated itself upon me; and having produced heavy ropes, soon had me bound as securely as I was ever bound in the course of my life, either on the stage or off. I struggled at first, but soon saw that one man could make no headway against a band of over twenty sinewy barbarians. My hands were tied behind my back, my knees bent to their fullest extent, and my wrists and ankles stoutly linked together with unyielding cords. A stifling gag was forced into my mouth, and a blindfold fastened tightly over my eyes. Then, as the Arabs bore me aloft on their shoulders and began a jouncing descent of the pyramid, I heard the taunts of my late guide Abdul, who mocked and jeered delightedly in his hollow voice, and assured me that I was soon to have my "magic powers" put to a supreme test which would quickly remove any egotism I might have gained through triumphing over all the tests offered by America and Europe. Egypt, he reminded me, is very old; and full of inner mysteries and antique powers not even conceivable to the experts of today, whose devices had so uniformly failed to entrap me.

How far or in what direction I was carried, I cannot tell; for the circumstances were all against the formation of any accurate judgement. I know, however, that it could not have been a great distance; since my bearers at no point hastened beyond a walk, yet kept me aloft a surprisingly short time. It is this perplexing brevity which makes me feel almost like shuddering whenever I think of Gizeh and its plateau—for one is oppressed by hints of the closeness to every-day tourist routes of what existed then and must exist still.

The evil abnormality I speak of did not become manifest at first. Setting me down on a surface which I recognised as sand rather than rock, my captors passed a rope around my chest and dragged me a few feet to a ragged opening in the ground, into which they presently lowered me with much rough handling. For apparent aeons I bumped against the stony irregular sides of a narrow hewn well which I took to be one of the numerous burial shafts of the plateau until the prodigious, almost incredible depth of it robbed me of all bases of conjecture.

The horror of the experience deepened with every dragging second. That any descent through the sheer solid rock could be so vast without reaching the core of the planet itself, or that any rope made by man could be so long as to dangle me in these unholy and seemingly fathomless profundities of nether earth, were beliefs of such grotesqueness that it was easier to doubt my agitated senses than to accept them. Even now I am uncertain, for I know how deceitful the sense of time becomes when one or more of the usual perceptions or conditions of life is removed or distorted. But I am quite sure that I preserved a logical consciousness that far; that at least I did not add any full-grown phantoms of imagination to a picture hideous enough in its reality, and explicable by a type of cerebral illusion vastly short of actual hallucination.

All this was not the cause of my first bit of fainting. The shocking ordeal was cumulative, and the beginning of the later terrors was a very perceptible increase in my rate of descent. They were paying out that infinitely long rope very swiftly now, and I scraped cruelly against the rough and con-stricted sides of the shaft as I shot madly downward. My clothing was in tat-ters, and I felt the trickle of blood all over, even above the mounting and excruciating pain. My nostrils, too, were assailed by a scarcely definable menace; a creeping odour of damp and staleness curiously unlike anything I had ever smelt before, and having faint overtones of spice and incense that lent an element of mockery.

Then the mental cataclysm came. It was horrible—hideous beyond all articulate description because it was all of the soul, with nothing of detail to describe. It was the ecstasy of nightmare and the summation of the fiendish. The suddenness of it was apocalyptic and demoniac—one moment I was plunging agonisingly down that narrow well of million-toothed torture, yet the next moment I was soaring on bat-wings in the gulfs of hell; swinging free and swoopingly through illimitable miles of boundless, musty space; rising dizzily to measureless pinnacles of chilling ether, then diving gasp-ingly to sucking nadirs of ravenous, nauseous lower vacua. . . . Thank God for the mercy that shut out in oblivion those clawing Furies of consciousness which half unhinged my faculties, and tore Harpy-like at my spirit! That one respite, short as it was, gave me the strength and sanity to endure those still greater sublimations of cosmic panic that lurked and gibbered on the road ahead.

II

It was very gradually that I regained my senses after that eldritch flight through Stygian space. The process was infinitely painful, and coloured by fantastic dreams in which my bound and gagged condition found singular embodiment. The precise nature of these dreams was very clear while I was experiencing them, but became blurred in my recollection almost immedi-ately afterward, and was soon reduced to the merest outline by the terrible events—real or imaginary—which followed. I dreamed that I was in the grasp of a great and horrible paw; a yellow, hairy, five-clawed paw which had reached out of the earth to crush and engulf me. And when I stopped to reflect what the paw was, it seemed to me that it was Egypt. In the dream I looked back at the events of the preceding weeks, and saw myself lured and enmeshed little by little, subtly and insidiously, by some hellish ghoul-spirit of the elder Nile sorcery; some spirit that was in Egypt before ever man was, and that will be when man is no more.

I saw the horror and unwholesome antiquity of Egypt, and the grisly alliance it has always had with the tombs and temples of the dead. I saw phantom processions of priests with the heads of bulls, falcons, cats, and ibises; phantom processions marching interminably through subterraneous labyrinths and avenues of titanic propylaea beside which a man is as a fly, and offering unnamable sacrifices to indescribable gods. Stone colossi marched in endless night and drove herds of grinning androsphinxes down to the shores of illimitable stagnant rivers of pitch. And behind it all I saw the ineffable malignity of primordial necromancy, black and amorphous, and fumbling greedily after me in the darkness to choke out the spirit that had dared to mock it by emulation. In my sleeping brain there took shape a melodrama of sinister hatred and pursuit, and I saw the black soul of Egypt singling me out and calling me in inaudible whispers; calling and luring me, leading me on with the glitter and glamour of a Saracenic surface, but ever pulling me down to the age-mad catacombs and horrors of its dead and abysmal pharaonic heart.

Then the dream-faces took on human resemblances, and I saw my guide Abdul Reis in the robes of a king, with the sneer of the Sphinx on his features. And I knew that those features were the features of Khephren the Great, who raised the Second Pyramid, carved over the Sphinx's face in the likeness of his own, and built that titanic gateway temple whose myriad corridors the archaeologists think they have dug out of the cryptical sand and the uninformative rock. And I looked at the long, lean, rigid hand of Khephren; the long, lean, rigid hand as I had seen it on the diorite statue in the Cairo Museum—the statue they had found in the terrible gateway temple—and wondered that I had not shrieked when I saw it on Abdul Reis. . . . That hand! It was hideously cold, and it was crushing me; it was the cold and cramping of the sarcophagus . . . the chill and constriction of unrememberable Egypt. . . . It was nighted, necropolitan Egypt itself . . . that yellow paw . . . and they whisper such things of Khephren. . . .

But at this juncture I began to awake—or at least, to assume a condition less completely that of sleep than the one just preceding. I recalled the fight atop the pyramid, the treacherous Bedouins and their attack, my frightful descent by rope through endless rock depths, and my mad swinging and plunging in a chill void redolent of aromatic putrescence. I perceived that I now lay on a damp rock floor, and that my bonds were still biting into me with unloosened force. It was very cold, and I seemed to detect a faint current of noisome air sweeping across me. The cuts and bruises I had received from the jagged sides of the rock shaft were paining me woefully, their soreness enhanced to a stinging or burning acuteness by some pungent quality in the faint draught, and the mere act of rolling over was enough to set my whole frame throbbing with untold agony. As I turned I felt a tug from above, and concluded that the rope whereby I was lowered still reached to the surface. Whether or not the Arabs still held it, I had no idea; nor had I any idea how far within the earth I was. I knew that the darkness around me was wholly or nearly total, since no ray of moonlight penetrated my blindfold; but I did not trust my senses enough to accept as evidence of extreme depth the sensation of vast duration which had characterised my descent.

Knowing at least that I was in a space of considerable extent reached from the surface directly above by an opening in the rock, I doubtfully conjectured that my prison was perhaps the buried gateway chapel of old Khephren—the Temple of the Sphinx—perhaps some inner corridor which the guides had not shown me during my morning visit, and from which I might easily escape if I could find my way to the barred entrance. It would be a labyrinthine wandering, but no worse than others out of which I had in the past found my way. The first step was to get free of my bonds, gag, and blindfold; and this I knew would be no great task, since subtler experts than these Arabs had tried every known species of fetter upon me during my long and varied career as an exponent of escape, yet had never succeeded in defeating my methods.

Then it occurred to me that the Arabs might be ready to meet and attack me at the entrance upon any evidence of my probable escape from the binding cords, as would be furnished by any decided agitation of the rope which they probably held. This, of course, was taking for granted that my place of confinement was indeed Khephren's Temple of the Sphinx. The direct opening in the roof, wherever it might lurk, could not be beyond easy reach of the ordinary modern entrance near the Sphinx; if in truth it were any great distance at all on the surface, since the total area known to visitors is not at all enormous. I had not noticed any such opening during my daytime pilgrimage, but knew that these things are easily overlooked amidst the drifting sands. Thinking these matters over as I lay bent and bound on the rock floor, I nearly forgot the horrors of the abysmal descent and cavernous swinging which had so lately reduced me to a coma. My present thought was only to outwit the Arabs, and I accordingly determined to work myself free as quickly as possible, avoiding any tug on the descending line which might betray an effective or even problematical attempt at freedom.

This, however, was more easily determined than effected. A few preliminary trials made it clear that little could be accomplished without considerable motion; and it did not surprise me when, after one especially energetic struggle, I began to feel the coils of falling rope as they piled up about me and upon me. Obviously, I thought, the Bedouins had felt my movements and released their end of the rope; hastening no doubt to the temple's true entrance to lie murderously in wait for me. The prospect was not pleasing— but I had faced worse in my time without flinching, and would not flinch now. At present I must first of all free myself of bonds, then trust to ingenuity to escape from the temple unharmed. It is curious how implicitly I had come to believe myself in the old temple of Khephren beside the Sphinx, only a short distance below the ground.

That belief was shattered, and every pristine apprehension of preternatural depth and demoniac mystery revived, by a circumstance which grew in horror and significance even as I formulated my philosophical plan. I have said that the falling rope was piling up about and upon me. Now I saw that it was *continuing to pile,* as no rope of normal length could possibly do. It gained in momentum and became an avalanche of hemp, accumulating mountainously on the floor, and half burying me beneath its swiftly multiplying coils. Soon I was completely engulfed and gasping for breath as the increasing convolutions submerged and stifled me. My senses tottered again, and I vainly tried to fight off a menace desperate and ineluctable. It was not merely that I was tortured beyond human endurance—not merely that life and breath seemed to be crushed slowly out of me—it was the knowledge of *what those unnatural lengths of rope implied,* and the consciousness of what unknown and incalculable gulfs of inner earth must at this moment be surrounding me. My endless descent and swinging flight through goblin space, then, must have been real; and even now I must be lying helpless in some nameless cavern world toward the core of the planet. Such a sudden confirmation of ultimate horror was insupportable, and a second time I lapsed into merciful oblivion.

When I say oblivion, I do not imply that I was free from dreams. On the contrary, my absence from the conscious world was marked by visions of the most unutterable hideousness. God! . . . If only I had not read so much Egyptology before coming to this land which is the fountain of all darkness and terror! This second spell of fainting filled my sleeping mind anew with shivering realisation of the country and its archaic secrets, and through some damnable chance my dreams turned to the ancient notions of the dead and their sojournings in soul *and body* beyond those mysterious tombs which were more houses than graves. I recalled, in dream-shapes which it is well that I do not remember, the peculiar and elaborate construction of Egyptian sepulchres; and the exceedingly singular and terrific doctrines which determined this construction.

All these people thought of was death and the dead. They conceived of a literal resurrection of the body which made them mummify it with desperate care, and preserve all the vital organs in canopic jars near the corpse; whilst besides the body they believed in two other elements, the soul, which after its weighing and approval by Osiris dwelt in the land of the blest, and the obscure and portentous *ka* or life-principle which wandered about the upper and lower worlds in a horrible way, demanding occasional access to the preserved body, consuming the food offerings brought by priests and pious relatives to the mortuary chapel, and sometimes—as men whispered—taking its body or the wooden double always buried beside it and stalking noxiously abroad on errands peculiarly repellent.

For thousands of years those bodies rested gorgeously encased and staring glassily upward when not visited by the *ka,* awaiting the day when Osiris should restore both *ka* and soul, and lead forth the stiff legions of the dead from the sunken houses of sleep. It was to have been a glorious rebirth—but not all souls were approved, nor were all tombs inviolate, so that certain grotesque *mistakes* and fiendish *abnormalities* were to be looked for. Even today the Arabs murmur of unsanctified convocations and unwholesome worship in forgotten nether abysses, which only winged invisible *kas* and soulless mummies may visit and return unscathed.

Perhaps the most leeringly blood-congealing legends are those which relate to certain perverse products of decadent priestcraft—*composite mummies* made by the artificial union of human trunks and limbs with the heads of animals in imitation of the elder gods. At all stages of history the sacred animals were mummified, so that consecrated bulls, cats, ibises, crocodiles, and the like might return some day to greater glory. But only in the decadence did they mix the human and animal in the same mummy—only in the decadence, when they did not understand the rights and prerogatives of the *ka* and the soul. What happened to those composite mummies is not told of—at least publicly—and it is certain that no Egyptologist ever found one. The whispers of Arabs are very wild, and cannot be relied upon. They even hint that old Khephren—he of the Sphinx, the Second Pyramid, and the yawning gateway temple—lives far underground wedded to the ghoul-queen Nitokris and ruling over the mummies that are neither of man nor of beast.

It was of these—of Khephren and his consort and his strange armies of the hybrid dead—that I dreamed, and that is why I am glad the exact dream-shapes have faded from my memory. My most horrible vision was connected with an idle question I had asked myself the day before when looking at the great carven riddle of the desert and wondering with what unknown depths the temple so close to it might be secretly connected. That question, so innocent and whimsical then, assumed in my dream a meaning of frenetic and hysterical madness . . . *what huge and loathsome abnormality was the Sphinx originally carven to represent?*

My second awakening—if awakening it was—is a memory of stark hideousness which nothing else in my life—save one thing which came after—can parallel; and that life has been full and adventurous beyond most men's. Remember that I had lost consciousness whilst buried beneath a cascade of falling rope whose immensity revealed the cataclysmic depth of my present position. Now, as perception returned, I felt the entire weight gone; and realised upon rolling over that although I was still tied, gagged, and blindfolded, *some agency had removed completely the suffocating hempen landslide which had overwhelmed me.* The significance of this condition, of course, came to me only gradually; but even so I think it would have brought unconsciousness again had I not by this time reached such a state of emotional exhaustion that no new horror could make much difference. I was alone . . . with *what*?

Before I could torture myself with any new reflection, or make any fresh effort to escape from my bonds, an additional circumstance became manifest. Pains not formerly felt were racking my arms and legs, and I seemed coated with a profusion of dried blood beyond anything my former cuts and abrasions could furnish. My chest, too, seemed pierced by an hundred wounds, as though some malign, titanic ibis had been pecking at it. Assuredly the agency which had removed the rope was a hostile one, and had begun to wreak terrible injuries upon me when somehow impelled to desist. Yet at the time my sensations were distinctly the reverse of what one might expect. Instead of sinking into a bottomless pit of despair, I was stirred to a new courage and action; for now I felt that the evil forces were physical things which a fearless man might encounter on an even basis.

On the strength of this thought I tugged again at my bonds, and used all the art of a lifetime to free myself as I had so often done amidst the glare of lights and the applause of vast crowds. The familiar details of my escaping process commenced to engross me, and now that the long rope was gone I half regained my belief that the supreme horrors were hallucinations after all, and that there had never been any terrible shaft, measureless abyss, or interminable rope. Was I after all in the gateway temple of Khephren beside the Sphinx, and had the sneaking Arabs stolen in to torture me as I lay helpless there? At any rate, I must be free. Let me stand up unbound, ungagged, and with eyes open to catch any glimmer of light which might come trickling from any source, and I could actually delight in the combat against evil and treacherous foes!

How long I took in shaking off my encumbrances I cannot tell. It must have been longer than in my exhibition performances, because I was wounded, exhausted, and enervated by the experiences I had passed through. When I was finally free, and taking deep breaths of a chill, damp, evilly spiced air all the more horrible when encountered without the screen of gag and blindfold edges, I found that I was too cramped and fatigued to move at once. There I lay trying to stretch a frame bent and mangled, for an indefinite period, and straining my eyes to catch a glimpse of some ray of light which would give a hint as to my position.

By degrees my strength and flexibility returned, but my eyes beheld nothing. As I staggered to my feet I peered diligently in every direction, yet met only an ebony blackness as great as that I had known when blindfolded. I tried my legs, blood-encrusted, beneath my shredded trousers, and found that I could walk; yet could not decide in what direction to go. Obviously I ought not to walk at random, and perhaps retreat directly from the entrance I sought; so I paused to note the direction of the cold, foetid, natron-scented air-current which I had never ceased to feel. Accepting the point of its source as the possible entrance to the abyss, I strove to keep track of this landmark and to walk consistently toward it.

I had had a match box with me, and even a small electric flashlight; but of course the pockets of my tossed and tattered clothing were long since emptied of all heavy articles. As I walked cautiously in the blackness, the draught grew stronger and more offensive, till at length I could regard it as nothing less than a tangible stream of detestable vapour pouring out of some aperture like the smoke of the genie from the fisherman's jar in the Eastern tale. The East . . . Egypt . . . truly, this dark cradle of civilisation was ever the wellspring of horrors and marvels unspeakable! The more I reflected on the nature of this cavern wind, the greater my sense of disquiet became; for although despite its odour I had sought its source as at least an indirect clue to the outer world, I now saw plainly that this foul emanation could have no admixture or connection whatsoever with the clean air of the Libyan Desert, but must be essentially a thing vomited from sinister gulfs still lower down. I had, then, been walking in the wrong direction!

After a moment's reflection I decided not to retrace my steps. Away from the draught I would have no landmarks, for the roughly level rock floor was devoid of distinctive configurations. If, however, I followed up the strange current, I would undoubtedly arrive at an aperture of some sort, from whose gate I could perhaps work round the walls to the opposite side of this Cyclopean and otherwise unnavigable hall. That I might fail, I well realised. I saw that this was no part of Khephren's gateway temple which tourists know, and it struck me that this particular hall might be unknown even to archaeologists, and merely stumbled upon by the inquisitive and malignant Arabs who had imprisoned me. If so, was there any present gate of escape to the known parts or to the outer air?

What evidence, indeed, did I now possess that this was the gateway temple at all? For a moment all my wildest speculations rushed back upon me, and I thought of that vivid mélange of impressions—descent, suspension in space, the rope, my wounds, and the dreams that were frankly dreams. Was this the end of life for me? Or indeed, would it be merciful if this moment *were* the end? I could answer none of my own questions, but merely kept on till Fate for a third time reduced me to oblivion. This time there were no dreams, for the suddenness of the incident shocked me out of all thought either conscious or subconscious. Tripping on an unexpected descending step at a point where the offensive draught became strong enough to offer an actual physical resistance, I was precipitated headlong down a black flight of huge stone stairs into a gulf of hideousness unrelieved.

That I ever breathed again is a tribute to the inherent vitality of the healthy human organism. Often I look back to that night and feel a touch of actual *humour* in those repeated lapses of consciousness; lapses whose succession reminded me at the time of nothing more than the crude cinema melodramas of that period. Of course, it is possible that the repeated lapses never occurred; and that all the features of that underground nightmare were merely the dreams of one long coma which began with the shock of my descent into that abyss and ended with the healing balm of the outer air and of the rising sun which found me stretched on the sands of Gizeh before the sardonic and dawn-flushed face of the Great Sphinx.

I prefer to believe this latter explanation as much as I can, hence was glad when the police told me that the barrier to Khephren's gateway temple had been found unfastened, and that a sizeable rift to the surface did actually exist in one corner of the still buried part. I was glad, too, when the doctors pronounced my wounds only those to be expected from my seizure, blindfolding, lowering, struggling with bonds, falling some distance—perhaps into a depression in the temple's inner gallery—dragging myself to the outer barrier and escaping from it, and experiences like that . . . a very soothing diagnosis. And yet I know that there must be more than appears on the surface. That extreme descent is too vivid a memory to be dismissed—and it is odd that no one has ever been able to find a man answering the description of my guide Abdul Reis el Drogman—the tomb-throated guide who looked and smiled like King Khephren.

I have digressed from my connected narrative—perhaps in the vain hope of evading the telling of that final incident; that incident which of all is most certainly an hallucination. But I promised to relate it, and do not break promises. When I recovered—or seemed to recover—my senses after that fall down the black stone stairs, I was quite as alone and in darkness as before. The windy stench, bad enough before, was now fiendish; yet I had acquired enough familiarity by this time to bear it stoically. Dazedly I began to crawl away from the place whence the putrid wind came, and with my bleeding hands felt the colossal blocks of a mighty pavement. Once my head struck against a hard object, and when I felt of it I learned that it was the base of a column—a column of unbelievable immensity—whose surface was covered with gigantic chiselled hieroglyphics very perceptible to my touch. Crawling on, I encountered other titan columns at incomprehensible distances apart; when suddenly my attention was captured by the realisation of something which must have been impinging on my subconscious hearing long before the conscious sense was aware of it.

From some still lower chasm in earth's bowels were proceeding certain *sounds,* measured and definite, and like nothing I had ever heard before. That they were very ancient and distinctly ceremonial, I felt almost intuitively; and much reading in Egyptology led me to associate them with the flute, the sambuke, the sistrum, and the tympanum. In their rhythmic piping, droning, rattling, and beating I felt an element of terror beyond all the known terrors of earth—a terror peculiarly dissociated from personal fear, and taking the form of a sort of objective pity for our planet, that it should hold within its depths such horrors as must lie beyond these aegipanic cacophonies. The sounds increased in volume, and I felt that they were approaching. Then—and may all the gods of all pantheons unite to keep the like from my ears again—I began to hear, faintly and afar off, *the morbid and millennial tramping of the marching things.*

It was hideous that footfalls *so dissimilar* should move in such perfect rhythm. The training of unhallowed thousands of years must lie behind that march of earth's inmost monstrosities . . . padding, clicking, walking, stalking, rumbling, lumbering, crawling . . . and all to the abhorrent discords of those mocking instruments. And then . . . God keep the memory of those Arab legends out of my head! The mummies without souls . . . the meeting-place of the wandering *kas* . . . the hordes of the devil-cursed pharaonic dead of forty centuries . . . the *composite mummies* led through the uttermost onyx voids by King Khephren and his ghoul-queen Nitokris. . . .

The tramping drew nearer—heaven save me from the sound of those feet and paws and hooves and pads and talons as it commenced to acquire detail! Down limitless reaches of sunless pavement a spark of light flickered in the malodorous wind, and I drew behind the enormous circumference of a Cyclopic column that I might escape for a while the horror that was stalking million-footed toward me through gigantic hypostyles of inhuman dread and phobic antiquity. The flickers increased, and the tramping and dissonant rhythm grew sickeningly loud. In the quivering orange light there stood faintly forth a scene of such stony awe that I gasped from a sheer wonder that conquered even fear and repulsion. Bases of columns whose middles were higher than human sight . . . mere bases of things that must each dwarf the Eiffel Tower to insignificance . . . hieroglyphics carved by unthinkable hands in caverns where daylight can be only a remote legend. . . .

I *would not* look at the marching things. That I desperately resolved as I heard their creaking joints and nitrous wheezing above the dead music and the dead tramping. It was merciful that they did not speak . . . but God! *their crazy torches began to cast shadows on the surface of those stupendous columns.* Heaven take it away! *Hippopotami should not have human hands and carry torches . . . men should not have the heads of crocodiles. . . .*

I tried to turn away, but the shadows and the sounds and the stench were everywhere. Then I remembered something I used to do in half-conscious nightmares as a boy, and began to repeat to myself, "This is a dream! This is a dream!" But it was of no use, and I could only shut my eyes and pray . . . at least, that is what I think I did, for one is never sure in visions—and I know this can have been nothing more. I wondered whether I should ever reach the world again, and at times would furtively open my eyes to see if I could discern any feature of the place other than the wind of spiced putrefaction, the topless columns, and the thaumatropically grotesque shadows of abnormal horror. The sputtering glare of multiplying torches now shone, and unless this hellish place were wholly without walls, I could not fail to see some boundary or fixed landmark soon. But I had to shut my eyes again when I realised *how many* of the things were assembling—and when I glimpsed a certain object walking solemnly and steadily *without any body above the waist.*

A fiendish and ululant corpse-gurgle or death-rattle now split the very atmosphere—the charnel atmosphere poisonous with naphtha and bitumen blasts—in one concerted chorus from the ghoulish legion of hybrid blasphemies. My eyes, perversely shaken open, gazed for an instant upon a sight which no human creature could even imagine without panic, fear and physical exhaustion. The things had filed ceremonially in one direction, the direction of the noisome wind, where the light of their torches showed their bended heads . . . or the bended heads of such as had heads. . . . They were worshipping before a great black foetor-belching aperture which reached up almost out of sight, and which I could see was flanked at right angles by two giant staircases whose ends were far away in shadow. One of these was indubitably the staircase I had fallen down.

The dimensions of the hole were fully in proportion with those of the columns—an ordinary house would have been lost in it, and any average public building could easily have been moved in and out. It was so vast a surface that only by moving the eye could one trace its boundaries . . . so vast, so hideously black, and so aromatically stinking. . . . Directly in front of this yawning Polyphemus-door the things were throwing objects—evidently sacrifices or religious offerings, to judge by their gestures. Khephren was their leader; sneering King Khephren *or the guide Abdul Reis,* crowned with a golden pshent and intoning endless formulae with the hollow voice of the dead. By his side knelt beautiful Queen Nitokris, whom I saw in profile for a moment, noting that the right half of her face was eaten away by rats or other ghouls. And I shut my eyes again when I saw *what* objects were being thrown as offerings to the foetid aperture or its possible local deity.

It occurred to me that judging from the elaborateness of this worship, the concealed deity must be one of considerable importance. Was it Osiris or Isis, Horus or Anubis, or some vast unknown God of the Dead still more central and supreme? There is a legend that terrible altars and colossi were reared to an Unknown One before ever the known gods were worshipped. . . .

And now, as I steeled myself to watch the rapt and sepulchral adorations of those nameless things, a thought of escape flashed upon me. The hall was dim, and the columns heavy with shadow. With every creature of that nightmare throng absorbed in shocking raptures, it might be barely possible for me to creep past to the faraway end of one of the staircases and ascend unseen; trusting to Fate and skill to deliver me from the upper reaches. Where I was, I neither knew nor seriously reflected upon—and for a moment it struck me as amusing to plan a serious escape from that which I knew to be a dream. Was I in some hidden and unsuspected lower realm of Khephren's gateway temple—that temple which generations have persistently called the Temple of the Sphinx? I could not conjecture, but I resolved to ascend to life and consciousness if wit and muscle could carry me.

Wriggling flat on my stomach, I began the anxious journey toward the foot of the left-hand staircase, which seemed the more accessible of the two. I cannot describe the incidents and sensations of that crawl, but they may be guessed when one reflects on *what I had to watch steadily in that malign, wind-blown torchlight* in order to avoid detection. The bottom of the staircase was, as I have said, far away in shadow; as it had to be to rise without a bend to the dizzy parapeted landing above the titanic aperture. This placed the last stages of my crawl at some distance from the noisome herd, though the spectacle chilled me even when quite remote at my right.

At length I succeeded in reaching the steps and began to climb; keeping close to the wall, on which I observed decorations of the most hideous sort, and relying for safety on the absorbed, ecstatic interest with which the monstrosities watched the foul-breezed aperture and the impious objects of nourishment they had flung on the pavement before it. Though the staircase was huge and steep, fashioned of vast porphyry blocks as if for the feet of a giant, the ascent seemed virtually interminable. Dread of discovery and the pain which renewed exercise had brought to my wounds combined to make that upward crawl a thing of agonising memory. I had intended, on reaching the landing, to climb immediately onward along whatever upper staircase might mount from there; stopping for no last look at the carrion abominations that pawed and genuflected some seventy or eighty feet below—yet a sudden repetition of that thunderous corpse-gurgle and death-rattle chorus, coming as I had nearly gained the top of the flight and showing by its ceremonial rhythm that it was not an alarm of my discovery, caused me to pause and peer cautiously over the parapet.

The monstrosities were hailing something which had poked itself out of the nauseous aperture to seize the hellish fare proffered it. It was something quite ponderous, even as seen from my height; something yellowish and hairy, and endowed with a sort of nervous motion. It was as large, perhaps, as a good-sized hippopotamus, but very curiously shaped. It seemed to have no neck, but five separate shaggy heads springing in a row from a roughly cylindrical trunk; the first very small, the second good-sized, the third and fourth equal and largest of all, and the fifth rather small, though not so small as the first. Out of these heads darted curious rigid tentacles which seized ravenously on the *excessively great* quantities of unmentionable food placed before the aperture. Once in a while the thing would leap up, and occasionally it would retreat into its den in a very odd manner. Its locomotion was so inexplicable that I stared in fascination, wishing it would emerge farther from the cavernous lair beneath me.

Then it *did* emerge . . . it *did* emerge, and at the sight I turned and fled into the darkness up the higher staircase that rose behind me; fled unknowingly up incredible steps and ladders and inclined planes to which no human sight or logic guided me, and which I must ever relegate to the world of dreams for want of any confirmation. It must have been a dream, or the dawn would never have found me breathing on the sands of Gizeh before the sardonic dawn-flushed face of the Great Sphinx.

The Great Sphinx! God!—that *idle question* I asked myself on that sun-blest morning before . . . *what huge and loathsome abnormality was the Sphinx originally carven to represent?* Accursed is the sight, be it in dream or not, that revealed to me the supreme horror—the Unknown God of the Dead, which licks its colossal chops in the unsuspected abyss, fed hideous morsels by soulless absurdities that should not exist. The five-headed monster that emerged . . . that five-headed monster as large as a hippopotamus . . . the five-headed monster—*and that of which it is the merest fore paw.* . . .

But I survived, and I know it was only a dream.

OPENING KING TUTANKHAMEN'S TOMB

Howard Carter

WITH A. C. MACE

As chief inspector for Egypt's antiquities department, Howard Carter discovered the tombs of Mentuhotep I, Queen Hatshepsut, and Pharaoh Thutmose IV. When he was fired from his post after an altercation with some drunken French tourists, he and his sponsor, Lord Carnarvon (also known as "Porchy," short for Baron Porchester of Highclere), discovered the tomb of Amenhotep I, the Valley Temple of Queen Hatshepsut, and the cemetery of the eighteenth-dynasty queens. But their greatest achievement was the discovery of Pharaoh Tutankhamen's tomb, which consisted of several chambers full of treasures that took ten years to preserve and remove. In this account—written with the help of archaeologist Arthur C. Mace, who was an associate curator of the Metropolitan Museum of Art of New York and one of the supposed victims of the mummy's curse—Carter tells in vivid detail what it was like to be the first to enter the unexplored tomb.

This was to be our final season in The Valley. Six full seasons we had excavated there, and season after season had drawn a blank; we had worked for months at a stretch and found nothing, and only an excavator knows how desperately depressing that can be; we had almost made up our minds that we were beaten, and were preparing to leave The Valley and try our luck elsewhere; and then—hardly had we set hoe to ground in our last despairing effort than we made a discovery that far exceeded our wildest dreams. Surely, never before in the whole history of excavation has a full digging season been compressed within the space of five days.

Let me try and tell the story of it all. It will not be easy, for the dramatic suddenness of the initial discovery left me in a dazed condition, and the months that have followed have been so crowded with incident that I have hardly had time to think. Setting it down on paper will perhaps give me a chance to realize what has happened and all that it means.

I [had] arrived in Luxor on October 28th, and by November 1st I had enrolled my workmen and was ready to begin. Our former excavations had stopped short at the north-east corner of the tomb of Rameses VI, and from this point I started trenching southwards. It will be remembered that in this area there were a number of roughly constructed workmen's huts, used probably by the laborers in the tomb of Rameses. These huts, built about three feet above bed-rock, covered the whole area in front of the Rameside tomb, and continued in a southerly direction to join up with a similar group of huts on the opposite side of The Valley, discovered by [American millionaire Theodore] Davis in connection with his work on the Akhenaton cache. By the evening of November 3rd we had laid bare a sufficient number of these huts for experimental purposes, so, after we had planned and noted them, they were removed, and we were ready to clear away the three feet of soil that lay beneath them.

Hardly had I arrived on the work next morning than the unusual silence, due to the stoppage of the work, made me realize that something out of the ordinary had happened, and I was greeted by the announcement that a step cut in the rock had been discovered underneath the very first hut to be attacked. This seemed too good to be true, but a short amount of extra clearing revealed the fact that we were actually in the entrance of a steep cut in the rock, some thirteen feet below the entrance to the tomb of Rameses VI, and a similar depth from the present bed level of The Valley. The manner of cutting was that of the sunken stairway entrance so common in The Valley, and I almost dared to hope that we had found our tomb at last. Work continued feverishly throughout the whole of that day and the morning of the next, but it was not until the afternoon of November 5th that we succeeded in clearing away the masses of rubbish that overlay the cut, and were able to demarcate the upper edges of the stairway on all its four sides.

It was clear by now beyond any question that we actually had before us the entrance to a tomb, but doubts, born of previous disappointments, persisted in creeping in. There was always the horrible possibility, suggested by our experience in the Thothmes III Valley, that the tomb was an unfinished one, never completed and never used: if it had been finished there was the depressing probability that it had been completely plundered in ancient times. On the other hand, there was just the chance of an untouched or only partially plundered tomb, and it was with ill-suppressed excitement that I watched the descending steps of the staircase, as one by one they came to light. The cutting was excavated in the side of a small hillock, and, as the work progressed, its western edge receded under the slope of the rock until it was, first partially, and then completely, roofed in, and became a passage, ten feet high by six feet wide. Work progressed more rapidly now; step succeeded step, and at the level of the twelfth, towards sunset, there was disclosed the upper part of a doorway, blocked, plastered, and sealed.

A sealed doorway—it was actually true, then! Our years of patient labor were to be rewarded after all, and I think my first feeling was one of congratulation that my faith in The Valley had not been unjustified. With excitement growing to fever heat I searched the seal impressions on the door for evidence of the identity of the owner, but could find no name: the only decipherable ones were those of the well-known royal necropolis seal, the jackal and nine captives. Two facts, however, were clear: first, the employment of this royal seal was certain evidence that the tomb had been constructed for a person of very high standing; and second, that the sealed door was entirely screened from above by workmen's huts of the Twentieth Dynasty was sufficiently clear proof that at least from that date it had never been entered. With that for the moment I had to be content.

While examining the seals I noticed, at the top of the doorway, where some of the plaster had fallen away, a heavy wooden lintel. Under this, to assure myself of the method by which the doorway had been blocked, I made a small peephole, just large enough to insert an electric torch [i.e., flashlight], and discovered that the passage beyond the door was filled completely from floor to ceiling with stones and rubble—additional proof this of the care with which the tomb had been protected.

It was a thrilling moment for an excavator. Alone, save for my native workmen, I found myself, after years of comparatively unproductive labor, on the threshold of what might prove to be a magnificent discovery. Anything, literally anything, might lie beyond that passage, and it needed all my self-control to keep from breaking down the doorway, and investigating then and there.

One thing puzzled me, and that was the smallness of the opening in comparison with the ordinary Valley tombs. The design was certainly of the Eighteenth Dynasty. Could it be the tomb of a noble buried here by royal consent? Was it a royal cache, a hiding-place to which a mummy and its equipment had been removed for safety? Or was it actually the tomb of the king for whom I had spent so many years in search?

Once more I examined the seal impressions for a clue, but on the part of the door so far laid bare only those of the royal necropolis seal already mentioned were clear enough to read. Had I but known that a few inches lower down there was a perfectly clear and distinct impression of the seal of Tutankhamen, the king I most desired to find, I would have cleared on, had a much better night's rest in consequence, and saved myself nearly three weeks of uncertainty. It was late, however, and darkness was already upon us. With some reluctance I re-closed the small hole that I had made, filled in our excavation for protection during the night, selected the most trustworthy of my workmen—themselves almost as excited as I was—to watch all night above the tomb, and so home by moonlight, riding down The Valley.

Naturally my wish was to go straight ahead with our clearing to find out the full extent of the discovery, but Lord Carnarvon was in England, and in fairness to him I had to delay matters until he could come. Accordingly, on the morning of November 6th I sent him the following cable: "At last have made wonderful discovery in Valley; a magnificent tomb with seals intact; re-covered same for your arrival; congratulations."

My next task was to secure the doorway against interference until such time as it could finally be re-opened. This we did by filling our excavation up again to surface level, and rolling on top of it the large flint boulders of which the workmen's huts had been composed. By the evening of the same day, exactly forty-eight hours after we had discovered the first step of the staircase, this was accomplished. The tomb had vanished. So far as the appearance of the ground was concerned there never had been any tomb, and I found it hard to persuade myself at times that the whole episode had not been a dream.

I was soon to be reassured on this point. News travels fast in Egypt, and within two days of the discovery congratulations, inquiries, and offers of help descended upon me in a steady stream from all directions. It became clear, even at this early stage, that I was in for a job that could not be tackled single-handed, so I wired to [A. R.] Callender, who had helped me on various previous occasions, asking him if possible to join me without delay, and to my relief he arrived on the very next day. On the 8th I had received two messages from Lord Carnarvon in answer to my cable, the first of which read, "Possibly come soon," and the second, received a little later, "Propose arrive Alexandria 20th."

We had thus nearly a fortnight's grace, and we devoted it to making preparations of various kinds, so that when the time of re-opening came, we should be able, with the least possible delay, to handle any situation that might arise. On the night of the 18th I went to Cairo for three days, to meet Lord Carnarvon and make a number of necessary purchases, returning to Luxor on the 21st. On the 23rd Lord Carnarvon arrived in Luxor with his daughter, Lady Evelyn Herbert, his devoted companion in all his Egyptian work, and everything was in hand for the beginning of the second chapter of the discovery of the tomb. Callender had been busy all day clearing away the upper layer of rubbish, so that by morning we should be able to get into the staircase without any delay.

By the afternoon of the 24th the whole staircase was clear, sixteen steps in all, and we were able to make a proper examination of the sealed doorway. On the lower part the seal impressions were much clearer, and we were able without any difficulty to make out on several of them the name of Tutankhamen. This added enormously to the interest of the discovery. If we had found, as seemed almost certain, the tomb of that shadowy monarch, whose tenure of the throne coincided with one of the most interesting periods in the whole of Egyptian history, we should indeed have reason to congratulate ourselves.

With heightened interest, if that were possible, we renewed our investigation of the doorway. Here for the first time a disquieting element made its appearance. Now that the whole door was exposed to light it was possible to discern a fact that had hitherto escaped notice—that there had been two successive openings and re-closings of a part of its surface: furthermore, that the sealing originally discovered, the jackal and nine captives, had been applied to the re-closed portions, whereas the sealings of Tutankhamen covered the untouched part of the doorway, and were therefore those with which the tomb had been originally secured. The tomb then was not absolutely intact, as we had hoped. Plunderers had entered it, and entered it more than once—from the evidence of the huts above, plunderers of a date not later than the reign of Rameses VI—but that they had not rifled it completely was evident from the fact that it had been re-sealed.[6]

Then came another puzzle. In the lower strata of rubbish that filled the staircase we found masses of broken potsherds and boxes, the latter bearing the names of Akhenaton, Smenkhkare, and Tutankhamen, and, what was much more upsetting, a scarab of Thothmes III and a fragment with the name of Amenhotep III. Why this mixture of names? The balance of evidence so far would seem to indicate a cache rather than a tomb, and at this stage in the proceedings we inclined more and more to the opinion that we were about to find a miscellaneous collection of objects of the Eighteenth Dynasty kings, brought from Tell el Amarna by Tutankhamen and deposited here for safety.

So matters stood on the evening of the 24th. On the following day the sealed doorway was to be removed, so Callender set carpenters to work making a heavy wooden grille to be set up in its place. Mr. Engelbach, Chief Inspector of the Antiquities Department, paid us a visit during the afternoon, and witnessed part of the final clearing of rubbish from the doorway.

On the morning of the 25th the seal impressions on the doorway were carefully noted and photographed, and then we removed the actual blocking of the door, consisting of rough stones carefully built from floor to lintel, and heavily plastered on their outer faces to take the seal impressions.

This disclosed the beginning of a descending passage (not a staircase), the same width as the entrance stairway, and nearly seven feet high. As I had already discovered from my hole in the doorway, it was filled completely with stone and rubble, probably the chip from its own excavation. This filling, like the doorway, showed distinct signs of more than one opening and re-closing of the tomb, the untouched part consisting of clean white chip, mingled with dust, whereas the disturbed part was composed mainly of dark flint. It was clear that an irregular tunnel had been cut through the original filling at the upper corner on the left side, a tunnel corresponding in position with that of the hole in the doorway.

As we cleared the passage we found, mixed with the rubble of the lower

---

[6] From later evidence we found that this re-sealing could not have taken place later than the reign of Horemheb, i.e., from ten to fifteen years after the burial.

levels, broken potsherds, jar scalings, alabaster jars, whole and broken, vases of painted pottery, numerous fragments of smaller articles, and water skins, these last having obviously been used to bring up the water needed for the plastering of the doorways. These were clear evidence of plundering, and we eyed them askance. By night we had cleared a considerable distance down the passage, but as yet saw no sign of second doorway or of chamber.

The day following (November 26th) was the day of days, the most wonderful that I have ever lived through, and certainly one whose like I can never hope to see again. Throughout the morning the work of clearing continued, slowly perforce, on account of the delicate objects that were mixed with the filling. Then, in the middle of the afternoon, thirty feet down from the outer door, we came upon a second sealed doorway, almost an exact replica of the first. The seal impressions in this case were less distinct, but still recognizable as those of Tutankhamen and of the royal necropolis. Here again the signs of opening and re-closing were clearly marked upon the plaster. We were firmly convinced by this time that it was a cache that we were about to open, and not a tomb. The arrangement of stairway, entrance passage, and doors reminded us very forcibly of the cache of Akhenaton and Tyi material found in the very near vicinity of the present excavation by Davis, and the fact that Tutankhamen's seals occurred there likewise seemed almost certain proof that we were right in our conjecture. We were soon to know. There lay the sealed doorway, and behind it was the answer to the question.

Slowly, desperately slowly it seemed to us as we watched, the remains of passage debris that encumbered the lower part of the doorway were removed, until at last we had the whole door clear before us. The decisive moment had arrived. With trembling hands I made a tiny breach in the upper left hand corner. Darkness and blank space, as far as an iron testing-rod could reach, showed that whatever lay beyond was empty, and not filled like the passage we had just cleared. Candle tests were applied as a precaution against possible foul gases, and then, widening the hole a little, I inserted the candle and peered in, Lord Carnarvon, Lady Evelyn, and Callender standing anxiously beside me to hear the verdict. At first I could see nothing, the hot air escaping from the chamber causing the candle flame to flicker, but presently, as my eyes grew accustomed to the light, details of the room within emerged slowly from the mist, strange animals, statues, and gold—everywhere the glint of gold. For the moment—an eternity it must have seemed to the others standing by—I was struck dumb with amazement, and when Lord Carnarvon, unable to stand the suspense any longer, inquired anxiously, "Can you see anything?" it was all I could do to get out the words, "Yes, wonderful things." Then widening the hole a little further, so that we both could see, we inserted an electric torch.

I suppose most excavators would confess to a feeling of awe—embarrassment almost—when they break into a chamber closed and sealed by pious hands so many centuries ago. For the moment, time as a factor in human life has lost its meaning. Three thousand, four thousand years maybe, have passed and gone since human feet last trod the floor on which you stand, and yet, as you note the signs of recent life around you—the half-filled bowl of mortar for the door, the blackened lamp, the finger-mark upon the freshly painted surface, the farewell garland dropped upon the threshold—you feel it might have been but yesterday. The very air you breathe, unchanged throughout the centuries, you share with those who laid the mummy to its rest. Time is annihilated by little intimate details such as these, and you feel an intruder.

That is perhaps the first and dominant sensation, but others follow thick and fast—the exhilaration of discovery, the fever of suspense, the almost overmastering impulse, born of curiosity, to break down seals and lift the lids of boxes, the thought—pure joy to the investigator—that you are about to add a page to history, or solve some problem of research, the strained expectancy—why not confess it? of the treasure-seeker. Did these thoughts actually pass through our minds at the time, or have I imagined them since? I cannot tell. It was the discovery that my memory was blank, and not the mere desire for dramatic chapter-ending, that occasioned this digression.

Surely never before in the whole history of excavation had such an amazing sight been seen as the light of our torch revealed to us. . . . Imagine how . . . [it] appeared to us as we looked down . . . from our spy-hole in the blocked doorway, casting the beam of light from our torch—the first light that had pierced the darkness of the chamber for three thousand years—from one group of objects to another, in a vain attempt to interpret the treasure that lay before us. The effect was bewildering, overwhelming. I suppose we had never formulated exactly in our minds just what we had expected or hoped to see, but certainly we had never dreamed of anything like this, a roomful—a whole museumful it seemed—of objects, some familiar, but some the like of which we had never seen, piled one upon another in seemingly endless profusion.

Gradually the scene grew clearer, and we could pick out individual objects. First, right opposite to us—we had been conscious of them all the while but refused to believe in them—were three great gilt couches, their sides carved in the form of monstrous animals, curiously attenuated in body, as they had to be to serve their purpose, but with heads of startling realism. Uncanny beasts enough to look upon at any time: seen as we saw them, their brilliant gilded surfaces picked out of the darkness by our electric torch, as though by limelight, their heads throwing grotesque distorted shadows on the wall behind them, they were almost terrifying. Next, on the right, two statues caught and held our attention; two life-sized figures of a king in black, facing each other like sentinels, gold killed, gold sandaled, armed with mace and staff, the protective sacred cobra upon their foreheads.

By the middle of February our work in the Antechamber was finished. With the exception of the two sentinel statues, left for a special reason, all its contents had been removed to the laboratory, every inch of its floor had been swept and sifted for the last bead or fallen piece of inlay, and it now stood bare and empty. We were ready at last to penetrate the mystery of the sealed door.

Friday, the 17th, was the day appointed, and at two o'clock those who were to be privileged to witness the ceremony met by appointment above the tomb. . . . By a quarter past two the whole company had assembled, so we removed our coats and filed down the sloping passage into the tomb.

In the Antechamber everything was prepared and ready, and to those who had not visited it since the original opening of the tomb it must have presented a strange sight. We had screened the statues with boarding to protect them from possible damage, and between them we had erected a small platform, just high enough to enable us to reach the upper part of the doorway, having determined, as the safest plan, to work from the top downwards. A short distance back from the platform there was a barrier, and beyond, knowing that there might be hours of work ahead of us, we had provided chairs for the visitors. On either side standards had been set up for our lamps, their light shining full upon the doorway. Looking back, we realize what a strange, incongruous picture the chamber must have presented, but at the time I question whether such an idea even crossed our minds. One thought and one only was possible. There before us lay the sealed door, and with its opening we were to blot out the centuries and stand in the presence of a king who reigned three thousand years ago. My own feelings as I mounted the platform were a strange mixture, and it was with a trembling hand that I struck the first blow.

My first care was to locate the wooden lintel above the door: then very carefully I chipped away the plaster and picked out the small stones which formed the uppermost layer of the filling. The temptation to stop and peer inside at every moment was irresistible, and when, after about ten minutes' work, I had made a hole large enough to enable me to do so, I inserted an electric torch. An astonishing sight its light revealed, for there, within a yard of the doorway, stretching as far as one could see and blocking the entrance to the chamber, stood what to all appearance was a solid wall of gold. For the moment there was no clue as to its meaning, so as quickly as I dared I set to work to widen the hole. This had now become an operation of considerable difficulty, for the stones of the masonry were not accurately squared blocks built regularly upon one another, but rough slabs of varying size, some so heavy that it took all one's strength to lift them: many of them, too, as the weight above was removed, were left so precariously balanced that the least false movement would have sent them sliding inwards to crash upon the contents of the chamber below. We were also endeavoring to preserve the seal-impressions upon the thick mortar of the outer face, and this added considerably to the difficulty of handling the stones. [Arthur C.] Mace and [A. R.] Callender were helping me by this time, and each stone was cleared on a regular system. With a crowbar I gently eased it up, Mace holding it to prevent it falling forwards; then he and I lifted it out and passed it back to Callender, who transferred it on to one of the foremen, and so, by a chain of workmen, up the passage and out of the tomb altogether.

With the removal of a very few stones the mystery of the golden wall was solved. We were at the entrance of the actual burial-chamber of the king, and that which barred our way was the side of an immense gilt shrine built to cover and protect the sarcophagus. It was visible now from the Antechamber by the light of the standard lamps, and as stone after stone was removed, and its gilded surface came gradually into view, we could, as though by electric current, feel the tingle of excitement which thrilled the spectators behind the barrier. . . . We who were doing the work were probably less excited, for our whole energies were taken up with the task in hand—that of removing the blocking without an accident. The fall of a single stone might have done irreparable damage to the delicate surface of the shrine, so, directly the hole was large enough, we made an additional protection for it by inserting a mattress on the inner side of the door-blocking, suspending it from the wooden lintel of the doorway. Two hours of hard work it took us to clear away the blocking, or at least as much of it as was necessary for the moment; and at one point, when near the bottom, we had to delay operations for a space while we collected the scattered beads from a necklace brought by the plunderers from the chamber within and dropped upon the threshold. This last was a terrible trial to our patience, for it was a slow business, and we were all of us excited to see what might be within; but finally it was done, the last stones were removed, and the way to the innermost chamber lay open before us.

In clearing away the blocking of the doorway we had discovered that the level of the inner chamber was about four feet lower than that of the Antechamber, and this, combined with the fact that there was but a narrow space between door and shrine, made an entrance by no means easy to effect. Fortunately, there were no smaller antiquities at this end of the chamber, so I lowered myself down, and then, taking one of the portable lights, I edged cautiously to the corner of the shrine and looked beyond it. At the corner two beautiful alabaster vases blocked the way, but I could see that if these were removed we should have a clear path to the other end of the chamber; so, carefully marking the spot on which they stood, I picked them up—with the exception of the king's wishing-cup they were of finer quality and more graceful shape than any we had yet found—and passed them back to the Antechamber. Lord Carnarvon and M. Lacau now joined me, and, picking our way along the narrow passage between shrine and wall, paying out the wire of our light behind us, we investigated further.

It was, beyond any question, the sepulchral chamber in which we stood, for there, towering above us, was one of the great gilt shrines beneath which kings were laid. So enormous was this structure (seventeen feet by eleven feet, and nine feet high, we found afterwards) that it filled within a little the entire area of the chamber, a space of some two feet only separating it from the walls on all four sides, while its roof, with cornice top and torus molding, reached almost to the ceiling. From top to bottom it was overlaid with gold, and upon its sides there were inlaid panels of brilliant blue faience, in which were represented, repeated over and over, the magic symbols which would ensure its strength and safety. Around the shrine, resting upon the ground, there were a number of funerary emblems, and, at the north end, the seven magic oars the king would need to ferry himself across the waters of the underworld. The walls of the chamber, unlike those of the Antechamber, were decorated with brightly painted scenes and inscriptions, brilliant in their colors, but evidently somewhat hastily executed.

These last details we must have noticed subsequently, for at the time our one thought was of the shrine and of its safety. Had the thieves penetrated within it and disturbed the royal burial? Here, on the eastern end, were the great folding doors, closed and bolted, but not sealed, that would answer the question for us. Eagerly we drew the bolts, swung back the doors, and there within was a second shrine with similar bolted doors, and upon the bolts a seal, intact. This seal we determined not to break, for our doubts were resolved, and we could not penetrate further without risk of serious damage to the monument. I think at the moment we did not even want to break the seal, for a feeling of intrusion had descended heavily upon us with the opening of the doors, heightened, probably, by the almost painful impressiveness of a linen pall, decorated with golden rosettes, which drooped above the inner shrine. We felt that we were in the presence of the dead King and must do him reverence, and in imagination could see the doors of the successive shrines open one after the other till the innermost disclosed the King himself. Carefully, and as silently as possible, we re-closed the great swing doors, and passed on to the farther end of the chamber.

Here a surprise awaited us, for a low door, eastwards from the sepulchral chamber, gave entrance to yet another chamber, smaller than the outer ones and not so lofty. This doorway, unlike the others, had not been closed and sealed. We were able, from where we stood, to get a clear view of the whole of the contents, and a single glance sufficed to tell us that here, within this little chamber, lay the greatest treasures of the tomb. Facing the doorway, on the farther side, stood the most beautiful monument that I have ever seen— so lovely that it made one gasp with wonder and admiration. The central portion of it consisted of a large shrine-shaped chest, completely overlaid with gold, and surmounted by a cornice of sacred cobras. Surrounding this, freestanding, were statues of the four tutelary goddesses of the dead—gracious figures with outstretched protective arms, so natural and lifelike in their pose, so pitiful and compassionate the expression upon their faces, that one felt it almost sacrilege to look at them. One guarded the shrine on each of its four sides, but whereas the figures at front and back kept their gaze firmly fixed upon their charge, an additional note of touching realism was imparted by the other two, for their heads were turned sideways, looking over their shoulders towards the entrance, as though to watch against surprise. There is a simple grandeur about this monument that made an irresistible appeal to the imagination, and I am not ashamed to confess that it brought a lump to my throat. It is undoubtedly the Canopic chest and contains the jars which play such an important part in the ritual of mummification.

There were a number of other wonderful things in the chamber, but we found it hard to take them in at the time, so inevitably were one's eyes drawn back again and again to the lovely little goddess figures. Immediately in front of the entrance lay the figure of the jackal god Anubis, upon his shrine, swathed in linen cloth, and resting upon a portable sled, and behind this the head of a bull upon a stand—emblems, these, of the underworld. In the south side of the chamber lay an endless number of black shrines and chests, all closed and sealed save one, whose open doors revealed statues of Tutankhamen standing upon black leopards. On the farther wall were more shrine-shaped boxes and miniature coffins of gilded wood, these last undoubtedly containing funerary statuettes of the king. In the center of the room, left of the Anubis and the bull, there was a row of magnificent caskets of ivory and wood, decorated and inlaid with gold and blue faience, one, whose lid we raised, containing a gorgeous ostrich-feather fan with ivory handle, fresh and strong to all appearance as when it left the maker's hand. There were also, distributed in different quarters of the chamber, a number of model boats with sails and rigging all complete, and, at the north side, yet another chariot.

Such, from a hurried survey, were the contents of this innermost chamber. We looked anxiously for evidence of plundering, but on the surface there was none. Unquestionably the thieves must have entered, but they cannot have done more than open two or three of the caskets. Most of the boxes, as has been said, have still their seals intact, and the whole contents of the chamber, in fortunate contrast to those of the Antechamber and the Annex, still remain in position exactly as they were placed at the time of burial.

How much time we occupied in this first survey of the wonders of the tomb I cannot say, but it must have seemed endless to those anxiously waiting in the Antechamber. Not more than three at a time could be admitted with safety, so, when Lord Carnarvon and M. Lacau came out, the others came in pairs: first Lady Evelyn Herbert, the only woman present, with Sir William Garstin, and then the rest in turn. It was curious, as we stood in the Antechamber, to watch their faces as, one by one, they emerged from the door. Each had a dazed, bewildered look in his eyes, and each in turn, as he came out, threw up his hands before him, an unconscious gesture of impotence to describe in words the wonders that he had seen. They were indeed indescribable, and the emotions they had aroused in our minds were of too intimate a nature to communicate, even though we had the words at our command. It was an experience which, I am sure, none of us who were present is ever likely to forget, for in imagination—and not wholly in imagination either—we had been present at the funeral ceremonies of a king long dead and almost forgotten.

Fiction

THE ADVENTURE OF THE EGYPTIAN TOMB

Agatha Christie

Dame Agatha Christie is probably the most famous mystery writer of all time. Originally she studied singing in Paris, but she eventually abandoned this to become an author. Early in her career she divorced Col. Archibald Christie and two years later married archaeologist Max (later Sir Max) Mallowan, though she kept the Christie name. She was made Dame Commander, Order of the British Empire, in 1971. Of her approximately one hundred books, sixty-six were full-length detective novels, nineteen were collections of short stories, and fourteen were mystery plays. They include Murder on the Orient Express, The Mirror Crack'd from Side to Side, The Mousetrap, Evil Under the Sun, Akhnaton, *and* Death on the Nile. *Her most famous characters were the spinster-sleuth Jane Marple and the egotistical Belgian detective Hercule Poirot. It is the latter of these two who is featured in this story involving a mummy's curse.*

I have always considered that one of the most thrilling and dramatic of the many adventures I have shared with Poirot was that of our investigation into the strange series of deaths which followed upon the discovery and opening of the Tomb of King Men-her-Ra.

Hard upon the discovery of the Tomb of Tutankh-Amen by Lord Carnarvon, Sir John Willard and Mr. Bleibner of New York, pursuing their excavations not far from Cairo, in the vicinity of the Pyramids of Giza, came unexpectedly on a series of funeral chambers. The greatest interest was aroused by their discovery. The Tomb appeared to be that of King Men-her-Ra, one of those shadowy kings of the Eighth Dynasty, when the

Old Kingdom was falling to decay. Little was known about this period, and the discoveries were fully reported in the newspapers.

An event soon occurred which took a profound hold on the public mind. Sir John Willard died quite suddenly of heart failure.

The more sensational newspapers immediately took the opportunity of reviving all the old superstitious stories connected with the ill luck of certain Egyptian treasures. The unlucky Mummy at the British Museum, that hoary old chestnut, was dragged out with fresh zest, was quietly denied by the Museum, but nevertheless enjoyed all its usual vogue.

A fortnight later Mr. Bleibner died of acute blood poisoning, and a few days afterwards a nephew of his shot himself in New York. The "Curse of Men-her-Ra" was the talk of the day, and the magic power of dead and gone Egypt was exalted to a fetish point.

It was then that Poirot received a brief note from Lady Willard, widow of the dead archaeologist, asking him to go and see her at her house in Kensington Square. I accompanied him.

Lady Willard was a tall, thin woman, dressed in deep mourning. Her haggard face bore eloquent testimony to her recent grief.

"It is kind of you to have come so promptly, Monsieur Poirot."

"I am at your service, Lady Willard. You wished to consult me?"

"You are, I am aware, a detective, but it is not only as a detective that I wish to consult you. You are a man of original views, I know, you have imagination, experience of the world—tell me, Monsieur Poirot, what are your views on the supernatural?"

Poirot hesitated for a moment before he replied. He seemed to be considering. Finally he said:

"Let us not misunderstand each other, Lady Willard. It is not a general question that you are asking me there. It has a personal application, has it not? You are referring obliquely to the death of your late husband?"

"That is so," she admitted.

"You want me to investigate the circumstances of his death?"

"I want you to ascertain for me exactly how much is newspaper chatter, and how much may be said to be founded on fact. Three deaths, Monsieur Poirot—each one explicable taken by itself, but taken together surely an almost unbelievable coincidence, and all within a month of the opening of the tomb! It may be mere superstition, it may be some potent curse from the past that operates in ways undreamed of by modern science. The fact remains—three deaths! And I am afraid, Monsieur Poirot, horribly afraid. It may not yet be the end."

"For whom do you fear?"

"For my son. When the news of my husband's death came I was ill. My son, who has just come down from Oxford, went out there. He brought the—the body home, but now he has gone out again, in spite of my prayers and entreaties. He is so fascinated by the work that he intends to take his father's place and carry on the system of excavations. You may think me a foolish, credulous woman, but, Monsieur Poirot, I am afraid. Supposing that the spirit of the dead king is not yet appeased? Perhaps to you I seem to be talking nonsense—"

"No, indeed, Lady Willard," said Poirot quickly. "I, too, believe in the force of superstition, one of the greatest forces the world has ever known."

I looked at him in surprise. I should never have credited Poirot with being superstitious. But the little man was obviously in earnest.

"What you really demand is that I shall protect your son? I will do my utmost to keep him from harm."

"Yes, in the ordinary way, but against an occult influence?"

"In volumes of the Middle Ages, Lady Willard, you will find many ways of counteracting black magic. Perhaps they knew more than we moderns with all our boasted science. Now let us come to facts, that I may have guidance. Your husband had always been a devoted Egyptologist, hadn't he?"

"Yes, from his youth upwards. He was one of the greatest living authorities upon the subject."

"But Mr. Bleibner, I understand, was more or less of an amateur?"

"Oh, quite. He was a very wealthy man who dabbled freely in any subject that happened to take his fancy. My husband managed to interest him in Egyptology, and it was his money that was so useful in financing the expedition."

"And the nephew? What do you know of his tastes? Was he with the party at all?"

"I do not think so. In fact I never knew of his existence till I read of his death in the paper. I do not think he and Mr. Bleibner can have been at all intimate. He never spoke of having any relations."

"Who are the other members of the party?"

"Well, there is Dr. Tosswill, minor official connected with the British Museum; Mr. Schneider of the Metropolitan Museum in New York; a young American secretary; Dr. Ames, who accompanies the expedition in his professional capacity; and Hassan, my husband's devoted native servant."

"Do you remember the name of the American secretary?"

"Harper, I think, but I cannot be sure. He had not been with Mr. Bleibner very long, I know. He was a very pleasant young fellow."

"Thank you, Lady Willard."

"If there is anything else—?"

"For the moment, nothing. Leave it now in my hands, and be assured that I will do all that is humanly possible to protect your son."

They were not exactly reassuring words, and I observed Lady Willard wince as he uttered them. Yet, at the same time, the fact that he had not pooh-poohed her fears seemed in itself to be a relief to her.

For my part I had never before suspected that Poirot had so deep a vein of superstition in his nature. I tackled him on the subject as we went homewards. His manner was grave and earnest.

"But yes, Hastings. I believe in these things. You must not underrate the force of superstition."

"What are we going to do about it?"

"*Toujours pratique,* the good Hastings! *Eh bien,* to begin with we are going to cable to New York for fuller details of young Mr. Bleibner's death."

He duly sent off his cable. The reply was full and precise. Young Rupert Bleibner had been in low water for several years. He had been a beachcomber and a remittance man in several South Sea islands, but had returned to New York two years ago, where he had rapidly sunk lower and lower. The most significant thing, to my mind, was that he had recently managed to borrow enough money to take him to Egypt. "I've a good friend there I can borrow from," he had declared. Here, however, his plans had gone awry. He had returned to New York cursing his skinflint of an uncle who cared more for the bones of dead and gone kings than his own flesh and blood. It was during his sojourn in Egypt that the death of Sir John Willard occurred. Rupert had plunged once more into his life of dissipation in New York, and then, without warning, he had committed suicide, leaving behind him a letter which contained some curious phrases. It seemed written in a sudden fit of remorse. He referred to himself as a leper and an outcast, and the letter ended by declaring that such as he were better dead.

A shadowy theory leapt into my brain. I had never really believed in the vengeance of a long dead Egyptian king. I saw here a more modern crime. Supposing this young man had decided to do away with his uncle—preferably by poison. By mistake, Sir John Willard receives the fatal dose. The young man returns to New York, haunted by his crime. The news of his uncle's death reaches him. He realizes how unnecessary his crime has been, and stricken with remorse takes his own life.

I outlined my solutions to Poirot. He was interested.

"It is ingenious what you have thought of there—decidedly it is ingenious. It may even be true. But you leave out of count the fatal influence of the Tomb."

I shrugged my shoulders.

"You still think that has something to do with it?"

"So much so, *mon ami,* that we start for Egypt tomorrow."

"What?" I cried, astonished.

"I have said it." An expression of conscious heroism spread over Poirot's face. Then he groaned. "But, oh," he lamented, "the sea! The hateful sea!"

It was a week later. Beneath our feet was the golden sand of the desert. The hot sun poured down overhead. Poirot, the picture of misery, wilted by my side. The little man was not a good traveler. Our four days' voyage from Marseilles had been one long agony to him. He had landed at Alexandria the wraith of his former self, even his usual neatness had deserted him. We had arrived in Cairo and had driven out at once to the Mena House Hotel, right in the shadow of the Pyramids.

The charm of Egypt had laid hold of me. Not so Poirot. Dressed precisely the same as in London, he carried a small clothes-brush in his pocket and waged an unceasing war on the dust which accumulated on his dark apparel.

"And my boots," he wailed. "Regard them, Hastings. My boots, of the neat patent leather, usually so smart and shining. See, the sand is inside them, which is painful, and outside them, which outrages the eyesight. Also the heat, it causes my mustaches to become limp—but limp!"

"Look at the Sphinx," I urged. "Even I can feel the mystery and the charm it exhales."

Poirot looked at it discontentedly.

"It has not the air happy," he declared. "How could it, half-buried in sand in that untidy fashion. Ah, this cursed sand!"

"Come, now, there's a lot of sand in Belgium," I reminded him, mindful of a holiday spent at Knocke-sur-mer in the midst of "*les dunes impeccables*" as the guide-book had phrased it.

"Not in Brussels," declared Poirot. He gazed at the Pyramids thoughtfully. "It is true that they, at least, are of a shape solid and geometrical, but their surface is of an unevenness most unpleasing. And the palm trees I like them not. Not even do they plant them in rows!"

I cut short his lamentations, by suggesting that we should start for the camp. We were to ride there on camels, and the beasts were patiently kneeling, waiting for us to mount, in charge of several picturesque boys headed by a voluble dragoman.

I pass over the spectacle of Poirot on a camel. He started by groans and lamentations and ended by shrieks, gesticulations and invocations to the Virgin Mary and every saint in the calendar. In the end, he descended ignominiously and finished the journey on a diminutive donkey. I must admit that a trotting camel is no joke for the amateur. I was stiff for several days.

At last we neared the scene of the excavations. A sunburnt man with a gray beard, in white clothes and wearing a helmet, came to meet us.

"Monsieur Poirot and Captain Hastings? We received your cable. I'm sorry that there was no one to meet you in Cairo. An unforeseen event occurred which completely disorganized our plans."

Poirot paled. His hand, which had stolen to his clothes-brush, stayed its course.

"Not another death?" he breathed.

"Yes."

"Sir Guy Willard?" I cried.

"No, Captain Hastings. My American colleague, Mr. Schneider."

"And the cause?" demanded Poirot.

"Tetanus."

I blanched. All around me I seemed to feel an atmosphere of evil, subtle and menacing. A horrible thought flashed across me. Supposing I were the next?

"*Mon Dieu,*" said Poirot, in a very low voice, "I do not understand this. It is horrible. Tell me, monsieur, there is no doubt that it was tetanus?"

"I believe not. But Dr. Ames will tell you more than I can do."

"Ah, of course, you are not the doctor."

"My name is Tosswill."

This, then, was the British expert described by Lady Willard as being a minor official at the British Museum. There was something at once grave and steadfast about him that took my fancy.

"If you will come with me," continued Dr. Tosswill, "I will take you to Sir Guy Willard. He was most anxious to be informed as soon as you should arrive."

We were taken across the camp to a large tent. Dr. Tosswill lifted up the flap and we entered. Three men were sitting inside.

"Monsieur Poirot and Captain Hastings have arrived, Sir Guy," said Tosswill.

The youngest of the three men jumped up and came forward to greet us. There was a certain impulsiveness in his manner which reminded me of his mother. He was not nearly so sunburnt as the others, and that fact, coupled with a certain haggardness round the eyes, made him look older than his twenty-two years. He was clearly endeavoring to bear up under a severe mental strain.

He introduced his two companions, Dr. Ames, a capable-looking man of thirty odd, with a touch of graying hair at the temples, and Mr. Harper, the secretary, a pleasant lean young man wearing the national insignia of horn-rimmed spectacles.

After a few minutes' desultory conversation the latter went out, and Dr. Tosswill followed him. We were left alone with Sir Guy and Dr. Ames.

"Please ask any questions you want to ask, Monsieur Poirot," said Willard. "We are utterly dumfounded at this strange series of disasters, but it isn't—it can't be, anything but coincidence."

There was a nervousness about his manner which rather belied the words. I saw that Poirot was studying him keenly.

"Your heart is really in this work, Sir Guy?"

"Rather. No matter what happens, or what comes of it, the work is going on. Make up your mind to that."

Poirot wheeled round on the other.

"What have you to say to that, *monsieur le docteur?*"

"Well," drawled the doctor, "I'm not for quitting myself."

Poirot made one of those expressive grimaces of his.

"Then, *évidemment,* we must find out just how we stand. When did Mr. Schneider's death take place?"

"Three days ago."

"You are sure it was tetanus?"

"Dead sure."

"It couldn't have been a case of strychnine poisoning, for instance?"

"No, Monsieur Poirot. I see what you're getting at. But it was a clear case of tetanus."

"Did you not inject anti-serum?"

"Certainly we did," said the doctor dryly. "Every conceivable thing that could be done was tried."

"Had you the anti-serum with you?"

"No. We procured it from Cairo."

"Have there been any other cases of tetanus in the camp?"

"No, not one."

"Are you certain that the death of Mr. Bleibner was not due to tetanus?"

"Absolutely plumb certain. He had a scratch upon his thumb which became poisoned, and septicemia set in. It sounds pretty much the same to a layman, I dare say, but the two things are entirely different."

"Then we have four deaths—all totally dissimilar, one heart failure, one blood poisoning, one suicide and one tetanus.

"Exactly, Monsieur Poirot."

"Are you certain that there is nothing which might link the four together?"

"I don't quite understand you."

"I will put it plainly. Was any act committed by those four men which might seem to denote disrespect to the spirit of Men-her-Ra?"

The doctor gazed at Poirot in astonishment.

"You're talking through your hat, Monsieur Poirot. Surely you've not been guyed into believing all that fool talk?"

"Absolute nonsense," muttered Willard angrily.

Poirot remained placidly immovable, blinking a little out of his green cat's eyes.

"So you do not believe it, *monsieur le docteur?*"

"No, sir, I do not," declared the doctor emphatically. "I am a scientific man, and I believe only what science teaches."

"Was there no science then in Ancient Egypt?" asked Poirot softly. He did not wait for a reply, and indeed Dr. Ames seemed rather at a loss for the moment. "No, no, do not answer me, but tell me this. What do the native workmen think?"

"I guess," said Dr. Ames, "that, where white folk lose their heads, natives aren't going to be far behind. I'll admit that they're getting what you might call scared—but they've no cause to be."

"I wonder," said Poirot noncommittally.

Sir Guy leant forward.

"Surely," he cried incredulously, "you cannot believe in—oh, but the thing's absurd! You can know nothing of Ancient Egypt if you think that."

For answer Poirot produced a little book from his pocket—an ancient tattered volume. As he held it out I saw its title, *The Magic of the Egyptians and Chaldeans*. Then, wheeling round, he strode out of the tent. The doctor stared at me.

"What is his little idea?"

The phrase, so familiar on Poirot's lips, made me smile as it came from another.

"I don't know exactly," I confessed. "He's got some plan of exorcising the evil spirits, I believe."

I went in search of Poirot, and found him talking to the lean-faced young man who had been the late Mr. Bleibner's secretary.

"No," Mr. Harper was saying, "I've only been six months with the expedition. Yes, I knew Mr. Bleibner's affairs pretty well."

"Can you recount to me anything concerning his nephew?"

"He turned up here one day, not a bad-looking fellow. I'd never met him before, but some of the others had—Ames, I think, and Schneider. The old man wasn't at all pleased to see him. They were at it in no time, hammer and tongs. 'Not a cent,' the old man shouted. 'Not one cent now or when I'm dead. I intend to leave my money to the furtherance of my life's work. I've been talking it over with Mr. Schneider today.' And a bit more of the same. Young Bleibner lit out for Cairo right away."

"Was he in perfectly good health at the time?"

"The old man?"

"No, the young one."

"I believe he did mention there was something wrong with him. But it couldn't have been anything serious, or I should have remembered."

"One thing more, has Mr. Bleibner left a will?"

"So far as we know, he has not."

"Are you remaining with the expedition, Mr. Harper?"

"No, sir, I am not. I'm for New York as soon as I can square up things here. You may laugh if you like, but I'm not going to be this blasted old Men-her-Ra's next victim. He'll get me if I stop here."

The young man wiped the perspiration from his brow.

Poirot turned away. Over his shoulder he said with a peculiar smile: "Remember, he got one of his victims in New York."

"Oh, hell!" said Mr. Harper forcibly.

"That young man is nervous," said Poirot thoughtfully. "He is on the edge, but absolutely on the edge."

I glanced at Poirot curiously, but his enigmatical smile told me nothing. In company with Sir Guy Willard and Dr. Tosswill we were taken round the excavations. The principal finds had been removed to Cairo, but some of the tomb furniture was extremely interesting. The enthusiasm of the young baronet was obvious, but I fancied that I detected a shade of nervousness in his manner as though he could not quite escape from the feeling of menace in the air. As we entered the tent which had been assigned to us, for a wash before joining the evening meal, a tall dark figure in white robes stood aside to let us pass with a graceful gesture and a murmured greeting in Arabic. Poirot stopped.

"You are Hassan, the late Sir John Willard's servant?"

"I served my Lord Sir John, now I serve his son." He took a step nearer to us and lowered his voice. "You are a wise one, they say, learned in dealing with evil spirits. Let the young master depart from here. There is evil in the air around us."

And with an abrupt gesture, not waiting for a reply, he strode away.

"Evil in the air," muttered Poirot. "Yes, I feel it."

Our meal was hardly a cheerful one. The floor was left to Dr. Tosswill, who discoursed at length upon Egyptian antiquities. Just as we were preparing to retire to rest, Sir Guy caught Poirot by the arm and pointed. A shadowy figure was moving amidst the tents. It was no human one: I recognized distinctly the dog-headed figure I had seen carved on the walls of the tomb.

My blood literally froze at the sight.

"Mon Dieu!" murmured Poirot, crossing himself vigorously. "Anubis, the jackal-headed, the god of departing souls."

"Some one is hoaxing us," cried Dr. Tosswill, rising indignantly to his feet.

"It went into your tent, Harper," muttered Sir Guy, his face dreadfully pale.

"No," said Poirot, shaking his head, "into that of the Dr. Ames."

The doctor stared at him incredulously; then, repeating Dr. Tosswill's words, he cried:

"Some one is hoaxing us. Come, we'll soon catch the fellow."

He dashed energetically in pursuit of the shadowy apparition. I followed him, but, search as we would, we could find no trace of any living thing having passed that way. We returned, somewhat disturbed in mind, to find Poirot taking energetic measures, in his own way, to ensure his personal safety. He was busily surrounding our tent with various diagrams and inscriptions which he was drawing in the sand. I recognized the five-pointed star or Pentagon many times repeated. As was his wont, Poirot was at the same time delivering an impromptu lecture on witchcraft and magic in general, White Magic as opposed to Black, with various references to the Ka and the Book of the Dead thrown in.

It appeared to excite the liveliest contempt in Dr. Tosswill, who drew me aside, literally snorting with rage.

"Balderdash, sir," he exclaimed angrily. "Pure balderdash. The man's an impostor. He doesn't know the difference between the superstitions of the Middle Ages and the beliefs of Ancient Egypt. Never have I heard such a hotch-potch of ignorance and credulity."

I calmed the excited expert, and joined Poirot in the tent. My little friend was beaming cheerfully.

"We can now sleep in peace," he declared happily. "And I can do with some sleep. My head, it aches abominably. Ah, for a good *tisane!*"

As though in answer to prayer, the flap of the tent was lifted and Hassan appeared, bearing a steaming cup which he offered to Poirot. It proved to be chamomile tea, a beverage of which he is inordinately fond. Having thanked Hassan and refused his offer of another cup for myself, we were left alone once more. I stood at the door of the tent some time after undressing, looking out over the desert.

"A wonderful place," I said aloud, "and a wonderful work. I can feel the fascination. This desert life, this probing into the heart of a vanished civilization. Surely, Poirot, you, too, must feel the charm?"

I got no answer, and I turned, a little annoyed. My annoyance was quickly changed to concern. Poirot was lying back across the rude couch, his face horribly convulsed. Beside him was the empty cup. I rushed to his side, then dashed out and across the camp to Dr. Ames's tent.

"Dr. Ames!" I cried. "Come at once."

"What's the matter?" said the doctor, appearing in pajamas.

"My friend. He's ill. Dying. The chamomile tea. Don't let Hassan leave the camp."

Like a flash the doctor ran to our tent. Poirot was lying as I left him.

"Extraordinary," cried Ames. "Looks like a seizure—or—what did you say about something he drank?" He picked up the empty cup.

"Only I did not drink it!" said a placid voice.

We turned in amazement. Poirot was sitting up on the bed. He was smiling.

"No," he said gently. "I did not drink it. While my good friend Hastings was apostrophizing the night, I took the opportunity of pouring it, not down my throat, but into a little bottle. That little bottle will go to the analytical chemist. No"—as the doctor made a sudden movement—"as a sensible man, you will understand that violence will be of no avail. During Hastings' brief absence to fetch you, I have had time to put the bottle in safe keeping. Ah, quick, Hastings, hold him!"

I misunderstood Poirot's anxiety. Eager to save my friend, I flung myself in front of him. But the doctor's swift movement had another meaning. His hand went to his mouth, a smell of bitter almonds filled the air, and he swayed forward and fell.

"Another victim," said Poirot gravely, "but the last. Perhaps it is the best way. He has three deaths on his head."

"Dr. Ames?" I cried, stupefied. "But I thought you believed in some occult influence?"

"You misunderstood me, Hastings. What I meant was that I believe in the terrific force of superstition. Once get it firmly established that a series of deaths are supernatural, and you might almost stab a man in broad daylight, and it would still be put down to the curse, so strongly is the instinct of the supernatural implanted in the human race. I suspected from the first that a man was taking advantage of that instinct. The idea came to him, I imagine, with the death of Sir John Willard. A fury of superstition arose at once. As far as I could see, nobody could derive any particular profit from Sir

John's death. Mr. Bleibner was a different case. He was a man of great wealth. The information I received from New York contained several suggestive points. To begin with, young Bleibner was reported to have said he had a good friend in Egypt from whom he could borrow. It was tacitly understood that he meant his uncle, but it seemed to me that in that case he would have said so outright. The words suggest some boon companion of his own. Another thing, he scraped up enough money to take him to Egypt, his uncle refused outright to advance him a penny, yet he was able to pay the return passage to New York. Some one must have lent him the money."

"All that was very thin," I objected.

"But there was more. Hastings, there occur often enough words spoken metaphorically which are taken literally. The opposite can happen too. In this case, words which were meant literally were taken metaphorically. Young Bleibner wrote plainly enough: 'I am a leper,' but nobody realized that he shot himself because he believed that he had contracted the dread disease of leprosy."

"What?" I ejaculated.

"It was the clever invention of a diabolical mind. Young Bleibner was suffering from some minor skin trouble, he had lived in the South Sea Islands, where the disease is common enough. Ames was a former friend of his, and a well-known medical man, he would never have dreamed of doubting his word. When I arrived here, my suspicions were divided between Harper and Dr. Ames, but I soon realized that only the doctor could have perpetrated and concealed the crimes, and I learnt from Harper that he was previously acquainted with young Bleibner. Doubtless the latter at some time or another had made a will or had insured his life in favor of the doctor. The latter saw his chance of acquiring wealth. It was easy for him to inoculate Mr. Bleibner with the deadly germs. Then the nephew, overcome with despair at the dread news his friend had conveyed to him, shot himself. Mr. Bleibner, whatever his intentions, had made no will. His fortune would pass to his nephew and from him to the doctor."

"And Mr. Schneider?"

"We cannot be sure. He knew young Bleibner too, remember, and may have suspected something, or, again, the doctor may have thought that a further death motiveless and purposeless would strengthen the coils of superstition. Furthermore, I will tell you an interesting psychological fact, Hastings. A murderer has always a strong desire to repeat his successful crime, the performance of it grows upon him. Hence my fears for young Willard. The figure of Anubis you saw tonight was Hassan, dressed up by my orders. I wanted to see if I could frighten the doctor. But it would take more than the supernatural to frighten him. I could see that he was not entirely taken in by my pretenses of belief in the occult. The little comedy I played for him did not deceive him. I suspected that he would endeavor to make me the next victim. Ah, but in spite of *la mer maudite,* the heat abominable, and the annoyances of the sand, the little gray cells still functioned!"

Poirot proved to be perfectly right in his premises. Young Bleibner, some years ago, in a fit of drunken merriment, had made a jocular will, leaving "my cigarette case you admire so much and everything else of which I die possessed which will be principally debts to my good friend Robert Ames who once saved my life from drowning."

The case was hushed up as far as possible, and, to this day, people talk of the remarkable series of deaths in connection with the Tomb of Men-her-Ra as a triumphal proof of the vengeance of a bygone king upon the desecrators of his tomb—a belief which, as Poirot pointed out to me, is contrary to all Egyptian belief and thought.

Fiction

THE DEMON-POSSESSED PRINCESS

An Ancient Egyptian Priest

This story was written in about 300 B.C., during the final period of Ancient Egypt, by an unknown priest (or priests). He was attempting to honor his god by reviving an old legend that may have been based on an actual incident. In order to make his tale more convincing, the priest wrote this story down on papyrus and forged it to make it look like it was written during the Great Empire, one thousand years earlier. While this may have fooled his contemporaries, it didn't fool modern Egyptologists, who knew much more about the Great Empire than the priest did. Still, it is possible that the country of Bekhten in the tale is actually Bactria and that the princess of the title was the sister of an actual Hittite princess who married Ramses II. Because this story was translated many years ago, I have rewritten it so it is much easier to read.

As was his yearly custom, the Pharaoh Ramses II was in Naharin where the lords of every country came and bowed down before him in peace because of his fame. From the marshes at the northern limits of the earth, they brought their tribute of silver, gold, lapis lazuli, malachite, and every sweet wood of God's Land. They carried these on their backs, each one leading his neighbor.

When the Lord of Bekhten had his tribute brought forward, he placed his eldest daughter in front, and praising His Majesty, requested life from him. Now, the Pharaoh saw that she was extremely beautiful—more so than any woman he'd ever seen—so he accepted her as his wife. They then chose an Egyptian name for her—"The Great Pharaoh's Wife,

Nefrure"—and when they returned to Egypt, she assumed all the functions of a queen.

When the twenty-second day of the tenth month of year 23 came, Ramses went to that exalted mistress of cities, Thebes, to perform the ceremonies of his father, Amon-Re, who was that city's lord. This beautiful feast celebrating the beginning of the world was held at Southern Opet Luxor, which was the Pharaoh's favorite court. During the ceremony, Ramses was told that one of the Lord of Bekhten's messengers had come, bearing many gifts for his wife, so His Majesty asked that the man be brought forward. The messenger approached His Majesty and bowed down on his knees with his nose to the ground, saying, "Praise you, Sun of the Nine Bows! Give us life! I have come to you, my lord Pharaoh, on account of the queen's oldest sister, Bentresh. Sickness has penetrated her limbs. We request that Your Majesty please send a wise man to see her."

The Pharaoh replied, "Bring me the sacred scribes and the officials of the court," and they were brought to him immediately. He said to them, "Who among you has experience in his heart and can write with his fingers?" The Pharaoh's scribe, Thutemhab, stepped forward and His Majesty commanded him to go to Bekhten with the messenger.

When the wise man finally arrived in Bekhten after a seventeen-month journey, he found that Bentresh was possessed by a spirit, but it was too powerful for him to deal with.

As Thutemhab was unable to exorcise the spirit, the Lord of Bekhten sent another messenger into Ramses' presence, saying, "O Pharaoh, my lord, let His Majesty command that the great god Khonsu be brought to my country to cast the demon out from my daughter." Then in the ninth month of the year 26, while Ramses was at the feast of Amon, the wise man returned from Bekhten.

There were two gods named Khonsu and both had temples in Thebes, so the Pharaoh went before Khonsu-in-Beautiful-Thebes, saying, "O my good lord, I repeat before you the matter concerning the daughter of the Lord of Bekhten." He then had this Khonsu taken to the temple of Khonsu-the-Plan-Maker, a powerful god for smiting evil spirits. Ramses then said to the first Khonsu, "O great lord, if you incline your face toward Khonsu-the-Plan-Maker, then he shall be conveyed to Bekhten." There was a violent nodding and His Majesty said, "Send your protection with him, that he may go to Bekhten to save the daughter of the Lord of Bekhten." Again the first

Khonsu nodded his head violently. The Pharaoh repeated his request for the protection of Khonsu-the-Plan-Maker four times.

So His Majesty commanded that the second Khonsu be escorted to a great ship, along with five transports, numerous chariots and horses of the east and west, and they set off on their journey.

After a year and five months, the god arrived in Bekhten and the Lord of Bekhten, with his soldiers and his nobles, came before Khonsu-the-Plan-Maker. He threw himself upon his belly, saying, "You have come to us by command of the Pharaoh Usermare-Setepnere Ramses II and you are welcome here."

The god went to the place where Bentresh was and cast out the demon. Giving her protection, she became well immediately. Then the spirit said to Khonsu-the-Plan-Maker-of-Thebes, "You come in peace, O great god, smiting the barbarians. Your city is in Bekhten. Your servants are its people and I am your servant. I will go back to where I came from to satisfy your heart because you have come here, but let Your Majesty command that a feast be celebrated with me and with the Lord of Bekhten." Then the god nodded to his priest, saying, "Let the Lord of Bekhten make a great offering before this spirit." While all these things were happening, the Lord of Bekhten stood by with his soldiers, in great fear. Then he made a great offering before Khonsu and celebrated a feast-day with them. The spirit departed in peace as commanded by Khonsu, and the Lord of Bekhten and all his people rejoiced.

The Lord then thought to himself, "I'm going to keep this god here in Bekhten with me and will not permit him to return to Egypt." So the god remained there for three years and nine months.

Eventually the Lord had a nightmare where he saw Khonsu leave his shrine and come into his bedroom. The god appeared as a hawk of gold and he then flew upward toward Egypt. The Lord awoke in a great fright.

The next day he called the priest of Khonsu-the-Plan-Maker and said, "Let the god depart for Egypt." He then gave Khonsu lots of wonderful gifts, including many soldiers and horses.

When the god arrived back in Thebes, he was taken to the temple of Khonsu-in-Beautiful-Thebes and set before him many of the gifts the Lord of Bekhten had given to him. Khonsu-the-Plan-Maker then returned to his own temple, arriving in the ninth day of the second month in the year 33 of King Usermare-Setepnere, that he might be given life, like Re, forever.

Nonfiction

THE MAJESTIC SPHINX

Mark Twain

In spite of having virtually no formal education, Mark Twain (whose real name was Samuel Clemens) went on to become one of America's greatest authors. His classic works include The Adventures of Huckleberry Finn, The Adventures of Tom Sawyer, The Prince and the Pauper, A Connecticut Yankee in King Arthur's Court, *and "The Celebrated Jumping Frog of Calaveras County." He came to prominence during a period when America was still strongly divided into North and South, but oddly he was a blend of the two, with a heavy dose of the West thrown in. After the Civil War broke out, he found himself in the Confederate Army, but after two weeks he deserted (or "resigned" as he called it) and went to the Nevada Territory as a prospector and miner. Unsuccessful, he turned to writing and created his pen name. His form of humor soon almost landed him in several duels. It was his jumping frog story that really launched his career as a humorist. This was followed by his humorous travelogue through the Holy Land entitled* The Innocents Abroad, *from which this selection is taken. It was a tremendous success and brought him international fame.*

After years of waiting, it [the sphinx] was before me at last. The great face was so sad, so earnest, so longing, so patient. There was a dignity not of earth in its mien, and in its countenance a benignity such as never any thing human wore. It was stone, but it seemed sentient. If ever image of stone thought, it was thinking. It was looking toward the verge of the landscape, yet looking *at* nothing—nothing but distance and vacancy. It was looking over and beyond every thing of the present, and far into the past. It was gazing out over the ocean of Time—over lines of century-waves which, further and further receding, closed nearer and nearer together, and blended at last into one unbroken tide, away toward the horizon of remote antiquity. It was thinking of the wars of departed ages; of the empires it had seen created and destroyed; of the nations whose birth it had witnessed, whose progress it had watched, whose annihilation it had noted; of the joy and sorrow, the life and death, the grandeur and decay, of five thousand slow revolving years. It was the type of an attribute of man—of a faculty of his heart and brain. It was MEMORY—RETROSPECTION—wrought into visible, tangible form. All who know what pathos there is in memories of days that are accomplished and faces that have vanished—albeit only a trifling score of years gone by—will have some appreciation of the pathos that dwells in these grave eyes that look so steadfastly back upon the things they knew before History was born—before Tradition had being—things that were, and forms that moved, in a vague era which even Poetry and Romance scarce know of—and passed one by one away and left the stony dreamer solitary in the midst of a strange new age, and uncomprehended scenes.

The Sphinx is grand in its loneliness; it is imposing in its magnitude; it is impressive in the mystery that hangs over its story. And there is that in the overshadowing majesty of this eternal figure of stone, with its accusing memory of the deeds of all ages, which reveals to one something of what he shall feel when he shall stand at last in the awful presence of God.

There are some things which, for the credit of America, should be left unsaid, perhaps; but these very things happen sometimes to be the very things which, for the real benefit of Americans, ought to have prominent notice. While we stood looking, a wart, or an excrescence of some kind, appeared on the jaw of the Sphinx. We heard the familiar clink of a hammer, and understood the case at once. One of our well-meaning reptiles—I mean relic-hunters—had crawled up there and was trying to break a "specimen" from the face of this the most majestic creation the hand of man has wrought. But the great image contemplated the dead ages as calmly as ever, unconscious of the small insect that was fretting at its jaw. Egyptian granite that has defied the storms and earthquakes of all time has nothing to fear from the tack-hammers of ignorant excursionists—highwaymen like this specimen. He failed in his enterprise. We sent a sheik to arrest him if he had the authority, or to warn him, if he had not, that by the laws of Egypt the crime he was attempting to commit was punishable with imprisonment or the bastinado. Then he desisted and went away.

The Sphinx: a hundred and twenty-five feet long, sixty feet high, and a hundred and two feet around the head, if I remember rightly—carved out of one solid block of stone harder than any iron. The block must have been as large as the Fifth Avenue Hotel before the usual waste (by the necessities of sculpture) of a fourth or a half of the original mass was begun. I only set down these figures and these remarks to suggest the prodigious labor the carving of it so elegantly, so symmetrically, so faultlessly, must have cost. This species of stone is so hard that figures cut in it remain sharp and un-marred after exposure to the weather for two or three thousand years. Now did it take a hundred years of patient toil to carve the Sphinx? It seems prob-able.

Fiction

SMITH AND
THE PHARAOHS

Sir H. Rider Haggard

Sir H. Rider Haggard is one of the best-known action and adventure writers and the creator of the South African big game hunter Allan Quartermain. His more than sixty books include Queen Sheba's Ring, She, Ayesha, *and* King Solomon's Mines. *They are based on his own experiences in Africa. And, of course, he couldn't write about Africa without writing about that great country in the north.*

I

Scientists, or some scientists—for occasionally one learned person differs from other learned persons—tell us they know all that is worth knowing about man, which statement, of course, includes woman. They trace him from his remotest origin; they show us how his bones changed and his shape modified, also how, under the influence of his needs and passions, his intelligence developed from something very humble. They demonstrate conclusively that there is nothing in man which the dissecting table will not explain; that his aspirations towards another life have their root in the fear of death, or, say others of them, in that of earthquake or thunder; that his affinities with the past are merely inherited from remote ancestors who lived in that past, perhaps a million years ago; and that everything noble about him is but the fruit of expediency or of a veneer of civilization, while everything base must be attributed to the instincts of his dominant and primeval nature. Man, in short, is an animal who, like every other animal, is finally subdued by his environment and takes his color from his surroundings, as cattle do from the red soil of Devon. Such are the facts, they (or some of them) declare; all the rest is rubbish.

At times we are inclined to agree with these sages, especially after it has been our privilege to attend a course of lectures by one of them. Then perhaps something comes within the range of our experience which gives us pause and causes doubts, the old divine doubts, to arise again deep in our hearts, and with them a yet diviner hope.

Perchance when all is said, so we think to ourselves, man *is* something more than an animal. Perchance he has known the past, the far past, and will know the future, the far, far future. Perchance the dream is true, and he does indeed possess what for convenience is called an immortal soul, that may manifest itself in one shape or another; that may sleep for ages, but, waking or sleeping, still remains itself, indestructible as the matter of the Universe.

An incident in the career of Mr. James Ebenezer Smith might well occasion such reflections, were any acquainted with its details, which until this, its setting forth, was not the case. Mr. Smith is a person who knows when to be silent. Still, undoubtedly it gave cause for thought to one individual—namely, to him to whom it happened. Indeed, James Ebenezer Smith is still thinking over it, thinking very hard indeed.

J. E. Smith was well born and well educated. When he was a good-looking and able young man at college, but before he had taken his degree, trouble came to him, the particulars of which do not matter, and he was thrown penniless, also friendless, upon the rocky bosom of the world. No, not quite friendless, for he had a godfather, a gentleman connected with business whose Christian name was Ebenezer. To him, as a last resource, Smith went, feeling that Ebenezer owed him something in return for the awful appellation wherewith he had been endowed in baptism.

To a certain extent Ebenezer recognized the obligation. He did nothing heroic, but he found his godson a clerkship in a bank of which he was one of the directors—a modest clerkship, no more. Also, when he died a year later, he left him a hundred pounds to be spent upon some souvenir.

Smith, being of a practical turn of mind, instead of adorning himself with memorial jewelry for which he had no use, invested the hundred pounds in an exceedingly promising speculation. As it happened, he was not misinformed, and his talent returned to him multiplied by ten. He repeated the experiment, and, being in a position to know what he was doing, with considerable success. By the time that he was thirty he found himself possessed of a fortune of something over twenty-five thousand pounds. Then (and this shows the wise and practical nature of the man) he stopped speculating and put out his money in such a fashion that it brought him a safe and clear four per cent.

By this time Smith, being an excellent man of business, was well up in the service of his bank—as yet only a clerk, it is true, but one who drew his four hundred pounds a year, with prospects. In short, he was in a position to marry had he wished to do so. As it happened, he did not wish—perhaps because, being very friendless, no lady who attracted him crossed his path: perhaps for other reasons.

Shy and reserved in temperament, he confided only in himself. None, not even his superiors at the bank or the Board of Management, knew how well off he had become. No one visited him at the flat which he was understood to occupy somewhere in the neighborhood of Putney; he belonged to no club, and possessed not a single intimate. The blow which the world had dealt him in his early days, the harsh repulses and the rough treatment he had then experienced, sank so deep into his sensitive soul that never again did he seek close converse with his kind. In fact, while still young, he fell into a condition of old-bachelorhood of a refined type.

Soon, however, Smith discovered—it was after he had given up speculating—that a man must have something to occupy his mind. He tried philanthropy, but found himself too sensitive for a business which so often resolves itself into rude inquiry as to the affairs of other people. After a struggle, therefore, he compromised with his conscience by setting aside a liberal portion of his income for anonymous distribution among deserving persons and objects.

While still in this vacant frame of mind Smith chanced one day, when the bank was closed, to drift into the British Museum, more to escape the vile weather that prevailed without than for any other reason. Wandering hither and thither at hazard, he found himself in the great gallery devoted to Egyptian stone objects and sculpture. The place bewildered him somewhat, for he knew nothing of Egyptology; indeed, there remained upon his mind only a sense of wonderment not unmixed with awe. It must have been a great people, he thought to himself, that executed these works, and with the thought came a desire to know more about them. Yet he was going away when suddenly his eye fell on the sculptured head of a woman which hung upon the wall.

Smith looked at it once, twice, thrice, and at the third look he fell in love. Needless to say, he was not aware that such was his condition. He knew only that a change had come over him, and never, never could he forget the face which that carven mask portrayed. Perhaps it was not really beautiful save for its wondrous and mystic smile; perhaps the lips were too thick and the nostrils too broad. Yet to him that face was Beauty itself, beauty which drew him as with a cart-rope, and awoke within him all kinds of wonderful imaginings, some of them so strange and tender that almost they partook of the nature of memories. He stared at the image, and the image smiled back sweetly at him, as doubtless it, or rather its original—for this was but a plaster cast—had smiled at nothingness in some tomb or hiding-hole for over thirty centuries, and as the woman whose likeness it was had once smiled upon the world.

A short, stout gentleman bustled up and, in tones of authority, addressed some workmen who were arranging a base for a neighboring statue. It occurred to Smith that he must be someone who knew about these objects. Overcoming his natural diffidence with an effort, he raised his hat and asked the gentleman if he could tell him, who was the original of the mask.

The official—who, in fact, was a very great man in the Museum—glanced at Smith shrewdly, and, seeing that his interest was genuine, answered:

"I don't know. Nobody knows. She has been given several names, but none of them have authority. Perhaps one day the rest of the statue may be found, and then we shall learn—that is, if it is inscribed. Most likely, however, it has been burnt for lime long ago."

"Then you can't tell me anything about her?" said Smith.

"Well, only a little. To begin with, that's a cast. The original is in the Cairo Museum. Mariette found it, I believe at Karnak, and gave it a name after his fashion. Probably she was a queen—of the eighteenth dynasty, by the work. But you can see her rank for yourself from the broken *uræus*." (Smith did not stop him to explain that he had not the faintest idea what a *uræus* might be, seeing that he was utterly unfamiliar with the snake-headed crest of Egyptian royalty.) "You should go to Egypt and study the head for your-self. It is one of the most beautiful things that ever was found. Well, I must be off. Good day."

And he bustled down the long gallery.

Smith found his way upstairs and looked at mummies and other things. Somehow it hurt him to reflect that the owner of yonder sweet, alluring face must have become a mummy long, long before the Christian era. Mummies did not strike him as attractive.

He returned to the statuary and stared at his plaster cast till one of the workmen remarked to his fellow that if he were the gent he'd go and look at "a live 'un" for a change.

Then Smith retired abashed.

On his way home he called at his bookseller's and ordered "all the best works on Egyptology." When, a day or two later, they arrived in a packing-case, together with a bill for thirty-eight pounds, he was somewhat dis-mayed. Still, he tackled those books like a man, and, being clever and industrious, within three months had a fair working knowledge of the sub-ject, and had even picked up a smattering of hieroglyphics.

In January—that was, at the end of those three months—Smith aston-ished his Board of Directors by applying for ten weeks' leave, he who had hitherto been content with a fortnight in the year. When questioned he ex-plained that he had been suffering from bronchitis, and was advised to take a change in Egypt.

"A very good idea," said the manager; "but I'm afraid you'll find it ex-pensive. They fleece one in Egypt."

"I know," answered Smith; "but I've saved a little and have only myself to spend it upon."

So Smith went to Egypt and saw the original of the beauteous head and a thousand other fascinating things. Indeed, he did more. Attaching himself to some excavators who were glad of his intelligent assistance, he actually dug for a month in the neighborhood of ancient Thebes, but without find-ing anything in particular.

It was not till two years later that he made his great discovery, that which is known as Smith's Tomb. Here it may be explained that the state of his health had become such as to necessitate an annual visit to Egypt, or so his superiors understood.

However, as he asked for no summer holiday, and was always ready to do another man's work or to stop overtime, he found it easy to arrange for these winter excursions.

On this, his third visit to Egypt, Smith obtained from the Director-General of Antiquities at Cairo a license to dig upon his own account. Being already well known in the country as a skilled Egyptologist, this was granted upon the usual terms—namely, that the Department of Antiquities should have a right to take any of the objects which might be found, or all of them, if it so desired.

Such preliminary matters having been arranged by correspondence, Smith, after a few days spent in the Museum at Cairo, took the night train to Luxor, where he found his head-man, an ex-dragoman named Mahomet, waiting for him and his fellaheen laborers already hired. There were but forty of them, for his was a comparatively small venture. Three hundred pounds was the amount that he had made up his mind to expend, and such a sum does not go far in excavations.

During his visit of the previous year Smith had marked the place where he meant to dig. It was in the cemetery of old Thebes, at the wild spot not far from the temple of Medinet Habu, that is known as the Valley of the Queens. Here, separated from the resting-places of their royal lords by the bold mass of the intervening hill, some of the greatest ladies of Egypt have been laid to rest, and it was their tombs that Smith desired to investigate. As he knew well, some of these must yet remain to be discovered. Who could say? Fortune favors the bold. It might be that he would find the holy grave of that beauteous, unknown Royalty whose face had haunted him for three long years!

For a whole month he dug without the slightest success. The spot that he selected had proved, indeed, to be the mouth of a tomb. After twenty-five days of laborious exploration it was at length cleared out, and he stood in a rude unfinished cave. The queen for whom it had been designed must have died quite young and been buried elsewhere, or she had chosen herself another sepulchre, or mayhap the rock had proved unsuitable for sculpture.

Smith shrugged his shoulders and moved on, sinking trial pits and trenches here and there, but still finding nothing. Two-thirds of his time and money had been spent when at last the luck turned. One day, towards evening, with some half-dozen of his best men he was returning after a fruitless morning of labor, when something seemed to attract him towards a little wadi, or bay, in the hillside that was filled with tumbled rocks and sand. There were scores of such places, and this one looked no more promising than any of the others had proved to be. Yet it attracted him. Thoroughly dispirited, he walked past it twenty paces or more, then turned.

"Where go you, sah?" asked his head-man, Mahomet.

He pointed to the recess in the cliff.

"No good, sah," said Mahomet. "No tomb there. Bed-rock too near top. Too much water run in there; dead queen like keep dry!"

But Smith went on, and the others followed obediently.

He walked down the little slope of sand and boulders and examined the cliff. It was virgin rock; never a tool mark was to be seen. Already the men were going, when the same strange instinct which had drawn him to the spot caused him to take a spade from one of them and begin to shovel away the sand from the face of the cliff—for here, for some unexplained reason, were no boulders or debris. Seeing their master, to whom they were attached, at work, they began to work too, and for twenty minutes or more dug on cheerfully enough, just to humor him, since all were sure that here there was no tomb. At length Smith ordered them to desist, for, although now they were six feet down, the rock remained of the same virgin character.

With an exclamation of disgust he threw out a last shovelful of sand. The edge of his spade struck on something that projected. He cleared away a little more sand, and there appeared a rounded ledge which seemed to be a cornice. Calling back the men, he pointed to it, and without a word all of them began to dig again. Five minutes more of work made it clear that it was a cornice, and half an hour later there appeared the top of the doorway of a tomb.

"Old people wall him up," said Mahomet, pointing to the flat stones set in mud for mortar with which the doorway had been closed, and to the undecipherable impress upon the mud of the scarab seals of the officials whose duty it had been to close the last resting-place of the royal dead for ever.

"Perhaps queen all right inside," he went on, receiving no answer to his remark.

"Perhaps," replied Smith, briefly. "Dig, man, dig! Don't waste time in talking."

So they dug on furiously till at length Smith saw something which caused him to groan aloud. There was a hole in the masonry—the tomb had been broken into. Mahomet saw it too, and examined the top of the aperture with his skilled eye.

"Very old thief," he said. "Look, he try build up wall again, but run away before he have time finish." And he pointed to certain flat stones which had been roughly and hurriedly replaced.

"Dig . . . dig!" said Smith.

Ten minutes more and the aperture was cleared. It was only just big enough to admit the body of a man.

By now the sun was setting. Swiftly, swiftly it seemed to tumble down the sky. One minute it was above the rough crests of the western hills behind them; the next, a great ball of glowing fire, it rested on their topmost ridge. Then it was gone. For an instant a kind of green spark shone where it had been. This too went out, and the sudden Egyptian night was upon them.

The fellaheen muttered among themselves, and one or two of them wandered off on some pretext. The rest threw down their tools and looked at Smith. "Men say they no like stop here. They afraid of ghost! Too many *afreet* live in these tomb. That what they say. Come back finish tomorrow morning when it light. Very foolish people, these common fellaheen," remarked Mahomet, in a superior tone.

"Quite so," replied Smith, who knew well that nothing that he could offer would tempt his men to go on with the opening of a tomb after sunset. "Let them go away. You and I will stop and watch the place till morning."

"Sorry, sah," said Mahomet, "but I not feel quite well inside; I think I got fever. I go to camp and lie down and pray under plenty blanket."

"All right, go," said Smith; "but if there is anyone who is not a coward, let him bring me my big coat, something to eat and drink, and the lantern that hangs in my tent. I will meet him there in the valley."

Mahomet, though rather doubtfully, promised that this should be done, and, after begging Smith to accompany them, lest the spirit of whoever slept in the tomb should work him a mischief during the night, they departed quickly enough.

Smith lit his pipe, sat down on the sand, and waited. Half an hour later he heard a sound of singing, and through the darkness, which was dense, saw lights coming up the valley.

"My brave men," he thought to himself, and scrambled up the slope to meet them.

He was right. These were his men, no less than twenty of them, for with a fewer number they did not dare to face the ghosts which they believed haunted the valley after nightfall. Presently the light from the lantern which one of them carried (not Mahomet, whose sickness had increased too suddenly to enable him to come) fell upon the tall form of Smith, who, dressed in his white working clothes, was leaning against a rock. Down went the lantern, and with a howl of terror the brave company turned and fled.

"Sons of cowards!" roared Smith after them, in his most vigorous Arabic. "It is I, your master, not an *afreet*."

They heard, and by degrees crept back again. Then he perceived that in order to account for their number each of them carried some article. Thus one had the bread, another the lantern, another a tin of sardines, another the sardine-opener, another a box of matches, another a bottle of beer, and so on. As even thus there were not enough things to go round, two of them bore his big coat between them, the first holding it by the sleeves and the second by the tail as though it were a stretcher.

"Put them down," said Smith, and they obeyed. "Now," he added, "run for your lives; I thought I heard two *afreets* talking up there just now of what they would do to any followers of the Prophet who mocked their gods, if perchance they should meet them in their holy place at night."

This kindly counsel was accepted with much eagerness. In another minute Smith was alone with the stars and the dying desert wind.

Collecting his goods, or as many of them as he wanted, he thrust them into the pockets of the greatcoat and returned to the mouth of the tomb. Here he made his simple meal by the light of the lantern, and afterwards tried to go to sleep. But sleep he could not. Something always woke him. First it was a jackal howling amongst the rocks; next a sand-fly bit him on the ankle so sharply that he thought he must have been stung by a scorpion. Then, notwithstanding his warm coat, the cold got hold of him, for the clothes beneath were wet through with perspiration, and it occurred to him that unless he did something he would probably contract an internal chill or perhaps fever. He rose and walked about.

By now the moon was up, revealing all the sad, wild scene in its every detail. The mystery of Egypt entered his soul and oppressed him. How much dead majesty lay in the hill upon which he stood? Were they all really dead, he wondered, or were those fellaheen right? Did their spirits still come forth at night and wander through the land where once they ruled? Of course that was the Egyptian faith according to which the *Ka,* or Double, eternally haunted the place where its earthly counterpart had been laid to rest. When one came to think of it, beneath a mass of unintelligible symbolism there was much in the Egyptian faith which it was hard for a Christian to disbelieve. Salvation through a Redeemer, for instance, and the resurrection of the body. Had he, Smith, not already written a treatise upon these points of similarity which he proposed to publish one day, not under his own name? Well, he would not think of them now; the occasion seemed scarcely fitting—they came home too pointedly to one who was engaged in violating a tomb.

His mind, or rather his imagination—of which he had plenty—went off at a tangent. What sights had this place seen thousands of years ago! Once, thousands of years ago, a procession had wound up along the roadway which was doubtless buried beneath the sand whereon he stood towards the dark door of this sepulchre. He could see it as it passed in and out between the rocks. The priests, shaven-headed and robed in leopards' skins, or some of them in pure white, bearing the mystic symbols of their office. The funeral sledge drawn by oxen, and on it the great rectangular case that contained the outer and the inner coffins, and within them the mummy of some departed Majesty; in the Egyptian formula, "the hawk that had spread its wings and flown into the bosom of Osiris," God of Death. Behind, the mourners, rending the air with their lamentations. Then those who bore the funeral furniture and offerings. Then the high officers of State and the first priests of Amen and of the other gods. Then the sister queens, leading by the hand a wondering child or two. Then the sons of Pharaoh, young men carrying the emblems of their rank.

Lastly, walking alone, Pharaoh himself in his ceremonial robes, his apron, his double crown of linen surmounted by the golden snake, his inlaid bracelets and his heavy, tinkling earrings. Pharaoh, his head bowed, his feet traveling wearily, and in his heart—what thoughts? Sorrow, perhaps, for her who had departed. Yet he had other queens and fair women without count. Doubtless she was sweet and beautiful, but sweetness and beauty were not given to her alone. Moreover, was she not wont to cross his will and to question his divinity? No, surely it is not only of her that he thinks, her for whom he had prepared this splendid tomb with all things needful to unite her with the gods. Surely he thinks also of himself and that other tomb on the farther side of the hill whereat the artists labor day by day—yes, and have labored these many years; that tomb to which before so very long he too must travel in just this fashion, to seek his place beyond the doors of Death, who lays his equal hand on king and queen and slave.

The vision passed. It was so real that Smith thought he must have been dreaming. Well, he was awake now, and colder than ever. Moreover, the jackals had multiplied. There were a whole pack of them, and not far away. Look! One crossed in the ring of the lamplight, a slinking, yellow beast that smelt the remains of dinner. Or perhaps it smelt him. Moreover, there were bad characters who haunted these mountains, and he was alone and quite unarmed. Perhaps he ought to put out the light which advertised his where-abouts. It would be wise and yet in this particular he rejected wisdom. After all, the light was some company.

Since sleep seemed to be out of the question, he fell back upon poor hu-manity's other anodyne, work, which has the incidental advantage of gener-ating warmth. Seizing a shovel, he began to dig at the doorway of the tomb, whilst the jackals howled louder than ever in astonishment. They were not used to such a sight. For thousands of years, as the old moon above could have told, no man, or at least no solitary man, had dared to rob tombs at such an unnatural hour.

When Smith had been digging for about twenty minutes something tinkled on his shovel with a noise which sounded loud in that silence.

"A stone which may come in handy for the jackals," he thought to him-self, shaking the sand slowly off the spade until it appeared. There it was, and not large enough to be of much service. Still, he picked it up, and rubbed it in his hands to clear off the encrusting dirt. When he opened them he saw that it was no stone, but a bronze.

"Osiris," reflected Smith, "buried in front of the tomb to hallow the ground. No, an Isis. No, the head of a statuette, and a jolly good one, too—at any rate, in moonlight. Seems to have been gilded." And, reaching out for the lamp, he held it over the object.

Another minute, and he found himself sitting at the bottom of the hole, lamp in one hand and statuette, or rather head, in the other.

"The Queen of the Mask!" he gasped. "The same—the same! By heav-ens, the very same!"

Oh, he could not be mistaken. There were the identical lips, a little thick and pouted; the identical nostrils, curved and quivering, but a little wide; the identical arched eyebrows and dreamy eyes set somewhat far apart. Above all, there was the identical alluring and mysterious smile. Only on this masterpiece of ancient art was set a whole crown of *uræi* surrounding the entire head. Beneath the crown and pressed back behind the ears was a full-bottomed wig or royal head-dress, of which the ends descended to the breasts. The statuette, that, having been gilt, remained quite perfect and uncorroded, was broken just above the middle, apparently by a single violent blow, for the fracture was very clean.

At once it occurred to Smith that it had been stolen from the tomb by a thief who thought it to be gold; that outside of the tomb doubt had overtaken him and caused him to break it upon a stone or otherwise. The rest was clear. Finding that it was but gold-washed bronze he had thrown away the fragments, rather than be at the pains of carrying them. This was his theory, probably not a correct one, as the sequel seems to show.

Smith's first idea was to recover the other portion. He searched quite a long while, but without success. Neither then nor afterwards could it be found. He reflected that perhaps this lower half had remained in the thief's hand, who, in his vexation, had thrown it far away, leaving the head to lie where it fell. Again Smith examined this head, and more closely. Now he saw that just beneath the breasts was a delicately cut cartouche.

Being by this time a master of hieroglyphics, he read it without trouble. It ran: "Ma-Mee, Great Royal Lady. Beloved of . . ." Here the cartouche was broken away.

"Ma-Mé, or it might be Ma-Mi," he reflected. "I never heard of a queen called Ma-Mé, or Ma-Mi, or Ma-Mu. She must be quite new to history. I wonder of whom she was beloved? Amen, or Horus, or Isis, probably. Of some god, I have no doubt, at least I hope so!"

He stared at the beautiful portrait in his hand, as once he had stared at the cast on the Museum wall, and the beautiful portrait, emerging from the dust of ages, smiled back at him there in the solemn moonlight as once the cast had smiled from the Museum wall.

Only that had been but a cast, whereas this was real. This had slept with the dead from whose features it had been fashioned, the dead who lay, or who had lain, within.

A sudden resolution took hold of Smith. He would explore that tomb, at once and alone. No one should accompany him on this his first visit; it would be a sacrilege that anyone save himself should set foot there until he had looked on what it might contain.

Why should he not enter? His lamp, of what is called the "hurricane" brand, was very good and bright, and would burn for many hours. Moreover, there had been time for the foul air to escape through the hole that they had cleared. Lastly, something seemed to call on him to come and see. He placed the bronze head in his breast-pocket over his heart, and, thrusting the lamp through the hole, looked down. Here there was no difficulty, since sand had drifted in to the level of the bottom of the aperture. Through it he struggled, to find himself upon a bed of sand that only just left him room to push himself along between it and the roof. A little farther on the passage was almost filled with mud.

Mahomet had been right when, from his knowledge of the bed-rock, he said that any tomb made in this place must be flooded. It *had* been flooded by some ancient rain-storm, and Smith began to fear that he would find it quite filled with soil caked as hard as iron. So, indeed, it was to a certain depth, a result that apparently had been anticipated by those who hollowed it, for this entrance shaft was left quite undecorated. Indeed, as Smith found afterwards, a hole had been dug beneath the doorway to allow the mud to enter after the burial was completed. Only a miscalculation had been made. The natural level of the mud did not quite reach the roof of the tomb, and therefore still left it open.

After crawling for forty feet or so over this caked mud, Smith suddenly found himself on a rising stair. Then he understood the plan; the tomb itself was on a higher level.

Here began the paintings. Here the Queen Ma-Mee, wearing her crowns and dressed in diaphanous garments, was presented to god after god. Between her figure and those of the divinities the wall was covered with hieroglyphs as fresh today as on that when the artist had limned them. A glance told him that they were extracts from the Book of the Dead. When the thief of bygone ages had broken into the tomb, probably not very long after the interment, the mud over which Smith had just crawled was still wet. This he could tell, since the clay from the rascal's feet remained upon the stairs, and that upon his fingers had stained the paintings on the wall against which he had supported himself; indeed, in one place was an exact impression of his hand, showing its shape and even the lines of the skin.

At the top of the flight of steps ran another passage at a higher level, which the water had never reached, and to right and left were the beginnings of unfinished chambers. It was clear to him that this queen had died young. Her tomb, as she or the king had designed it, was never finished. A few more paces, and the passage enlarged itself into a hall about thirty feet square. The ceiling was decorated with vultures, their wings outspread, the looped Cross of Life hanging from their talons. On one wall her Majesty Ma-Mee stood expectant while Anubis weighed her heart against the feather of truth, and Thoth, the Recorder, wrote down the verdict upon his tablets. All her titles were given to her here, such as "Great Royal Heiress, Royal Sister, Royal Wife, Royal Mother, Lady of the Two Lands, Palm-branch of Love, Beautiful exceedingly."

Smith read them hurriedly and noted that nowhere could he see the name of the king who had been her husband. It would almost seem as though this had been purposely omitted. On the other walls Ma-Mee, accompanied by her *Ka,* or Double, made offerings to the various gods, or uttered propitiatory speeches to the hideous demons of the underworld, declaring their names to them and forcing them to say: "Pass on. Thou art pure!"

Lastly, on the end wall, triumphant, all her trials done, she, the justified Osiris, or Spirit, was received by the god Osiris, Savior of Spirits.

All these things Smith noted hurriedly as he swung the lamp to and fro in that hallowed place. Then he saw something else which filled him with dismay. On the floor of the chamber where the coffins had been—for this was the burial chamber—lay a heap of black fragments charred with fire. Instantly he understood. After the thief had done his work he had burned the mummy-cases, and with them the body of the queen. There could be no doubt that this was so, for look! among the ashes lay some calcined human bones, while the roof above was blackened with the smoke and cracked by the heat of the conflagration. There was nothing left for him to find!

Oppressed with the closeness of the atmosphere, he sat down upon a little bench or table cut in the rock that evidently had been meant to receive offerings to the dead. Indeed, on it still lay the scorched remains of some votive flowers. Here, his lamp between his feet, he rested a while, staring at those calcined bones. See, yonder was the lower jaw, and in it some teeth, small, white, regular, and but little worn. Yes, she had died young. Then he turned to go, for disappointment and the holiness of the place overcame him; he could endure no more of it that night.

Leaving the burial hall, he walked along the painted passage, the lamp swinging and his eyes fixed upon the floor. He was disheartened, and the paintings could wait till the morrow. He descended the steps and came to the foot of the mud slope. Here suddenly he perceived, projecting from some sand that had drifted down over the mud, what seemed to be the corner of a reed box or basket. To clear away the sand was easy, and—yes, it was a basket, a foot or so in length, such a basket as the old Egyptians used to contain the funeral figures which are called *ushaptis,* or other objects connected with the dead. It looked as though it had been dropped, for it lay upon its side. Smith opened it—not very hopefully, for surely nothing of value would have been abandoned thus.

The first thing that met his eyes was a mummied hand, broken off at the wrist, a woman's little hand, most delicately shaped. It was withered and paper-white, but the contours still remained; the long fingers were perfect, and the almond-shaped nails had been stained with henna, as was the embalmers' fashion. On the hand were two gold rings, and for those rings it had been stolen. Smith looked at it for a long while, and his heart swelled within him, for here was the hand of that royal lady of his dreams.

Indeed, he did more than look; he kissed it, and as his lips touched the holy relic it seemed to him as though a wind, cold but scented, blew upon his brow. Then, growing fearful of the thoughts that arose within him, he hurried his mind back to the world, or rather to the examination of the basket.

Here he found other objects roughly wrapped in fragments of mummy-cloth that had been torn from the body of the queen. These it is needless to describe, for are they not to be seen in the gold room of the Museum, labelled "Bijouterie de la Reine Ma-Mé, XVIIIème Dynastie. Thebes (Smith's Tomb)"? It may be mentioned, however, that the set was incomplete. For instance, there was but one of the great gold ceremonial earrings fashioned like a group of pomegranate blooms, and the most beautiful of the necklaces had been torn in two—half of it was missing.

It was clear to Smith that only a portion of the precious objects which were buried with the mummy had been placed in this basket. Why had these been left where he found them? A little reflection made that clear also. Something had prompted the thief to destroy the desecrated body and its coffin with fire, probably in the hope of hiding his evil handiwork. Then he fled with his spoil. But he had forgotten how fiercely mummies and their trappings can burn. Or perhaps the thing was an accident. He must have had a lamp, and if its flame chanced to touch this bituminous tinder!

At any rate, the smoke overtook the man in that narrow place as he began to climb the slippery slope of clay. In his haste he dropped the basket, and dared not return to search for it. It could wait till the morrow, when the fire would be out and the air pure. Only for this desecrator of the royal dead that morrow never came, as was discovered afterwards.

When at length Smith struggled into the open air the stars were paling before the dawn. An hour later, after the sky was well up, Mahomet (recovered from his sickness) and his myrmidons arrived.

"I have been busy while you slept," said Smith, showing them the mummied hand (but not the rings which he had removed from the shrunk fingers), and the broken bronze, but not the priceless jewellery which was hidden in his pockets.

For the next ten days they dug till the tomb and its approach were quite clear. In the sand, at the head of a flight of steps which led down to the doorway, they found the skeleton of a man, who evidently had been buried there in a hurried fashion. His skull was shattered by the blow of an axe, and the shaven scalp that still clung to it suggested that he might have been a priest.

Mahomet thought, and Smith agreed with him, that this was the person who had violated the tomb. As he was escaping from it the guards of the holy place surprised him after he had covered up the hole by which he had entered and purposed to return. There they executed him without trial and divided up the plunder, thinking that no more was to be found. Or perhaps his confederates killed him.

Such at least were the theories advanced by Mahomet. Whether they were right or wrong none will ever know. For instance, the skeleton may not have been that of the thief, though probability appears to point the other way.

Nothing more was found in the tomb, not even a scarab or a mummy-bead. Smith spent the remainder of his time in photographing the pictures and copying the inscriptions, which for various reasons proved to be of extraordinary interest. Then, having reverently buried the charred bones of the queen in a secret place of the sepulchre, he handed it over to the care of the local Guardian of Antiquities, paid off Mahomet and the fellaheen, and departed for Cairo. With him went the wonderful jewels of which he had breathed no word, and another relic to him yet more precious—the hand of her Majesty Ma-Mee, Palm-branch of Love.

And now follows the strange sequel of this story of Smith and the queen Ma-Mee.

II

Smith was seated in the sanctum of the distinguished Director-General of Antiquities at the new Cairo Museum. It was a very interesting room. Books piled upon the floor; objects from tombs awaiting examination, lying here and there; a hoard of Ptolemaic silver coins, just dug up at Alexandria, standing on the table in the pot that had hidden them for two thousand years; in the corner the mummy of a royal child, aged six or seven, not long ago discovered, with some inscription scrawled upon the wrappings (brought here to be deciphered by the Master), and the withered lotus-bloom, love's last offering, thrust beneath one of the pink retaining bands.

"A touching object," thought Smith to himself. "Really, they might have left the dear little girl in peace."

Smith had a tender heart, but even as he reflected he became aware that some of the jewellery hidden in an inner pocket of his waistcoat (designed for bank notes) was fretting his skin. He had a tender conscience also.

Just then the Director, a French savant, bustled in, alert, vigorous, full of interest.

"Ah, my dear Mr. Smith!" he said, in his excellent English. "I am indeed glad to see you back again, especially as I understand that you are come rejoicing and bringing your sheaves with you. They tell me you have been extraordinarily successful. What do you say is the name of this queen whose tomb you have found—Ma-Mee? A very unusual name. How do you get the extra vowel? Is it for euphony—eh? Did I not know how good a scholar you are, I should be tempted to believe that you had misread it. Me-Mee,

Ma-Mee! That would be pretty in French, would it not? *Ma mie*—my darling! Well, I dare say she was somebody's *mie* in her time. But tell me the story."

Smith told him shortly and clearly; also he produced his photographs and copies of inscriptions.

"This is interesting—interesting truly," said the Director, when he had glanced through them. "You must leave them with me to study. Also you will publish them, is it not so? Perhaps one of the Societies would help you with the cost, for it should be done in facsimile. Look at this vignette! Most unusual. Oh, what a pity that scoundrelly priest got off with the jewelery and burnt her Majesty's body!"

"He didn't get off with all of it."

"What, Mr. Smith? Our inspector reported to me that you found nothing."

"I dare say, sir; but your inspector did not know what I found."

"Ah, you are a discreet man! Well, let us see."

Slowly Smith unbuttoned his waistcoat. From its inner pocket and elsewhere about his person he extracted the jewels wrapped in mummy-cloth as he had found them. First he produced a scepter-head of gold, in the shape of a pomegranate fruit and engraved with the throne name and titles of Ma-Mee.

"What a beautiful object!" said the Director. "Look! the handle was of ivory, and that *sacré* thief of a priest smashed it out at the socket. It was fresh ivory then; the robbery must have taken place not long after the burial. See, this magnifying-glass shows it. Is that all?"

Smith handed him the surviving half of the marvelous necklace that had been torn in two.

"I have re-threaded it," he muttered, "but every bead is in its place."

"Oh, heavens! How lovely! Note the cutting of those carnelian heads of Hathor and the gold lotus-blooms between—yes, and the enameled flies beneath. We have nothing like it in the Museum."

So it went on.

"Is that all?" gasped the Director at last, when every object from the basket glittered before them on the table.

"Yes," said Smith. "That is—no. I found a broken statuette hidden in the sand outside the tomb. It is of the queen, but I thought perhaps you would allow me to keep this."

"But certainly, Mr Smith; it is yours indeed. We are not niggards here. Still, if I might see it—"

From yet another pocket Smith produced the head. The Director gazed at it, then he spoke with feeling.

"I said just now that you were discreet, Mr. Smith, and I have been reflecting that you are honest. But now I must add that you are very clever. If you had not made me promise that this bronze should be yours before you showed it to me—well, it would never have gone into that pocket again. And, in the public interest, won't you release me from the promise?"

"*No,*" said Smith.

"You are perhaps not aware," went on the Director, with a groan, "that this is a portrait of Mariette's unknown queen whom we are thus able to identify. It seems a pity that the two should be separated; a replica we could let you have."

"I am quite aware," said Smith, "and I will be sure to send *you* a replica, with photographs. Also I promise to leave the original to some museum by will."

The Director clasped the image tenderly, and, holding it to the light, read the broken cartouche beneath the breasts.

"'Ma-Mé, Great Royal Lady. Beloved of—' Beloved of whom? Well, of Smith, for one. Take it, monsieur, and hide it away at once, lest soon there should be another mummy in this collection, a modern mummy called Smith; and, in the name of Justice, let the museum which inherits it be not the British, but that of Cairo, for this queen belongs to Egypt. By the way, I have been told that you are delicate in the lungs. How is your health now? Our cold winds are very trying. Quite good? Ah, that is excellent! I suppose that you have no more articles that you can show me?"

"I have nothing more except a mummied hand, which I found in the basket with the jewels. The two rings off it lie there. Doubtless it was removed to get at that bracelet. I suppose you will not mind my keeping the hand—"

"Of the beloved of Smith," interrupted the Director drolly. "No, I suppose not, though for my part I should prefer one that was not quite so old. Still, perhaps *you* will not mind my seeing it. That pocket of yours still looks a little bulky; I thought that it contained books!"

Smith produced a cigar-box; in it was the hand wrapped in cotton wool.

"Ah," said the Director, "a pretty, well-bred hand. No doubt this Ma-Mee was the real heiress to the throne, as she describes herself. The Pharaoh was somebody of inferior birth, half-brother—she is called 'Royal Sister,' you remember—son of one of the Pharaoh's slave-women, perhaps. Odd that she never mentioned him in the tomb. It looks as though they didn't get on in life, and that she was determined to have done with him in death. Those were the rings upon that hand, were they not?"

He replaced them on the fingers, then took off one, a royal signet in a cartouche, and read the inscription on the other: "'Bes Ank, Ank Bes.' 'Bes the Living, the living Bes.'

"Your Ma-Mee had some human vanity about her," he added. "Bes, among other things, as you know, was the god of beauty and of the adornments of women. She wore that ring that she might remain beautiful, and that her dresses might always fit, and her rouge never cake when she was dancing before the gods. Also it fixes her period pretty closely, but then so do other things. It seems a pity to rob Ma-Mee of her pet ring, does it not? The royal signet will be enough for us."

With a little bow he gave the hand back to Smith, leaving the Bes ring on the finger that had worn it for more than three thousand years. At least, Smith was so sure it was the Bes ring that at the time he did not look at it again.

Then they parted, Smith promising to return upon the morrow, which, owing to events to be described, he did not do.

"Ah!" said the Master to himself, as the door closed behind his visitor. "He's in a hurry to be gone. He has fear lest I should change my mind about that ring. Also there is the bronze. Monsieur Smith was *rusé* there. It is worth a thousand pounds, that bronze. Yet I do not believe he was thinking of the money. I believe he is in love with that Ma-Mee and wants to keep her picture. *Mon Dieu!* A well-established affection. At least he is what the English call an odd fish, one whom I could never make out, and of whom no one seems to know anything. Still, honest, I am sure—quite honest. Why, he might have kept every one of those jewels and no one have been the wiser.

And what things! What a find! *Ciel!* what a find! There has been nothing like it for years. Benedictions on the head of Odd-fish Smith!"

Then he collected the precious objects, thrust them into an inner compartment of his safe, which he locked and double-locked, and, as it was nearly five o'clock, departed from the Museum to his private residence in the grounds, there to study Smith's copies and photographs, and to tell some friends of the great things that had happened.

When Smith found himself outside the sacred door, and had presented its venerable guardian with a baksheesh of five piastres, he walked a few paces to the right and paused a while to watch some native laborers who were dragging a huge sarcophagus upon an improvised tramway. As they dragged they sang an echoing rhythmic song, whereof each line ended with an invocation to Allah.

Just so, reflected Smith, had their forefathers sung when, millenniums ago, they dragged that very sarcophagus from the quarries to the Nile, and from the Nile to the tomb whence it reappeared today, or when they slid the casing blocks of the pyramids up the great causeway and smooth slope of sand, and laid them in their dizzy resting-places. Only then each line of the immemorial chant of toil ended with an invocation to Amen, now transformed to Allah.

The East may change its masters and its gods, but its customs never change, and if today Allah wore the feathers of Amen one wonders whether the worshippers would find the difference so very great.

Thus thought Smith as he hurried away from the sarcophagus and those blue-robed, dark-skinned fellaheen, down the long gallery that is filled with a thousand sculptures. For a moment he paused before the wonderful white statue of Queen Amenartas, then, remembering that his time was short, hastened on to a certain room, one of those which opened out of the gallery.

In a corner of this room, upon the wall, amongst many other beautiful objects, stood that head which Mariette had found, whereof in past years the cast had fascinated him in London. Now he knew whose head it was; to him it had been given to find the tomb of her who had sat for that statue. Her very hand was in his pocket—yes, the hand that had touched yonder marble, pointing out its defects to the sculptor, or perhaps swearing that he flattered her. Smith wondered who that sculptor was; surely he must have been a happy man. Also he wondered whether the statuette was also this master's work. He thought so, but he wished to make sure.

Near to the end of the room he stopped and looked about him like a thief. He was alone in the place; not a single student or tourist could be seen, and its guardian was somewhere else. He drew out the box that contained the hand. From the hand he slipped the ring which the Director-General had left there as a gift to himself. He would much have preferred the other with the signet, but how could he say so, especially after the episode of the statuette?

Replacing the hand in his pocket without looking at the ring—for his eyes were watching to see whether he was observed—he set it upon his little finger, which it exactly fitted. (Ma-Mee had worn both of them upon the third finger of her left hand, the Bes ring as a guard to the signet.) He had the fancy to approach the effigy of Ma-Mee wearing a ring which she had worn and that came straight from her finger to his own.

Smith found the head in its accustomed place. Weeks had gone by since he looked upon it, and now, to his eyes, it had grown more beautiful than ever, and its smile was more mystical and loving. He drew out the statuette and began to compare them point by point. Oh, no doubt was possible! Both were likenesses of the same woman, though the statuette might have been executed two or three years later than the statue. To him the face of it looked a little older and more spiritual. Perhaps illness, or some premonition of her end had then thrown its shadow on the queen. He compared and compared. He made some rough measurements and sketches in his pocketbook, and set himself to work out a canon of proportions.

So hard and earnestly did he work, so lost was his mind that he never heard the accustomed warning sound which announces that the Museum is about to close. Hidden behind an altar as he was, in his distant, shadowed corner, the guardian of the room never saw him as he cast a last perfunctory glance about the place before departing till the Saturday morning; for the morrow was Friday, the Mohammedan Sabbath, on which the Museum remains shut, and he would not be called upon to attend. So he went. Everybody went. The great doors clanged, were locked and bolted, and, save for a watchman outside, no one was left in all that vast place except Smith in his corner, engaged in sketching and in measurements.

The difficulty of seeing, owing to the increase of shadow, first called his attention to the fact that time was slipping away. He glanced at his watch and saw that it was ten minutes to the hour.

"Soon be time to go," he thought to himself, and resumed his work.

How strangely silent the place seemed! Not a footstep to be heard or the sound of a human voice. He looked at his watch again, and saw that it was six o'clock, not five, or so the thing said. But that was impossible, for the Museum shut at five; evidently the desert sand had got into the works. The room in which he stood was that known as Room I, and he had noticed that its Arab custodian often frequented Room K or the gallery outside. He would find him and ask what was the real time.

Passing round the effigy of the wonderful Hathor cow, perhaps the finest example of an ancient sculpture of a beast in the whole world, Smith came to the doorway and looked up and down the gallery. Not a soul to be seen. He ran to Room K, to Room H, and others. Still not a soul to be seen. Then he made his way as fast as he could go to the great entrance. The doors were locked and bolted.

"Watch must be right after all. I'm shut in," he said to himself. "However, there's sure to be someone about somewhere. Probably the *salle des ventes* is still open. Shops don't shut till they are obliged."

Thither he went, to find its door as firmly closed as a door can be. He knocked on it, but a sepulchral echo was the only answer.

"I know," he reflected. "The Director must still be in his room. It will take him a long while to examine all that jewelry and put it away."

So for the room he headed, and, after losing his path twice, found it by help of the sarcophagus that the Arabs had been dragging, which now stood as deserted as it had done in the tomb, a lonesome and impressive object in the gathering shadows. The Director's door was shut, and again his knockings produced nothing but an echo. He started on a tour round the Museum, and, having searched the ground floors, ascended to the upper galleries by the great stairway.

Presently he found himself in that devoted to the royal mummies, and, being tired, rested there a while. Opposite to him, in a glass case in the middle of the gallery, reposed Rameses II. Near to, on shelves in a side case, were Rameses' son, Meneptah, and above, his son, Seti II, while in other cases were the mortal remains of many more of the royalties of Egypt. He looked at the proud face of Rameses and at the little fringe of white locks turned yellow by the embalmer's spices, also at the raised left arm. He remembered how the Director had told him that when they were unrolling this mighty monarch they went away to lunch, and that presently the man who had been left in charge of the body rushed into the room with his hair on end, and said that the dead king had lifted his arm and pointed at him.

Back they went, and there, true enough, was the arm lifted; nor were they ever able to get it quite into its place again. The explanation given was that the warmth of the sun had contracted the withered muscles, a very natural and correct explanation.

Still, Smith wished that he had not recollected the story just at this moment, especially as the arm seemed to move while he contemplated it— a very little, but still to move.

He turned round and gazed at Meneptah, whose hollow eyes stared at him from between the wrappings carelessly thrown across the parchment-like and ashen face. There, probably, lay the countenance that had frowned on Moses. There was the heart which God had hardened. Well, it was hard enough now, for the doctors said he died of ossification of the arteries, and that the vessels of the heart were full of lime!

Smith stood upon a chair and peeped at Seti II above. His weaker countenance was very peaceful, but it seemed to wear an air of reproach. In getting down Smith managed to upset the heavy chair. The noise it made was terrific. He would not have thought it possible that the fall of such an article could produce so much sound. Satisfied with his inspection of these particular kings, who somehow looked quite different now from what they had ever done before—more real and imminent, so to speak—he renewed his search for a living man.

On he went, mummies to his right, mummies to his left, of every style and period, till he began to feel as though he never wished to see another dried remnant of mortality. He peeped into the room where lay the relics of Iouiya and Touiyou, the father and mother of the great Queen Taia. Cloths had been drawn over these, and really they looked worse and more suggestive thus draped than in their frigid and unadorned blackness. He came to the coffins of the priest-kings of the twentieth dynasty, formidable painted coffins with human faces. There seemed to be a vast number of these priest-kings, but perhaps they were better than the gold masks of the great Ptolemaic ladies which glinted at him through the gathering gloom.

Really, he had seen enough of the upper floors. The statues downstairs were better than all these dead, although it was true that, according to the Egyptian faith, every one of those statues was haunted eternally by the *Ka*, or Double, of the person whom it represented. He descended the great stairway. Was it fancy, or did something run across the bottom step in front of him—an animal of some kind, followed by a swift-moving and indefinite shadow? If so, it must have been the Museum cat hunting a Museum mouse. Only then what on earth was that very peculiar and unpleasant shadow?

He called, "Puss! puss! puss!" for he would have been quite glad of its company; but there came no friendly "miau" in response. Perhaps it was only the *Ka* of a cat and the shadow was—oh! never mind what. The Egyptians worshipped cats, and there were plenty of their mummies about on the shelves. But the shadow!

Once he shouted in the hope of attracting attention, for there were no windows to which he could climb. He did not repeat the experiment, for it seemed as though a thousand voices were answering him from every corner and roof of the gigantic edifice.

Well, he must face the thing out. He was shut in a museum, and the question was in what part of it he should camp for the night. Moreover, as it was growing rapidly dark, the problem must be solved at once. He thought with affection of the lavatory, where, before going to see the Director, only that afternoon he had washed his hands with the assistance of a kindly Arab who watched the door and gracefully accepted a piastre. But there was no Arab there now, and the door, like every other in this confounded place, was locked. He marched on to the entrance.

Here, opposite to each other, stood the red sarcophagi of the great Queen Hatshepu and her brother and husband, Thotmes III. He looked at them. Why should not one of these afford him a night's lodging? They were deep and quiet, and would fit the human frame very nicely. For a while Smith wondered which of these monarchs would be the more likely to take offense at such a use of a private sarcophagus, and, acting on general principles, concluded that he would rather throw himself on the mercy of the lady.

Already one of his legs was over the edge of that solemn coffer, and he was squeezing his body beneath the massive lid that was propped above it on blocks of wood, when he remembered a little, naked, withered thing with long hair that he had seen in a side chamber of the tomb of Amenhotep II in the Valley of Kings at Thebes. This caricature of humanity many thought, and he agreed with them, to be the actual body of the mighty Hatshepu as it appeared after the robbers had done with it.

Supposing now, that when he was lying at the bottom of that sarcophagus, sleeping the sleep of the just, this little personage should peep over its edge and ask him what he was doing there! Of course the idea was absurd; he was tired, and his nerves were a little shaken. Still, the fact remained that for centuries the hallowed dust of Queen Hatshepu had slept where he, a modern man, was proposing to sleep.

He scrambled down from the sarcophagus and looked round him in despair. Opposite to the main entrance was the huge central hall of the Museum. Now the cement roof of this hall had, he knew, gone wrong, with the result that very extensive repairs had become necessary. So extensive were they, indeed, that the Director-General had informed him that they would take several years to complete. Therefore this hall was boarded up, only a little doorway being left by which the workmen could enter. Certain statues, of Seti II and others, too large to be moved, were also roughly boarded over, as were some great funeral boats on either side of the entrance. The rest of the place, which might be two hundred feet long with a proportionate breadth, was empty save for the colossi of Amenhotep III and his queen Taia that stood beneath the gallery at its farther end.

It was an appalling place in which to sleep, but better, reflected Smith, than a sarcophagus or those mummy chambers. If, for instance, he could creep behind the deal boards that enclosed one of the funeral boats he would be quite comfortable there. Lifting the curtain, he slipped into the hall, where the gloom of evening had already settled. Only the sky-lights and the outline of the towering colossi at the far end remained visible. Close to him were the two funeral boats which he had noted when he looked into the hall earlier on that day, standing at the head of a flight of steps which led to the sunk floor of the center. He groped his way to that on the right. As he expected, the projecting planks were not quite joined at the bow. He crept in between them and the boat and laid himself down.

Presumably, being altogether tired out, Smith did ultimately fall asleep, for how long he never knew. At any rate, it is certain that, if so, he woke up again. He could not tell the time, because his watch was not a repeater, and the place was as black as the pit. He had some matches in his pocket, and might have struck one and even have lit his pipe. To his credit be it said, however, he remembered that he was the sole tenant of one of the most valuable museums in the world, and his responsibilities with reference to fire. So he refrained from striking that match under the keel of a boat which had become very dry in the course of five thousand years.

Smith found himself very wide awake indeed. Never in all his life did he remember being more so, not even in the hour of its great catastrophe, or when his godfather, Ebenezer, after much hesitation, had promised him a clerkship in the bank of which he was a director. His nerves seemed strung tight as harp-strings, and his every sense was painfully acute. Thus he could even smell the odor of mummies that floated down from the upper galleries and the earthly scent of the boat which had been buried for thousands of years in sand at the foot of the pyramid of one of the fifth dynasty kings.

Moreover, he could hear all sorts of strange sounds, faint and far-away sounds which at first he thought must emanate from Cairo without. Soon, however, he grew sure that their origin was more local. Doubtless the cement work and the cases in the galleries were cracking audibly, as is the unpleasant habit of such things at night.

Yet why should these common manifestations be so universal and affect him so strangely? Really, it seemed as though people were stirring all about him. More, he could have sworn that the great funeral boat beneath which he lay had become repeopled with the crew that once it bore.

He heard them at their business above him. There were trampings and a sound as though something heavy were being laid on the deck, such, for instance, as must have been made when the mummy of Pharaoh was set there for its last journey to the western bank of the Nile. Yes, and now he could have sworn again that the priestly crew were getting out the oars.

Smith began to meditate flight from the neighborhood of that place when something occurred which determined him to stop where he was.

The huge hall was growing light, but not, as at first he hoped, with the rays of dawn. This light was pale and ghostly, though very penetrating. Also it had a blue tinge, unlike any other he had ever seen. At first it arose in a kind of fan or fountain at the far end of the hall, illumining the steps there and the two noble colossi which sat above.

But what was this that stood at the head of the steps, radiating glory? By heavens! it was Osiris himself or the image of Osiris, god of the Dead, the Egyptian savior of the world!

There he stood, in his mummy-cloths, wearing the feathered crown, and holding in his hands, which projected from an opening in the wrappings, the crook and the scourge of power. Was he alive, or was he dead? Smith could not tell, since he never moved, only stood there, splendid and fearful, his calm, benignant face staring into nothingness.

Smith became aware that the darkness between him and the vision of this god was peopled; that a great congregation was gathering, or had gathered there. The blue light began to grow; long tongues of it shot forward, which joined themselves together, illumining all that huge hall.

Now, too, he saw the congregation. Before him, rank upon rank of them, stood the kings and queens of Egypt. As though at a given signal, they bowed themselves to the Osiris, and ere the tinkling of their ornaments had died away, lo! Osiris was gone. But in his place stood another, Isis, the Mother of Mystery, her deep eyes looking forth from beneath the jeweled vulture-cap. Again the congregation bowed, and, lo! she was gone. But in her place stood yet another, a radiant, lovely being, who held in her hand the Sign of Life, and wore upon her head the symbol of the shining disc— Hathor, Goddess of Love. A third time the congregation bowed, and she, too, was gone; nor did any other appear in her place.

The Pharaohs and their queens began to move about and speak to each other; their voices came to his ears in one low, sweet murmur.

In his amazement Smith had forgotten fear. From his hiding-place he watched them intently. Some of them he knew by their faces. There, for instance, was the long-necked Khu-en-aten, talking somewhat angrily to the imperial Rameses II. Smith could understand what he said, for this power seemed to have been given to him. He was complaining in a high, weak voice that on this, the one night of the year when they might meet, the gods, or the magic images of the gods who were put up for them to worship, should not include *his* god, symbolized by the "Aten," or the sun's disc.

"I have heard of your Majesty's god," replied Rameses; "the priests used to tell me of him, also that he did not last long after your Majesty flew to heaven. The Fathers of Amen gave you a bad name; they called you 'the heretic' and hammered out your cartouches. They were quite rare in my time. Oh, do not let your Majesty be angry! So many of us have been heretics. My grandson, Seti, there,"—and he pointed to a mild, thoughtful-faced man—"for example. I am told that he really worshipped the god of those Hebrew slaves whom I used to press to build my cities. Look at that lady with him.

"Beautiful, isn't she? Observe her large, violet eyes! Well, she was the one who did the mischief, a Hebrew herself. At least, they tell me so."

"I will talk with him," answered Khu-en-aten. "It is more than possible that we may agree on certain points. Meanwhile, let me explain to your Majesty—"

"Oh, I pray you, not now. There is my wife."

"Your wife?" said Khu-en-aten, drawing himself up. "Which wife? I am told that your Majesty had many and left a large family; indeed, I see some hundreds of them here tonight. Now, I—but let me introduce Nefertiti to your Majesty. I may explain that she was my *only* wife."

"So I have understood. Your Majesty was rather an invalid, were you not? Of course, in those circumstances, one prefers the nurse whom one can trust. Oh, pray, no offense! Nefertari, my love—oh, I beg pardon!—Astnefert—Nefertari has gone to speak to some of her children—let me introduce you to your predecessor, the Queen Nefertiti, wife of Amenhotep IV—I mean Khu-en-aten (he changed his name, you know, because half of it was that of the father of the gods). She is interested in the question of plural marriage. Goodbye! I wish to have a word with my grandfather, Rameses I. He was fond of me as a little boy."

At this moment Smith's interest in that queer conversation died away, for of a sudden he beheld none other than the queen of his dreams, Ma-Mee. Oh! there she stood, without a doubt, only ten times more beautiful than he had ever pictured her. She was tall and somewhat fair-complexioned, with slumberous, dark eyes, and on her face gleamed the mystic smile he loved. She wore a robe of simple white and a purple-broidered apron, a crown of golden *uræi* with turquoise eyes was set upon her dark hair as in her statue, and on her breast and arms were the very necklace and bracelets that he had taken from her tomb. She appeared to be somewhat moody, or rather thoughtful, for she leaned by herself against a balustrade, watching the throng without much interest.

Presently a Pharaoh, a black-browed, vigorous man with thick lips, drew near.

"I greet your Majesty," he said.

She started, and answered:

"Oh, it is you! I make my obeisance to your Majesty," and she curtsied to him, humbly enough, but with a suggestion of mockery in her movements.

"Well, you do not seem to have been very anxious to find me, Ma-Mee, which, considering that we meet so seldom——"

"I saw that your Majesty was engaged with my sister queens," she interrupted, in a rich, low voice, "and with some other ladies in the gallery there, whose faces I seem to remember, but who I think were *not* queens. Unless, indeed, you married them after I was drawn away."

"One must talk to one's relations," replied the Pharaoh.

"Quite so. But, you see, I have no relations—at least, none whom I know well. My parents, you will remember, died when I was young, leaving me Egypt's heiress, and they are still vexed at the marriage which I made on the advice of my counsellors. But, is it not annoying? I have lost one of my rings, that which had the god Bes on it. Some dweller on the earth must be wearing it today, and that is why I cannot get it back from him."

"Him! Why 'him'? Hush; the business is about to begin."

"What business, my lord?"

"Oh, the question of the violation of our tombs, I believe."

"Indeed! That is a large subject, and not a very profitable one, I should say. Tell me, who is that?" And she pointed to a lady who had stepped forward, a very splendid person, magnificently arrayed.

"Cleopatra the Greek," he answered, "the last of Egypt's Sovereigns, one of the Ptolemys. You can always know her by that Roman who walks about after her."

"Which?" asked Ma-Mee. "I see several—also other men. She was the wretch who rolled Egypt in the dirt and betrayed her. Oh, if it were not for the law of peace by which we abide when we meet thus!"

"You mean that she would be torn to shreds, Ma-Mee, and her very soul scattered like the limbs of Osiris? Well, if it were not for that law of peace, so perhaps would many of us, for never have I heard a single king among these hundreds speak altogether well of those who went before or followed after him."

"Especially of those who went before if they happen to have hammered out their cartouches and usurped their monuments," said the queen, dryly, and looking him in the eyes.

At this home-thrust the Pharaoh seemed to wince. Making no answer, he pointed to the royal woman who had mounted the steps at the end of the hall.

Queen Cleopatra lifted her hand and stood thus for a while. Very splendid she was, and Smith, on his hands and knees behind the boarding of the boat, thanked his stars that alone among modern men it had been his lot to look upon her rich and living loveliness. There she shone, she who had changed the fortunes of the world, she who, whatever she did amiss, at least had known how to die.

III

Silence fell upon that glittering galaxy of kings and queens and upon all the hundreds of their offspring, their women, and their great officers who crowded the double tier of galleries around the hall.

"Royalties of Egypt," she began, in a sweet, clear voice which penetrated to the farthest recesses of the place, "I, Cleopatra, the sixth of that name and the last monarch who ruled over the Upper and the Lower Lands before Egypt became a home of slaves, have a word to say to your Majesties, who, in your mortal days, all of you more worthily filled the throne on which once I sat. I do not speak of Egypt and its fate, or of our sins—whereof mine were not the least—that brought her to the dust. Those sins I and others expiate elsewhere, and of them, from age to age, we hear enough. But on this one night of the year, that of the feast of him whom we call Osiris, but whom other nations have known and know by different names, it is given to us once more to be mortal for an hour, and, though we be but shadows, to renew the loves and hates of our long-perished flesh. Here for an hour we strut in our forgotten pomp; the gems that were ours still adorn our brows, and once more we seem to listen to our people's praise. Our hopes are the hopes of mortal life, our foes are the foes we feared, our gods grow real again, and our lovers whisper in our ears. Moreover, this joy is given to us—to see each other as we are, to know as the gods know, and therefore to forgive, even where we despise and hate. Now I have done, and I, the youngest of the rulers of ancient Egypt, call upon him who was the first of her kings to take my place."

She bowed, and the audience bowed back to her. Then she descended the steps and was lost in the throng. Where she had been appeared an old man, simply-clad, long-bearded, wise-faced, and wearing on his gray hair no crown save a plain band of gold, from the center of which rose the snake-headed *uræus* crest.

"Your Majesties who came after me," said the old man, "I am Menes, the first of the accepted Pharaohs of Egypt, although many of those who went before me were more truly kings than I. Yet as the first who joined the Upper and the Lower Lands, and took the royal style and titles, and ruled as well as I could rule, it is given to me to talk with you for a while this night whereon our spirits are permitted to gather from the uttermost parts of the uttermost worlds and see each other face to face. First, in darkness and in secret, let us speak of the mystery of the gods and of its meanings. Next, in darkness and in secret, let us speak of the mystery of our lives, of whence they come, of where they tarry by the road, and whither they go at last. And afterwards, let us speak of other matters face to face in light and openness, as we were wont to do when we were men. Then hence to Thebes, there to celebrate our yearly festival. Is such your will?"

"Such is our will," they answered.

It seemed to Smith that dense darkness fell upon the place, and with it a silence that was awful. For a time that he could not reckon, that might have been years or might have been moments, he sat there in the utter darkness and the utter silence.

At length the light came again, first as a blue spark, then in upward pouring rays, and lastly pervading all. There stood Menes on the steps, and there in front of him was gathered the same royal throng.

"The mysteries are finished," said the old king. "Now, if any have ought to say, let it be said openly."

A young man dressed in the robes and ornaments of an early dynasty came forward and stood upon the steps between the Pharaoh Menes and all those who had reigned after him. His face seemed familiar to Smith, as was the side lock that hung down behind his right ear in token of his youth. Where had he seen him? Ah, he remembered. Only a few hours ago lying in one of the cases of the Museum, together with the bones of the Pharaoh Unas.

"Your Majesties," he began, "I am the King Metesuphis. The matter that I wish to lay before you is that of the violation of our sepulchres by those men who live upon the earth. The mortal bodies of many who are gathered here tonight lie in this place to be stared at and mocked by the curious. I myself am one of them, jawless, broken, hideous to behold. Yonder, day by day, must my *Ka* sit watching my desecrated flesh, torn from the pyramid that, with cost and labor, I raised up to be an eternal house wherein I might hide till the hour of resurrection. Others of us lie in far lands. Thus, as he can tell you, my predecessor, Man-kau-ra, he who built the third of the great pyramids, the Pyramid of Her, sleeps, or rather wakes in a dark city, called London, across the seas, a place of murk where no sun shines. Others have been burnt with fire, others are scattered in small dust. The ornaments that were ours are stole away and sold to the greedy; our sacred writings and our symbols are their jest. Soon there will not be one holy grave in Egypt that remains undefiled."

"That is so," said a voice from the company. "But four months gone the deep, deep pit was opened that I had dug in the shadow of the Pyramid of Cephren, who begat me in the world. There in my chamber I slept alone, two handfuls of white bones, since when I died they did not preserve the body with wrappings and with spices. Now I see those bones of mine, beside which my Double has watched for these five thousand years, hid in the blackness of a great ship and tossing on a sea that is strewn with ice."

"It is so," echoed a hundred other voices.

"Then," went on the young king, turning to Menes, "I ask of your Majesty whether there is no means whereby we may be avenged on those who do us this foul wrong."

"Let him who has wisdom speak," said the old Pharaoh.

A man of middle age, short in stature and of a thoughtful brow, who held in his hand a wand and wore the feathers and insignia of the heir to the throne of Egypt and of a high priest of Amen, moved to the steps. Smith knew him at once from his statues. He was Khaemuas, son of Rameses the Great, the mightiest magician that ever was in Egypt, who of his own will withdrew himself from earth before the time came that he should sit upon the throne.

"I have wisdom, your Majesties, and I will answer," he said. "The time draws on when, in the land of Death which is Life, the land that we call Amenti, it will be given to us to lay our wrongs as to this matter before Those who judge, knowing that they will be avenged. On this night of the year also, when we resume the shapes we were, we have certain powers of vengeance, or rather of executing justice. But our time is short, and there is much to say and do before the sun-god Ra arises and we depart each to his place. Therefore it seems best that we should leave these wicked ones in their wickedness till we meet them face to face beyond the world."

Smith, who had been following the words of Khaemuas with the closest attention and considerable anxiety, breathed again, thanking Heaven that the engagements of these departed monarchs were so numerous and pressing. Still, as a matter of precaution, he drew the cigar-box which contained Ma-Mee's hand from his pocket, and pushed it as far away from him as he could. It was a most unlucky act. Perhaps the cigar-box grated on the floor, or perhaps the fact of his touching the relic put him into psychic communication with all these spirits. At any rate, he became aware that the eyes of that dreadful magician were fixed upon him, and that a bone had a better chance of escaping the search of a Röntgen ray than he of hiding himself from their baleful glare.

"As it happens, however," went on Khaemuas, in a cold voice, "I now perceive that there is hidden in this place, and spying on us, one of the worst of these vile thieves. I say to your Majesties that I see him crouched beneath your funeral barge, and that he has with him at this moment the hand of one of your Majesties, stolen by him from her tomb at Thebes."

Now every queen in the company became visibly agitated (Smith, who was watching Ma-Mee, saw her hold up her hands and look at them), while all the Pharaohs pointed with their fingers and exclaimed together, in a voice that rolled round the hall like thunder:

"Let him be brought forth to judgment!"

Khaemuas raised his wand and, holding it towards the boat where Smith was hidden, said:

"Draw near, Vile One, bringing with thee that thou hast stolen."

Smith tried hard to remain where he was. He sat himself down and set his heels against the floor. As the reader knows, he was always shy and retiring by disposition, and never had these weaknesses oppressed him more than they did just then. When a child his favorite nightmare had been that the foreman of a jury was in the act of proclaiming him guilty of some dreadful but unstated crime. Now he understood what that nightmare foreshadowed. He was about to be convicted in a court of which all the kings and queens of Egypt were the jury, Menes was Chief Justice, and the magician Khaemuas played the role of Attorney-General.

In vain did he sit down and hold fast. Some power took possession of him which forced him first to stretch out his arm and pick up the cigar-box containing the hand of Ma-Mee, and next drew him from the friendly shelter of the deal boards that were about the boat.

Now he was on his feet and walking down the flight of steps opposite to those on which Menes stood far away. Now he was among all that throng of ghosts, which parted to let him pass, looking at him as he went with cold and wondering eyes. They were very majestic ghosts; the ages that had gone by since they laid down their scepters had taken nothing from their royal dignity. Moreover, save one, none of them seemed to have any pity for his plight. She was a little princess who stood by her mother, that same little princess whose mummy he had seen and pitied in the Director's room with a lotus flower thrust beneath her bandages. As he passed Smith heard her say:

"This Vile One is frightened. Be brave, Vile One!"

Smith understood, and pride come to his aid. He, a gentleman of the modern world, would not show the white feather before a crowd of ancient Egyptian ghosts. Turning to the child, he smiled at her, then drew himself to his full height and walked on quietly. Here it may be stated that Smith was a tall man, still comparatively young, and very good-looking, straight and spare in frame, with dark, pleasant eyes and a little black beard.

"At least he is a well-favored thief," said one of the queens to another.

"Yes," answered she who had been addressed. "I wonder that a man with such a noble air should find pleasure in disturbing graves and stealing the offerings of the dead," words that gave Smith much cause for thought. He had never considered the matter in this light.

Now he came to the place where Ma-Mee stood, the black-browed Pharaoh who had been her husband at her side. On his left hand which held the cigar-box was the gold Bes ring, and that box he felt constrained to carry pressed against him just over his heart.

As he went by he turned his head, and his eyes met those of Ma-Mee. She started violently. Then she saw the ring upon his hand and again started still more violently.

"What ails your Majesty?" asked the Pharaoh.

"Oh, naught," she answered. "Yet does this earth-dweller remind you of anyone?"

"Yes, he does," answered the Pharaoh. "He reminds me very much of that accursed sculptor about whom we had words."

"Do you mean a certain Horu, the Court artist; he who worked the image that was buried with me, and whom you sent to carve your statues in the deserts of Kush, until he died of fevers—or was it poison?"

"Aye; Horu and no other, may Set take and keep him!" growled the Pharaoh.

Then Smith passed on and heard no more. Now he stood before the venerable Menes. Some instinct caused him to bow to the royal company, and they also bowed back to him, coldly, but very gravely and courteously.

"Dweller on the world where once we had our place, and therefore brother of us, the dead," began Menes, "this divine priest and magician"—and he pointed to Khaemuas—"declares that you are one of those who foully violate our sepulchres and desecrate our ashes. He declares, moreover, that at this very moment you have with you a portion of the mortal flesh of a certain Majesty whose spirit is present here. Say, now, are these things true?"

To his astonishment Smith found that he had not the slightest difficulty in answering in the same sweet tongue.

"O King, they are true, and not true. Hear me, rulers of Egypt. It is true that I have searched in your graves, because my heart has been drawn towards you, and I would learn all that I could concerning you, for it comes to me now that once I was one of you—no king, indeed, yet perchance of the blood of kings. Also—for I would hide nothing even if I could—I searched for one tomb above all others."

"Why, O man?" asked the Judge.

"Because a face drew me, a lovely face that was cut in stone."

Now all that great audience turned their eyes towards him and listened as though his words moved them.

"Did you find that holy tomb?" asked Menes. "If so, what did you find therein?"

"Aye, Pharaoh, and in it I found these," and he took from the box the withered hand, from his pocket the broken bronze, and from his finger the ring.

"Also I found other things which I delivered to the keeper of this place, articles of jewelry that I seem to see tonight upon one who is present here among you."

"Is the face of this figure the face you sought?" asked the Judge.

"It is the lovely face," he answered.

Menes took the effigy in his hand and read the cartouche that was engraved beneath its breast.

"If there be here among us," he said, presently, "one who long after my day ruled as queen in Egypt, one who was named Ma-Mé, let her draw near."

Now from where she stood glided Ma-Mee and took her place opposite to Smith.

"Say, O Queen," asked Menes, "do you know ought of this matter?"

"I know that hand; it was my own hand," she answered. "I know that ring; it was my ring. I know that image in bronze; it was my image. Look on me and judge for yourselves whether this be so. A certain sculptor fashioned it, the son of a king's son, who was named Horu, the first of sculptors and the head artist of my Court. There, clad in strange garments, he stands before you. Horu, or the Double of Horu, he who cut the image when I ruled in Egypt, is he who found the image and the man who stands before you; or, mayhap, his Double cast in the same mold."

The pharaoh Menes turned to the magician Khaemuas and said:

"Are these things so, O Seer?"

"They are so," answered Khaemuas. "This dweller on the earth is he who, long ago, was the sculptor Horu. But what shall that avail? He, once more a living man, is a violator of the hallowed dead. I say, therefore, that judgment should be executed on his flesh, so that when the light comes here tomorrow he himself will again be gathered to the dead."

Menes bent his head upon his breast and pondered. Smith said nothing. To him the whole play was so curious that he had no wish to interfere with its development. If these ghosts wished to make him of their number, let them do so. He had no ties on earth, and now when he knew full surely that there was a life beyond this of earth he was quite prepared to explore its mysteries. So he folded his arms upon his breast and awaited the sentence.

But Ma-Mee did not wait. She raised her hand so swiftly that the bracelets jingled on her wrists, and spoke out with boldness.

"Royal Khaemuas, prince and magician," she said, "hearken to one who, like you, was Egypt's heir centuries before you were born, one also who ruled over the Two Lands, and not so ill—which, Prince, never was your lot. Answer me! Is all wisdom centered in your breast? Answer me! Do you alone know the mysteries of Life and Death? Answer me! Did your god

Amen teach you that vengeance went before mercy? Answer me! Did he teach you that men should be judged unheard? That they should be hurried by violence to Osiris ere their time, and thereby separated from the dead ones whom they loved and forced to return to live again upon this evil Earth?

"Listen: when the last moon was near her full my spirit sat in my tomb in the burying-place of queens. My spirit saw this man enter into my tomb, and what he did there. With bowed head he looked upon my bones that a thief of the priesthood of Amen had robbed and burnt within twenty years of their burial, in which he himself had taken part. And what did this man with those bones, he who was once Horu? I tell you that he hid them away there in the tomb where he thought they could not be found again. Who, then, was the thief and the violator? He who robbed and burnt my bones, or he who buried them with reverence? Again, he found the jewels that the priest of your brotherhood had dropped in his flight, when the smoke of the burning flesh and spices overpowered him, and with them the hand which that wicked one had broken off from the body of my Majesty. What did this man then? He took the jewels. Would you have had him leave them to be stolen by some peasant? And the hand? I tell you that he kissed that poor dead hand which once had been part of the body of my Majesty, and that now he treasures it as a holy relic. My spirit saw him do these things and made report thereof to me. I ask you, therefore, Prince, I ask you all, Royalties of Egypt—whether for such deeds this man should die?"

Now Khaemuas, the advocate of vengeance, shrugged his shoulders and smiled meaningly, but the congregation of kings and queens thundered an answer, and it was: "No!"

Ma-Mee looked to Menes to give judgment. Before he could speak the dark-browed Pharaoh who had named her wife strode forward and addressed them.

"Her Majesty, Heiress of Egypt, Royal Wife, Lady of the Two Lands, has spoken," he cried. "Now let me speak who was the husband of her Majesty. Whether this man was once Horu the sculptor I know not. If so he was also an evil-doer who, by my decree, died in banishment in the land of Kush. Whatever be the truth as to that matter, he admits that he violated the tomb of her Majesty and stole what the old thieves had left. Her Majesty says also—and he does not deny it—that he dared to kiss her hand, and for a man to kiss the hand of a wedded Queen of Egypt the punishment is death. I claim that this man should die to the World before his time, that in a day to come again he may live and suffer in the World. Judge, O Menes."

Menes lifted his head and spoke, saying:

"Repeat to me the law, O Pharaoh, under which a living man must die for the kissing of a dead hand. In my day and in that of those who went before me there was no such law in Egypt. If a living man, who was not her husband, or of her kin, kissed the living hand of a wedded Queen of Egypt, save in ceremony, then perchance he might be called upon to die. Perchance for such a reason a certain Horu once was called upon to die. But in the grave there is no marriage, and therefore even if he had found her alive within the tomb and kissed her hand, or even her lips, why should he die for the crime of love?

"Hear me, all; this is my judgment in the matter. Let the soul of that priest who first violated the tomb of the royal Ma-Mee be hunted down and given to the jaws of the Destroyer, that he may know the last depths of Death, if so the gods declare. But let this man go from among us unharmed, since what he did he did in reverent ignorance and because Hathor, Goddess of Love, guided him from of old. Love rules this world wherein we meet tonight, with all the worlds whence we have gathered or whither we still must go. Who can defy its power? Who can refuse its rites? Now hence to Thebes!"

There was a rushing sound as of a thousand wings, and all were gone. No, not all, since Smith yet stood before the draped colossi and the empty steps, and beside him, glorious, unearthly, gleamed the vision of Ma-Mee.

"I, too, must away," she whispered; "yet ere I go a word with you who once were a sculptor in Egypt. You loved me then, and that love cost you your life, you who once dared to kiss this hand of mine that again you kissed in yonder tomb. For I was Pharaoh's wife in name only; understand me well, in name only; since that title of Royal Mother, which they gave me is but a graven lie. Horu, I never was a wife, and when you died, swiftly I followed you to the grave. Oh, you forget, but I remember! I remember many things. You think that the priestly thief broke this figure of me which you found in the sand outside my tomb. Not so. I broke it, because, daring greatly, you had written thereon, 'Beloved' not 'of *Horus* the God' as you should have done, but of '*Horu* the Man.' So when I came to be buried, Pharaoh, knowing all, took the image from my wrappings and hurled it away. I remember, too, the casting of that image, and how you threw a gold chain I had given you into the crucible with the bronze, saying that gold alone was fit to fashion me. And this signet that I bear—it was you who cut it. Take it, take it, Horu, and in its place give me back that which is on your hand, the Bes ring that I also wore. Take it and wear it ever till you die again, and let it go to the grave with you as once it went to the grave with me.

"Now hearken. When Ra the great sun arises again and you awake you will think that you have dreamed a dream. You will think that in this dream you saw and spoke with a lady of Egypt who died more than three thousand years ago, but whose beauty, carved in stone and bronze, has charmed your heart today. So let it be, yet know, O man, who once was named Horu, that such dreams are oft-times a shadow of the truth. Know that this Glory which shines before you is mine indeed in the land that is both far and near, the land wherein I dwell eternally, and that what is mine has been, is, and shall be yours for ever. Gods may change their kingdoms and their names; men may live and die, and live again once more to die; empires may fall and those who ruled them be turned to forgotten dust. Yet true love endures immortal as the souls in which it was conceived, and from it for you and me, the night of woe and separation done, at the daybreak which draws on, there shall be born the splendor and the peace of union. Till that hour foredoomed seek me no more, though I be ever near you, as I have ever been. Till that most blessed hour, Horu, farewell."

She bent towards him; her sweet lips touched his brow; the perfume from her breath and hair beat upon him; the light of her wondrous eyes searched out his very soul, reading the answer that was written there.

He stretched out his arms to clasp her, and lo! she was gone.

It was a very cold and a very stiff Smith who awoke on the following morning, to find himself exactly where he had lain down—namely, on a cement floor beneath the keel of a funeral boat in the central hall of the Cairo Museum. He crept from his shelter shivering, and looked at this hall, to find it quite as empty as it had been on the previous evening. Not a sign or a token was there of Pharaoh Menes and all those kings and queens of whom he had dreamed so vividly.

Reflecting on the strange fantasies that weariness and excited nerves can summon to the mind in sleep, Smith made his way to the great doors and waited in the shadow, praying earnestly that, although it was the Mohammedan Sabbath, someone might visit the Museum to see that all was well.

As a matter of fact, someone did, and before he had been there a minute—a watchman going about his business. He unlocked the place carelessly, looking over his shoulder at a kite fighting with two nesting crows. In an instant Smith, who was not minded to stop and answer questions, had slipped past him and was gliding down the portico, from monument to monument, like a snake between boulders, still keeping in the shadow as he headed for the gates.

The attendant caught sight of him and uttered a yell of fear; then, since it is not good to look upon an *afreet,* appearing from whence no mortal man could be, he turned his head away. When he looked again Smith was through those gates and had mingled with the crowd in the street beyond.

The sunshine was very pleasant to one who was conscious of having contracted a chill of the worst Egyptian order from long contact with a damp stone floor. Smith walked on through it towards his hotel—it was Shepheard's, and more than a mile away—making up a story as he went to tell the hall-porter of how he had gone to dine at Mena House by the Pyramids, missed the last tram, and stopped the night there.

Whilst he was thus engaged his left hand struck somewhat sharply against the corner of the cigar-box in his pocket, that which contained the relic of the queen Ma-Mee. The pain caused him to glance at his fingers to see if they were injured, and to perceive on one of them the ring he wore. Surely, surely it was not the same that the Director-General had given him! *That* ring was engraved with the image of the god Bes. On *this* was cut the cartouche of her Majesty Ma-Mee! And he had dreamed—oh, he had dreamed—!

To this day Smith is wondering whether, in the hurry of the moment, he made a mistake as to which of those rings the Director-General had given him as part of his share of the spoil of the royal tomb he discovered in the Valley of Queens. Afterward Smith wrote to ask, but the Director-General could only remember that he gave him one of the two rings, and assured him that that inscribed *"Bes Ank, Ank Bes,"* was with Ma-Mee's other jewels in the Gold Room of the Museum.

Also Smith is wondering whether any other bronze figure of an old Egyptian royalty shows so high a percentage of gold as, on analysis, the broken image of Ma-Mee was proved to do. For had she not seemed to tell him a tale of the melting of a golden chain when that effigy was cast?

Was it all only a dream, or was it—something more—by day and by night he asks of Nothingness.

But, be she near or far, no answer comes from the Queen Ma-Mee, whose proud titles were: "Her Majesty the Good God, the Justified Dweller in Osiris; Daughter of Amen, Royal Heiress, Royal Sister, Royal Wife, Royal Mother; Lady of the Two Lands; Wearer of the Double Crown, of the White Crown, of the Red Crown; Sweet Flower of Love, Beautiful Eternally."

So, like the rest of us, Smith must wait to learn the truth concerning many things, and more particularly as to which of those two circles of ancient gold the Director-General gave him yonder at Cairo.

It seems but a little matter, yet it is more than all the worlds to him!

To the astonishment of his colleagues in antiquarian research, Smith has never returned to Egypt. He explains to them that his health is quite restored, and that he no longer needs this annual change to a more temperate clime.

Now, *which* of the two royal rings did the Director-General return to Smith on the mummied hand of her late Majesty Ma-Mee?

Fiction

SOME WORDS
WITH A MUMMY

Edgar Allan Poe

Edgar Allan Poe was born in Boston, but was soon orphaned and subsequently raised by a foster family, which he did not get along well with. While his foster family lived in England for five years, he went to a private school near London. When he returned to the United States, he entered the University of Virginia. He took to gambling to support himself, but his drinking and mounting debts forced him to leave. Poe spent two years in the Army and rose to the rank of sergeant major. Shortly after he received an honorable discharge, he entered West Point in an effort to please his foster father. When he realized he would never receive an inheritance, he deliberately broke regulations and was thrown out of the academy. After being refused by the Polish army, he focused more on his writing and began working as a magazine editor. When he was twenty-seven, he married his fourteen-year-old cousin. It was during this period that he wrote his great horror stories, including "The Tell-Tale Heart," "The Pit and the Pendulum," "The Fall of the House of Usher," "The Murders in the Rue Morgue," and his classic poem "The Raven." His drinking increased throughout his wife's long illness and eventual death from tuberculosis. Poe was on the way to his wedding with his childhood sweetheart when he disappeared; he was found unconscious several days later. He never regained consciousness and the cause of his death at the age of forty remains a mystery. Poe's complete works fill seventeen volumes, with only one novel, which is actually more of a novella. He is credited with having invented the detective story. Although he was just beginning to be recognized when he died, Poe is now considered to be one of America's greatest writers and poets. In the beginning of this tale Poe mentions Welsh rabbit—also known as rarebit—which is a meatless dish consisting of cheese and beer. It was once commonly believed that eating Welsh rabbit right before going to sleep would produce particularly vivid dreams and nightmares.

The symposium of the preceding evening had been a little too much for my nerves. I had a wretched headache, and was desperately drowsy. Instead of going out, therefore, to spend the evening as I had proposed, it occurred to me that I could not do a wiser thing than just eat a mouthful of supper and go immediately to bed.

A *light* supper of course. I am exceedingly fond of Welsh rabbit. More than a pound at once, however, may not at all times be advisable. Still, there can be no material objection to two. And really between two and three, there is merely a single unit of difference. I ventured, perhaps, upon four. My wife will have it five;—but, clearly, she has confounded two very distinct affairs. The abstract number, five, I am willing to admit; but, concretely, it has reference to bottles of Brown Stout, without which, in the way of condiment, Welsh rabbit is to be eschewed.

Having thus concluded a frugal meal, and donned my night-cap, with the serene hope of enjoying it till noon the next day, I placed my head upon the pillow, and, through the aid of a capital conscience, fell into a profound slumber forthwith.

But when were the hopes of humanity fulfilled? I could not have completed my third snore when there came a furious ringing at the street-door bell, and then an impatient thumping at the knocker, which awakened me at once. In a minute afterward, and while I was still rubbing my eyes, my wife thrust in my face a note, from my old friend, Doctor Ponnonner. It ran thus:

> *Come to me by all means, my dear good friend, as soon as you receive this. Come and help us to rejoice. At last, by long persevering diplomacy, I have gained the assent of the Directors of the City Museum, to my examination of the Mummy—you know the one I mean. I have permission to unswathe it and open it, if desirable. A few friends only will be present—you, of course. The Mummy is now at my house, and we shall begin to unroll it at eleven to-night.*
>
> *Yours ever,*
> Ponnonner

By the time I had reached the "Ponnonner," it struck me that I was as wide awake as a man need be. I leaped out of bed in an ecstasy, overthrowing all in my way; dressed myself with a rapidity truly marvelous; and set off, at the top of my speed, for the Doctor's.

There I found a very eager company assembled. They had been awaiting me with much impatience; the Mummy was extended upon the dining-table; and the moment I entered its examination was commenced.

It was one of a pair brought, several years previously, by Captain Arthur Sabretash, a cousin of Ponnonner's, from a tomb near Eleithias, in the Lybian Mountains, a considerable distance above Thebes on the Nile. The grottoes at this point, although less magnificent than the Theban sepulchres, are of higher interest, on account of affording more numerous illustrations of the private life of the Egyptians. The chamber from which our specimen was taken, was said to be very rich in such illustrations; the walls being completely covered with fresco paintings and bas-reliefs, while statues, vases, and Mosaic work of rich patterns, indicated the vast wealth of the deceased.

The treasure had been deposited in the Museum precisely in the same condition in which Captain Sabretash had found it;—that is to say, the coffin had not been disturbed. For eight years it had thus stood, subject only externally to public inspection. We had now, therefore, the complete Mummy at our disposal; and to those who are aware how very rarely the unransacked antique reaches our shores, it will be evident, at once, that we had great reason to congratulate ourselves upon our good fortune.

Approaching the table, I saw on it a large box, or case, nearly seven feet long, and perhaps three feet wide, by two feet and a half deep. It was oblong—not coffin-shaped. The material was at first supposed to be the wood of the sycamore (*platanus*), but, upon cutting into it, we found it to be pasteboard, or more properly, *papier mâché,* composed of papyrus. It was thickly ornamented with paintings, representing funeral scenes, and other mournful subjects, interspersed among which, in every variety of position, were certain series of hieroglyphical characters intended, no doubt, for the name of the departed. By good luck, Mr. Gliddon formed one of our party; and he had no difficulty in translating the letters, which were simply phonetic, and represented the word *Allamistakeo.*

We had some difficulty in getting this case open without injury, but, having at length accomplished the task, we came to a second, coffin-shaped, and very considerably less in size than the exterior one, but resembling it precisely in every other respect. The interval between the two was filled with resin, which had, in some degree, defaced the colors of the interior box.

Upon opening this latter (which we did quite easily), we arrived at a third case, also coffin-shaped, and varying from the second one in no particular, except in that of its material, which was cedar, and still emitted the peculiar and highly aromatic odor of that wood. Between the second and the third case there was no interval; the one fitting accurately within the other.

Removing the third case, we discovered and took out the body itself. We had expected to find it, as usual, enveloped in frequent rolls, or bandages, of linen, but, in place of these, we found a sort of sheath, made of papyrus, and coated with a layer of plaster, thickly gilt and painted. The paintings represented subjects connected with the various supposed duties of the soul, and its presentation to different divinities, with numerous identical human figures, intended, very probably, as portraits of the persons embalmed. Extending from head to foot, was a columnar, or perpendicular inscription in phonetic hieroglyphics, giving again his name and titles, and the names and titles of his relations.

Around the neck thus ensheathed, was a collar of cylindrical glass beads, diverse in color, and so arranged as to form images of deities, of the scarabæus, etc., with the winged globe. Around the small of the waist was a similar collar or belt.

Stripping off the papyrus, we found the flesh in excellent preservation, with no perceptible odor. The color was reddish. The skin was hard, smooth, and glossy. The teeth and hair were in good condition. The eyes (it seemed) had been removed, and glass ones substituted, which were very beautiful and wonderfully life-like, with the exception of somewhat too determined a stare. The fingers and the nails were brilliantly gilded.

Mr. Gliddon was of the opinion, from the redness of the epidermis, that the embalmment had been effected altogether by asphaltum; but, on scraping the surface with a steel instrument, and throwing into the fire some of the powder thus obtained, the flavor of camphor and other sweet-scented gums became apparent.

We searched the corpse very carefully for the usual openings through which the entrails are extracted, but, to our surprise, we could discover none. No member of the party was at that period aware that entire or unopened mummies are not infrequently met. The brain it was customary to withdraw through the nose; the intestines through an incision in the side;

the body was then shaved, washed, and salted; then laid aside for several weeks, when the operation of embalming, properly so called, began.

As no trace of an opening could be found, Doctor Ponnonner was preparing his instruments for dissection, when I observed that it was then past two o'clock. Hereupon it was agreed to postpone the internal examination until the next evening; and we were about to separate for the present, when some one suggested an experiment or two with the Voltaic pile.

The application of electricity to a Mummy three or four thousand years old at the least, was an idea, if not very sage, still sufficiently original, and we all caught it at once. About one-tenth in earnest and nine-tenths in jest, we arranged a battery in the Doctor's study, and conveyed thither the Egyptian.

It was only after much trouble that we succeeded in laying bare some portions of the temporal muscle which appeared of less stony rigidity than other parts of the frame, but which, as we had anticipated, of course, gave no indication of galvanic susceptibility when brought in contact with the wire. This, the first trial, indeed, seemed decisive, and, with a hearty laugh at our own absurdity, we were bidding each other good night, when my eyes, happening to fall upon those of the Mummy, were there immediately riveted in amazement. My brief glance, in fact, had sufficed to assure me that the orbs which we had all supposed to be glass, and which were originally noticeable for a certain wild stare, were now so far covered by the lids, that only a small portion of the *tunica albuginea* [whites of the eyes] remained visible.

With a shout I called attention to the fact, and it became immediately obvious to all.

I cannot say that I was *alarmed* at the phenomenon, because "alarmed" is, in my case, not exactly the word. It is possible, however, that, but for the Brown Stout, I might have been a little nervous. As for the rest of the company, they really made no attempt at concealing the downright fright which possessed them. Doctor Ponnonner was a man to be pitied. Mr. Gliddon, by some peculiar process, rendered himself invisible. Mr. Silk Buckingham, I fancy, will scarcely be so bold as to deny that he made his way, upon all fours, under the table.

After the first shock of astonishment, however, we resolved, as a matter of course, upon further experiment forthwith. Our operations were now directed against the great toe of the right foot. We made an incision over the outside of the exterior *os sesamoideum pollicis pedis* [bones of the foot], and thus got at the root of the *abductor* muscle. Readjusting the battery, we now applied the fluid to the bisected nerves—when, with a movement of exceeding life-likeness, the Mummy first drew up its right knee so as to bring it nearly in contact with the abdomen, and then, straightening the limb with inconceivable force, bestowed a kick upon Doctor Ponnonner, which had the effect of discharging that gentleman, like an arrow from a catapult, through a window into the street below.

We rushed out *en masse* to bring in the mangled remains of the victim, but had the happiness to meet him upon the staircase, coming up in an unaccountable hurry, brimful of the most ardent philosophy, and more than ever impressed with the necessity of prosecuting our experiment with vigor and with zeal.

It was by his advice, accordingly, that we made, upon the spot, a profound incision into the tip of the subject's nose, while the Doctor himself, laying violent hands upon it, pulled it into vehement contact with the wire.

Morally and physically—figuratively and literally—was the effect electric. In the first place, the corpse opened its eyes and winked very rapidly for several minutes, as does Mr. Barnes in the pantomime; in the second place, it sneezed; in the third, it sat upon end; in the fourth, it shook its fist in Doctor Ponnonner's face; in the fifth, turning to Messieurs Gliddon and Buckingham, it addressed them, in very capital Egyptian, thus:

"I must say, gentlemen, that I am as much surprised as I am mortified at your behavior. Of Doctor Ponnonner nothing better was to be expected. He is a poor little fat fool who *knows* no better. I pity and forgive him. But you, Mr. Gliddon—and you, Silk—who have traveled and resided in Egypt until one might imagine you to the manner born—you, I say who have been so much among us that you speak Egyptian fully as well, I think, as you write your mother tongue—you, whom I have always been led to regard as the firm friend of the mummies—I really did anticipate more gentlemanly conduct from *you*. What am I to think of your standing quietly by and seeing me thus unhandsomely used? What am I to suppose by your permitting Tom, Dick, and Harry to strip me of my coffins, and my clothes, in this wretchedly cold climate? In what light (to come to the point) am I to regard your aiding and abetting that miserable little villain, Doctor Ponnonner, in pulling me by the nose?"

It will be taken for granted, no doubt, that upon hearing this speech under the circumstances, we all either made for the door, or fell into violent hysterics, or went off in a general swoon. One of these three things was, I say, to be expected. Indeed each and all of these lines of conduct might have been very plausibly pursued. And, upon my word, I am at a loss to know how or why it was that we pursued neither the one nor the other. But, perhaps, the true reason is to be sought in the spirit of the age, which proceeds by the rule of contraries altogether, and is now usually admitted as the solution of every thing in the way of paradox and impossibility. Or, perhaps, after all, it was only the Mummy's exceedingly natural and matter-of-course air that divested his words of the terrible. However this may be, the facts are clear, and no member of our party betrayed any very particular trepidation, or seemed to consider that any thing had gone very especially wrong.

For my part I was convinced it was all right, and merely stepped aside, out of the range of the Egyptian's fist. Doctor Ponnonner thrust his hands into his breeches' pockets, looked hard at the Mummy, and grew excessively red in the face. Mr. Glidden stroked his whiskers and drew up the collar of his shirt. Mr. Buckingham hung down his head, and put his right thumb into the left corner of his mouth.

The Egyptian regarded him with a severe countenance for some minutes and at length, with a sneer, said:

"Why don't you speak, Mr. Buckingham? Did you hear what I asked you, or not? *Do* take your thumb out of your mouth!"

Mr. Buckingham, hereupon, gave a slight start, took his right thumb out of the left corner of his mouth, and, by way of indemnification inserted his left thumb in the right corner of the aperture above-mentioned.

Not being able to get an answer from Mr. B., the figure turned peevishly to Mr. Gliddon, and, in a peremptory tone, demanded in general terms what we all meant.

Mr. Gliddon replied at great length, in phonetics; and but for the deficiency of American printing-offices in hieroglyphical type, it would afford me much pleasure to record here, in the original, the whole of his very excellent speech.

I may as well take this occasion to remark, that all the subsequent conversation in which the Mummy took a part, was carried on in primitive Egyptian, through the medium (so far as concerned myself and other untraveled members of the company)—through the medium, I say, of Messieurs Gliddon and Buckingham, as interpreters. These gentlemen spoke the mother tongue of the Mummy with inimitable fluency and grace; but I could not help observing that (owing, no doubt, to the introduction of images entirely modern, and, of course, entirely novel to the stranger) the two travelers were reduced, occasionally, to the employment of sensible forms for the purpose of conveying a particular meaning. Mr. Gliddon, at one period, for example, could not make the Egyptian comprehend the term "politics," until he sketched upon the wall, with a bit of charcoal a little carbuncle-nosed gentleman, out at elbows, standing upon a stump, with his left leg drawn back, right arm thrown forward, with his fist shut, the eyes rolled up toward Heaven, and the mouth open at an angle of ninety degrees. Just in the same way Mr. Buckingham failed to convey the absolutely modern idea, "wig," until (at Doctor Ponnonner's suggestion) he grew very pale in the face, and consented to take off his own.

It will be readily understood that Mr. Gliddon's discourse turned chiefly upon the vast benefits accruing to science from the unrolling and disemboweling of mummies; apologizing, upon this score, for any disturbance that might have been occasioned *him*, in particular, the individual Mummy called Allamistakeo; and concluding with a mere hint (for it could scarcely be considered more) that, as these little matters were now explained, it might be as well to proceed with the investigation intended. Here Doctor Ponnonner made ready his instruments.

In regard to the latter suggestions of the orator, it appears that Allamistakeo had certain scruples of conscience, the nature of which I did not distinctly learn; but he expressed himself satisfied with the apologies tendered, and, getting down from the table, shook hands with the company all round.

When this ceremony was at an end, we immediately busied ourselves in repairing the damages which our subject had sustained from the scalpel. We sewed up the wound in his temple, bandaged his foot, and applied a square inch of black plaster to the tip of his nose.

It was now observed that the Count (this was the title, it seems, of Allamistakeo) had a slight fit of shivering—no doubt from the cold. The Doctor immediately repaired to his wardrobe, and soon returned with a black dress coat, made in Jennings' best manner, a pair of sky-blue plaid pantaloons with straps, a pink gingham *chemise,* a flapped vest of brocade, a white sack overcoat, a walking cane with a hook, a hat with no brim, patent-leather boots, straw-colored kid gloves, an eye-glass, a pair of whiskers, and a waterfall cravat. Owing to the disparity of size between the Count and the Doctor (the proportion being as two to one), there was some little difficulty in adjusting these habiliments upon the person of the Egyptian; but when all was arranged, he might have been said to be dressed. Mr. Gliddon, therefore, gave him his arm, and led him to a comfortable chair by the fire, while the Doctor rang the bell upon the spot and ordered a supply of cigars and wine.

The conversation soon grew animated. Much curiosity was, of course, expressed in regard to the somewhat remarkable fact of Allamistakeo's still remaining alive.

"I should have thought," observed Mr. Buckingham, "that it is high time you were dead."

"Why," replied the Count, very much astonished, "I am little more than seven hundred years old! My father lived a thousand, and was by no means in his dotage when he died."

Here ensued a brisk series of questions and computations, by means of which it became evident that the antiquity of the Mummy had been grossly misjudged. It had been five thousand and fifty years and some months since he had been consigned to the catacombs at Eleithias.

"But my remark," resumed Mr. Buckingham, "had no reference to your age at the period of interment (I am willing to grant, in fact, that you are still a young man), and my allusion was to the immensity of time during which, by your own showing, you must have been done up in asphaltum."

"In what?" said the Count.

"In asphaltum," persisted Mr. B.

"Ah, yes; I have some faint notion of what you mean; it might be made to answer, no doubt—but in my time we employed scarcely any thing else than the Bichloride of Mercury."

"But what we are especially at a loss to understand," said Doctor Ponnonner, "is how it happens that, having been dead and buried in Egypt five thousand years ago, you are here today all alive and looking so delightfully well."

"Had I been, as you say, *dead,*" replied the Count, "it is more than probable that dead, I should still be; for I perceive you are yet in the infancy of Galvanism, and cannot accomplish with it what was a common thing among us in the old days. But the fact is, I fell into catalepsy, and it was considered by my best friends that I was either dead or should be; they accordingly embalmed me at once—I presume you are aware of the chief principle of the embalming process?"

"Why, not altogether."

"Ah, I perceive;—a deplorable condition of ignorance! Well I cannot enter into details just now: but it is necessary to explain that to embalm (properly speaking), in Egypt, was to arrest indefinitely *all* the animal functions subjected to the process. I use the word 'animal' in its widest sense, as including the physical not more than the moral and *vital* being. I repeat that the leading principle of embalmment consisted, with us, in the immediately arresting, and holding in perpetual *abeyance, all* the animal functions subjected to the process. To be brief, in whatever condition the individual was, at the period of embalmment, in that condition he remained. Now, as it is my good fortune to be of the blood of the Scarabæus, I was embalmed *alive,* as you see me at present."

"The blood of the Scarabæus!" exclaimed Doctor Ponnonner.

"Yes. The Scarabæus was the *insignium* or the 'arms,' of a very distinguished and very rare patrician family. To be 'of the blood of the Scarabæus,' is merely to be one of that family of which the Scarabæus is the *insignium.* I speak figuratively."

"But what has this to do with you being alive?"

"Why, it is the general custom in Egypt to deprive a corpse, before embalmment, of its bowels and brains; the race of the Scarabæi alone did not coincide with the custom. Had I not been a Scarabæus, therefore, I should have been without bowels and brains; and without either it is inconvenient to live."

"I perceive that," said Mr. Buckingham, "and I presume that all the *entire* mummies that come to hand are of the race of Scarabæi."

"Beyond doubt."

"I thought," said Mr. Gliddon, very meekly, "that the Scarabæus was one of the Egyptian *gods.*"

"One of the Egyptian *what?*" exclaimed the Mummy, starting to its feet.

"Gods!" repeated the traveler.

"Mr. Gliddon, I really am astonished to hear you talk in this style," said the Count, resuming his chair. "No nation upon the face of the earth has ever acknowledged more than *one god*. The Scarabæus, the Ibis, etc., were with us (as similar creatures have been with others) the symbols, or *media,* through which we offered worship to the Creator too august to be more directly approached."

There was here a pause. At length the colloquy was renewed by Doctor Ponnonner.

"It is not improbable, then, from what you have explained," said he, "that among the catacombs near the Nile there may exist other mummies of the Scarabæus tribe, in a condition of vitality?"

"There can be no question of it," replied the Count; "all the Scarabæi embalmed accidentally while alive, are alive now. Even some of those *purposely* so embalmed, may have been overlooked by their executors, and still remain in the tomb."

"Will you be kind enough to explain," I said, "what you mean by 'purposely so embalmed'?"

"With great pleasure!" answered the Mummy, after surveying me leisurely through his eye-glass—for it was the first time I had ventured to address him a direct question.

"With great pleasure," he said. "The usual duration of man's life, in my time, was about eight hundred years. Few men died, unless by most extraordinary accident, before the age of six hundred; few lived longer than a decade of centuries; but eight were considered the natural term. After the discovery of the embalming principle, as I have already described it to you, it occurred to our philosophers that a laudable curiosity might be gratified, and, at the same time, the interests of science much advanced, by living this natural term in installments. In the case of history, indeed, experience demonstrated that something of this kind was indispensable. A historian, for example, having attained the age of five hundred, would write a book with great labor and then get himself carefully embalmed; leaving instructions to his executors *pro tem,* that they should cause him to be revivified after the lapse of a certain period—say five or six hundred years. Resuming existence at the expiration of this time, he would invariably find his great work converted into a species of hap-hazard notebook—that is to say, into a kind of literary arena for the conflicting guesses, riddles, and personal squabbles of whole herds of exasperated commentators. These guesses, etc., which passed under the name of annotations, or emendations, were found so completely to have enveloped, distorted, and overwhelmed the text, that the author had to go about with a lantern to discover his own book. When discovered, it was never worth the trouble of the search. After re-writing it throughout, it was regarded as the bounden duty of the historian to set himself to work immediately in correcting, from his own private knowledge and experience, the traditions of the day concerning the epoch at which he had originally lived. Now this process of re-scription and personal rectification, pursued by various individual sages from time to time, had the effect of preventing our history from degenerating into absolute fable."

"I beg your pardon," said Doctor Ponnonner at this point, laying his hand gently upon the arm of the Egyptian—"I beg your pardon, sir, but may I presume to interrupt you for one moment?"

"By all means, *sir*," replied the Count, drawing up.

"I merely wished to ask you a question," said the Doctor. "You mentioned the historian's personal correction of *traditions* respecting his own epoch. Pray, sir, upon an average, what proportion of these Kabbala were usually found to be right?"

"The Kabbala, as you properly term them, sir, were generally discovered to be precisely on a par with the facts recorded in the un-re-written histories themselves;—that is to say, not one individual iota of either was ever known, under any circumstances, to be not totally and radically wrong."

"But since it is quite clear," resumed the Doctor, "that at least five thousand years have elapsed since your entombment, I take it for granted that your histories at that period, if not your traditions were sufficiently explicit on that one topic of universal interest, the Creation, which took place, as I presume you are aware, only about ten centuries before."

"Sir!" said the Count Allamistakeo.

The Doctor repeated his remarks, but it was only after much additional explanation that the foreigner could be made to comprehend them. The latter at length said, hesitatingly:

"The ideas you have suggested are to me, I confess, utterly novel. During my time I never knew any one to entertain so singular a fancy as that the universe (or this world if you will have it so) ever had a beginning at all. I remember once, and once only, hearing something remotely hinted, by a man of many speculations, concerning the origin *of the human race;* and by this individual, the very word *Adam* (or Red Earth), which you make use of, was employed. He employed it, however, in a generical sense, with reference to the spontaneous germination from rank soil (just as a thousand of the lower *genera* of creatures are germinated)—the spontaneous germination, I say, of five vast hordes of men, simultaneously upspringing in five distinct and nearly equal divisions of the globe."

Here, in general, the company shrugged their shoulders, and one or two of us touched our foreheads with a very significant air. Mr. Silk Buckingham, first glancing slightly at the occiput and then at the sinciput of Allamistakeo, spoke as follows:—

"The long duration of human life in your time, together with the occasional practice of passing it, as you have explained, in installments, must have had, indeed, a strong tendency to the general development and conglomeration of knowledge. I presume, therefore, that we are to attribute the marked inferiority of the old Egyptians in all particulars of science, when compared with the moderns, and more especially with the Yankees, altogether to the superior solidity of the Egyptian skull."

"I confess again," replied the Count, with much suavity, "that I am somewhat at a loss to comprehend you; pray, to what particulars of science do you allude?"

Here our whole party, joining voices, detailed, at great length, the assumptions of phrenology and the marvels of animal magnetism.

Having heard us to an end, the Count proceeded to relate a few anecdotes, which rendered it evident that prototypes of Gall and Spurzheim had flourished and faded in Egypt so long ago as to have been nearly forgotten, and that the maneuvers of Mesmer were really very contemptible tricks when put in collation with the positive miracles of the Theban *savants,* who created lice and a great many other similar things.

I here asked the Count if his people were able to calculate eclipses. He smiled rather contemptuously, and said they were.

This put me a little out, but I began to make other inquiries in regard to his astronomical knowledge, when a member of the company, who had never as yet opened his mouth, whispered in my ear, that for information on this head, I had better consult Ptolemy (whoever Ptolemy is), as well as one Plutarch *de facie lunæ*.

I then questioned the Mummy about burning-glasses and lenses, and, in general, about the manufacture of glass; but I had not made an end of my queries before the silent member again touched me quietly on the elbow, and begged me for God's sake to take a peep at Diodorus Siculus. As for the Count, he merely asked me, in the way of reply, if we moderns possessed any such microscopes as would enable us to cut cameos in the style of the Egyptians. While I was thinking how I should answer this question, little Doctor Ponnonner committed himself in a very extraordinary way.

"Look at our architecture!" he exclaimed, greatly to the indignation of both the travelers, who pinched him black and blue to no purpose.

"Look," he cried with enthusiasm, "at the Bowling-Green Fountain in New York! or if this be too vast a contemplation, regard for a moment the Capitol at Washington, D.C.!"—and the good little medical man went on to detail very minutely, the proportions of the fabric to which he referred. He explained that the portico alone was adorned with no less than four and twenty columns, five feet in diameter, and ten feet apart.

The Count said that he regretted not being able to remember, just at that moment, the precise dimensions of any one of the principal buildings of the city of Aznac, whose foundations were laid in the night of Time, but the ruins of which were still standing, at the epoch of his entombment, in a vast plain of sand to the westward of Thebes. He recollected, however, (talking of the porticoes,) that one affixed to an inferior palace in a kind of suburb called Carnac, consisted of a hundred and forty-four columns, thirty-seven feet in circumference, and twenty-five feet apart. The approach to this portico, from the Nile, was through an avenue two miles long, composed of sphynxes, statues, and obelisks, twenty, sixty, and a hundred feet in height. The palace itself (as well as he could remember) was, in one direction, two miles long, and might have been altogether about seven in circuit. Its walls were richly painted all over, within and without, with hieroglyphics. He would not pretend to *assert* that even fifty or sixty of the Doctor's Capitols might have been built within these walls, but he was by no means sure that two or three hundred of them might not have been squeezed in with some trouble. That palace at Carnac was an insignificant little building after all. He (the

Count), however, could not conscientiously refuse to admit the ingenuity, magnificence, and superiority of the Fountain at the Bowling Green, as described by the Doctor. Nothing like it, he was forced to allow, had ever been seen in Egypt or elsewhere.

I here asked the Count what he had to say to our railroads.

"Nothing," he replied, "in particular." They were rather slight, rather ill-conceived, and clumsily put together. They could not be compared, of course, with the vast, level, direct, iron-grooved causeways upon which the Egyptians conveyed entire temples and solid obelisks of a hundred and fifty feet in altitude.

I spoke of our gigantic mechanical forces.

He agreed that we knew something in that way, but inquired how I should have gone to work in getting up the imposts on the lintels of even the little palace at Carnac.

This question I concluded not to hear, and demanded if he had any idea of Artesian wells; but he simply raised his eyebrows; while Mr. Gliddon winked at me very hard and said, in a low tone, that one had been recently discovered by the engineers employed to bore for water in the Great Oasis.

I then mentioned our steel; but the foreigner elevated his nose, and asked me if our steel could have executed the sharp carved work seen on the obelisks, and which was wrought altogether by edge-tools of copper.

This disconcerted us so greatly that we thought it advisable to vary the attack to Metaphysics. We sent for a copy of a book called the *Dial,* and read out of it a chapter or two about something that is not very clear, but which the Bostonians call the Great Movement of Progress.

The Count merely said that Great Movements were awfully common things in his day, and as for Progress, it was at one time quite a nuisance, but it never progressed.

We then spoke of the great beauty and importance of Democracy, and were at much trouble in impressing the Count with a due sense of the advantages we enjoyed in living where there was suffrage *ad libitum* [as far as pleases], and no king.

He listened with marked interest, and in fact seemed not a little amused. When we had done, he said that, a great while ago, there had occurred something of a very similar sort. Thirteen Egyptian provinces determined all at once to be free, and to set a magnificent example to the rest of mankind. They assembled their wise men, and concocted the most ingenious constitution it is possible to conceive. For a while they managed remarkably well; only their habit of bragging was prodigious. The thing ended, however, in the consolidation of the thirteen states, with some fifteen or twenty others, in the most odious and insupportable despotism that was ever heard of upon the face of the Earth.

I asked what was the name of the usurping tyrant.

As well as the Count could recollect, it was *Mob*.

Not knowing what to say to this, I raised my voice, and deplored the Egyptian ignorance of steam.

The Count looked at me with much astonishment, but made no answer. The silent gentleman, however, gave me a violent nudge in the ribs with his elbows—told me I had sufficiently exposed myself for once—and demanded if I was really such a fool as not to know that the modern steam-engine is derived from the invention of Hero, through Solomon de Caus.

We were now in imminent danger of being discomfited; but, as good luck would have it, Doctor Ponnonner, having rallied, returned to our rescue, and inquired if the people of Egypt would seriously pretend to rival the moderns in the all-important particular of dress.

The Count, at this, glanced downward to the straps of his pantaloons, and then, taking hold of the end of one of his coat-tails, held it up close to his eyes for some minutes. Letting it fall, at last, his mouth extended itself very gradually from ear to ear; but I do not remember that he said any thing in the way of reply.

Hereupon we recovered our spirits, and the Doctor, approaching the Mummy with great dignity, desired it to say candidly, upon its honor as a gentleman, if the Egyptians had comprehended, at *any* period, the manufacture of either Ponnonner's lozenges or Brandreth's pills.

We looked, with profound anxiety, for an answer;—but in vain. It was not forthcoming. The Egyptian blushed and hung down his head. Never was triumph more consummate; never was defeat borne with so ill a grace. Indeed, I could not endure the spectacle of the poor Mummy's mortification. I reached my hat, bowed to him stiffly, and took leave.

Upon getting home I found it past four o'clock, and went immediately to bed. It is now ten, A.M. I have been up since seven, penning these memoranda for the benefit of my family and of mankind. The former I shall behold no more. My wife is a shrew. The truth is, I am heartily sick of this life and of the nineteenth century in general. I am convinced that every thing is going wrong. Besides, I am anxious to know who will be President in 2045. As soon, therefore, as I shave and swallow a cup of coffee, I shall just step over to Ponnonner's and get embalmed for a couple of hundred years.

Fiction

COLONEL STONESTEEL'S GENUINE HOMEMADE TRULY EGYPTIAN MUMMY

Ray Bradbury

Ray Bradbury is one of the greatest and most popular science fiction writers in the world. He started out writing for pulp magazines in the 1940s and gradually gained in popularity. His books include such classics as The Martian Chronicles, Fahrenheit 451, R is for Rocket, The Illustrated Man, *plus two of my favorites—*Dandelion Wine *and* Something Wicked This Way Comes. *Many of his short stories have been dramatized in the television series* Ray Bradbury Theater, *hosted, of course, by Ray Bradbury himself. His works are in a large way responsible for bringing science fiction to a mainstream audience, but he has never restricted himself to this genre. Though he's spent most of his life living in Los Angeles, he often writes about the Midwest, where he spent his early childhood. In this nostalgic story he takes the mystery of Ancient Egypt and introduces it into Green Town, Illinois.*

That was the autumn they found the genuine Egyptian mummy out past Loon Lake.

How the mummy got there, and how long it had been there, no one knew. But there it was, all wrapped up in its creosote rags, looking a bit spoiled by time, and just waiting to be found by someone.

The day before, it had been just another autumn day with the trees blazing and dropping down their burnt-looking leaves when Charlie Flagstaff, aged twelve, stepped to the middle of a pretty empty street, stared at the sky, the horizon, the whole world, and shouted, "Okay! I'm waiting. Come on!"

Nothing happened. So Charlie kicked the leaves ahead of him across town until he came to the tallest house on the greatest street, the house where everyone in Green Town came with his troubles. Charlie scowled, shut his eyes, and yelled at the big house windows. "Colonel Stonesteel!"

The front door burst open, as if the old man had been waiting there, like Charlie, for something incredible to happen in Green Town, Illinois.

"Charlie," Colonel Stonesteel called. "You're old enough to knock. What's there about boys makes them shout around houses?"

The door slammed shut.

Charlie sighed, walked up, and knocked softly.

"Why, Charlie Flagstaff, is that you?" The door opened a squint for the Colonel. "Good gravy, look at that weather!"

The old man strode forth to hone his fine hatchet nose on the sharp wind. "Don't you just love autumn, son? Just smell that air."

He remembered to glance down at the boy's pale face.

"Why, son, you look as if your last friend drowned and your dog died. What's wrong? School starts next week? On top of which, Halloween's not coming fast enough?"

"Still eight long weeks off. Might as well be ten years," the boy sighed, staring out at the autumn town. "You ever notice, Colonel, not much ever happens around here?"

"Why, hell's bell's son, it's Labor Day tomorrow, big parade, seven almost-brand-new cars, mayor in his next-best suit, fireworks, maybe—er . . ."

The Colonel stopped, not impressed with his own grocery list. "How old are you, Charlie?"

"Thirteen. Almost."

"Things do tend to run down, come thirteen. Meanwhile, Charlie, what do we do to survive until noon today?"

"If anyone knows, it's you, Colonel."

"Charlie . . ." The old man flinched from the boy's clear-water stare. "I can move politicians big as prize hogs, shake town hall skeletons, make locomotives run back uphill. But small boys on long, dry autumn weekends, suffering from a bad attack of the desperate empties? Well . . ."

Colonel Stonesteel eyed the future in the clouds.

"Charlie," he said at last, "I am touched and moved by the circumstance of your lying there on the damn railway tracks, waiting for a murderous train that will never come. So, listen. I'll bet you six Baby Ruth candy bars that Green Town, upper Illinois, population one thousand dogs, will be changed forever, changed for the best, by God, sometime in the next twenty-four miraculous hours! Bet?"

"A bet!" Charlie seized and pumped the old man's hand. "Colonel, I knew you could do it!"

"Ain't done yet, but look. This town's the Red Sea. I herewith order it to part. Gangway!"

The Colonel marched (Charlie ran) into the house, where the Colonel sniffed a vast door leading up to a dry-timber attic. "Listen, Charlie. Hear. The attic storms."

The Colonel yanked the door wide on autumn whispers, high winds trapped and shuddering in the beams.

"What's it say?"

Just then a gust of wind hurled the Colonel, like so much flimsy chaff, up the dark stairs. He was philosophical along the way: "Time, it says, mostly. Oldness. Memory. Dust. Pain. Listen to those beams. When the weather cracks a roof's skeleton on a fine fall day, you truly got time-talk, Bombay snuffs, tombyard flowers gone to ghost—"

"Boy, Colonel," Charlie gasped, climbing, "you oughta write for *Top Notch Magazine*!"

"Did once. Got rejected. Here we are!"

And there they were indeed, in a place with no calendar, no days, no months, no years, but only vast spider shadows and glints of light from collapsed chandeliers lying about like shed tears in the dust.

"Boy!" Charlie cried, scared, and glad of it.

"Charles," the Colonel said, "you ready for me to birth you a real live, half-dead, sockdolager, on-the-spot mystery?"

"Ready!"

"Now!"

The Colonel swept charts, maps, agate marbles, glass eyes, and sneezes of dust off a table, then rolled up his sleeves.

"Great thing about midwifing mysteries is you don't have to boil water or wash up. Hand me that papyrus scroll there, boy, that darning needle just beyond, that old rickshaw blueprint on the wall, that plug of fired cannonball-cotton underfoot. Jump!"

"I'm jumping!" Charlie ran and fetched, fetched and ran.

"Here, here, and here! There, there, and there!"

Bindles of dry twigs, clutches of pussy willow, and cattails flew. The Colonel's sixteen hands were wild in the air, flashing sixteen bright suture needles, flakes of meadow grass, flickers of owl feather, glares of bright yellow fox eye.

"There, by God. Half-done!"

The Colonel pointed with a chop of his nose.

"Peel an eye, son. What's it commence to start to resemble?"

Charlie circled the table, eyes stretched so wide his mouth gaped.

"Why . . . why—" he sputtered. And then: "A mummy! Can't be!"

"Is, boy! Is!"

Wrist-deep in his creation, the Colonel listened to its reeds and thistles, its dry-flower whispers.

"Now, why did I build this mummy? You, you inspired it, Charlie. Go look out the attic window."

Charlie spat on the dusty pane, wiped a clear viewing spot, and peered out.

"What do you see out there in the damn town?" the Colonel asked. "Any murders being transacted?"

"Heck, no—"

"Anyone falling off church steeples or being run down by maniac lawn mowers?"

"Nope."

"Any *Monitors* or *Merrimacks* sailing up the dry lake, dirigibles falling on the Masonic Temple and squashing six thousand Masons flat?"

"Heck, there's only five thousand folks in Green Town!"

"Don't unhinge me with facts. Stare, boy. Spy. Report!"

"No dirigibles." Charlie stared. "No squashed Masonic temples."

"Right you are, boy."

The Colonel trotted over to join Charlie, surveying the dire territory. He pointed with his great hound nose.

"In all Green Town, in all your life, not one murder, not one orphanage fire, not one mad fiend carving his initials on librarian ladies' wooden legs.

Face it, son, Green Town, upper Illinois, is the most common, mean, ordinary, plain old bore of a graveyard in the eternal history of the Roman, Greek, Russian, Anglo-American empires. If Napoleon had been born here, he'd have committed hari-kari by the age of nine. Boredom. If Caesar had been raised here, he'd have raced to the Forum at the age of ten, shoved in his *own* dagger—"

"Boredom," said Charlie.

"Kee-rect!" Colonel Stonesteel ran back to flailing and pushing and cramming a strange lumpish shape around on the groaning table. "Boredom by the pound and ton. Boredom by the doomsday yard and the funeral mile. Lawns, homes, dog fur, men's haircuts, cheap suits in dark store windows, all cut from the same cloth—"

"Boredom," said Charlie, on cue.

"And what do you do when you're bored, son?"

"Er . . . break a window in a haunted house?"

"We got no haunted houses in Green Town!"

"Used to be. Old Higley's place. Torn down."

"See my point?! What else should we try? Quick!"

"Hold a massacre?"

"No massacre here in dogs' years. Lord, even our police chief's honest. Mayor? Not corrupt. Madness. Whole damn town faced with stark-raving ennuis and lulls. Last chance, Charlie. What's our salvation?"

Charlie smiled. "Build a mummy?"

"Bulldogs in the belfry! Yes! Lend a hand. Help me to finish, boy!"

While the old man cackled and sewed and swooped, Charlie seized and snatched and grabbed and hauled more lizard tails, old nicotine bandages left from a skiing accident that had busted the Colonel's ankle and broken a romance in 1895, some patches from a 1922 Kissel Kar inner tube, a few burned-out sparklers from the last peaceful summer of 1913, and a collection of gypsy moths and death's-head beetles that once had labels and now flew nameless as Charlie and the old man kneaded and wove, shuttled and tapped and molded a brittle, dry wicker shape.

"*Voilà,* Charlie! Finished. Done."

"Oh, Colonel!" The boy stared and gasped with love. "Can I make him a crown?"

"Make him a crown, boy. Make him a crown."

The sun was setting when the Colonel and Charlie and their Egyptian friend came down the dusky backstairs of the old man's house. Two of them were walking iron-heavy, the third was floating light as toasted cornflakes on the September air.

"Colonel," Charlie wondered aloud. "What we going to do with this pharaoh, now we got him? It ain't as if he could talk much, or run around doing things—"

"No need. Let folks talk, let folks run. Peek out."

They cracked the door and peered out at a town smothered in peace and ruined by nothing to do.

"All right, son, now you have recovered from your almost-fatal seizure of desperate empties. But that whole blasted population out there lies up to its elbows in glum and despond, fearful to rise each morn and find it's always and forever Sunday! Who'll save 'em, boy?"

"Amon Bubistis Rameses Ra the Third, just arrived on the Four O'Clock Limited?"

"God love your sprightly tongue, Charles. What we got here is a giant seed. Seed's no good unless we—"

"*Plant* it?" Charles asked.

"Plant. Then watch it grow. Then what? Harvest time. Harvest! Come on, boy. Er . . . bring your friend."

The Colonel crept out into the first nightfall.

The mummy came soon after, helped by Charlie.

Labor Day at high noon, Osiris Bubastis Amon-Ra-Tut arrived from the Land of the Dead.

An autumn wind stirred the land and flapped doors wide, not with the sound of the usual Labor Day parade, seven touring cars, a fife-and-drum corps, and the mayor, but with a mob that grew as it flowed through the streets and fell in a tide to inundate the lawn in front of Colonel Stonesteel's house. The Colonel and Charlie were sitting on the front porch; they had been sitting there for some hours, waiting, for the conniption fits to arrive, the storming of the Bastille to occur. Now with dogs going mad and biting boys' ankles and boys dancing around the fringes of the mob, the Colonel gazed down upon the Creation (his and Charlie's) and gave his secret smile.

"Well, Charlie. Do I win my bet?"

"You sure do, Colonel!"

"Come on."

Phones rang all across town and lunches burned on stoves as the Colonel strode forth to give the annual Labor Day parade his papal blessing.

At the center of the mob was a horse-drawn wagon. On top of the wagon, his eyes wild with discovery, was Tom Tuppen, owner of a half-dead farm just beyond town. Tom was babbling, and the crowd was babbling, because in the back of the wagon was the special harvest delivered out of four thousand lost years of time.

"Well, flood the Nile and plant the Delta," the Colonel gasped, eyes wide, staring. "Is or is it not that a genuine old Egyptian mummy lying there in its original papyrus and coal-tar wrappings?"

"Sure is!" Charlie cried.

"Sure is!" everyone yelled.

"I was plowing the field this morning," said Tom Tuppen. "Plowing, just plowing and—bang! Plow turned this up, right before me! Like to have had a stroke! Think! The Egyptians must've marched through Illinois three thousand years ago, and no one knew! Revelations, I call it! Outa the way, kids! I'm taking this find to the post office lobby. Setting it up on display! Giddap, now, git!"

The horse, the wagon, the mummy, the crowd moved away, leaving the Colonel behind, his eyes still pretend-wide, his mouth open.

"Hot dog," the Colonel whispered, "we did it, Charles. This uproar, babble, talk, and hysterical gossip will last for a thousand days or Armageddon, whichever comes first!"

"Yes, *sir,* Colonel!"

"Michelangelo couldn't've done better. Boy David's a castaway, lost and forgotten wonder compared to our Egyptian surprise and—"

The Colonel stopped as the mayor rushed by.

"Colonel, Charlie, howdy! Just phoned Chicago. Newsfolks here tomorrow breakfast! Museum folks by lunch! Glory Hallelujah for the Green Town Chamber of Commerce!"

The mayor ran off after the mob.

An autumn cloud crossed the Colonel's face and settled around his mouth.

"End of Act One, Charlie. Start thinking fast. Act Two coming up. We *do* want this commotion to last forever, don't we?"

"Yes, sir—"

"Crack your brain, boy. What does Uncle Wiggily say?"

"Uncle Wiggily says—ah—go back two hops?"

"Give the boy an A-plus, a gold star, and a brownie! The Lord giveth and the Lord taketh away, eh?"

Charlie looked into the old man's face and saw visitations of plagues there. "Yes, sir."

The Colonel watched the mob milling around the post office, two blocks away. The fife-and-drum corps arrived and played some tune vaguely inclined toward the Egyptian.

"Sundown, Charlie," the Colonel murmured, his eyes shut. "We make our final move."

What a day it was! Years later people said, "That was a day!" The mayor went home and got dressed up and came back and made three speeches and held two parades, one going up Main Street toward the end of the trolley line, the other coming back, and Osiris Bubastis Amon-Ra-Tut was at the center of both, smiling now to the right as gravity shifted his flimsy weight and then to the left as they rounded a corner. The fife-and-drum corps, now heavily augmented by accumulated brass, had spent an hour drinking beer and learning the Triumphal March from *Aida*, and this they played so many times that mothers took their screaming babies into the house and men retired to bars to soothe their nerves. There was talk of a third parade and a fourth speech, but sunset took the town unawares, and everyone, including Charlie, went home to a dinner mostly talk and short on eats.

By eight o'clock Charlie and the Colonel were driving along the leafy streets in the fine darkness, taking the air in the old man's 1924 Moon, a car that took up trembling where the Colonel left off.

"Where we going, Colonel?"

"Well," the Colonel mused, steering at ten philosophical miles per hour, nice and easy, "everyone, including your folks, is out at Grossett's Meadow right now, right? Final Labor Day speeches. Some one'll light the gasbag mayor, and he'll go up about forty feet, kee-rect? Fire Department'll be setting off the big skyrockets. Which means the post office, plus the mummy, plus the sheriff sitting there with him, will be empty and vulnerable. Then the miracle will happen, Charlie. It *has* to. Now ask me why the miracle will happen."

"Why?"

"Glad you asked. Well, boy, folks from Chicago'll be jumping off the train steps tomorrow, hot and fresh as pancakes, with their pointy noses and glass eyes and microscopes. Those museum snoopers plus the Associated Press, will rummage our Egyptian pharaoh seven ways from Christmas and blow their fuse boxes. That being so, Charles—"

"We're on our way to mess around with the evidence."

"You put it indelicately, boy, but truth is at the core. Look at it this way, child. Life is a magic show, or *should* be if people didn't go to sleep on each other. Always leave folks with a bit of mystery, son. Now, before people get used to our ancient friend, before he wears out the wrong bath towel, like any smart weekend guest, he should grab the next scheduled camel west and hightail it out of town. There!"

The post office stood silent, with one light shining in the foyer. Through the great window they could see the sheriff seated alongside the mummy on display, neither of them talking, abandoned at last by the attentive mobs that had gone for suppers and fireworks.

The Colonel brought forth a brown bag, in which a mysterious liquid gurgled. "Give me thirty-five minutes to mellow the sheriff down, Charlie. Then you creep in, listen, follow my cues, and work the miracle. Here goes nothing!"

And the Colonel stole away.

Beyond town, the mayor sat down and the fireworks went up.

Charlie stood on top of the Moon and watched them for half an hour. Then, figuring the mellowing time was over, he dogtrotted across the street and moused himself into the post office to stand in the shadows.

"Well, now," the Colonel was saying, seated between the Egyptian pharaoh and the sheriff, "why don't you just finish that bottle, sir?"

"It's finished," said the sheriff, obeying without hesitation.

The Colonel leaned forward in the half-light and peered at the gold amulet on the mummy's breast.

"You believe them old sayings?"

"What old sayings?" the sheriff inquired.

"If you read them hieroglyphics out loud, the mummy comes alive and walks."

"Horseradish," said the sheriff.

"Just look at all those fancy Egyptian symbols!" the Colonel pursued.

"Someone stole my glasses," the sheriff blurted. "You read that stuff to me. Make the fool mummy walk."

Charlie took this as a signal to move, and he sidled around through the shadows, closer to the Egyptian king.

"Here goes." The Colonel bent even closer to the pharaoh's amulet, meanwhile slipping the sheriff's glasses out of his cupped hand into his side pocket. "First symbol on here is a hawk. Second one's a jackal. That third's an owl. Fourth's a yellow fox eye—"

"Continue," the sheriff commanded.

The Colonel did so, and his voice rose and fell, and the sheriff's head nodded, and all the ancient Egyptian pictures and words flowed and touched around the mummy until at last the Colonel gave a great gasp and pointed.

"Good grief, Sheriff. Look!"

The sheriff blinked both eyes wide.

"The mummy," said the Colonel. "It's going for a walk!"

"Can't be!" the sheriff cried. "Can't be!"

"Is," said a voice, somewhere. Maybe the pharaoh under his breath.

And the mummy lifted up, suspended, and drifted toward the door.

"Why," the sheriff suggested, tears in his eyes, "I think he might just *fly*!"

"I'd better follow and bring him back," the Colonel said.

"*Do* that!" the sheriff replied.

The mummy was gone. The Colonel ran. The door slammed.

"Oh, dear." The sheriff lifted the bottle and shook it. "Empty."

They drove through avenues of autumn leaves that were suddenly the temples of dusting Egypt and the lily-sculpted pillars of time. Charlie let the car motor hum in his soul while over his shoulder, in the backseat, taking the ancient air, enjoying the warm river of wind, the mummy leaned this way and that as the car swerved.

"Say it, Colonel," said Charlie at last.

"What?" asked the old man.

"I love to hear you talk. Say what I want to hear. About the mummy. What he truly is. What he's really made of. Where he comes from—"

"Why, boy, you were there, you helped make, you saw—"

But the boy was looking at him steadily with bright autumn eyes. The mummy, their ancient harvest-tobacco dried-up Nile River bottom old-time masterpiece, leaned in the wind over their shoulder, waiting as much as the boy for the talk to come.

"You want to know who he truly was, once upon a time?"

The Colonel gathered a handful of dust in his lungs and softly filtered it out before he answered.

"He was everyone, no one, someone. You. Me."

"Go on," Charlie whispered.

Continue, said the lapis-lazuli gleam in the mummy's eyes.

"He was, he is," the Colonel murmured, "a bundle of old Sunday comic pages stashed in the attic to spontaneously combust from all those forgotten notions and stuffs. He's a stand of papyrus left in an autumn field long before Moses, a papier-mâché tumbleweed blown out of time, this way long-gone dusk, that way come-again dawn . . . a chart map of Siam, Blue River Nile source, hot desert dustdevil . . . all the confetti from lost trolley transfers, dried-up yellow cross-country road maps petering off in sand dunes . . . dry crushed flowers from wedding memory books . . . funeral wreaths . . . ticker tapes unraveled from gone-off-forever parades to Far Rockaway . . . lost scrolls from the great burned library at Alexandria . . . smell the chars? His rib cage, covered with what?! Posters torn off seed barns in North Storm, Ohio, shuttled south toward Fulfilment, Texas . . . dead gold-mine certificates, wedding and birth announcements . . . all the things that were once need, hope, dream. . . . first nickel in the pocket, dollar on the wall . . . wrapped and ribboned yellow-skinned letters from failed old men, time-orphaned women saying Tomorrow and Tomorrow . . . there'll be a ship in the harbor, horse on the road, knock on the door. . . . He's . . . he's telegrams you're afraid to open . . . poems you wrote and threw away . . . all the dumb, strange shadows you ever grew, boy, or I ever inked out inside my head at three A.M., crushed, stashed, and now shaped in one form under our hands and here in our gaze. That, that, that is what old King Pharaoh Seventh Dynasty Holy Dust *is*!"

"Wow," Charlie sighed.

As they drove up and parked in front of his house, Colonel Stonesteel peered out cautiously.

"Your folks ever go up in your attic, boy?"

"Too small. They poke me up to rummage."

"Good. Hoist our ancient Egyptian friend out of the backseat there. Don't weigh much, twenty pounds at the most. You carried him fine, Charlie. Oh, that was a sight. You running out of the post office, making the mummy walk. You shoulda seen the sheriff's face!"

"I hope he don't get in trouble because of this."

"Oh, he'll bump his head and make up a fine story. Can't very well admit he saw the mummy go for a walk, can he? He'll think of something—organize a posse. You'll see. But right now, son, get our ancient friend here up, hide him, good, visit him weekly. Feed him night talk. Then thirty, forty years from now—"

"What?" Charlie asked.

"In a bad year so brimmed up with boredom it drips out your ears, when the town has long forgotten this first arrival and departure, on a morning, I say, when you lie in bed and don't want to get up, don't even want to twitch your ears or blink, you're so damned bored . . . well, on *that* morning, Charlie, you just climb up in your rummage-sale attic and shake this mummy out of bed, toss him in a cornfield, and watch new hellfire mobs break loose. Life starts over that hour, that day, for you, the town, everyone. Now grab, git, and hide, boy! Hop to it!"

"I hate for the night to be over," Charlie said very quietly. "Can't we circle a few more blocks and then finish off some lemonade on your porch, and *him* along, too?"

"Lemonade!" Colonel Stonesteel banged his heel on the car floor. The car exploded and surged. "For the Lost and Found King, and the Pharaoh's Illinois Son!"

It was late on Labor Day evening, the two of them seated on the Colonel's front porch again, rocking up a fair breeze, lemonades in hand, ice in mouth, sucking the sweet savor of the night's incredible adventures. A wind blew. The mummy, behind Charlie's rocker, propped against the porch wall, almost seemed to be listening.

"Boy!" Charlie exclaimed. "I can see tomorrow's *Clarion* headlines: PRICELESS MUMMY KIDNAPPED. RAMESES-TUT VANISHES. GREAT FIND GONE. REWARD OFFERED. SHERIFF NONPLUSSED. BLACKMAIL EXPECTED."

"Talk on, boy. Like I taught you."

The last Labor Day fireworks were dying in the sky. Their light faded in the lapis-lazuli eyes of boy and man and their withered friend, all fixed in shadow.

"Colonel." Charlie gazed into the future. "What if, even in my old age, I don't ever *need* my own particular mummy?"

"Eh?"

"What if I have a life chock-full of things, never bored, find what I want to do, *do* it, make every day count, every night swell, sleep tight, wake up yelling, laugh lots, grow old, still running fast, what *then*, Colonel?"

"Why then, boy, you'll be one of God's luckiest people!"

"For you see, Colonel," Charlie said, looking at him with pure round, unblinking eyes, "I made up my mind. I'm going to be the greatest writer that ever lived."

The Colonel braked his rocker and searched the innocent fire in that small face.

"Lord, I see it. Yes. You *will*. Well, then, Charles, when you are very old, you must find some lad, not as lucky as you, to give Osiris-Ra to. Your life may be full, but others, lost on the road, will need our Egyptian friend. Agreed? Agreed."

The last skyrockets soared and fell, the last fire balloons went sailing out among the gentle stars. Cars and people were driving or walking home, some fathers or mothers carrying their tired and already-sleeping children. As the quiet parade passed Colonel Stonesteel's porch, some folks glanced in and waved at the old man and the boy and the tall, dim-shadowed servant who stood between. The night was over forever.

Charlie said, "Say some more, Colonel."

"No. I'm shut. Listen to what *he* has to say now. Let *him* tell your future, Charlie. Let him start you on stories. Ready?"

A wind came up and blew in the dry papyrus and sifted the ancient wrappings and trembled the curious hands and softly twitched the lips of their old/new four-thousand year nighttime visitor, whispering.

"What's he saying, Charles?"

Charlie shut his eyes, waited, listened, nodded, let a single tear slide down his cheek, and at last said, "Everything . . . Everything I always wanted to hear."

Nonfiction

DEAD KINGS

(Excerpt)

Rudyard Kipling

Joseph Rudyard Kipling was born in Bombay, India, the son of a clergyman. When he was five years old, he was sent to school in England, where he suffered six years of mental torture and beatings from his guardians before his parents moved to England and rescued him. He returned to India as a journalist in 1882 and stayed for eight years before moving back to England. His stories and poems of India made him famous. His works include Kim, The Jungle Book, The Light That Failed, Plain Tales from the Hills, *and* Captains Courageous. *He also wrote the short story "The Man Who Would Be King" and the poem "Gunga Din," both of which were made into movies. In 1907 he was awarded the Nobel Prize for Literature. In these excerpts from the* Idler, *a 1914 magazine article entitled "Egypt of the Magicians," he describes a bit of his travels through Egypt. They are taken from the section he titled "Dead Kings."*

Granted that all Egypt is one big undertaker's emporium, what could be more fascinating than to get Government leave to rummage in a corner of it, to form a little company and spend the cold weather trying to pay dividends in the shape of amethyst necklaces, lapis-lazuli scarabs, pots of pure gold, and priceless bits of statuary? Or, if one is rich, what better fun than to grub-stake an expedition on the supposed site of a dead city and see what turns up? There was a big-game hunter who had used most of the Continent, quite carried away by this sport.

"I'm going to take shares in a city next year, and watch the digging myself," he said. "It beats elephants to pieces. In *this* game you're digging up dead things and making them alive. Aren't you going to have a flutter?"

He showed me a seductive little prospectus. Myself, I would sooner not lay hands on a dead man's kit or equipment, especially when he has gone to his grave in the belief that the trinkets guarantee salvation. Of course, there is the other argument, put forward by skeptics, that the Egyptian was a blatant self-advertiser, and that nothing would please him more than the thought that he was being looked at and admired after all these years. Still, one might rob some shrinking soul who didn't see it in that light.

At the end of spring the diggers flock back out of the Desert and exchange chaff and news in the gorgeous verandahs. For example, A's company has made a find of priceless stuff, Heaven knows how old, and is—not too meek about it. Company B, less fortunate, hints that if only A knew to what extent their native diggers had been stealing and disposing of the thefts, under their very archeological noses, they would not be so happy.

"Nonsense," says Company A. "Our diggers are above suspicion. Besides, we watched 'em."

"*Are* they?" is the reply. "Well, next time you are in Berlin, go to the Museum and you'll see what the Germans have got hold of. It must have come out of your ground. The Dynasty proves it!" So A's cup is poisoned—till next year.

No collector or curator of a museum should have any moral scruples whatever; and I have never met one who had; though I have been informed by deeply-shocked informants of four nationalities that the Germans are the most flagrant pirates of all.

The business of exploration is about as romantic as earth-work on Indian railways. There are the same narrow-gauge trams and donkeys, the same shining gangs in the borrow-pits and the same skirling dark-blue crowds of women and children with the little earth-baskets. But the hoes are not driven in, nor the clods jerked aside at random, and when the work fringes along the base of some mighty wall, men use their hands carefully. A white man—or he was white at breakfast-time—patrols through the continually renewed dust-haze. Weeks may pass without a single bead, but anything may turn up at any moment, and it is his to answer the shout of discovery.

We had the good fortune to stay a while at the Headquarters of the Metropolitan Museum (New York) in a valley riddled like a rabbit-warren with tombs. Their stables, store-houses, and servants' quarters are old tombs, their talk is of tombs, and their dream (the diggers' dream always) is to discover a virgin tomb where the untouched dead lie with their jewels upon them. Four miles away are the wide-winged, rampant hotels. Here is nothing whatever but the rubbish of death that died thousands of years ago, on whose grave no green thing has ever grown. Villages, expert in two hundred generations of grave-robbing, cower among the mounds of wastage, and whoop at the daily tourist. Paths made by bare feet run, from one half-tomb, half-mud-heap to the next, not much more distinct than snail smears, but they have been used since. . . .

Time is a dangerous thing to play with. That morning the concierge had toiled for us among steamer-sailings to see if we could save three days. That evening we sat with folk for whom Time had stood still since the Ptolemies. I wondered, at first, how it concerned them or any man if such and such a Pharaoh had used to his own glory the plinths and columns of such another Pharaoh before or after Melchizedek. Their whole background was too inconceivably remote for the mind to work on. But the next morning we were taken to the painted tomb of a noble—a Minister of Agriculture—who died four or five thousand years ago. He said to me, in so many words: "Observe! I was very like your friend, the late Mr. Samuel Pepys, of your Admiralty. I took an enormous interest in life, which I most thoroughly enjoyed, on its human and on its spiritual side. I do not think you will find many departments of State better managed than mine, or a better-kept house, or a nicer set of young people. . . . My daughters! The eldest, as you can see, takes after her mother. The youngest, my favorite, is supposed to favor me. Now I will show you all the things that I did, and delighted in, till it was time for me to present my accounts elsewhere." And he showed me, detail by detail, in color and in drawing, his cattle, his horses, his crops, his tours in the district, his accountants presenting the revenue returns, and he himself, busiest of the busy, in the good day.

But when we left that broad, gay ante-room and came to the narrower passage where once his body had lain and where all his doom was portrayed, I could not follow him so well. I did not see how he, so experienced in life, could be cowed by friezes of brute-headed apparitions or satisfied by files of repeated figures. He explained, something to this effect:

"We live on the River—a line without breadth or thickness. Behind us is the Desert, which nothing can affect; whither no man goes till he is dead. (One does not use good agricultural ground for cemeteries.) Practically, then, we only move in two dimensions—up stream and down. Take away the Desert, which we don't consider any more than a healthy man considers death, and you will see that we have no background whatever. Our world is all one straight bar of brown or green earth, and, for some months, mere sky-reflecting water that wipes out everything. You have only to look at the Colossi to realize how enormously and extravagantly man and his works must scale in such a country. Remember, too, that our crops are sure, and our life is very, very easy. Above all, we have no neighbors. That is to say, we must give out, for we cannot take in. Now, I put it to you, what is left for a priest with imagination, except to develop ritual and multiply gods on friezes? Unlimited leisure, limited space of two dimensions, divided by the hypnotizing line of the River, and bounded by visible, unalterable death— must, *ipso facto*—"

"Even so," I interrupted. "I do not comprehend your Gods—your direct worship of beasts, for instance?"

"You prefer the indirect? The worship of Humanity with a capital H? My Gods, or what I saw in them, contented me."

"What did you see in your Gods as affecting belief and conduct?"

"You know the answer to the riddle of the Sphinx?"

"No," I murmured. "What is it?"

"All sensible men are of the same religion, but no sensible man ever tells," he replied. With that I had to be content, for the passage ended in solid rock. . . .

There is a valley of rocks and stones in every shade of red and brown, called the Valley of the Kings, where a little oil-engine coughs behind its hand all day long, grinding electricity to light the faces of dead Pharaohs a hundred feet underground. All down the valley, during the tourist season, stand char-a-bancs and donkeys and sand-carts, with here and there exhausted couples who have dropped out of the processions and glisten and fan themselves in some scrap of shade. Along the sides of the valley are the tombs of the kings neatly numbered, as it might be mining adits with concrete steps leading up to them, and iron grilles that lock of nights, and doorkeepers of the Department of Antiquities demanding the proper tickets. One enters, and from deeps below deeps hears the voice of dragomans booming through the names and titles of the illustrious and thrice-puissant dead. Rock-cut steps go down into hot, still darkness, passages twist and are led over blind pits which, men say, the wise builders childishly hoped would be taken for the real tombs by thieves to come. Up and down these alley-ways clatter all the races of Europe with a solid backing of the United States.

Their footsteps are suddenly blunted on the floor of a hall paved with immemorial dust that will never dance in any wind. They peer up at the blazoned ceilings, stoop down to the minutely decorated walls, crane and follow the somber splendors of a cornice, draw in their breaths and climb up again to the fierce sunshine to re-dive into the next adit on their program. What they think proper to say, they say aloud—and some of it is very interesting. What they feel you can guess from a certain haste in their movements—something between the shrinking modesty of a man under fire and the Hadn't-we-better-be-getting-on attitude of visitors to a mine. After all, it is not natural for man to go underground except for business or for the last time. He is conscious of the weight of mother-earth overhead, and when to her expectant bulk is added the whole beaked, horned, winged, and crowned hierarchy of a lost faith flaming at every turn of his eye, he naturally wishes to move away. Even the sight of a very great king indeed, sarcophagused under electric light in a hall full of most fortifying pictures, does not hold him too long.

Some men assert, that the crypt of St. Peter's, with only nineteen centuries bearing down on the groining, and the tombs of early popes and kings all about, is more impressive than the Valley of the Kings because it explains how and out of what an existing creed grew. But the Valley of the Kings explains nothing except that most terrible line in Macbeth:

To the last syllable of recorded time.

Earth opens her dry lips and says it.

LOT NO. 249

Sir Arthur Conan Doyle

Scottish author Sir Arthur Conan Doyle is most famous as the creator of Sherlock Holmes. Doyle was a physician who began writing while he was trying to establish his medical practice. He was much more successful as a writer than as a doctor so he eventually abandoned his practice, though he took it up again briefly during the Boer War in South Africa. His works include The Hound of the Baskervilles, A Study in Scarlet, The Sign of the Four, *and* The White Company. *Conan Doyle was fascinated by the supernatural and that comes out in many of his stories—including this one. Both this story and Conan Doyle's "The Ring of Thoth" directly influenced Anne Rice's novel* The Mummy, or Ramses the Damned.

O f the dealings of Edward Bellingham with William Monkhouse Lee, and of the cause of the great terror of Abercrombie Smith, it may be that no absolute and final judgment will ever be delivered. It is true that we have the full and clear narrative of Smith himself, and such corroboration as he could look for from Thomas Styles the servant, from the Reverend Plumptree Peterson, Fellow of Old's, and from such other people as chanced to gain some passing glance at this or that incident in a singular chain of events. Yet, in the main, the story must rest upon Smith alone, and the most will think that it is more likely that one brain, however outwardly sane, has some subtle warp in its texture, some strange flaw in its workings, than that the path of Nature has been overstepped in open day in so famed a center of learning and light as the University of Oxford. Yet when we think how narrow and how devious this path of Nature is, how dimly we can trace it, for all our lamps of science, and how from the darkness which girds it round great and terrible possibilities loom ever shadowly upwards, it is a bold and confident man who will put a limit to the strange by-paths into which the human spirit may wander.

In a certain wing of what we will call Old College in Oxford there is a corner turret of an exceeding great age. The heavy arch which spans the open door has bent downwards in the center under the weight of its years, and the gray, lichen-blotched blocks of stone are bound and knitted together with withes and strands of ivy, as though the old mother had set herself to brace them up against wind and weather. From the door a stone stair curves upward spirally, passing two landings, and terminating in a third one, its steps all shapeless and hollowed by the tread of so many generations of the seekers after knowledge. Life has flowed like water down this winding stair, and, water-like, has left these smooth-worn grooves behind it. From the long-gowned, pedantic scholars of Plantagenet days down to the young bloods of a later age, how full and strong had been that tide of young English life. And what was left now of all those hopes, those strivings, those fiery energies, save here and there in some old-world churchyard a few scratches upon a stone, and perchance a handful of dust in a moldering coffin? Yet here were the silent stair and the gray old wall, with bend and saltire and many another heraldic device still to be read upon its surface, like grotesque shadows thrown back from the days that had passed.

In the month of May, in the year 1884, three young men occupied the sets of rooms which opened on to the separate landings of the old stair. Each set consisted simply of a sitting-room and of a bedroom, while the two corresponding rooms upon the ground-floor were used, the one as a coal-cellar, and the other as the living-room of the servant, or gyp, Thomas Styles, whose duty it was to wait upon the three men above him. To right and to left was a line of lecture-rooms and of offices, so that the dwellers in the old turret enjoyed a certain seclusion, which made the chambers popular among the more studious undergraduates. Such were the three who occupied them now—Abercrombie Smith above, Edward Bellingham beneath him, and William Monkhouse Lee upon the lowest story.

It was ten o'clock on a bright spring night, and Abercrombie Smith lay back in his arm-chair, his feet upon the fender, and his briar-root pipe between his lips. In a similar chair, and equally at his ease, there lounged on the other side of the fireplace his old school friend Jephro Hastie. Both men were in flannels, for they had spent their evening upon the river, but apart from their dress no one could look at their hard-cut, alert faces without seeing that they were open-air men—men whose minds and tastes turned naturally to all that was manly and robust. Hastie, indeed, was stroke of his college boat, and Smith was an even better oar, but a coming examination had already cast its shadow over him and held him to his work, save for the few hours a week which health demanded. A litter of medical books upon the table, with scattered bones, models, and anatomical plates, pointed to the extent as well as the nature of his studies, while a couple of single-sticks and a set of boxing-gloves above the mantelpiece hinted at the means by which, with Hastie's help, he might take his exercise in its most compressed and least distant form. They knew each other very well—so well that they could sit now in that soothing silence which is the very highest development of companionship.

"Have some whisky," said Abercrombie Smith at last between two cloudbursts. "Scotch in the jug and Irish in the bottle."

"No, thanks. I'm in for the skulls. I don't liquor when I'm training. How about you?"

"I'm reading hard. I think it best to leave it alone."

Hastie nodded, and they relapsed into a contented silence.

"By-the-way, Smith," asked Hastie, presently, "have you made the acquaintance of either of the fellows on your stair yet?"

"Just a nod when we pass. Nothing more."

"Hum! I should be inclined to let it stand at that. I know something of them both. Not much, but as much as I want. I don't think I should take them to my bosom if I were you. Not that there's much amiss with Monkhouse Lee."

"Meaning the thin one?"

"Precisely. He is a gentlemanly little fellow. I don't think there is any vice in him. But then you can't know him without knowing Bellingham."

"Meaning the fat one?"

"Yes, the fat one. And he's a man whom I, for one, would rather not know."

Abercrombie Smith raised his eyebrows and glanced across at his companion.

"What's up, then?" he asked. "Drink? Cards? Cad? You used not to be censorious."

"Ah! You evidently don't know the man, or you wouldn't ask. There's something damnable about him—something reptilian. My gorge always rises at him. I should put him down as a man with secret vices—an evil liver. He's no fool, though. They say that he is one of the best men in his line that they have ever had in the college."

"Medicine or classics?"

"Eastern languages. He's a demon at them. Chillingworth met him somewhere above the second cataract last long, and he told me that he just prattled to the Arabs as if he had been born and nursed and weaned among them. He talked Coptic to the Copts, and Hebrew to the Jews, and Arabic to the Bedouins, and they were all ready to kiss the hem of his frock-coat. There are some old hermit Johnnies up in those parts who sit on rocks and scowl and spit at the casual stranger. Well, when they saw this chap Bellingham, before he had said five words they just lay down on their bellies and wriggled. Chillingworth said that he never saw anything like it. Bellingham seemed to take it as his right, too, and strutted about among them and talked down to them like a Dutch uncle. Pretty good for an undergrad of Old's, wasn't it?"

"Why do you say you can't know Lee without knowing Bellingham?"

"Because Bellingham is engaged to his sister Eveline. Such a bright little girl, Smith! I know the whole family well. It's disgusting to see that brute with her. A toad and a dove, that's what they always remind me of."

Abercrombie Smith grinned and knocked his ashes out against the side of the grate.

"You show every card in your hand, old chap," said he. "What a prejudiced, green-eyed, evil-thinking old man it is! You have really nothing against the fellow except that."

"Well, I've known her ever since she was as long as that cherry-wood pipe, and I don't like to see her taking risks. And it is a risk. He looks beastly. And he has a beastly temper, a venomous temper. You remember his row with Long Norton?"

"No; you always forget that I am a freshman."

"Ah, it was last winter. Of course. Well, you know the towpath along by the river. There were several fellows going along it, Bellingham in front, when they came on an old market-woman coming the other way. It had been raining—you know what those fields are like when it has rained—and the path ran between the river and a great puddle that was nearly as broad. Well, what does this swine do but keep the path, and push the old girl into the mud, where she and her marketings came to terrible grief. It was a blackguard thing to do, and Long Norton, who is as gentle a fellow as ever stepped, told him what he thought of it. One word led to another, and it ended in Norton laying his stick across the fellow's shoulders. There was the deuce of a fuss about it, and it's a treat to see the way in which Bellingham looks at Norton when they meet now. By Jove, Smith, it's nearly eleven o'clock!"

"No hurry. Light your pipe again."

"Not I. I'm supposed to be in training. Here I've been sitting gossiping when I ought to have been safely tucked up. I'll borrow your skull, if you can share it. Williams has had mine for a month. I'll take the little bones of your ear, too, if you are sure you won't need them. Thanks very much. Never mind a bag, I can carry them very well under my arm. Good-night, my son, and take my tip as to your neighbor."

When Hastie, bearing his anatomical plunder, had clattered off down the winding stair, Abercrombie Smith hurled his pipe into the wastepaper basket, and drawing his chair nearer to the lamp, plunged into a formidable green-covered volume, adorned with great colored maps of that strange internal kingdom of which we are the hapless and helpless monarchs. Though a freshman at Oxford, the student was not so in medicine, for he had worked for four years at Glasgow and at Berlin, and this coming examination would place him finally as a member of his profession. With his firm mouth, broad forehead, and clear-cut, somewhat hard-featured face, he was a man who, if he had no brilliant talent, was yet so dogged, so patient, and so strong that he might in the end overtop a more showy genius. A man who can hold his own among Scotchmen and North Germans is not a man to be easily set back. Smith had left a name at Glasgow and at Berlin, and he was bent now upon doing as much at Oxford, if hard work and devotion could accomplish it.

He had sat reading for about an hour, and the hands of the noisy carriage clock upon the side table were rapidly closing together upon the twelve, when a sudden sound fell upon the student's ear—a sharp, rather shrill sound, like the hissing intake of a man's breath who gasps under some strong emotion. Smith laid down his book and slanted his ear to listen. There was no one on either side or above him, so that the interruption came certainly from the neighbor beneath—the same neighbor of whom Hastie had given so unsavory an account. Smith knew him only as a flabby, pale-faced man of silent and studious habits, a man whose lamp threw a golden bar from the old turret even after he had extinguished his own. This community in lateness had formed a certain silent bond between them. It was soothing to Smith when the hours stole on towards dawning to feel that there was another so close who set as small a value upon his sleep as he did. Even now, as his thoughts turned towards him, Smith's feelings were kindly. Hastie was a good fellow, but he was rough, strong-fibered, with no imagination or sympathy. He could not tolerate departures from what he looked upon as the model type of manliness. If a man could not be measured by a public-school standard, then he was beyond the pale with Hastie. Like so many who are themselves robust, he was apt to confuse the constitution with the character, to ascribe to want of principle what was really a want of circulation. Smith, with his stronger mind, knew his friend's habit, and made allowance for it now as his thoughts turned towards the man beneath him.

There was no return of the singular sound, and Smith was about to turn to his work once more, when suddenly there broke out in the silence of the night a hoarse cry, a positive scream—the call of a man who is moved and shaken beyond all control. Smith sprang out of his chair and dropped his book. He was a man of fairly firm fiber, but there was something in this sudden, uncontrollable shriek of horror which chilled his blood and pringled in his skin. Coming in such a place and at such an hour, it brought a thousand fantastic possibilities into his head. Should he rush down, or was it better to wait? He had all the national hatred of making a scene, and he knew so little of his neighbor that he would not lightly intrude upon his affairs. For a moment he stood in doubt and even as he balanced the matter there was a quick rattle of footsteps upon the stairs, and young Monkhouse Lee, half dressed and as white as ashes, burst into his room.

"Come down!" he gasped. "Bellingham's ill."

Abercrombie Smith followed him closely down stairs into the sitting-room which was beneath his own, and intent as he was upon the matter in hand, he could not but take an amazed glance around him as he crossed the threshold. It was such a chamber as he had never seen before—a museum rather than a study. Walls and ceiling were thickly covered with a thousand strange relics from Egypt and the East. Tall, angular figures bearing burdens or weapons stalked in an uncouth frieze round the apartments. Above were bull-headed, stork-headed, cat-headed, owl-headed statues, with viper-crowned, almond-eyed monarchs, and strange, beetle-like deities cut out of the blue Egyptian lapis lazuli. Horus and Isis and Osiris peeped down from every niche and shelf, while across the ceiling a true son of Old Nile, a great, hanging-jawed crocodile, was slung in a double noose.

In the center of this singular chamber was a large, square table, littered with papers, bottles, and the dried leaves of some graceful, palm-like plant. These varied objects had all been heaped together in order to make room for a mummy case, which had been conveyed from the wall, as was evident from the gap there, and laid across the front of the table. The mummy itself, a horrid, black, withered thing, like a charred head on a gnarled bush, was lying half out of the case, with its claw-like hand and bony forearm resting upon the table. Propped up against the sarcophagus was an old yellow scroll of papyrus, and in front of it, in a wooden armchair, sat the owner of the room, his head thrown back, his widely-opened eyes directed in a horrified stare to the crocodile above him, and his blue, thick lips puffing loudly with every expiration.

"My God! he's dying!" cried Monkhouse Lee distractedly.

He was a slim, handsome young fellow, olive-skinned and dark-eyed, of a Spanish rather than of an English type, with a Celtic intensity of manner which contrasted with the Saxon phlegm of Abercrombie Smith.

"Only a faint, I think," said the medical student. "Just give me a hand with him. You take his feet. Now on to the sofa. Can you kick all those little wooden devils off? What a litter it is! Now he will be all right if we undo his collar and give him some water. What has he been up to at all?"

"I don't know. I heard him cry out. I ran up. I know him pretty well, you know. It is very good of you to come down."

"His heart is going like a pair of castanets," said Smith, laying his hand on the breast of the unconscious man. "He seems to me to be frightened all to pieces. Chuck the water over him! What a face he has got on him!"

It was indeed a strange and most repellent face, for color and outline were equally unnatural. It was white, not with the ordinary pallor of fear but with an absolutely bloodless white, like the under side of a sole. He was very fat, but gave the impression of having at some time been considerably fatter, for his skin hung loosely in creases and folds, and was shot with a meshwork of wrinkles. Short, stubbly brown hair bristled up from his scalp, with a pair of thick, wrinkled ears protruding on either side. His light gray eyes were still open, the pupils dilated and the balls projecting in a fixed and horrid stare. It seemed to Smith as he looked down upon him that he had never seen nature's danger signals flying so plainly upon a man's countenance, and his thoughts turned more seriously to the warning which Hastie had given him an hour before.

"What the deuce can have frightened him so?" he asked.

"It's the mummy."

"The mummy? How, then?"

"I don't know. It's beastly and morbid. I wish he would drop it. It's the second fright he has given me. It was the same last winter. I found him just like this, with that horrid thing in front of him."

"What does he want with the mummy, then?"

"Oh, he's a crank, you know. It's his hobby. He knows more about these things than any man in England. But I wish he wouldn't! Ah, he's beginning to come to."

A faint tinge of color had begun to steal back into Bellingham's ghastly cheeks, and his eyelids shivered like a sail after a calm. He clasped and unclasped his hands, drew a long, thin breath between his teeth, and suddenly jerking up his head, threw a glance of recognition around him. As his eyes fell upon the mummy, he sprang off the sofa, seized the roll of papyrus, thrust it into a drawer, turned the key, and then staggered back on to the sofa.

"What's up?" he asked. "What do you chaps want?"

"You've been shrieking out and making no end of a fuss," said Monkhouse Lee. "If our neighbor here from above hadn't come down, I'm sure I don't know what I should have done with you."

"Ah, it's Abercrombie Smith," said Bellingham, glancing up at him. "How very good of you to come in! What a fool I am! Oh, my God, what a fool I am!"

He sunk his head on to his hands, and burst into peal after peal of hysterical laughter.

"Look here! Drop it!" cried Smith, shaking him roughly by the shoulder. "Your nerves are all in a jangle. You must drop these little midnight games with mummies, or you'll be going off your chump. You're all on wires now."

"I wonder," said Bellingham, "whether you would be as cool as I am if you had seen—"

"What then?"

"Oh, nothing. I meant that I wonder if you could sit up at night with a mummy without trying your nerves. I have no doubt that you are quite right. I dare say that I have been taking it out of myself too much lately. But I am all right now. Please don't go, though. Just wait for a few minutes until I am quite myself."

"The room is very close," remarked Lee, throwing open the window and letting in the cool night air.

"It's balsamic resin," said Bellingham. He lifted up one of the dried palmate leaves from the table and frizzled it over the chimney of the lamp. It broke away into heavy smoke wreaths, and a pungent, biting odor filled the chamber. "It's the sacred plant—the plant of the priests," he remarked. "Do you know anything of Eastern languages, Smith?"

"Nothing at all. Not a word."

The answer seemed to lift a weight from the Egyptologist's mind.

"By-the-way," he continued, "how long was it from the time that you ran down, until I came to my senses?"

"Not long. Some four or five minutes."

"I thought it could not be very long," said he, drawing a long breath. "But what a strange thing unconsciousness is! There is no measurement to it. I could not tell from my own sensations if it were seconds or weeks. Now that gentleman on the table was packed up in the days of the eleventh dynasty, some forty centuries ago, and yet if he could find his tongue he would tell us that this lapse of time has been but a closing of the eyes and a reopening of them. He is a singularly fine mummy, Smith."

Smith stepped over to the table and looked down with a professional eye at the black and twisted form in front of him. The features, though horribly discolored, were perfect, and two little nut-like eyes still lurked in the depths of the black, hollow sockets. The blotched skin was drawn tightly from bone to bone, and a tangled wrap of black coarse hair fell over the ears. Two thin teeth, like those of a rat, overlay the shriveled lower lip. In its crouching position, with bent joints and craned head, there was a suggestion of energy about the horrid thing which made Smith's gorge rise. The gaunt ribs, with their parchment-like covering, were exposed, and the sunken, leaden-hued abdomen, with the long slit where the embalmer had left his mark; but the lower limbs were wrapped round with coarse yellow bandages. A number of little clove-like pieces of myrrh and of cassia were sprinkled over the body, and lay scattered on the inside of the case.

"I don't know his name," said Bellingham, passing his hand over the shriveled head. "You see the outer sarcophagus with the inscriptions is missing. Lot 249 is all the title he has now. You see it printed on his case. That was his number in the auction at which I picked him up."

"He has been a very pretty sort of fellow in his day," remarked Abercrombie Smith.

"He has been a giant. His mummy is six feet seven in length, and that would be a giant over there, for they were never a very robust race. Feel these great knotted bones, too. He would be a nasty fellow to tackle."

"Perhaps these very hands helped to build the stones into the pyramids," suggested Monkhouse Lee, looking down with disgust in his eyes at the crooked, unclean talons.

"No fear. This fellow has been pickled in natron, and looked after in the most approved style. They did not serve hodsmen in that fashion. Salt or bitumen was enough for them. It has been calculated that this sort of thing cost about seven hundred and thirty pounds in our money. Our friend was a noble at the least. What do you make of that small inscription near his feet, Smith?"

"I told you that I know no Eastern tongue."

"Ah, so you did. It is the name of the embalmer, I take it. A very conscientious worker he must have been. I wonder how many modern works will survive four thousand years?"

He kept on speaking lightly and rapidly, but it was evident to Abercrombie Smith that he was still palpitating with fear. His hands shook, his lower lip trembled, and look where he would, his eye always came sliding round to his gruesome companion. Through all his fear, however, there was a suspicion of triumph in his tone and manner. His eye shone, and his footstep, as he paced the room, was brisk and jaunty. He gave the impression of a man who has gone through an ordeal, the marks of which he still bears upon him, but which has helped him to his end.

"You're not going yet?" he cried, as Smith rose from the sofa.

At the prospect of solitude, his fears seemed to crowd back upon him, and he stretched out a hand to detain him.

"Yes, I must go. I have my work to do. You are all right now. I think that with your nervous system you should take up some less morbid study."

"Oh, I am not nervous as a rule; and I have unwrapped mummies before."

"You fainted last time," observed Monkhouse Lee.

"Ah, yes, so I did. Well, I must have a nerve tonic or a course of electricity. You are not going, Lee?"

"I'll do whatever you wish, Ned."

"Then I'll come down with you and have a shake-down on your sofa. Good-night, Smith. I am so sorry to have disturbed you with my foolishness."

They shook hands, and as the medical student stumbled up the spiral and irregular stair he heard a key turn in a door, and the steps of his two new acquaintances as they descended to the lower floor.

In this strange way began the acquaintance between Edward Bellingham and Abercrombie Smith, an acquaintance which the latter, at least, had no desire to push further. Bellingham, however, appeared to have taken a fancy to his rough-spoken neighbor, and made his advances in such a way that he could hardly be repulsed without absolute brutality. Twice he called to thank Smith for his assistance, and many times afterwards he looked in with books, papers, and such other civilities as two bachelor neighbors can offer each other. He was, as Smith soon found, a man of wide reading, with catholic tastes and an extraordinary memory. His manner, too, was so pleasing and suave that one came, after a time, to overlook his repellent appearance. For a jaded and wearied man he was no unpleasant companion, and Smith found himself, after a time, looking forward to his visits, and even returning them.

Clever as he undoubtedly was, however, the medical student seemed to detect a dash of insanity in the man. He broke out at times into a high, inflated style of talk which was in contrast with the simplicity of his life.

"It is a wonderful thing," he cried, "to feel that one can command powers of good and of evil—a ministering angel or a demon of vengeance." And again, of Monkhouse Lee, he said, "Lee is a good fellow, an honest fellow, but he is without strength or ambition. He would not make a fit partner for a man with a great enterprise. He would not make a fit partner for me."

At such hints and innuendoes stolid Smith, puffing solemnly at his pipe, would simply raise his eyebrows and shake his head, with little interjections of medical wisdom as to earlier hours and fresher air.

One habit Bellingham had developed of late which Smith knew to be a frequent herald of a weakening mind. He appeared to be forever talking to himself. At late hours of the night, when there could be no visitor with him, Smith could still hear his voice beneath him in a low, muffled monologue, sunk almost to a whisper, and yet very audible in the silence. This solitary babbling annoyed and distracted the student, so that he spoke more than once to his neighbor about it. Bellingham, however, flushed up at the charge, and denied curtly that he had uttered a sound; indeed, he showed more annoyance over the matter than the occasion seemed to demand.

Had Abercrombie Smith had any doubt as to his own ears he had not to go far to find corroboration. Tom Styles, the little wrinkled man-servant who had attended to the wants of the lodgers in the turret for a longer time than any man's memory could carry him, was sorely put to it over the same matter.

"If you please, sir," said he, as he tidied down the top chamber one morning, "do you think Mr. Bellingham is all right, sir?"

"All right, Styles?"

"Yes sir. Right in his head, sir."

"Why should he not be, then?"

"Well, I don't know, sir. His habits has changed of late. He's not the same man he used to be, though I make free to say that he was never quite one of my gentlemen, like Mr. Hastie or yourself, sir. He's took to talkin' to himself something awful. I wonder it don't disturb you. I don't know what to make of him, sir."

"I don't know what business it is of yours, Styles."

"Well, I takes an interest, Mr. Smith. It may be forward of me, but I can't help it. I feel sometimes as if I was mother and father to my young gentlemen. It all falls on me when things go wrong and the relations come. But Mr. Bellingham, sir. I want to know what it is that walks about his room sometimes when he's out and when the door's locked on the outside."

"Eh? You're talking nonsense, Styles."

"Maybe so, sir; but I heard it more'n once with my own ears."

"Rubbish, Styles."

"Very good, sir. You'll ring the bell if you want me."

Abercrombie Smith gave little heed to the gossip of the old man-servant, but a small incident occurred a few days later which left an unpleasant effect upon his mind, and brought the words of Styles forcibly to his memory.

Bellingham had come up to see him late one night, and was entertaining him with an interesting account of the rock tombs of Beni Hassan in Upper Egypt, when Smith, whose hearing was remarkably acute, distinctly heard the sound of a door opening on the landing below.

"There's some fellow gone in or out of your room," he remarked.

Bellingham sprang up and stood helpless for a moment, with the expression of a man who is half-incredulous and half-afraid.

"I surely locked it. I am almost positive that I locked it," he stammered. "No one could have opened it."

"Why, I hear someone coming up the steps now," said Smith.

Bellingham rushed out through the door, slammed it loudly behind him, and hurried down the stairs. About half-way down Smith heard him stop, and thought he caught the sound of whispering. A moment later the door beneath him shut, a key creaked in a lock, and Bellingham, with beads of moisture upon his pale face, ascended the stairs once more, and re-entered the room.

"It's all right," he said, throwing himself down in a chair. "It was that fool of a dog. He had pushed the door open. I don't know how I came to forget to lock it."

"I didn't know you kept a dog," said Smith, looking very thoughtfully at the disturbed face of his companion.

"Yes, I haven't had him long. I must get rid of him. He's a great nuisance."

"He must be, if you find it so hard to shut him up. I should have thought that shutting the door would have been enough, without locking it."

"I want to prevent old Styles from letting him out. He's of some value, you know, and it would be awkward to lose him."

"I am a bit of a dog-fancier myself," said Smith, still gazing hard at his companion from the corner of his eyes. "Perhaps you'll let me have a look at it."

"Certainly. But I am afraid it cannot be tonight; I have an appointment. Is that clock right? Then I am a quarter of an hour late already. You'll excuse me, I am sure."

He picked up his cap and hurried from the room. In spite of his appointment, Smith heard him re-enter his own chamber and lock his door upon the inside.

This interview left a disagreeable impression upon the medical student's mind. Bellingham had lied to him, and lied so clumsily that it looked as if he had desperate reasons for concealing the truth. Smith knew that his neighbor had no dog. He knew, also, that the step which he had heard upon the stairs was not the step of an animal. But if it were not, then what could it be? There was old Styles's statement about the something which used to pace the room at times when the owner was absent. Could it be a woman? Smith rather inclined to the view. If so, it would mean disgrace and expulsion to Bellingham if it were discovered by the authorities, so that his anxiety and falsehoods might be accounted for. And yet it was inconceivable that an undergraduate could keep a woman in his rooms without being instantly detected. Be the explanation what it might, there was something ugly about it, and Smith determined, as he turned to his books, to discourage all further attempts at intimacy on the part of his soft-spoken and ill-favored neighbor.

But his work was destined to interruption that night. He had hardly caught up the broken threads when a firm, heavy footfall came three steps at a time from below, and Hastie, in blazer and flannels, burst into the room.

"Still at it!" said he, plumping down into his wonted arm-chair. "What a chap you are to stew! I believe an earthquake might come and knock Oxford into a cocked hat, and you would sit perfectly placid with your books among the ruins. However, I won't bore you long. Three whiffs of baccy, and I am off."

"What's the news, then?" asked Smith, cramming a plug of bird's-eye into his briar with his forefinger.

"Nothing very much. Wilson made seventy for the freshmen against the eleven. They say that they will play him instead of Buddicomb, for Buddicomb is clean off color. He used to be able to bowl a little, but it's nothing but half-vollies and long hops now."

"Medium right," suggested Smith, with the intense gravity which comes upon a varsity man when he speaks of athletics.

"Inclining to fast, with a work from leg. Comes with the arm about three inches or so. He used to be nasty on a wet wicket. Oh, by-the-way, have you heard about Long Norton?"

"What's that?"

"He's been attacked."

"Attacked?"

"Yes, just as he was turning out of the High Street, and within a hundred yards of the gate of Old's."

"But who—"

"Ah, that's the rub! If you said 'what,' you would be more grammatical. Norton swears that it was not human, and, indeed, from the scratches on his throat, I should be inclined to agree with him."

"What, then? Have we come down to spooks?"

Abercrombie Smith puffed his scientific contempt.

"Well, no; I don't think that is quite the idea, either. I am inclined to think that if any showman has lost a great ape lately, and the brute is in these parts, a jury would find a true bill against it. Norton passes that way every night, you know, about the same hour. There's a tree that hangs low over the path—the big elm from Rainy's garden. Norton thinks the thing dropped on him out of the tree. Anyhow, he was nearly strangled by two arms, which, he says, were as strong and as thin as steel bands. He saw nothing; only those beastly arms that tightened and tightened on him. He yelled his head nearly off, and a couple of chaps came running, and the thing went over the wall like a cat. He never got a fair sight of it the whole time. It gave Norton a shake up, I can tell you. I tell him it has been as good as a change at the sea-side for him."

"A garrotter, most likely," said Smith.

"Very possibly. Norton says not; but we don't mind what he says. The garrotter had long nails, and was pretty smart at swinging himself over walls. By-the-way, your beautiful neighbor would be pleased if he heard about it. He had a grudge against Norton, and he's not a man, from what I know of him, to forget his little debts. But hallo, old chap, what have you got in your noodle?"

"Nothing," Smith answered curtly.

He had started in his chair, and the look had flashed over his face which comes upon a man who is struck suddenly by some unpleasant idea.

"You looked as if something I had said had taken you on the raw. By-the-way, you have made the acquaintance of Master B. since I looked in last, have you not? Young Monkhouse Lee told me something to that effect."

"Yes; I know him slightly. He has been up here once or twice."

"Well, you're big enough and ugly enough to take care of yourself. He's not what I should call exactly a healthy sort of Johnny, though, no doubt, he's very clever, and all that. But you'll soon find out for yourself. Lee is all right; he's a very decent little fellow. Well, so long, old chap! I row Mullins for the Vice-Chancellor's pot on Wednesday week, so mind you come down, in case I don't see you before."

Bovine Smith laid down his pipe and turned stolidly to his books once more. But with all the will in the world, he found it very hard to keep his mind upon his work. It would slip away to brood upon the man beneath him, and upon the little mystery which hung round his chambers. Then his thoughts turned to this singular attack of which Hastie had spoken, and to the grudge which Bellingham was said to owe the object of it. The two ideas would persist in rising together in his mind, as though there were some close and intimate connection between them. And yet the suspicion was so dim and vague that it could not be put down in words.

"Confound the chap!" cried Smith, as he shied his book on pathology across the room. "He has spoiled my night's reading, and that's reason enough, if there were no other, why I should steer clear of him in the future."

For ten days the medical student confined himself so closely to his studies that he neither saw nor heard anything of either of the men beneath him. At the hours when Bellingham had been accustomed to visit him, he took care to sport his oak, and though he more than once heard a knocking at his outer door, he resolutely refused to answer it. One afternoon, however, he was descending the stairs when, just as he was passing it, Bellingham's door flew open, and young Monkhouse Lee came out with his eyes sparkling and a dark flush of anger upon his olive cheeks. Close at his heels followed Bellingham, his fat, unhealthy face all quivering with malignant passion.

"You fool!" he hissed. "You'll be sorry."

"Very likely," cried the other. "Mind what I say. It's off! I won't hear of it!"

"You've promised, anyhow."

"Oh, I'll keep that! I won't speak. But I'd rather little Eva was in her grave. Once for all, it's off. She'll do what I say. We don't want to see you again."

So much Smith could not avoid hearing, but he hurried on, for he had no wish to be involved in their dispute. There had been a serious breach between them, that was clear enough, and Lee was going to cause the engagement with his sister to be broken off. Smith thought of Hastie's comparison of the toad and the dove, and was glad to think that the matter was at an end. Bellingham's face when he was in a passion was not pleasant to look upon. He was not a man to whom an innocent girl could be trusted for life. As he walked, Smith wondered languidly what could have caused the quarrel, and what the promise might be which Bellingham had been so anxious that Monkhouse Lee should keep.

It was the day of the sculling match between Hastie and Mullins, and a stream of men were making their way down to the banks of the Isis. A May sun was shining brightly, and the yellow path was barred with the black shadows of the tall elm-trees. On either side the gray colleges lay back from the road, the hoary old mothers of minds looking out from their high, mullioned windows at the tide of young life which swept so merrily past them. Black-clad tutors, prim officials, pale reading men, brown-faced, straw-hatted young athletes in white sweaters or many-colored blazers, all were hurrying towards the blue winding river which curves through the Oxford meadows.

Abercrombie Smith, with the intuition of an old oarsman, chose his position at the point where he knew that the struggle, if there were a struggle, would come. Far off he heard the hum which announced the start, the gathering roar of the approach, the thunder of running feet, and the shouts of the men in the boats beneath him. A spray of half-clad, deep-breathing runners shot past him, and craning over their shoulders, he saw Hastie pulling a steady thirty-six, while his opponent, with a jerky forty, was a good boat's length behind him. Smith gave a cheer for his friend, and pulling out his watch, was starting off again for his chambers, when he felt a touch upon his shoulder, and found that young Monkhouse Lee was beside him.

"I saw you there," he said, in a timid, deprecating way. "I wanted to speak to you, if you could spare me a half-hour. This cottage is mine. I share it with Harrington of King's. Come in and have a cup of tea."

"I must be back presently," said Smith. "I am hard on the grind at present. But I'll come in for a few minutes with pleasure. I wouldn't have come out only Hastie is a friend of mine."

"So he is of mine. Hasn't he a beautiful style? Mullins wasn't in it. But come into the cottage. It's a little den of a place, but it is pleasant to work in during the summer months."

It was a small, square, white building, with green doors and shutters, and a rustic trellis-work porch, standing back some fifty yards from the river's bank. Inside, the main room was roughly fitted up as a study—deal table, unpainted shelves with books, and a few cheap oleographs upon the wall. A kettle sang upon a spirit-stove, and there were tea things upon a tray on the table.

"Try that chair and have a cigarette," said Lee. "Let me pour you out a cup of tea. It's so good of you to come in, for I know that your time is a good deal taken up. I wanted to say to you that, if I were you, I should change my rooms at once."

"Eh?"

Smith sat staring with a lighted match in one hand and his unlit cigarette in the other.

"Yes; it must seem very extraordinary, and the worst of it is that I cannot give my reasons, for I am under a solemn promise—a very solemn promise. But I may go so far as to say that I don't think Bellingham is a very safe man to live near. I intend to camp out here as much as I can for a time."

"Not safe! What do you mean?"

"Ah, that's what I mustn't say. But do take my advice, and move your rooms. We had a grand row today. You must have heard us, for you came down the stairs."

"I saw that you had fallen out."

"He's a horrible chap, Smith. That is the only word for him. I have had doubts about him ever since that night when he fainted—you remember, when you came down. I taxed him today, and he told me things that made my hair rise, and wanted me to stand in with him. I'm not strait-laced, but I am a clergyman's son, you know, and I think there are some things which are quite beyond the pale. I only thank God that I found him out before it was too late, for he was to have married into my family."

"This is all very fine, Lee," said Abercrombie Smith curtly. "But either you are saying a great deal too much or a great deal too little."

"I give you a warning."

"If there is real reason for warning, no promise can bind you. If I see a rascal about to blow a place up with dynamite no pledge will stand in my way of preventing him."

"Ah, but I cannot prevent him, and I can do nothing but warn you."

"Without saying what you warn me against."

"Against Bellingham."

"But that is childish. Why should I fear him, or any man?"

"I can't tell you. I can only entreat you to change your rooms. You are in danger where you are. I don't even say that Bellingham would wish to injure you. But it might happen, for he is a dangerous neighbor just now."

"Perhaps I know more than you think," said Smith, looking keenly at the young man's boyish, earnest face. "Suppose I tell you that some one else shares Bellingham's rooms."

Monkhouse Lee sprang from his chair in uncontrollable excitement.

"You know, then?" he gasped.

"A woman."

Lee dropped back again with a groan.

"My lips are sealed," he said. "I must not speak."

"Well, anyhow," said Smith, rising, "it is not likely that I should allow myself to be frightened out of rooms which suit me very nicely. It would be a little too feeble for me to move out all my goods and chattels because you say that Bellingham might in some unexplained way do me an injury. I think that I'll just take my chance, and stay where I am, and as I see that it's nearly five o'clock, I must ask you to excuse me."

He bade the young student adieu in a few curt words, and made his way homeward through the sweet spring evening feeling half-ruffled, half-amused, as any other strong, unimaginative man might who has been menaced by a vague and shadowy danger.

There was one little indulgence which Abercrombie Smith always allowed himself, however closely his work might press upon him. Twice a week, on the Tuesday and the Friday, it was his invariable custom to walk over to Farlingford, the residence of Dr. Plumptree Peterson, situated about a mile and a half out of Oxford. Peterson had been a close friend of Smith's elder brother Francis, and as he was a bachelor, fairly well-to-do, with a good cellar and a better library, his house was a pleasant goal for a man who was in need of a brisk walk. Twice a week, then, the medical student would swing out there along the dark country roads, and spend a pleasant hour in Peterson's comfortable study, discussing, over a glass of old port, the gossip of the varsity or the latest developments of medicine or of surgery.

On the day which followed his interview with Monkhouse Lee, Smith shut up his books at a quarter past eight, the hour when he usually started for his friend's house. As he was leaving his room, however, his eyes chanced to fall upon one of the books which Bellingham had lent him, and his conscience pricked him for not having returned it. However repellent the man might be, he should not be treated with discourtesy. Taking the book, he walked downstairs and knocked at his neighbor's door. There was no answer; but on turning the handle he found that it was unlocked. Pleased at the thought of avoiding an interview, he stepped inside, and placed the book with his card upon the table.

The lamp was turned half down, but Smith could see the details of the room plainly enough. It was all much as he had seen it before—the frieze, the animal-headed gods, the banging crocodile, and the table littered over with papers and dried leaves. The mummy case stood upright against the wall, but the mummy itself was missing. There was no sign of any second occupant of the room, and he felt as he withdrew that he had probably done Bellingham an injustice. Had he a guilty secret to preserve, he would hardly leave his door open so that all the world might enter.

The spiral stair was as black as pitch, and Smith was slowly making his way down its irregular steps, when he was suddenly conscious that something had passed him in the darkness. There was a faint sound, a whiff of air, a light brushing past his elbow, but so slight that he could scarcely be certain of it. He stopped and listened, but the wind was rustling among the ivy outside, and he could hear nothing else.

"Is that you, Styles?" he shouted.

There was no answer, and all was still behind him. It must have been a sudden gust of air, for there were crannies and cracks in the old turret. And yet he could almost have sworn that he heard a footfall by his very side. He had emerged into the quadrangle, still turning the matter over in his head, when a man came running swiftly across the smooth-cropped lawn.

"Is that you, Smith?"

"Hello, Hastie!"

"For God's sake come at once! Young Lee is drowned! Here's Harrington of King's with the news. The doctor is out. You'll do, but come along at once. There may be life in him."

"Have you brandy?"

"No."

"I'll bring some. There's a flask on my table."

Smith bounded up the stairs, taking three at a time, seized the flask, and was rushing down with it, when, as he passed Bellingham's room, his eyes fell upon something which left him gasping and staring upon the landing.

The door, which he had closed behind him, was now open, and right in front of him, with the lamp-light shining upon it, was the mummy case. Three minutes ago it had been empty. He could swear to that. Now it framed the lank body of its horrible occupant, who stood, grim and stark, with his black shriveled face towards the door. The form was lifeless and inert, but it seemed to Smith as he gazed that there still lingered a lurid spark of vitality, some faint sign of consciousness in the little eyes which lurked in the depths of the hollow sockets. So astounded and shaken was he that he had forgotten his errand, and was still staring at the lean, sunken figure when the voice of his friend below recalled him to himself.

"Come on, Smith!" he shouted. "It's life and death, you know. Hurry up! Now, then," he added, as the medical student reappeared, "let us do a sprint. It is well under a mile, and we should do it in five minutes. A human life is better worth running for than a pot."

Neck and neck they dashed through the darkness, and did not pull up until, panting and spent, they had reached the little cottage by the river. Young Lee, limp and dripping like a broken water-plant, was stretched upon the sofa, the green scum of the river upon his black hair, and a fringe of white foam upon his leaden-hued lips. Beside him knelt his fellow-student Harrington, endeavoring to chafe some warmth back into his rigid limbs.

"I think there's life in him," said Smith, with his hand to the lad's side. "Put your watch glass to his lips. Yes, there's dimming on it. You take one arm, Hastie. Now work it as I do, and we'll soon pull him round."

For ten minutes they worked in silence, inflating and depressing the chest of the unconscious man. At the end of that time a shiver ran through his body, his lips trembled, and he opened his eyes. The three students burst out into an irrepressible cheer.

"Wake up, old chap. You've frightened us quite enough."

"Have some brandy. Take a sip from the flask."

"He's all right now," said his companion Harrington. "Heavens, what a fright I got! I was reading here, and he had gone for a stroll as far as the river, when I heard a scream and a splash. Out I ran, and by the time that I could find him and fish him out, all life seemed to have gone. Then Simpson couldn't get a doctor, for he has a game-leg, and I had to run, and I don't know what I'd have done without you fellows. That's right, old chap. Sit up."

Monkhouse Lee had raised himself on his hands, and looked wildly about him.

"What's up?" he asked. "I've been in the water. Ah, yes; I remember."

A look of fear came into his eyes, and he sank his face into his hands.

"How did you fall in?"

"I didn't fall in."

"How, then?"

"I was thrown in. I was standing by the bank, and something from behind picked me up like a feather and hurled me in. I heard nothing, and I saw nothing. But I know what it was, for all that."

"And so do I," whispered Smith.

Lee looked up with a quick glance of surprise. "You've learned, then!" he said. "You remember the advice I gave you?"

"Yes, and I begin to think that I shall take it."

"I don't know what the deuce you fellows are talking about," said Hastie, "but I think, if I were you, Harrington, I should get Lee to bed at once. It will be time enough to discuss the why and the wherefore when he is a little stronger. I think, Smith, you and I can leave him alone now. I am walking back to college; if you are coming in that direction, we can have a chat."

But it was little chat that they had upon their homeward path. Smith's mind was too full of the incidents of the evening, the absence of the mummy from his neighbor's rooms, the step that passed him on the stair, the reappearance—the extraordinary, inexplicable reappearance of the grisly thing—and then this attack upon Lee, corresponding so closely to the previous outrage upon another man against whom Bellingham bore a grudge. All this settled in his thoughts, together with the many little incidents which had previously turned him against his neighbor, and the singular circumstances under which he was first called in to him. What had been a dim suspicion, a vague, fantastic conjecture, had suddenly taken form, and stood out in his mind as a grim fact, a thing not to be denied. And yet, how monstrous it was! how unheard of! how entirely beyond all bounds of human experience. An impartial judge, or even the friend who walked by his side, would simply tell him that his eyes had deceived him, that the mummy had been there all the time, that young Lee had tumbled into the river as any other man tumbles into a river, and that a blue pill was the best thing for a disordered liver. He felt that he would have said as much if the positions had been reversed. And yet he could swear that Bellingham was a murderer at heart, and that he wielded a weapon such as no man had ever used in all the grim history of crime.

Hastie had branched off to his rooms with a few crisp and emphatic comments upon his friend's unsociability, and Abercrombie Smith crossed the quadrangle to his corner turret with a strong feeling of repulsion for his chambers and their associations. He would take Lee's advice, and move his quarters as soon as possible, for how could a man study when his ear was ever straining for every murmur or footstep in the room below? He observed, as he crossed over the lawn, that the light was still shining in Bellingham's window, and as he passed up the staircase the door opened, and the man himself looked out at him. With his fat, evil face he was like some bloated spider fresh from the weaving of his poisonous web.

"Good-evening," said he. "Won't you come in?"

"No," cried Smith, fiercely.

"No? You are busy as ever? I wanted to ask you about Lee. I was sorry to hear that there was a rumor that something was amiss with him."

His features were grave, but there was the gleam of a hidden laugh in his eyes as he spoke. Smith saw it, and he could have knocked him down for it.

"You'll be sorrier still to hear that Monkhouse Lee is doing very well, and is out of all danger," he answered. "Your hellish tricks have not come off this time. Oh, you needn't try to brazen it out. I know all about it."

Bellingham took a step back from the angry student, and half-closed the door as if to protect himself.

"You are mad," he said. "What do you mean? Do you assert that I had anything to do with Lee's accident?"

"Yes," thundered Smith. "You and that bag of bones behind you; you worked it between you. I tell you what it is, Master B., they have given up burning folk like you, but we still keep a hangman, and, by George! if any man in this college meets his death while you are here, I'll have you up, and if you don't swing for it, it won't be my fault. You'll find that your filthy Egyptian tricks won't answer in England."

"You're a raving lunatic," said Bellingham.

"All right. You just remember what I say, for you'll find that I'll be better than my word."

The door slammed, and Smith went fuming up to his chamber, where he locked the door upon the inside, and spent half the night in smoking his old briar and brooding over the strange events of the evening.

Next morning Abercrombie Smith heard nothing of his neighbor, but Harrington called upon him in the afternoon to say that Lee was almost himself again. All day Smith stuck fast to his work, but in the evening he determined to pay the visit to his friend Dr. Peterson upon which he had started the night before. A good walk and a friendly chat would be welcome to his jangled nerves.

Bellingham's door was shut as he passed, but glancing back when he was some distance from the turret, he saw his neighbor's head at the window outlined against the lamp-light, his face pressed apparently against the glass as he gazed out into the darkness. It was a blessing to be away from all contact with him, but if for a few hours, and Smith stepped out briskly, and breathed the soft spring air into his lungs. The half-moon lay in the west between two Gothic pinnacles, and threw upon the silvered street a dark tracery from the stone-work above. There was a brisk breeze, and light, fleecy clouds drifted swiftly across the sky. Old's was on the very border of the town, and in five minutes Smith found himself beyond the houses and between the hedges of a May-scented, Oxfordshire lane.

It was a lonely and little frequented road which led to his friend's house. Early as it was, Smith did not meet a single soul upon his way. He walked briskly along until he came to the avenue gate, which opened into the long gravel drive leading up to Farlingford. In front of him he could see the cozy red light of the windows glimmering through the foliage. He stood with his hand upon the iron latch of the swinging gate, and he glanced back at the road along which he had come. Something was coming swiftly down it.

It moved in the shadow of the hedge, silently and furtively, a dark, crouching figure, dimly visible against the black background. Even as he gazed back at it, it had lessened its distance by twenty paces, and was fast closing upon him. Out of the darkness he had a glimpse of a scraggy neck, and of two eyes that will ever haunt him in his dreams. He turned, and with a cry of terror he ran for his life up the avenue. There were the red lights, the signals of safety, almost within a stone's throw of him. He was a famous runner, but never had he run as he ran that night.

The heavy gate had swung into place behind him, but he heard it dash open again before his pursuer. As he rushed madly and wildly through the night, he could hear a swift, dry patter behind him, and could see, as he threw back a glance, that this horror was bounding like a tiger at his heels, with blazing eyes and one stringy arm out thrown. Thank God, the door was ajar. He could see the thin bar of light which shot from the lamp in the hall. Nearer yet sounded the clatter from behind. He heard a hoarse gurgling at his very shoulder. With a shriek he flung himself against the door, slammed and bolted it behind him, and sank half-fainting on to the hall chair.

"My goodness, Smith, what's the matter?" asked Peterson, appearing at the door of his study.

"Give me some brandy!"

Peterson disappeared, and came rushing out again with a glass and a decanter.

"You need it," he said, as his visitor drank off what he poured out for him. "Why, man, you are as white as a cheese."

Smith laid down his glass, rose up, and took a deep breath.

"I am my own man again now," said he. "I was never so unmanned before. But, with your leave, Peterson, I will sleep here tonight, for I don't think I could face that road again except by daylight. It's weak, I know, but I can't help it."

Peterson looked at his visitor with a very questioning eye.

"Of course you shall sleep here if you wish. I'll tell Mrs. Burney to make up the spare bed. Where are you off to now?"

"Come up with me to the window that overlooks the door. I want you to see what I have seen."

They went up to the window of the upper hall whence they could look down upon the approach to the house. The drive and the fields on either side lay quiet and still, bathed in the peaceful moonlight.

"Well, really, Smith," remarked Peterson, "it is well that I know you to be an abstemious man. What in the world can have frightened you?"

"I'll tell you presently. But where can it have gone? Ah, now look, look! See the curve of the road just beyond your gate."

"Yes, I see; you needn't pinch my arm off. I saw someone pass. I should say a man, rather thin, apparently, and tall, very tall. But what of him? And what of yourself? You are still shaking like an aspen leaf."

"I have been within hand-grip of the devil, that's all. But come down to your study, and I shall tell you the whole story."

He did so. Under the cheery lamplight, with a glass of wine on the table beside him, and the portly form and florid face of his friend in front, he narrated, in their order, all the events, great and small, which had formed so singular a chain, from the night on which he had found Bellingham fainting in front of the mummy case until his horrid experience of an hour ago.

"There now," he said as he concluded, "that's the whole black business. It is monstrous and incredible, but it is true."

Doctor Plumptree Peterson sat for some time in silence with a very puzzled expression upon his face.

"I never heard of such a thing in my life, never!" he said at last. "You have told me the facts. Now tell me your inferences."

"You can draw your own."

"But I should like to hear yours. You have thought over the matter, and I have not."

"Well, it must be a little vague in detail, but the main points seem to me to be clear enough. This fellow Bellingham, in his Eastern studies, has got hold of some infernal secret by which a mummy—or possibly only this particular mummy—can be temporarily brought to life. He was trying this disgusting business on the night when he fainted. No doubt the sight of the creature moving had shaken his nerve, even though he had expected it. You remember that almost the first words he said were to call out upon himself as a fool. Well, he got more hardened afterwards, and carried the matter through without fainting. The vitality which he could put into it was evidently only a passing thing, for I have seen it continually in its case as dead as this table. He has some elaborate process, I fancy, by which he brings the thing to pass. Having done it, he naturally bethought him that he might use the creature as an agent. It has intelligence and it has strength. For some purpose he took Lee into his confidence; but Lee, like a decent Christian, would have nothing to do with such a business. Then they had a row, and Lee vowed that he would tell his sister of Bellingham's true character. Bellingham's game was to prevent him, and he nearly managed it, by setting this creature of his on his track. He had already tried its powers upon another man—Norton—towards whom he had a grudge. It is the merest chance that he has not two murders upon his soul. Then, when I taxed him with the matter, he had the strongest reasons for wishing to get me out of the way before I could convey my knowledge to anyone else. He got his chance when I went out, for he knew my habits, and where I was bound for. I have had a narrow shave, Peterson, and it is mere luck you didn't find me on your doorstep in the morning. I'm not a nervous man as a rule, and I never thought to have the fear of death put upon me as it was to-night."

"My dear boy, you take the matter too seriously," said his companion. "Your nerves are out of order with your work, and you make too much of it. How could such a thing as this stride about the streets of Oxford, even at night, without being seen?"

"It has been seen. There is quite a scare in the town about an escaped ape, as they imagine the creature to be. It is the talk of the place."

"Well, it's a striking chain of events. And yet, my dear fellow, you must allow that each incident in itself is capable of a more natural explanation."

"What! even my adventure of tonight?"

"Certainly. You come out with your nerves all unstrung, and your head full of this theory of yours. Some gaunt, half-famished tramp steals after you, and seeing you run, is emboldened to pursue you. Your fears and imagination do the rest."

"It won't do, Peterson; it won't do."

"And again, in the instance of your finding the mummy case empty, and then a few moments later with an occupant, you know that it was lamp-light, that the lamp was half turned down, and that you had no special reason to look hard at the case. It is quite possible that you may have over-looked the creature in the first instance."

"No, no; it is out of the question."

"And then Lee may have fallen into the river, and Norton been garroted. It is certainly a formidable indictment that you have against Bellingham; but if you were to place it before a police magistrate, he would simply laugh in your face."

"I know he would. That is why I mean to take the matter into my own hands."

"Eh?"

"Yes; I feel that a public duty rests upon me, and, besides, I must do it for my own safety, unless I choose to allow myself to be hunted by this beast out of the college, and that would be a little too feeble. I have quite made up my mind what I shall do. And first of all, may I use your paper and pens for an hour?"

"Most certainly. You will find all that you want upon that side-table."

Abercrombie Smith sat down before a sheet of foolscap, and for an hour, and then for a second hour his pen traveled swiftly over it. Page after page was finished and tossed aside while his friend leaned back in his arm-chair, looking across at him with patient curiosity. At last, with an exclamation of satisfaction, Smith sprang to his feet, gathered his papers up into order, and laid the last one upon Peterson's desk.

"Kindly sign this as a witness," he said.

"A witness? Of what?"

"Of my signature, and of the date. The date is the most important. Why, Peterson, my life might hang upon it."

"My dear Smith, you are talking wildly. Let me beg you to go to bed."

"On the contrary, I never spoke so deliberately in my life. And I will promise to go to bed the moment you have signed it."

"But what is it?"

"It is a statement of all that I have been telling you tonight. I wish you to witness it."

"Certainly," said Peterson, signing his name under that of his companion. "There you are! But what is the idea?"

"You will kindly retain it, and produce it in case I am arrested."

"Arrested? For what?"

"For murder. It is quite on the cards. I wish to be ready for every event. There is only one course open to me, and I am determined to take it."

"For Heaven's sake, don't do anything rash!"

"Believe me, it would be far more rash to adopt any other course. I hope that we won't need to bother you, but it will ease my mind to know that you have this statement of my motives. And now I am ready to take your advice and to go to roost, for I want to be at my best in the morning."

Abercrombie Smith was not an entirely pleasant man to have as an enemy. Slow and easy tempered, he was formidable when driven to action. He brought to every purpose in life the same deliberate resoluteness which had distinguished him as a scientific student. He had laid his studies aside for a day, but he intended that the day should not be wasted. Not a word did he say to his host as to his plans, but by nine o'clock he was well on his way to Oxford.

In the High Street he stopped at Clifford's, the gun-maker's, and bought a heavy revolver, with a box of central-fire cartridges. Six of them he slipped into the chambers, and half-cocking the weapon, placed it in the pocket of his coat. He then made his way to Hastie's rooms, where the big oarsman was lounging over his breakfast, with the *Sporting Times* propped up against the coffeepot.

"Hello! What's up?" he asked. "Have some coffee?"

"No, thank you. I want you to come with me, Hastie, and do what I ask you."

"Certainly, my boy."

"And bring a heavy stick with you."

"Hello!" Hastie stared. "Here's a hunting-crop that would fell an ox."

"One other thing. You have a box of amputating knives. Give me the longest of them."

"There you are. You seem to be fairly on the war trail. Anything else?"

"No; that will do." Smith placed the knife inside his coat, and led the way to the quadrangle. "We are neither of us chickens, Hastie," said he. "I think I can do this job alone, but I take you as a precaution. I am going to have a little talk with Bellingham. If I have only him to deal with, I won't, of course, need you. If I shout, however, up you come, and lam out with your whip as hard as you can lick. Do you understand?"

"All right. I'll come if I hear you bellow."

"Stay here, then. It may be a little time, but don't budge until I come down."

"I'm a fixture."

Smith ascended the stairs, opened Bellingham's door and stepped in. Bellingham was seated behind his table, writing. Beside him, among his litter of strange possessions, towered the mummy case, with its sale number 249 still stuck upon its front, and its hideous occupant stiff and stark within it. Smith looked very deliberately round him, closed the door, locked it, took the key from the inside, and then stepping across to the fireplace, struck a match and set the fire alight. Bellingham sat staring, with amazement and rage upon his bloated face.

"Well, really now, you make yourself at home," he gasped.

Smith sat himself deliberately down, placing his watch upon the table, drew out his pistol, cocked it, and laid it in his lap. Then he took the long amputating knife from his bosom, and threw it down in front of Bellingham.

"Now, then," said he, "just get to work and cut up that mummy."

"Oh, is that it?" said Bellingham with a sneer.

"Yes, that is it. They tell me that the law can't touch you. But I have a law that will set matters straight. If in five minutes you have not set to work, I swear by the God who made me that I will put a bullet through your brain!"

"You would murder me?"

Bellingham had half risen, and his face was the color of putty.

"Yes."

"And for what?"

"To stop your mischief. One minute has gone."

"But what have I done?"

"I know and you know."

"This is mere bullying."

"Two minutes are gone."

"But you must give reasons. You are a madman—a dangerous madman. Why should I destroy my own property? It is a valuable mummy."

"You must cut it up, and you must burn it."

"I will do no such thing."

"Four minutes are gone."

Smith took up the pistol and he looked towards Bellingham with an inexorable face. As the second-hand stole round, he raised his hand, and the finger twitched upon the trigger.

"There! there! I'll do it!" screamed Bellingham.

In frantic haste he caught up the knife and hacked at the figure of the mummy, ever glancing round to see the eye and the weapon of his terrible visitor bent upon him. The creature crackled and snapped under every stab of the keen blade. A thick yellow dust rose up from it. Spices and dried essences rained down upon the floor. Suddenly, with a rending crack, its backbone snapped asunder, and it fell, a brown heap of sprawling limbs, upon the floor.

"Now into the fire!" said Smith.

The flames leaped and roared as the dried and tinder-like debris was piled upon it. The little room was like the stoke-hole of a steamer and the sweat ran down the faces of the two men; but still the one stooped and worked, while the other sat watching him with a set face. A thick, fat smoke oozed out from the fire, and a heavy smell of burned rosin and singed hair filled the air. In a quarter of an hour a few charred and brittle sticks were all that was left of Lot No. 249.

"Perhaps that will satisfy you," snarled Bellingham, with hate and fear in his little gray eyes as he glanced back at his tormenter.

"No; I must make a clean sweep of all your materials. We must have no more devil's tricks. In with all these leaves! They may have something to do with it."

"And what now?" asked Bellingham, when the leaves also had been added to the blaze.

"Now the roll of papyrus which you had on the table that night. It is in that drawer, I think."

"No, no," shouted Bellingham. "Don't burn that! Why, man, you don't know what you do. It is unique; it contains wisdom which is nowhere else to be found."

"Out with it!"

"But look here, Smith, you can't really mean it. I'll share the knowledge with you. I'll teach you all that is in it. Or, stay, let me only copy it before you burn it!"

Smith stepped forward and turned the key in the drawer. Taking out the yellow, curled roll of paper, he threw it into the fire, and pressed it down with his heel. Bellingham screamed, and grabbed at it; but Smith pushed him back, and stood over it until it was reduced to a formless gray ash.

"Now, Master B.," said he, "I think I have pretty well drawn your teeth. You'll hear from me again, if you return to your old tricks. And now good-morning, for I must go back to my studies."

And such is the narrative of Abercrombie Smith as to the singular events which occurred in Old College, Oxford, in the spring of '84. As Bellingham left the university immediately afterwards, and was last heard of in the Sudan, there is no one who can contradict his statement. But the wisdom of men is small, and the ways of nature are strange, and who shall put a bound to the dark things which may be found by those who seek for them?

Fiction

THE LOCKED
TOMB MYSTERY

Elizabeth Peters

"Elizabeth Peters" is one of the pen names of Dr. Barbara Mertz, who is also known as "Barbara Michaels." Mertz received her doctorate in Egyptology and has written a couple of scholarly books on the subject. As Peters and Michaels she has written over fifty novels—everything from gothic to mystery to romance. Generally the twenty-seven Michaels books are more supernatural, while the Peters books are generally detective mysteries. Under the Elizabeth Peters name she has written a wonderful series of Egyptian mysteries featuring a Victorian feminist archaeologist named Amelia Peabody Emerson. So far this series includes The Hippopotamus Pool, Crocodile on the Sandbank, The Ape Who Guards the Balance, Lion in the Valley, Deeds of the Disturber, He Shall Thunder in the Sky, The Last Camel Died at Noon, The Snake, the Crocodile, and the Dog, Seeing a Large Cat, The Falcon at the Portal, The Curse of the Pharaohs, *and* The Mummy Case. *It just didn't seem right to me to put together an anthology of stories on mummies and Ancient Egypt without including something by her, so with the help of Mertz's assistant, I found the following story, which appears to be her only Egyptian short story. And of all the stories in this book, this one is probably the most historically accurate.*

Senebtisi's funeral was the talk of southern Thebes. Of course, it could not compare with the burials of Great Ones and Pharaohs, whose Houses of Eternity were furnished with gold and fine linen and precious gems, but ours was not a quarter where nobles lived; our people were craftsmen and small merchants, able to afford a chamber-tomb and a coffin and a few spells to ward off the perils of the Western Road—no more than that. We had never seen anything like the burial of the old woman who had been our neighbor for so many years.

The night after the funeral, the customers of Nehi's tavern could talk of nothing else. I remember that evening well. For one thing, I had just won my first appointment as a temple scribe. I was looking forward to boasting a little, and perhaps paying for a round of beer, if my friends displayed proper appreciation of my good fortune. Three of the others were already at the tavern when I arrived, my linen shawl wrapped tight around me. The weather was cold even for winter, with a cruel, dry wind driving sand into every crevice of the body.

"Close the door quickly," said Senu, the carpenter. "What weather! I wonder if the Western journey will be like this—cold enough to freeze a man's bones."

This prompted a ribald comment from Rennefer, the weaver, concerning the effects of freezing on certain of Senebtisi's vital organs. "Not that anyone would notice the difference," he added. "There was never any warmth in the old hag. What sort of mother would take all her possessions to the next world and leave her only son penniless?"

"Is it true, then?" I asked, signaling Nehi to fetch the beer jar. "I have heard stories—"

"All true," said the potter, Baenre. "It is a pity you could not attend the burial, Wadjsen; it was magnificent!"

"You went?" I inquired. "That was good of you, since she ordered none of her funerary equipment from you."

Baenre is a scanty little man with thin hair and sharp bones. It is said that he is a domestic tyrant, and that his wife cowers when he comes roaring home from the tavern, but when he is with us, his voice is almost a whisper. "My rough kitchenware would not be good enough to hold the wine and fine oil she took to the tomb. Wadjsen, you should have seen the boxes and jars and baskets—dozens of them. They say she had a gold mask, like the ones worn by great nobles, and that all her ornaments were of solid gold."

"It is true," said Rennefer. "I know a man who knows one of the servants of Bakenmut, the goldsmith who made the ornaments."

"How is her son taking it?" I asked. I knew Minmose slightly; a shy, serious man, he followed his father's trade of stone carving. His mother had lived with him all his life, greedily scooping up his profits, though she had money of her own, inherited from her parents.

"Why, as you would expect," said Senu, shrugging. "Have you ever heard him speak harshly to anyone, much less his mother? She was an old she-goat who treated him like a boy who has not cut off the side lock; but with him it was always 'Yes, honored mother,' and 'As you say, honored mother.' She would not even allow him to take a wife."

"How will he live?"

"Oh, he has the shop and the business, such as it is. He is a hard worker; he will survive."

In the following months I heard occasional news of Minmose.

Gossip said he must be doing well, for he had taken to spending his leisure time at a local house of prostitution—a pleasure he never had dared enjoy while his mother lived. Nefertiry, the loveliest and most expensive of the girls, was the object of his desire, and Rennefer remarked that the maiden must have a kind heart, for she could command higher prices than Minmose was able to pay. However, as time passed, I forgot Minmose and Senebtisi, and her rich burial. It was not until almost a year later that the matter was recalled to my attention.

The rumors began in the marketplace, at the end of the time of inundation, when the floodwater lay on the fields and the farmers were idle. They enjoy this time, but the police of the city do not; for idleness leads to crime, and one of the most popular crimes is tomb robbing. This goes on all the time in a small way, but when the Pharaoh is strong and stern, and the laws are strictly enforced, it is a very risky trade. A man stands to lose more than a hand or an ear if he is caught. He also risks damnation after he has entered his own tomb; but some men simply do not have proper respect for the gods.

The king, Nebmaatre (may he live forever!), was then in his prime, so there had been no tomb robbing for some time—or at least none had been detected. But, the rumors said, three men of west Thebes had been caught trying to sell ornaments such as are buried with the dead. The rumors turned out to be correct, for once. The men were questioned on the soles of their feet and confessed to the robbing of several tombs.

Naturally all those who had kin buried on the west bank—which included most of us—were alarmed by this news, and half the nervous matrons in our neighborhood went rushing across the river to make sure the family tombs were safe. I was not surprised to hear that that dutiful son Minmose had also felt obliged to make sure his mother had not been disturbed.

However, I was surprised at the news that greeted me when I paid my next visit to Nehi's tavern. The moment I entered, the others began to talk at once, each eager to be the first to tell the shocking facts.

"Robbed?" I repeated when I had sorted out the babble of voices. "Do you speak truly?"

"I do not know why you should doubt it," said Rennefer. "The richness of her burial was the talk of the city, was it not? Just what the tomb robbers like! They made a clean sweep of all the gold, and ripped the poor old hag's mummy to shreds."

At that point we were joined by another of the habitués, Merusir. He is a pompous, fat man who considers himself superior to the rest of us because he is Fifth Prophet of Amon. We put up with his patronizing ways because sometimes he knows court gossip. On that particular evening it was apparent that he was bursting with excitement. He listened with a supercilious sneer while we told him the sensational news. "I know, I know," he drawled. "I heard it much earlier—and with it, the other news which is known only to those in the confidence of the Palace."

He paused, ostensibly to empty his cup. Of course, we reacted as he had hoped we would, begging him to share the secret. Finally he condescended to inform us.

"Why, the amazing thing is not the robbery itself, but how it was done. The tomb entrance was untouched, the seals of the necropolis were unbroken. The tomb itself is entirely rock-cut, and there was not the slightest break in the walls or floor or ceiling. Yet when Minmose entered the burial chamber, he found the coffin open, the mummy mutilated, and the gold ornaments gone."

We stared at him, openmouthed.

"It is a most remarkable story," I said.

"Call me a liar if you like," said Merusir, who knows the language of polite insult as well as I do. "There was a witness—two, if you count Minmose himself. The sem-priest Wennefer was with him."

This silenced the critics. Wennefer was known to us all. There was not a man in southern Thebes with a higher reputation. Even Senebtisi had been fond of him, and she was not fond of many people. He had officiated at her funeral.

Pleased at the effect of his announcement, Merusir went on in his most pompous manner. "The king himself has taken an interest in the matter. He has called on Amenhotep Sa Hapu to investigate."

"Amenhotep?" I exclaimed. "But I know him well."

"You do?" Merusir's plump cheeks sagged like bladders punctured by a sharp knife.

Now, at that time Amenhotep's name was not in the mouth of everyone, though he had taken the first steps on that astonishing career that was to make him the intimate friend of Pharaoh. When I first met him, he had been a poor, insignificant priest at a local shrine. I had been sent to fetch him to the house where my master lay dead of a stab wound, presumably murdered. Amenhotep's fame had begun with that matter, for he had discovered the truth and saved an innocent man from execution. Since then he had handled several other cases, with equal success.

My exclamation had taken the wind out of Merusir's sails. He had hoped to impress us by telling us something we did not know. Instead it was I who enlightened the others about Amenhotep's triumphs. But when I finished, Rennefer shook his head.

"If this wise man is all you say, Wadjsen, it will be like inviting a lion to rid the house of mice. He will find there is a simple explanation. No doubt the thieves entered the burial chamber from above or from one side, tunneling through the rock. Minmose and Wennefer were too shocked to observe the hole in the wall, that is all."

We argued the matter for some time, growing more and more heated as the level of the beer in the jar dropped. It was a foolish argument, for none of us knew the facts; and to argue without knowledge is like trying to weave without thread.

This truth did not occur to me until the cool night breeze had cleared my head, when I was halfway home. I decided to pay Amenhotep a visit. The next time I went to the tavern, I would be the one to tell the latest news, and Merusir would be nothing!

Most of the honest householders had retired, but there were lamps burning in the street of the prostitutes, and in a few taverns. There was a light, as well, in one window of the house where Amenhotep lodged. Like the owl he resembled, with his beaky nose and large, close-set eyes, he preferred to work at night.

The window was on the ground floor, so I knocked on the wooden shutter, which of course was closed to keep out night demons. After a few moments the shutter opened, and the familiar nose appeared. I spoke my name, and Amenhotep went to open the door.

"Wadjsen! It has been a long time," he exclaimed. "Should I ask what brings you here, or shall I display my talents as a seer and tell you?"

"I suppose it requires no great talent," I replied. "The matter of Senebtisi's tomb is already the talk of the district."

"So I had assumed." He gestured me to sit down and hospitably indicated the wine jar that stood in the corner. I shook my head.

"I have already taken too much beer, at the tavern. I am sorry to disturb you so late—"

"I am always happy to see you, Wadjsen." His big dark eyes reflected the light of the lamp, so that they seemed to hold stars in their depths. "I have missed my assistant, who helped me to the truth in my first inquiry."

"I was of little help to you then," I said with a smile. "And in this case I am even more ignorant. The thing is a great mystery, known only to the gods."

"No, no!" He clapped his hands together, as was his habit when annoyed with the stupidity of his hearer. "There is no mystery. I know who robbed the tomb of Senebtisi. The only difficulty is to prove how it was done."

At Amenhotep's suggestion I spent the night at his house so that I could accompany him when he set out next morning to find the proof he needed. I required little urging, for I was afire with curiosity. Though I pressed him, he would say no more, merely remarking piously, "'A man may fall to ruin because of his tongue; if a passing remark is hasty and it is repeated, thou wilt make enemies.'"

I could hardly dispute the wisdom of this adage, but the gleam in Amenhotep's bulging black eyes made me suspect he took a malicious pleasure in my bewilderment.

After our morning bread and beer we went to the temple of Khonsu, where the sem-priest Wennefer worked in the records office. He was copying accounts from pottery ostraca onto a papyrus that was stretched across his lap. All scribes develop bowed shoulders from bending over their writing; Wennefer was folded almost double, his face scant inches from the surface of the papyrus. When Amenhotep cleared his throat, the old man started, smearing the ink. He waved our apologies aside and cleaned the papyrus with a wad of lint.

"No harm was meant, no harm is done," he said in his breathy, chirping voice. "I have heard of you, Amenhotep Sa Hapu; it is an honor to meet you."

"I, too, have looked forward to meeting you, Wennefer. Alas that the occasion should be such a sad one."

Wennefer's smile faded. "Ah, the matter of Senebtisi's tomb. What a tragedy! At least the poor woman can now have a proper reburial. If Minmose had not insisted on opening the tomb, her *ba* would have gone hungry and thirsty through eternity."

"Then the tomb entrance really was sealed and undisturbed?" I asked skeptically.

"I examined it myself," Wennefer said. "Minmose had asked me to meet him after the day's work, and we arrived at the tomb as the sun was setting; but the light was still good. I conducted the funeral service for Senebtisi, you know. I had seen the doorway blocked and mortared and with my own hands had helped to press the seals of the necropolis onto the wet plaster. All was as I had left it that day a year ago."

"Yet Minmose insisted on opening the tomb?" Amenhotep asked.

"Why, we agreed it should be done," the old man said mildly. "As you know, robbers sometimes tunnel in from above or from one side, leaving the entrance undisturbed. Minmose had brought tools. He did most of the work himself, for these old hands of mine are better with a pen than a chisel. When the doorway was clear, Minmose lit a lamp and we entered. We were crossing the hall beyond the entrance corridor when Minmose let out a shriek. 'My mother, my mother,' he cried—oh, it was pitiful to hear! Then I saw it too. The thing—the thing on the floor. . . ."

"You speak of the mummy, I presume," said Amenhotep. "The thieves had dragged it from the coffin out into the hall?"

"Where they despoiled it," Wennefer whispered. "The august body was ripped open from throat to groin, through the shroud and the wrappings and the flesh."

"Curious," Amenhotep muttered, as if to himself. "Tell me, Wennefer, what is the plan of the tomb?"

Wennefer rubbed his brush on the ink cake and began to draw on the back surface of one of the ostraca.

"It is a fine tomb, Amenhotep, entirely rock-cut. Beyond the entrance is a flight of stairs and a short corridor, thus leading to a hall broader than it is long, with two pillars. Beyond that, another short corridor; then the burial chamber. The august mummy lay here." And he inked in a neat circle at the beginning of the second corridor.

"Ha," said Amenhotep, studying the plan. "Yes, yes, I see. Go on, Wennefer. What did you do next?"

"I did nothing," the old man said simply. "Minmose's hand shook so violently that he dropped the lamp. Darkness closed in. I felt the presence of the demons who had defiled the dead. My tongue clove to the roof of my mouth and—"

"Dreadful," Amenhotep said. "But you were not far from the tomb entrance; you could find your way out?"

"Yes, yes, it was only a dozen paces; and by Amon, my friend, the sunset light has never appeared so sweet! I went at once to fetch the necropolis guards. When we returned to the tomb, Minmose had rekindled his lamp—"

"I thought you said the lamp was broken."

"Dropped, but fortunately not broken. Minmose had opened one of the jars of oil—Senebtisi had many such in the tomb, all of the finest quality—and had refilled the lamp. He had replaced the mummy in its coffin and was kneeling by it praying. Never was there so pious a son!"

"So then, I suppose, the guards searched for the tomb."

"We all searched," Wennefer said. "The tomb chamber was in a dreadful state; boxes and baskets had been broken open and the contents strewn about. Every object of precious metal had been stolen, including the amulets on the body."

"What about the oil, the linen, and the other valuables?" Amenhotep asked.

"The oil and the wine were in large jars, impossible to move easily. About the other things I cannot say; everything was in such confusion—and I do not know what was there to begin with. Even Minmose was not certain; his mother had filled and sealed most of the boxes herself. But I know what was taken from the mummy, for I saw the golden amulets and ornaments placed on it when it was wrapped by the embalmers. I do not like to speak evil of anyone, but you know, Amenhotep, that the embalmers . . ."

"Yes," Amenhotep agreed with a sour face. "I myself watched the wrapping of my father; there is no other way to make certain the ornaments will go on the mummy instead of into the coffers of the embalmers. Minmose did not perform this service for his mother?"

"Of course he did. He asked me to share in the watch, and I was glad to agree. He is the most pious—"

"So I have heard," said Amenhotep. "Tell me again, Wennefer, of the condition of the mummy. You examined it?"

"It was my duty. Oh, Amenhotep, it was a sad sight! The shroud was still tied firmly around the body; the thieves had cut straight through it and through the bandages beneath, baring the body. The arm bones were broken, so roughly had the thieves dragged the heavy gold bracelets from them."

"And the mask?" I asked. "It was said that she had a mask of solid gold."

"It, too, was missing."

"Horrible," Amenhotep said. "Wennefer, we have kept you from your work long enough. Only one more question. How do you think the thieves entered the tomb?"

The old man's eyes fell. "Through me," he whispered.

I gave Amenhotep a startled look. He shook his head warningly.

"It was not your fault," he said, touching Wennefer's bowed shoulder.

"It was. I did my best, but I must have omitted some vital part of the ritual. How else could demons enter the tomb?"

"Oh, I see." Amenhotep stroked his chin. "Demons."

"It could have been nothing else. The seals on the door were intact, the mortar untouched. There was no break of the smallest size in the stone of the walls or ceiling or floor."

"But—" I began.

"And there is this. When the doorway was clear and the light entered, the dust lay undisturbed on the floor. The only marks on it were the strokes of the broom with which Minmose, according to custom, had swept the floor as he left the tomb after the funeral service."

"Amon preserve us," I exclaimed, feeling a chill run through me.

Amenhotep's eyes moved from Wennefer to me, then back to Wennefer. "That is conclusive," he murmured.

"Yes," Wennefer said with a groan. "And I am to blame—I, a priest who failed at his task."

"No," said Amenhotep. "You did not fail. Be of good cheer, my friend. There is another explanation."

Wennefer shook his head despondently. "Minmose said the same, but he was only being kind, poor man! He was so overcome, he could scarcely walk. The guards had to take him by the arms to lead him from the tomb. I carried his tools. It was the least—"

"The tools," Amenhotep interrupted. "They were in a bag or a sack?"

"Why, no. He had only a chisel and a mallet. I carried them in my hand as he had done."

Amenhotep thanked him again, and we took our leave. As we crossed the courtyard I waited for him to speak, but he remained silent; and after a while I could contain myself no longer.

"Do you still believe you know who robbed the tomb?"

"Yes, yes, it is obvious."

"And it was not demons?"

Amenhotep blinked at me like an owl blinded by sunlight.

"Demons are a last resort."

He had the smug look of a man who thinks he has said something clever; but his remark smacked of heresy to me, and I looked at him doubtfully.

"Come, come," he snapped. "Senebtisi was a selfish, greedy old woman, and if there is justice in the next world, as our faith decrees, her path through the Underworld will not be easy. But why would diabolical powers play tricks with her mummy when they could torment her spirit? Demons have no need of gold."

"Well, but—"

"Your wits used not to be so dull. What do you think happened?"

"If it was not demons—"

"It was not."

"Then someone must have broken in."

"Very clever," said Amenhotep, grinning.

"I mean that there must be an opening, in the walls or the floor, that Wennefer failed to see."

"Wennefer, perhaps. The necropolis guards, no. The chambers of the tomb were cut out of solid rock. It would be impossible to disguise a break in such a surface, even if tomb robbers took the trouble to fill it in—which they never have been known to do."

"Then the thieves entered through the doorway and closed it again. A dishonest craftsman could make a copy of the necropolis seal. . . ."

"Good." Amenhotep clapped me on the shoulder. "Now you are beginning to think. It is an ingenious idea, but it is wrong. Tomb robbers work in haste, for fear of the necropolis guards. They would not linger to replace stones and mortar and seals."

"Then I do not know how it was done."

"Ah, Wadjsen, you are dense! There is only one person who could have robbed the tomb."

"I thought of that," I said stiffly, hurt by his raillery. "Minmose was the last to leave the tomb and the first to reenter it. He had good reason to desire the gold his mother should have left to him. But, Amenhotep, he could not have robbed the mummy on either occasion; there was not time. You know the funeral ritual as well as I. When the priests and mourners leave the tomb, they leave together. If Minmose had lingered in the burial chamber, even for a few minutes, his delay would have been noted and remarked upon."

"That is quite true," said Amenhotep.

"Also," I went on, "the gold was heavy as well as bulky. Minmose could not have carried it away without someone noticing."

"Again you speak truly."

"Then unless Wennefer the priest is conspiring with Minmose—"

"That good, simple man? I am surprised at you, Wadjsen. Wennefer is as honest as the Lady of Truth herself."

"Demons—"

Amenhotep interrupted with the hoarse hooting sound that passed for a laugh with him. "Stop babbling of demons. There is one man besides myself who knows how Senebtisi's tomb was violated. Let us go and see him."

He quickened his pace, his sandals slapping in the dust. I followed, trying to think. His taunts were like weights that pulled my mind to its farthest limits. I began to get an inkling of truth, but I could not make sense of it. I said nothing, not even when we turned into the lane south of the temple that led to the house of Minmose.

There was no servant at the door. Minmose himself answered our summons. I greeted him and introduced Amenhotep.

Minmose lifted his hands in surprise. "You honor my house, Amen-hotep. Enter and be seated."

Amenhotep shook his head. "I will not stay, Minmose. I came only to tell you who desecrated your mother's tomb."

"What?" Minmose gaped at him. "Already you know? But how? It is a great mystery, beyond—"

"You did it, Minmose."

Minmose turned a shade paler. But that was not out of the way; even the innocent might blanch at such an accusation.

"You are mad," he said. "Forgive me, you are my guest, but—"

"There is no other possible explanation," Amenhotep said. "You stole the gold when you entered the tomb two days ago."

"But, Amenhotep," I exclaimed. "Wennefer was with him, and Wen-nefer saw the mummy already robbed when—"

"Wennefer did not see the mummy," Amenhotep said. "The tomb was dark; the only light was that of a small lamp, which Minmose promptly dropped. Wennefer has poor sight. Did you not observe how he bent over his writing? He caught only a glimpse of a white shape, the size of a wrapped mummy, before the light went out. When next Wennefer saw the mummy, it was in the coffin, and his view of it then colored his confused memory of the first supposed sighting of it. Few people are good observers. They see what they expect to see."

"Then what did he see?" I demanded. Minmose might not have been there. Amenhotep avoided looking at him.

"A piece of linen in the rough shape of a human form, arranged on the floor by the last person who left the tomb. It would have taken him only a moment to do this before he snatched up the broom and swept himself out."

"So the tomb was sealed and closed," I exclaimed. "For almost a year he waited—"

"Until the next outbreak of tomb robbing. Minmose could assume this would happen sooner or later; it always does. He thought he was being clever by asking Wennefer to accompany him—a witness of irreproachable character who could testify that the tomb entrance was untouched. In fact, he was too careful to avoid being compromised; that would have made me doubt him, even if the logic of the facts had not pointed directly at him. Asking that same virtuous man to share his supervision of the mummy wrapping, lest he be suspected of connivance with the embalmers; feigning weakness so that the necropolis guards would have to support him, and thus be in a position to swear he could not have concealed the gold on his person. Only a guilty man would be so anxious to appear innocent. Yet there was reason for his precautions. Sometime in the near future, when that loving son Minmose discovers a store of gold hidden in the house, overlooked by his mother—the old do forget sometimes—then, since men have evil minds, it might be necessary for Minmose to prove beyond a shadow of a doubt that he could not have laid hands on his mother's burial equipment."

Minmose remained dumb, his eyes fixed on the ground. It was I who responded as he should have, questioning and objecting.

"But how did he remove the gold? The guards and Wennefer searched the tomb, so it was not hidden there, and there was not time for him to bury it outside."

"No, but there was ample time for him to do what had to be done in the burial chamber after Wennefer had tottered off to fetch the guards. He overturned boxes and baskets, opened the coffin, ripped through the mummy wrappings with his chisel, and took the gold. It would not take long, especially for one who knew exactly where each ornament had been placed."

Minmose's haggard face was as good as an admission of guilt. He did not look up or speak, even when Amenhotep put a hand on his shoulder.

"I pity you, Minmose," Amenhotep said gravely. "After years of devotion and self-denial, to see yourself deprived of your inheritance . . . And there was Nefertiry. You had been visiting her in secret, even before your mother died, had you not? Oh, Minmose, you should have remembered the words of the sage: 'Do not go in to a woman who is a stranger; it is a great crime, worthy of death.' She has brought you to your death, Minmose. You knew she would turn from you if your mother left you nothing."

Minmose's face was gray. "Will you denounce me, then? They will beat me to make me confess."

"Any man will confess when he is beaten," said Amenhotep, with a curl of his lip. "No, Minmose, I will not denounce you. The court of the vizier demands facts, not theories, and you have covered your tracks very neatly. But you will not escape justice. Nefertiry will consume your gold as the desert sands drink water, and then she will cast you off; and all the while Anubis, the Guide of the Dead, and Osiris, the Divine Judge, will be waiting for you. They will eat your heart, Minmose, and your spirit will hunger and thirst through all eternity. I think your punishment has already begun.

Do you dream, Minmose? Did you see your mother's face last night, wrinkled and withered, her sunken eyes accusing you, as it looked when you tore the gold mask from it?"

A long shudder ran through Minmose's body. Even his hair seemed to shiver and rise. Amenhotep gestured to me. We went away, leaving Minmose staring after us with a face like death.

After we had gone a short distance, I said, "There is one more thing to tell, Amenhotep."

"There is much to tell." Amenhotep sighed deeply. "Of a good man turned evil; of two women who, in their different ways, drove him to crime; of the narrow line that separates the virtuous man from the sinner. . . ."

"I do not speak of that. I do not wish to think of that. It makes me feel strange. . . . The gold, Amenhotep—how did Minmose bear away the gold from his mother's burial?"

"He put it in the oil jar," said Amenhotep. "The one he opened to get fresh fuel for his lamp. Who would wonder if, in his agitation, he spilled a quantity of oil on the floor? He has certainly removed it by now. He has had ample opportunity, running back and forth with objects to be repaired or replaced."

"And the piece of linen he had put down to look like the mummy?"

"As you well know," Amenhotep replied, "the amount of linen used to wrap a mummy is prodigious. He could have crumpled that piece and thrown it in among the torn wrappings. But I think he did something else. It was a cool evening, in winter, and Minmose would have worn a linen mantle. He took the cloth out in the same way he had brought it in. Who would notice an extra fold of linen over a man's shoulders?

"I knew immediately that Minmose must be the guilty party, because he was the only one who had the opportunity, but I did not see how he had managed it until Wennefer showed me where the supposed mummy lay. There was no reason for a thief to drag it so far from the coffin and the burial chamber—but Minmose could not afford to have Wennefer catch even a glimpse of that room, which was then undisturbed. I realized then that what the old man had seen was not the mummy at all, but a substitute."

"Then Minmose will go unpunished."

"I said he would be punished. I spoke truly." Again Amenhotep sighed.

"You will not denounce him to Pharaoh?"

"I will tell my lord the truth. But he will not choose to act. There will be no need."

He said no more. But six weeks later Minmose's body was found floating in the river. He had taken to drinking heavily, and people said he drowned by accident. But I knew it was otherwise. Anubis and Osiris had eaten his heart, just as Amenhotep had said.

Author's note: Amenhotep Sa Hapu was a real person who lived during the fourteenth century B.C. Later generations worshiped him as a sage and scholar; he seems like a logical candidate for the role of ancient Egyptian detective.

Fiction

THE DEATH-RING OF SNEFERU

Sax Rohmer

"Sax Rohmer" is the nom de plume of Arthur Sarsfield Ward, who was the creator of the diabolically evil villain Dr. Fu Manchu. He was the author of over fifty novels and short story collections—thirteen of them featuring Fu Manchu. Some were adapted for radio, movies, and a television series. Boris Karloff, Christopher Lee, and Peter Sellers all played the sinister Fu Manchu in various films. Rohmer's books include The Shadow of Fu-Manchu, The Golden Scorpion, Egyptian Nights, Tales of Secret Egypt, *and* The Green Eyes of Bast. *A number of his stories feature mummies, but the supernatural aspects generally turn out to have ordinary explanations. Of his many Egyptian tales, I have chosen this thrilling story of an antiquities dealer who jumps into an adventure that's over his head.*

I

The orchestra had just ceased playing; and, taking advantage of the lull in the music, my companion leaned confidentially forward, shooting suspicious glances all around him, although there was nothing about the well-dressed after-dinner throng filling Shepheard's that night to have aroused misgiving in the mind of a cinema anarchist.

"I have a very big thing in view," he said, speaking in a husky whisper. "I shall be one up on you, Kernaby, if I pull it off."

He glanced sideways, in the manner of a pantomime brigand, at a party of New York tourists, our immediate neighbors, and from them to an elderly peer with whom I was slightly acquainted and who, in addition to his being stone deaf, had never noticed anything in his life, much less attempted so fatiguing an operation as intrigue.

"Indeed," I commented; and rang the bell with the purpose in view of ordering another cooling beverage.

True, I might be the Egyptian representative of a Birmingham commercial enterprise, but I did not gladly suffer the society of this individual, whose only claim to my acquaintance lay in the fact that he was in the employ of a rival house. My lack of interest palpably disappointed him; but I thought little of the man's qualities as a connoisseur and less of his company. His name was Theo Bishop and I fancy that his family was associated with the tanning industry. I have since thought more kindly of poor Bishop, but at the time of which I write nothing could have pleased me better than his sudden dissolution.

Perhaps unconsciously I had allowed my boredom to become rudely apparent; for Bishop slightly turned his head aside, and—

"Right-o, Kernaby," he said; "I know you think I am an ass, so we will say no more about it. Another cocktail?"

And now I became conscience-stricken; for mingled with the disappointment in Bishop's tone and manner was another note. Vaguely it occurred to me that the man was yearning for sympathy of some kind, that he was bursting to unbosom himself, and that the vanity of a successful rival was by no means wholly responsible. I have since placed that ambiguous note and recognized it for a note of tragedy. But at the time I was deaf to its pleading.

We chatted then for some while longer on indifferent topics, Bishop being, as I have indicated, a man difficult to offend; when, having correspondence to deal with, I retired to my own room. I suppose I had been writing for about an hour, when a servant came to announce a caller. Taking an ordinary visiting-card from the brass salver, I read—

ABÛ TABÂH.

No title preceded the name, no address followed, but I became aware of something very like a nervous thrill as I stared at the name of my visitor. Personality is one of the profoundest mysteries of our being. Of the person whose card I held in my hand I knew little, practically nothing; his actions, if at times irregular, had never been wantonly violent; his manner was gentle as that of a mother to a baby and his singular reputation among the natives I thought I could afford to ignore; for the Egyptian, like the Celt, with all his natural endowments, is yet a child at heart. Therefore I cannot explain why, sitting there in my room in Shepheard's Hotel, I knew and recognized, at the name of Abû Tabâh, the touch of fear.

"I will see him downstairs," I said.

Then, as the servant was about to depart, recognizing that I had made a concession to that strange sentiment which the Imám Abû Tabâh had somehow inspired in me—

"No," I added; "show him up here to my room."

A few moments later the man returned again, carrying the brass salver, upon which lay a sealed envelope. I took it up in surprise, noting that it was one belonging to the hotel, and, ere opening it—

"Where is my visitor?" I said in Arabic.

"He regrets that he cannot stay," replied the man; "but he sends you this letter."

Greatly mystified, I dismissed the servant and tore open the envelope. Inside, upon a sheet of hotel notepaper I found this remarkable message—

KERNABY PASHA—

There are reasons why I cannot stay to see you personally, but I would have you believe that this warning is dictated by nothing but friendship. Grave peril threatens. It is associated with the hieroglyphic—

If you would avert it, and if you value your life, avoid all contact with anything bearing this figure.

ABÛ TABÂH

The mystery deepened. There had been something incongruous about
the modern European visiting-card used by this representative of Islam, this
living illustration of the *Arabian Nights;* now, his incomprehensible "warning" plunged me back again into the medieval Orient to which he properly
belonged. Yet I knew Abû Tabâh, for all his romantic aspect, to be emi-
nently practical, and I could not credit him with descending to the methods
of melodrama.

As I studied the precise wording of the note, I seemed to see the slim
figure of its author before me, black-robed, white-turbaned, and urbane, his
delicate ivory hands crossed and resting upon the head of the ebony cane
without which I had never seen him. Almost, I succumbed to a sort of sub-
jective hallucination; Abû Tabâh became a veritable presence, and the poetic
beauty of his face struck me anew, as, fixing upon me his eyes, which were
like the eyes of a gazelle, he spoke the strange words cited above, in the pure
and polished English which he held at command, and described in the air,
with a long nervous forefinger, the queer device which symbolized the Ancient Egyptian god, Set, the Destroyer.

Of course, it was the aura of a powerful personality, clinging even to the
written message; but there was something about the impression made upon
me which argued for the writer's sincerity.

That Abû Tabâh was some kind of agent, recognized—at any rate unof-
ficially—by the authorities, I knew or shrewdly surmised; but the exact nature of his activities, and how he reconciled them with his religious duties,
remained profoundly mysterious. The episode had rendered further work
impossible, and I descended to the terrace, with no more definite object in
view than that of finding a quiet corner where I might meditate in the congenial society of my briar, and at the same time seek inspiration from the
ever-changing throng in the Shâria Kâmel Pasha.

I had scarcely set my foot upon the terrace, however, ere a hand was laid
upon my arm. Turning quickly I recognized, in the dusk, Hassan es-Sugra,
for many years a trusted employee of the British Archeological Society.

His demeanor was at once excited and furtive, and I recognized with something akin to amazement that he, also, had a story to unfold. I mentally catalogued this eventful evening "the night of strange confidences."

Seated at a little table on the deserted balcony (for the evening was very chilly) and directly facing the shop of Philip, the dealer in Arab woodwork, Hassan es-Sugra told his wonder tale; and as he told it I knew that Fate had cast me, willy-nilly, for a part in some comedy upon which the curtain had already risen here in Cairo, and whereof the second act should be played in perhaps the most ancient setting which the hand of man has built. As the narrative unrolled itself before me, I perceived wheels within wheels; I was wholly absorbed, yet half incredulous.

". . . When the professor abandoned work on the pyramid, Kernaby Pasha," he said, bending eagerly forward and laying his muscular brown hand upon my sleeve, "it was not because there was no more to learn there."

"I am aware of this, O Hassan," I interrupted, "it was in order that they might carry on the work at the Pyramid of Illahûn, which resulted in a find of jewelry almost unique in the annals of Egyptology."

"Do I not know all this!" exclaimed Hassan impatiently; "and was not mine the hand that uncovered the golden uræus [i.e., serpent headdress]? But the work projected at the Pyramid of Méydûm was never completed, and I can tell you why."

I stared at him through the gloom; for I had already some idea respecting the truth of this matter.

"It was that the men, over two hundred of them, refused to enter the passage again," he whispered dramatically, "it was because misfortune and disaster visited more than one who had penetrated to a certain place therein." He bent further forward. "The Pyramid of Méydûm is the home of a powerful *Efreet*, Kernaby Pasha! But I who was the last to leave it, know what is concealed there. In a certain place, low down in the corner of the King's Chamber, is a ring of gold, bearing a cartouche. It is the royal ring of the Pharaoh who built the pyramid."

He ceased, watching me intently. I did not doubt Hassan's word, for I had always counted him a man of integrity; but there was much that was obscure and much that was mysterious in his story.

"Why did you not bring it away?" I asked.

"I feared to touch it, Kernaby Pasha; it is an evil talisman. Until today I have feared to speak of it."

"And today?"

Hassan extended his hands, palms upward.

"I am threatened with the loss of my house," he said simply, "if I do not find a certain sum of money within a period of twelve days."

I sat resting my chin on my hand and staring into the face of Hassan es-Sugra. Could it be that from superstitious motives such a treasure had indeed been abandoned? Could if be that Fate had delivered into my hands a relic so priceless as the signet-ring of Sneferu, one of the earliest Memphite Pharaohs? Since I had recently incurred the displeasure of my principals, Messrs. Moses, Murphy & Co., of Birmingham, the mere anticipation of such a "find" was sufficient to raise my professional enthusiasm to white heat, and in those few moments of silence I had decided upon instant action.

"Meet me at Rikka Station, tomorrow morning at nine o'clock," I said, "and arrange for donkeys to carry us to the pyramid."

II

On my arrival at Rikka, and therefore at the very outset of my inquiry, I met with what one slightly prone to superstition might have regarded as an unfortunate omen. A native funeral was passing out of the town amid the wailing of women and the chanting by the *Yemeneeyeh,* of the Profession of the Faith, with its queer monotonous cadences, a performance which despite its familiarity in the Near East never failed to affect me unpleasantly. By the token of the *tarbûsh* upon the bier, I knew that this was a man who was being hurried to his lonely resting-place on the fringe of the desert.

As the procession wound its way out across the sands, I saw to the removal of my baggage and joined Hassan es-Sugra, who awaited me by the wooden barrier. I perceived immediately that something was wrong with the man; he was palpably laboring under the influence of some strong excitement, and his dark eyes regarded me almost fearfully. He was muttering to himself like one suffering from an over-indulgence in hashish, and I detected the words *"Allahu akbar!"* (God is most great) several times repeated.

"What ails you, Hassan, my friend?" I said; and noting how his gaze persistently returned to the melancholy procession wending its way towards the little Moslem cemetery:—"Was the dead man some relation of yours?"

"No, no, Kernaby Pasha," he muttered gutturally, and moistened his lips with his tongue; "I was but slightly acquainted with him."

"Yet you are much disturbed."

"Not at all, Kernaby Pasha," he assured me; "not in the slightest."

By which familiar formula I knew that Hassan es-Sugra would conceal from me the cause of his distress, and therefore, since I had no appetite for further mysteries, I determined to learn it from another source.

"See to the loading of the donkey," I directed him—for three sleek little animals were standing beside him, patiently awaiting the toil of the day.

Hassan setting about the task with a cheerful alacrity obviously artificial, I approached the native station master, with whom I was acquainted, and put to him a number of questions respecting his important functions—in which I was not even mildly interested. But to the Oriental mind a direct inquiry is an affront, almost an insult; and to have inquired bluntly the name of the deceased and the manner of his death would have been the best way to have learned nothing whatever about the matter. Therefore having discussed in detail the slothful incompetence of Arab ticket collectors and the lazy condition and innate viciousness of Egyptian porters as a class, I mentioned incidentally that I had observed a funeral leaving Rikka.

The station master (who was bursting to talk about this very matter, but who would have declined on principle to do so had I definitely questioned him) now unfolded to me the strange particulars respecting the death of one, Ahmed Abdulla, who had been a retired dragoman though some time employed as an excavator.

"He rode out one night upon his white donkey," said my informant, "and no man knows whither he went. But it is believed, Kernaby Pasha, that it was to the Haram el-Kaddâb" (the False Pyramid)—extending his hand to where, beyond the belt of fertility, the tomb of Sneferu up-reared its three platforms from the fringe of the desert. "To enter the pyramid even in day time is to court misfortune; to enter at night is to fall into the hands of the powerful *Efreet* who dwells there. His donkey returned without him, and therefore search was made for Ahmed Abdulla. He was found the next day"—again the long arm shot out towards the desert—"dead upon the sands, near the foot of the pyramid."

I looked into the face of the speaker; beyond doubt he was in deadly earnest.

"Why should Ahmed Abdulla have wanted to visit such a place at night?" I asked.

My acquaintance lowered his voice, muttered "*Sahâm Allah fee 'adoo ed—dîn!*" (May God transfix the enemies of the religion) and touched his forehead, his mouth, and his breast with the iron ring which he wore.

"There is a great treasure concealed there, Kernaby Pasha," he replied; "a treasure hidden from the world in the days of Suleyman the Great, sealed with his seal, and guarded by the servants of Gânn Ibn-Gânn."

"So you think the guardian *jinn* killed Ahmed Abdulla?"

The station master muttered invocations, and—

"There are things which may not be spoken of," he said; "but those who saw him dead say that he was terrible to look upon. A great *Welee*, a man of wisdom famed throughout Egypt, has been summoned to avert the evil; for if the anger of the *jinn* is aroused they may visit the most painful and unfortunate penalties upon all Rikka. . . ."

Half an hour later I set out, having confidentially informed the station master that I sought to obtain a fine turquoise necklet which I knew to be in the possession of the Sheikh of Méydûm. Little did I suspect how it was written that I should indeed visit the house of the venerable Sheikh. Out through the fields of young green corn, the palm groves and the sycamore orchards I rode, Hassan plodding silently behind me and leading the donkey who bore the baggage. Curious eyes watched our passage, from field, doorway, and *shadûf;* but nothing of note marked our journey save the tremendous heat of the sun at noon, beneath which I knew myself a fool to travel.

I camped on the western side of the pyramid, but well clear of the marshes, which are the home of countless wild-fowl. I had no idea how long it would take me to extract the coveted ring from its hiding place (which Hassan had closely described to me); and, remembering the speculative glances of the villagers, I had no intention of exposing myself against the face of the pyramid until dusk should have come to cloak my operations.

Hassan es-Sugra, whose new taciturnity was remarkable and whose behavior was distinguished by an odd disquiet, set out with his gun to procure our dinner, and I mounted the sandy slope on the southwest of the pyramid, where from my cover behind a mound of rubbish, I studied through my field-glasses the belt of vegetation marking the course of the Nile. I could detect no sign of surveillance, but in view of the fact that the smuggling of relics out of Egypt is a punishable offense my caution was dictated by wisdom.

We dined excellently, Hassan the Silent and I, upon quail, tinned toma-toes, fresh dates, bread, and Vichy-water (to which in my own case was added a stiff three fingers of whisky).

When the newly risen moon cast an ebon shadow of the Pyramid of Sne-feru upon the carpet of the sands, I made my way around the angle of the ancient building towards the mound on the northern side whereby one ap-proaches the entrance. Three paces from the shadow's edge, I paused, trans-fixed, because of that which confronted me.

Outlined against the moon-bright sky upon a ridge of the desert behind and to the north of the great structure, stood the motionless figure of a man!

For a moment I thought that my mind had conjured up this phantasmal watcher, that he was a thing of moon-magic and not of flesh and blood. But as I stood regarding him, he moved, seemed to raise his head, then turned and disappeared beyond the crest.

How long I remained staring at the spot where he had been I know not; but I was aroused from my useless contemplation by the jingling of camel bells. The sound came from behind me, stealing sweetly through the still-ness from a great distance. I turned in a flash, whipped out my glasses and searched the remote fringe of the Fáyûm. Stately across the jeweled curtain of the night moved a caravan, blackly marked against that wondrous back-ground. Three walking figures I counted, three laden donkeys, and two camels. Upon the first of the camels a man was mounted, upon the second was a *shibreeyeh,* a sort of covered litter, which I knew must conceal a woman. The caravan passed out of sight into the palm grove which conceals the vil-lage of Méydûm.

I returned my glasses to their case, and stood for some moments deep in reflection; then I descended the slope, to the tiny encampment where I had left Hassan es-Sugra. He was nowhere to be seen; and having waited some ten minutes I grew impatient, and raising my voice:

"Hassan!" I cried; "Hassan es-Sugra!"

No answer greeted me, although in the desert stillness the call must have been audible for miles. A second and a third time I called his name . . . and the only reply was the shrill note of a pyramid bat that swooped low above my head; the vast solitude of the sands swallowed up my voice and the walls of the Tomb of Sneferu mocked me with their echo, crying eerily:

"Hassan! Hassan es-Sugra. . . . Hassan! . . ."

III

This mysterious episode affected me unpleasantly, but did not divert me from my purpose: I succeeded in casting out certain demons of superstition who had sought to lay hold upon me; and a prolonged scrutiny of the surrounding desert somewhat allayed my fears of human surveillance. For my visit to the chamber in the heart of the ancient building I had arrayed myself in rubber-soled shoes, an old pair of drill trousers, and a pajama jacket. A Colt repeater was in my hip pocket, and, in addition to several instruments which I thought might be useful in extracting the ring from its setting, I carried a powerful flashlight.

Seated on the threshold of the entrance, fifty feet above the desert level, I cast a final glance backward towards the Nile valley, then, the lighted flashlight carried in my jacket pocket, I commenced the descent of the narrow, sloping passage. Periodically, when some cranny between the blocks offered a foothold, I checked my progress, and inspected the steep path below for snake tracks.

Some two hundred and forty feet of labored descent discovered me in a sort of shallow cavern little more than a yard high and partly hewn out of the living rock which formed the foundation of the pyramid. In this place I found the heat to be almost insufferable, and the smell of remote mortality which assailed my nostrils from the sand-strewn floor threatened to choke me. For five minutes or more I lay there, bathed in perspiration, my nerves at high tension, listening for the slightest sound within or without. I cannot pretend that I was entirely master of myself. The stuff that fear is made of seemed to rise from the ancient dust; and I had little relish for the second part of my journey, which lay through a long horizontal passage rarely exceeding fourteen inches in height. The mere memory of that final crawl of forty feet or so is sufficient to cause me to perspire profusely; therefore let it suffice that I reached the end of the second passage, and breathing with difficulty the deathful, poisonous atmosphere of the place, found myself at the foot of the rugged shaft which gives access to the King's Chamber. Resting my flashlight upon a convenient ledge, I climbed up, and knew myself to be in one of the oldest chambers fashioned by human handiwork.

The journey had been most exhausting, but, allowing myself only a few moments' rest, I crossed to the eastern corner of the place and directed a ray of light upon the crevice which, from Hassan's description, I believed to conceal the ring. His account having been detailed, I experienced little difficulty in finding the cavity; but in the very moment of success the light of the flashlight grew dim . . . and I recognized with a mingling of chagrin and fear that it was burnt out and that I had no means of recharging it.

Ere the light expired, I had time to realize two things: that the cavity was empty . . . and that someone or something was approaching the foot of the shaft along the horizontal passage below!

Strictly though I have schooled my emotions, my heart was beating in a most uncomfortable fashion, as, crouching near the edge of the shaft, I watched the red glow fade from the delicate filament of the lamp. Retreat was impossible; there is but one entrance to the pyramid; and the darkness which now descended upon me was indescribable; it possessed horrific qualities; it seemed palpably to enfold me like the wings of some monstrous bat. The air of the King's Chamber I found to be almost unbearable, and it was no steady hand with which I gripped my pistol.

The sounds of approach continued. The suspense was becoming intolerable—when, into the Memphian gloom below me, there suddenly intruded a faint but ever-growing light. Between excitement and insufficient air, I regarded suffocation as imminent. Then, out into view beneath me, was thrust a slim ivory hand which held an electric pocket lamp. Fascinatedly I watched it, saw it joined by its fellow, then observed a white-turbaned head and a pair of black-robed shoulders follow. In my surprise I almost dropped the weapon which I held. The new arrival now standing upright and raising his head, I found myself looking into the face of *Abû Tabâh*!

"To Allah, the Great, the Compassionate, be all praise that I have found you alive," he said simply.

He exhibited little evidence of the journey which I had found so fatiguing, but an expression strongly like that of real anxiety rested upon his ascetic face.

"If life is dear to you," he continued, "answer me this, Kernaby Pasha; have you found the ring?"

"I have not," I replied; "my lamp failed me; but I think the ring is gone."

And now, as I spoke the words, the strangeness of his question came home to me, bringing with it an acute suspicion.

"What do you know of this ring, O my friend?" I asked.

Abû Tabâh shrugged his shoulders.

"I know much that is evil," he replied; "and because you doubt the purity of my motives, all that I have learned you shall learn also; for Allah the Great, the Merciful, this night has protected you from danger and spared you a frightful death. Follow me, Kernaby Pasha, in order that these things may be made manifest to you."

IV

A pair of fleet camels were kneeling at the foot of the slope below the entrance to the pyramid, and having recovered somewhat from the effect of the fatiguing climb out from the King's Chamber—

"It might be desirable," I said, "that I adopt a more suitable raiment for camel riding?"

Abû Tabâh slowly shook his head in that dignified manner which never deserted him. He had again taken up his ebony walking-stick and was now resting his crossed hands upon it and regarding me with his strange, melancholy eyes.

"To delay would be unwise," he replied. "You have mercifully been spared a painful and unfortunate end (all praise to Him who averted the peril); but the ring, which bears an ancient curse, is gone: for me there is no rest until I have found and destroyed it."

He spoke with a solemn conviction which bore the seal of verity.

"Your destructive theory may be perfectly sound," I said; "but as one professionally interested in relics of the past, I feel called upon to protest. Perhaps before we proceed any further you will enlighten me respecting this most obscure matter. Can you inform me, for example, what became of Hassan es-Sugra?"

"He observed my approach from a distance, and fled, being a man of little virtue. Respecting the other matters you shall be fully enlightened, tonight. The white camel is for you."

There was a gentle finality in his manner to which I succumbed. My feelings towards this mysterious being had undergone a slight change; and whilst I cannot truthfully say that I loved him as a brother, a certain respect for Abû Tabâh was taking possession of my mind. I began to understand his reputation with the natives; beyond doubt his uncanny wisdom was impressive; his lofty dignity awed. And no man is at his best arrayed in canvas shoes, very dirty drill trousers, and a pajama jacket.

As I had anticipated, the village of Méydûm proved to be our destination, and the gait of the magnificent creatures upon which we were mounted was exhausting. I shall always remember that moonlight ride across the desert to the palm groves of Méydûm. I entered the house of the Sheikh with misgivings; for my attire fell short of the ideal to which every representative of protective Britain looks up, but often fails to realize.

In a *mandarah,* part of it inlaid with fine mosaic and boasting a pretty fountain, I was presented to the imposing old man who was evidently the host of Abû Tabâh. Ere taking my seat upon the *dîwan,* I shed my canvas shoes, in accordance with custom, accepted a pipe and a cup of excellent coffee, and awaited with much curiosity the next development. A brief colloquy between Abû Tabâh and the Sheikh, at the further end of the apartment resulted in the disappearance of the Sheikh and the approach of my mysterious friend.

"Because, although you are not a Moslem, you are a man of culture and understanding," said Abû Tabâh, "I have ordered that my sister shall be brought into your presence."

"That is exceedingly good of you," I said, but indeed I knew it to be an honor which spoke volumes at once for Abû Tabâh's enlightenment and good opinion of myself.

"She is a virgin of great beauty," he continued; "and the excellence of her mind exceeds the perfection of her person."

"I congratulate you," I answered politely, "upon the possession of a sister in every way so desirable."

Abû Tabâh inclined his head in a characteristic gesture of gentle courtesy.

"Allah has indeed blessed my house," he admitted; "and because your mind is filled with conjectures respecting the source of certain information which you know me to possess, I desire that the matter shall be made clear to you."

How I should have answered this singular man I know not; but as he spoke the words, into the *mandarah* came the Sheikh, followed by a girl robed and veiled entirely in white. With gait slow and graceful she approached the *dîwan.* She wore a white *yelek* so closely wrapped about her that it concealed the rest of her attire, and a white *tarbar,* or head-veil, decorated with gold embroidery, almost entirely concealed her hair, save for one jet-black plait in which little gold ornaments were entwined and which hung down on the left of her forehead. A white *yashmak* reached nearly to her feet, which were clad in little red leather slippers.

As she approached me I was impressed, not so much with the details of her white attire, nor with the fine lines of a graceful figure which the gossamer robe quite failed to conceal, but with her wonderful gazelle-like eyes, which were uncannily like those of her brother, save that their bordering of *kohl* lent them an appearance of being larger and more luminous.

No form of introduction was observed; with modestly lowered eyes the girl saluted me and took her seat upon a heap of cushions before a small, coffee table set at one end of the *dîwan.* The Sheikh seated himself beside me, and Abû Tabâh, with a reed pen, wrote something rapidly on a narrow strip of paper. The Sheikh clapped his hands, a man entered bearing a brazier containing live charcoal, and, having placed it upon the floor, immediately withdrew. The *dîwan* was lighted by a lantern swung from the ceiling, and its light, pouring fully down upon the white figure of the girl, and leaving the other persons and objects in comparative shadow, produced a picture which I am unlikely to forget.

Amid a tense silence, Abû Tabâh took from a box upon the table some resinous substance. This he sprinkled upon the fire in the brazier; and the girl extending a small hand and round soft arm across the table, he again dipped his pen in the ink and drew upon the upturned palm a rough square which he divided into nine parts, writing in each an Arabic figure. Finally, in the center he poured a small drop of ink, upon which, in response to words rapidly spoken, the girl fixed an intent gaze.

Into the brazier Abû Tabâh dropped one by one fragments of the paper upon which he had written what I presumed to be a form of invocation. Immediately, standing between the smoking brazier and the girl, he commenced a subdued muttering. I recognized that I was about to be treated to an exhibition of *darb el-mendel,* Abû Tabâh being evidently a *sahhar,* or adept in the art called *er-roohânee.* Save for this indistinct muttering, no other sound disturbed the silence of the apartment, until suddenly the girl began to speak Arabic and in a sweet but monotonous voice.

"Again I see the ring," she said, "a hand is holding it before me. The ring bears a green scarab, upon which is written the name of a king of Egypt. . . . The ring is gone. I can see it no more."

"Seek it," directed Abû Tabâh in a low voice, and threw more incense upon the fire. "Are you seeking it?"

"Yes," replied the girl, who now began to tremble violently, "I am in a low passage which slopes downwards so steeply that I am afraid."

"Fear nothing," said Abû Tabâh; "follow the passage."

With marvelous fidelity the girl described the passage and the shaft leading to the King's Chamber in the Pyramid of Méydûm. She described the cavity in the wall where once (if Hassan es-Sugra was worthy of credence) the ring had been concealed.

"There is a freshly made hole in the stonework," she said. "The picture has gone; I am standing in some dark place and the same hand again holds the ring before me."

"Is it the hand of an Oriental," asked Abû Tabâh, "or of a European?"

"It is the hand of a European. It has disappeared; I see a funeral procession winding out from Rikka into the desert."

"Follow the ring," directed Abû Tabâh, a queer, compelling note in his voice.

Again he sprinkled perfume upon the fire and—

"I see a Pharaoh upon his throne," continued the monotonous voice, "upon the first finger of his left hand he wears the ring with the green scarab. A prisoner stands before him in chains; a woman pleads with the king, but he is deaf to her. He draws the ring from his finger and hands it to one standing behind the throne—one who has a very evil face. Ah! . . ."

The girl's voice died away in a low wail of fear or horror. But—

"What do you see?" demanded Abû Tabâh.

"The death-ring of Pharaoh!" whispered the soft voice tremulously; "it is the death-ring!"

"Return from the past to the present," ordered Abû Tabâh. "Where is the ring now?"

He continued his weird muttering, whilst the girl, who still shuddered violently, peered again into the pool of ink. Suddenly—

"I see a long line of dead men," she whispered, speaking in a kind of chant; "they are of all the races of the East, and some are swathed in mummy wrappings; the wrappings are scaled with the death ring of Pharaoh. They are passing me slowly, on their way across the desert from the Pyramid of Méydûm to a narrow ravine where a tent is erected. They go to summon one who is about to join their company. . . ."

I suppose the suffocating perfume of the burning incense was chiefly responsible, but at this point I realized that I was becoming dizzy and that immediate departure into a cooler atmosphere was imperative. Quietly, in order to avoid disturbing the séance, I left the *mandarah*. So absorbed were the three in their weird performance that my departure was apparently unnoticed. Out in the coolness of the palm grove I soon recovered. I doubt if I possess the temperament which enables one to contemplate with equanimity a number of dead men promenading in their shrouds.

V

"The truth is now wholly made manifest," said Abû Tabâh; "the revelation is complete."

Once more I was mounted upon the white camel and the mysterious *imám* rode beside me upon its fellow, which was of less remarkable color.

"I hear your words," I replied.

"The poor Ahmed Abdulla," he continued, "who was of little wisdom, knew, as Hassan es-Sugra knew, of the hidden ring; for he was one of those who fled from the pyramid refusing to enter it again. Greed spoke to him, however, and he revealed the secret to a certain Englishman, called Bishop, contracting to aid him in recovering the ring."

At last enlightenment was mine . . . and it brought in its train a dreadful premonition.

"Something I knew of the peril," said Abû Tabâh, "but not, at first, all. The Englishman I warned, but he neglected my warning. Already Ahmed Abdulla was dead, having been dispatched by his employer to the pyramid; and the people of Rikka had sent for me. Now, by means known to you, I learned that evil powers threatened your life also, in what form I knew not at that time save that the sign of Set had been revealed to me in conjunction with your death."

I shuddered.

"That the secret of the pyramid was a Pharaoh's ring I did not learn until later; but now it is made manifest that the thing of power is the death-ring of Sneferu. . . ."

The huge bulk of the Pyramid of Méydûm loomed above us as he spoke the words, for we were nearly come to our destination; and its proximity occasioned within me a physical chill. I do not think an open check for a thousand pounds would have tempted me to enter the place again. The death-ring of Sneferu possessed uncomfortable and supernatural properties. So far as I was aware, no example of such a ring (the *lettre de cachet* of the period) was included in any known collection. One dating much after Sneferu, and bearing the cartouche of Apepi II (one of the Hyksos, or Shepherd Kings), came to light late in the nineteenth century; it was reported to be the ring which, traditionally, Joseph wore as emblematic of the power vested in him by Pharaoh. Sir Gaston Maspero and other authorities considered it to be a "forgery" and it vanished from the ken of connoisseurs. I never learned by what firm it was manufactured.

A mile to the west of the pyramid we found Theo Bishop's encampment. I thought it to be deserted—until I entered the little tent. . . .

An oil-lamp stood upon a wooden box; and its rays made yellow the face of the man stretched upon the camp-bed. My premonition was realized; Bishop must have entered the pyramid less than an hour ahead of me; he it was who had stood upon the mound, silhouetted against the sky, when I had first approached the slope. He had met with the fate of Ahmed Abdulla.

He had been dead for at least two hours, and by the token of certain hideous glandular swellings, I knew that he had met his end by the bite of an Egyptian viper.

"Abû Tabâh!" I cried, my voice hoarsely unnatural—"the recess in the King's Chamber is a viper's nest!"

"You speak wisdom, Kernaby Pasha; the viper is the servant of the *jinn*."

Upon the third finger of his swollen right hand Bishop wore the ring of ghastly history; and the mysterious significance of the Sign of Set became apparent. For added to the usual cartouche of the Pharaoh was the symbol of the god of destruction, thus:

We buried him deeply, piling stones upon the grave, that the jackals of the desert might never disturb the last holder of the death-ring of Sneferu.

THE MUMMY
OR
RAMSES THE DAMNED
(Excerpt)

Anne Rice

Anne Rice is one of America's most popular horror writers. She is referred to as "the undisputed queen of vampire literature" and each of her seven vampire novels has been a bestseller. Interview with the Vampire *ranks only behind* Dracula *as the most popular vampire novel in recent history, and was made into a major motion picture. Rice's bestselling novels include* The Vampire Lestat, Queen of the Damned, The Tale of the Body Thief, Cry to Heaven, Feast of All Saints, Lasher, *and* The Witching Hour. *She has been called "the foremost practitioner of the Gothic style in the modern age." It seems logical that at some point she would turn her attention to Ancient Egypt. Of course she did so, and to great effect. The result was her wonderful novel* The Mummy or Ramses the Damned, *an excerpt of which is presented here.*

The camera flashes blinded him for a moment. If only he could get the photographers away.

But they had been at his side for months now—ever since the first artifacts had been found in these barren hills, south of Cairo. It was as if they too had known. Something was about to happen. After all these years, Lawrence Stratford was onto a major find.

And so they were there with the cameras, and the smoking flashes. They almost knocked him off balance as he made his way into the narrow rough-hewn passage towards the letters visible on the half-uncovered marble door.

The twilight seemed to darken suddenly. He could see the letters, but he couldn't make them out.

"Samir," he cried. "I need light."

"Yes, Lawrence." At once the torch exploded behind him, and in a flood of yellow illumination, the slab of stone was wonderfully visible. Yes, hieroglyphs, deeply etched and beautifully gilded, and in Italian marble. He had never seen such a sight.

He felt the hot silky touch of Samir's hand on his as he began to read aloud:

"'Robbers of the Dead, Look away from this tomb lest you wake its occupant, whose wrath cannot be contained. Ramses the Damned is my name.'"

He glanced at Samir. What could it mean?

"Go on, Lawrence, translate, you are far quicker than I am," Samir said.

"'Ramses the Damned is my name. Once Ramses the Great of Upper and Lower Egypt; Slayer of the Hittites, Builder of Temples; Beloved of the People; and immortal guardian of the kings and queens of Egypt throughout time. In the year of the death of the Great Queen Cleopatra, as Egypt becomes a Roman province, I commit myself to eternal darkness; beware, all those who would let the rays of the sun pass through this door.'"

"But it makes no sense," Samir whispered. "Ramses the Great ruled one thousand years before Cleopatra."

"Yet these are nineteenth-dynasty hieroglyphs without question," Lawrence countered. Impatiently, he scratched away at the loose rubble. "And look, the inscription's repeated—in Latin and in Greek." He paused, then quickly read the last few Latin lines.

"'Be Warned: I sleep as the earth sleeps beneath the night sky or the winter's snow; and once awakened, I am servant to no man.'"

For a moment Lawrence was speechless, staring at the words he'd read. Only vaguely did he hear Samir:

"I don't like it. Whatever it means, it's a curse."

Reluctantly Lawrence turned and saw that Samir's suspicion had turned to fear.

"The body of Ramses the Great is in the Cairo Museum," Samir said impatiently.

"No," Lawrence answered. He was aware of a chill moving slowly up his neck. "There's a body in the Cairo Museum, but it's not Ramses! Look at the cartouches, the seal! There was no one in the time of Cleopatra who could even write the ancient hieroglyphs. And these are perfect—and done like the Latin and the Greek with infinite care."

Oh, if only Julie were here, Lawrence thought bitterly. His daughter, Julie, was afraid of nothing. She would understand this moment as no one else could.

He almost stumbled as he backed out of the passage, waving the photographers out of his path. Again, the flashes went off around him. Reporters rushed towards the marble door.

"Get the diggers back to work," Lawrence shouted. "I want the passage cleared down to the threshold. I'm going into that tomb tonight."

"Lawrence, take your time with this," Samir cautioned. "There is something here which must not be dismissed."

"Samir, you astonish me," Lawrence answered. "For ten years we've been searching these hills for just such a discovery. And no one's touched that door since it was sealed two thousand years ago."

Almost angrily, he pushed past the reporters who caught up with him now, and tried to block the way. He needed the quiet of his tent until the door was uncovered; he needed his diary, the only proper confidant for the excitement he felt. He was dizzy suddenly from the long day's heat.

"No questions now, ladies and gentlemen," Samir said politely. As he always did, Samir came between Lawrence and the real world.

Lawrence hurried down the uneven path, twisting his ankle a little painfully, yet continuing, his eyes narrow as he looked beyond the flickering torches at the sombre beauty of the lighted tents under the violet evening sky.

Only one thing distracted him before he reached the safety zone of his camp chair and desk: a glimpse of his nephew, Henry, watching idly from a short distance away. Henry, so uncomfortable and out of place in Egypt; looking miserable in his fussy white linen suit. Henry, with the inevitable glass of Scotch in his hand, and the inevitable cheroot on his lip.

Undoubtedly the belly dancer was with him—the woman, Malenka, from Cairo, who gave her British gentleman all the money she made.

Lawrence could never entirely forget about Henry, but having Henry underfoot now was more than he could bear.

In a life well lived, Lawrence counted Henry as his only true disappointment—the nephew who cared for no one and nothing but gaming tables and the bottle; the sole male heir to the Stratford millions who properly couldn't be trusted with a one-pound note.

Sharp pain again as he missed Julie—his beloved daughter, who should have been here with him, and would have been if her young fiancé hadn't persuaded her to stay at home.

Henry had come to Egypt for money. Henry had company papers for Lawrence to sign. And Henry's father, Randolph, had sent him on this grim mission, desperate as always to cover his son's debts.

A fine pair they are, Lawrence thought grimly—the ne'er-do-well and the chairman of the board of Stratford Shipping who clumsily funneled the company's profits into his son's bottomless purse.

But in a very real way Lawrence could forgive his brother, Randolph, anything. Lawrence hadn't merely given the family business to Randolph. He had dumped it on Randolph, along with all its immense pressures and responsibilities, so that he, Lawrence, could spend his remaining years digging among the Egyptian ruins he so loved.

And to be perfectly fair, Randolph had done a tolerable job of running Stratford Shipping. That is, until his son had turned him into an embezzler and a thief. Even now, Randolph would admit everything if confronted. But Lawrence was too purely selfish for that confrontation. He never wanted to leave Egypt again for the stuffy London offices of Stratford Shipping. Not even Julie could persuade him to come home.

And now Henry stood there waiting for his moment. And Lawrence denied him that moment, entering the tent and eagerly pulling his chair up to the desk. He took out a leather-bound diary which he had been saving, perhaps for this discovery. Hastily he wrote what he remembered of the door's inscription and the questions it posed.

"Ramses the Damned." He sat back, looking at the name. And for the first time he felt just a little of the foreboding which had shaken Samir.

What on earth could all this mean?

Half-past midnight. Was he dreaming? The marble door of the tomb had been carefully removed, photographed, and placed on trestles in his tent. And now they were ready to blast their way in. The tomb! His at last.

He nodded to Samir. He felt the ripple of excitement move through the crowd. Flashes went off as he raised his hands to his ears, and then the blast caught them all off guard. He felt it in the pit of his stomach.

No time for that. He had the torch in hand and was going in, though Samir tried once again to stop him.

"Lawrence, there could be booby traps, there could be—"

"Get out of my way."

The dust was making him cough. His eyes were watering.

He thrust the torch through the gaping hole. Walls decorated with hieroglyphs—again, the magnificent nineteenth-dynasty style without question.

At once he stepped inside. How extraordinarily cool it felt; and the smell, what was it, a curious perfume after all these long centuries!

His heart beat too fast. The blood rushed to his face, and he had to cough again, as the press of reporters raised the dust in the passage.

"Keep back!" he shouted crossly. The flashes were going off all around him again. He could barely see the painted ceiling overhead with its tiny stars.

And there, a long table laden with alabaster jars and boxes. Heaps of rolled papyri. Dear God, all this alone confirmed a momentous discovery.

"But this is no tomb!" he whispered.

There was a writing table, covered with a thin film of dust, looking for all the world as if the scholar had only just left it. An open papyrus lay there, with sharpened pens, an ink bottle. And a goblet.

But the bust, the marble bust—it was unmistakably Graeco-Roman. A woman with her tight wavy hair drawn back beneath a metal band, her drowsy half-lidded eyes seemingly blind, and the name cut into the base:

CLEOPATRA

"Not possible," he heard Samir say. "But look, Lawrence, the mummy case!"

Lawrence had already seen it. He was staring speechless at the thing which lay serenely in the very middle of this puzzling room, this study, this library, with its stacks of scrolls and its dust-covered writing table.

Once again, Samir ordered the photographers back. The smoking flashes were maddening Lawrence.

"Get out, all of you, get out!" Lawrence said. Grumbling, they retreated out of sight of the door, leaving the two men standing there in stunned silence.

It was Samir who spoke first:

"This is Roman furniture. This is Cleopatra. Look at the coins, Lawrence, on the desk. With her image, and newly minted. Those alone are worth—"

"I know. But there lies an ancient Pharaoh, my friend. Every detail of the case—it's as fine as any ever found in the Valley of the Kings."

"But without a sarcophagus," Samir said. "Why?"

"This is no tomb," Lawrence answered.

"And so the King chose to be buried here!" Samir approached the mummy case, lifting the torch high above the beautifully painted face, with its darkly lined eyes and exquisitely modeled lips.

"I could swear this is the Roman period," he said.

"But the style . . ."

"Lawrence, it's too lifelike. It's a Roman artist who has imitated the nineteenth-dynastic style to perfection."

"And how could such a thing happen, my friend?"

"Curses," Samir whispered, as if he had not heard the question. He was staring at the rows of hieroglyphs that circled the painted figure. The Greek lettering appeared lower down, and finally came the Latin.

"'Touch not the remains of Ramses the Great,'" Samir read. "It's the same in all three tongues. Enough to give a sensible man pause."

"Not this sensible man," Lawrence replied. "Get those workers in here to lift this lid at once."

The dust had settled somewhat. The torches, in the old iron sconces on the wall, were sending far too much smoke onto the ceiling, but that he would worry about later.

The thing now was to cut open the bundled human shape, which had been propped against the wall, the thin wooden lid of the mummy case carefully laid upright beside it.

He no longer saw the men and women packed at the entrance, who peered at him and his find in silence.

Slowly, he raised the knife and sliced through the brittle husk of dried linen, which fell open immediately to reveal the tightly wrapped figure beneath.

There was a collective gasp from the reporters. Again and again the flashes popped. Lawrence could feel Samir's silence. Both men stared at the gaunt face beneath its yellowed linen bandages, at the withered arms so serenely laid across the breast.

It seemed one of the photographers was begging to be allowed into the chamber. Samir angrily demanded silence. But of these distractions, Lawrence was only dimly aware.

He gazed calmly at the emaciated form before him, its wrappings the color of darkened desert sand. It seemed he could detect an expression in the shrouded features; he could detect something eloquent of tranquillity in the set of the thin lips.

Every mummy was a mystery. Every desiccated yet preserved form a ghastly image of life in death. It never failed to chill him, to look upon these ancient Egyptian dead. But he felt a strange longing as he looked at this one—this mysterious being who called himself Ramses the Damned, Ramses the Great.

Something warm touched him inside. He drew closer, slashing again at the outer wrapping. Behind him, Samir ordered the photographers out of the passage. There was danger of contamination. *Yes, go, all of you, please.*

He reached out and touched the mummy suddenly; he touched it reverently with the very tips of his fingers. So curiously resilient! Surely the thick layer of bandages had become soft with time.

Again, he gazed at the narrow face before him, at the rounded lids, and the sombre mouth.

"Julie," he whispered. "Oh, my darling, if only you could see . . ."

It was cool now. There was noise out there; cars arriving. The braying of a donkey; and the sharp high-pitched sound of a woman laughing, an American woman, who had driven all the way from Cairo as soon as she had heard.

Lawrence and Samir sat together in their camp chairs at the ancient writing table, with the papyri spread out before them.

Careful not to put his full weight on the fragile piece of furniture, Lawrence hastily scribbled his translations in his leather-bound book.

Now and then he glanced over his shoulder at the mummy, the great

King who for all the world looked as if he merely slept. Ramses the Immortal! The very idea inflamed Lawrence. He knew that he would be in this strange chamber until well after dawn.

"But it must be a hoax," Samir said. "Ramses the Great guarding the royal families of Egypt for a thousand years. The lover of Cleopatra?"

"Ah, but it makes sublime sense!" Lawrence replied. He set down the pen for a moment, staring at the papyri. How his eyes ached. "If any woman could have driven an immortal man to entomb himself, Cleopatra would be that woman."

He looked at the marble bust before him. Lovingly he stroked Cleopatra's smooth white cheek. Yes, Lawrence could believe it. Cleopatra, beloved of Julius Caesar and beloved of Mark Antony; Cleopatra, who had held out against the Roman conquest of Egypt far longer than anyone dreamed possible; Cleopatra, the last ruler of Egypt in the ancient world. But the story—he must resume his translation. . . .

Samir rose and stretched uneasily. Lawrence watched him move towards the mummy. What was he doing? Examining the wrappings over the fingers, examining the brilliant scarab ring so clearly visible on the right hand? Now that was a nineteenth-dynasty treasure, no one could deny it, Lawrence thought.

Lawrence closed his eyes and massaged his eyelids gently. Then he opened them, focusing on the papyrus before him again.

"Samir, I tell you, the fellow is convincing me. Such a command of languages would dazzle anyone. And his philosophical perspective is quite as modern as my own." He reached for the older document, which he had examined earlier. "And this, Samir, I want you to examine it. This is none other than a letter from Cleopatra to Ramses."

"A hoax, Lawrence. Some sort of little Roman joke."

"No, my friend, nothing of the kind. She wrote this letter from Rome when Caesar was assassinated! She told Ramses she was coming home to him, and to Egypt."

He laid the letter aside. When Samir had time he would see for himself what these documents contained. All the world would see. He turned back to the original papyrus.

"But listen to this, Samir—Ramses' last thoughts: 'The Romans can not be condemned for the conquest of Egypt; we were conquered by time itself in the end. And all the wonders of this brave new century should draw me from my grief and yet I can not heal my heart; and so the mind suffers; the mind closes as if it were a flower without sun.'"

Samir was still looking at the mummy, looking at the ring. "Another reference to the sun. Again and again the sun." He turned to Lawrence. "But surely you don't believe it—!"

"Samir, if you can believe in the curse, why can't you believe in an immortal man?"

"Lawrence, you play with me. I have seen the workings of many a curse, my friend. But an immortal man who lived in Athens under Pericles and Rome under the Republic and Carthage under Hannibal? A man who taught Cleopatra the history of Egypt? Of this I know nothing at all."

"Listen again, Samir: 'Her beauty shall forever haunt me; as well as her courage and her frivolity; her passion for life, which seemed inhuman in its intensity while being only human after all.'"

Samir made no answer. His eyes were fixed on the mummy again, as if he could not stop looking at it. Lawrence understood perfectly, which is why he sat with his back to the thing in order to read the papyrus, so that he would get the crucial work done.

"Lawrence, this mummy is as dead as any I have ever seen in the Cairo Museum. A storyteller, that is what the man was. Yet these rings."

"Yes, my friend, I observed it very carefully earlier; it is the cartouche of Ramses the Great, and so we have not merely a storyteller but a collector of antiquities. Is that what you want me to believe?"

But what did Lawrence believe? He sat back against the sagging canvas of the camp chair and let his eyes drift over the contents of this strange room. Then again he translated from the scroll.

"'And so I retreat to this isolated chamber; and now my library shall become my tomb. My servants shall anoint my body and wrap it in fine funerary linen as was the custom of my time now so long forgotten. But no knife shall touch me. No embalmer shall extract the heart and brain from my immortal form.'"

A euphoria overcame Lawrence suddenly; or was it a state of waking dream? This voice—it seemed so real to him; he felt the personality, as one never did with the ancient Egyptians. Ah, but of course, this was an immortal man. . . .

* * *

"I love you, fine English," Malenka said to him. She kissed him, then helped him with his tie, the soft touch of her fingers against his chin making the hairs rise on his neck.

What lovely fools women were, Henry Stratford thought. But this Egyptian woman he had enjoyed more than most. She was dark-skinned, a dancer by profession—a quiet and luscious beauty with whom he could do exactly what he wanted. You never knew that kind of freedom with an English whore.

He could see himself settling someday in an Eastern country with such a woman—free of all British respectability. That is, after he had made his fortune at the tables—that one great win he needed to put him quite beyond the world's reach.

For the moment, there was work to be done. The crowd around the tomb had doubled in size since last evening. And the trick was to reach his uncle Lawrence before the man was swept up utterly by the museum people and the authorities—to reach him now when he just might agree to anything in return for being left alone.

"Go on, dearest." He kissed Malenka again and watched her wrap the dark cloak about herself and hurry to the waiting car. How grateful she was for these small Western luxuries. Yes, that kind of woman. Rather than Daisy, his London mistress, a spoilt and demanding creature who nevertheless excited him, perhaps because she was so difficult to please.

He took one last swallow of Scotch, picked up his leather briefcase, and left the tent.

The crowds were ghastly. All night long he'd been awakened by the grind and huff of automobiles, and frenzied voices. And now the heat was rising; and he could already feel sand inside his shoes.

How he loathed Egypt. How he loathed these desert camps and the filthy camel-riding Arabs, and the lazy dirty servants. How he loathed his uncle's entire world.

And there was Samir, that insolent, irritating assistant who fancied himself Lawrence's social equal, trying to quiet the foolish reporters. Could this really be the tomb of Ramses II? Would Lawrence grant an interview?

Henry didn't give a damn. He pushed past the men who were guarding the entrance to the tomb.

"Mr. Stratford, please," Samir called after him. A lady reporter was on his heels. "Let your uncle alone now," Samir said as he drew closer. "Let him savor his find."

"The hell I will."

He glared at the guard who blocked his path. The man moved. Samir turned back to hold off the reporters. Who was going into the tomb? they wanted to know.

"This is a family matter," he said quickly and coldly to the woman reporter trying to follow him. The guard stepped in her path.

So little time left. Lawrence stopped writing, wiped his brow carefully, folded his handkerchief and made one more brief note:

"Brilliant to hide the elixir in a wilderness of poisons. What safer place for a potion that confers immortality than among potions that bring death. And to think they were her poisons—those which Cleopatra tested before deciding to use the venom of the asp to take her life."

He stopped, wiped his brow again. Already so hot in here. And within a few short hours, they'd be upon him, demanding that he leave the tomb for the museum officials. Oh, if only he had made this discovery without the museum. God knows, he hadn't needed them. And they would take it all out of his hands.

The sun came in fine shafts through the rough-cut doorway. It struck the alabaster jars in front of him, and it seemed he heard something—faint, like a whispered breath.

He turned and looked at the mummy, at the features clearly molded beneath the tight wrappings. The man who claimed to be Ramses had been tall, and perhaps robust.

Not an old man, like the creature lying in the Cairo Museum. But then this Ramses claimed that he had never grown old. He was immortal, and merely slept within these bandages. Nothing could kill him, not even the poisons in this room, which he had tried in quantity, when grief for Cleopatra had left him half-mad. On his orders, his servants had wrapped his unconscious body; they had buried him alive, in the coffin he had had prepared for himself, supervising every detail; then they had sealed the tomb with the door that he himself had inscribed.

* * *

Dut what had rendered him unconscious? That was the mystery. Ah, what a delicious story. And what if—?

He found himself staring at the grim creature in its bindings of yellow linen. Did he really believe that something was alive there? Something that could move and speak?

It made Lawrence smile.

He turned back to the jars on the desk. The sun was making the little room an inferno. Taking his handkerchief, he carefully lifted the lid of the first jar before him. Smell of bitter almonds. Something as deadly as cyanide.

And the immortal Ramses claimed to have ingested half the contents of the jar in seeking to end his cursed life.

What if there were an immortal being under those wrappings?

There came that sound again. What was it? Not a rustling; no, nothing so distinct. Rather like an intake of breath.

Once again he looked at the mummy. The sun was shining full on it in long, beautiful dusty rays—the sun that shone through church windows, or through the branches of old oaks in dim forest glens.

It seemed he could see the dust rising from the ancient figure: a pale gold mist of moving particles. Ah, he was too tired!

And the thing, it did not seem so withered any longer; rather it had taken on the contour of a man.

"But what were you really, my ancient friend?" Lawrence asked softly. "Mad? Deluded? Or just what you claim to be—Ramses the Great?"

It gave him a chill to say it—what the French call a frisson. He rose and drew closer to the mummy.

The rays of the sun were positively bathing the thing. For the first time he noticed the contours of its eyebrows beneath the wrappings; there seemed more expression—hard, determined—to its face.

Lawrence smiled. He spoke to it in Latin, piecing together his sentences carefully. "Do you know how long you've slumbered, immortal Pharaoh? You who claimed to have lived one thousand years?"

Was he murdering the ancient language? He had spent so many years translating hieroglyphs that he was rusty with Caesar's tongue. "It's been twice that long, Ramses, since you sealed yourself in this chamber; since Cleopatra put the poisonous snake to her breast."

He stared at the figure, silent for a moment. Was there a mummy that did not arouse in one some deep, cold fear of death? You could believe life lingered there somehow; that the soul was trapped in the wrappings and could only be freed if the thing were destroyed.

Without thinking he spoke now in English.

"Oh, if only you were immortal. If only you could open your eyes on this modern world. And if only I didn't have to wait for permission to remove those miserable bandages, to look on . . . your face!"

The face. Had something changed in the face? No; it was only the full sunlight, wasn't it? But the face did seem fuller. Reverently, Lawrence reached out to touch it but then didn't, his hand poised there motionless.

He spoke in Latin again. "It's the year 1914, my great King. And the name Ramses the Great is still known to all the world; and so is the name of your last Queen."

Suddenly there was a noise behind him. Henry:

"Speaking to Ramses the Great in Latin, Uncle? Maybe the curse is already working on your brain."

"Oh, he understands Latin," Lawrence answered, still staring at the mummy. "Don't you, Ramses? And Greek also. And Persian and Etruscan, and tongues the world has forgotten. Who knows? Perhaps you knew the tongues of the ancient northern barbarians which became our own English centuries ago." Once again, he lapsed into Latin. "But oh, there are so many wonders in the world now, great Pharaoh. There are so many things I could show you. . . ."

"I don't think he can hear you, Uncle," Henry said coldly. There was a soft chink of glass touching glass. "Let's hope not, in any case."

Lawrence turned around sharply. Henry, a briefcase tucked under his left arm, held the lid of one of the jars in his right hand.

"Don't touch that!" Lawrence said crossly. "It's poison, you imbecile. They're all full of poisons. One pinch and you'll be as dead as he is. That is, if he's truly dead." Even the sight of his nephew made him angry. And at a time such as this. . . .

Lawrence turned back to the mummy. Why, even the hands seemed fuller. And one of the rings had almost broken through the wrapping. Only hours ago . . .

"Poisons?" Henry asked behind him.

"It's a veritable laboratory of poisons," Lawrence answered. "The very poisons Cleopatra tried, before her suicide, upon her helpless slaves!" But why waste this precious information on Henry?

"How incredibly quaint," his nephew answered. Cynical, sarcastic. "I thought she was bitten by an asp."

"You're an idiot, Henry. You know less history than an Egyptian camel driver. Cleopatra tried a hundred poisons before she settled on the snake."

He turned and watched coldly as his nephew touched the marble bust of Cleopatra, his fingers passing roughly over the nose, the eyes.

"Well, I fancy this is worth a small fortune, anyway. And these coins. You aren't going to give these things to the British Museum, are you?"

Lawrence sat down in the camp chair. He dipped the pen. Where had he stopped in his translation? Impossible to concentrate with these distractions.

"Is money all you think about?" he asked coldly. "And what have you ever done with it but gamble it away?" He looked up at his nephew. When had the youthful fire died in that handsome face? When had arrogance hardened it, and aged it; and made it so deadly dull? "The more I give you, the more you lose at the tables. Go back to London, for the love of heaven. Go back to your mistress and your music hall cronies. But get out."

There was sharp noise from outside—another motor car backfiring as it ground its way up the sandy road. A dark-faced servant in soiled clothes entered suddenly, with a full breakfast tray in his hands. Samir came behind him.

"I cannot hold them back much longer, Lawrence," Samir said. With a small graceful gesture, he bid the servant set down the breakfast on the edge of the portable desk. "The men from the British embassy are here also, Lawrence. So is every reporter from Alexandria to Cairo. It is quite a circus out there, I fear."

Lawrence stared at the silver dishes, the china cups. He wanted nothing now but to be alone with his treasures.

"Oh, just keep them out as long as you can, Samir. Give me a few more hours alone with these scrolls. Samir, the story is so sad, so poignant."

"I'll do my best," Samir answered. "But do take breakfast, Lawrence. You're exhausted. You need nourishment and rest."

"Samir, I've never been better. Keep them out of here till noon. Oh, and take Henry with you. Henry, go with Samir. He'll see that you have something to eat."

"Yes, do come with me, sir, please," Samir said quickly.

"I have to speak to my uncle alone."

Lawrence looked back at his notebook. And the scroll opened above it. Yes, the King had been talking of his grief after, that he had retreated here to a secret study far away from Cleopatra's mausoleum in Alexandria, far away from the Valley of the Kings.

"Uncle," Henry said frostily, "I'd be more than happy to go back to London if you would only take a moment to sign . . ."

Lawrence refused to look up from the papyrus. Maybe there would be some clue as to where Cleopatra's mausoleum had once stood.

"How many times must I say it?" he murmured indifferently. "No. I will sign no papers. Now take your briefcase with you and get out of my sight."

"Uncle, the Earl wants an answer regarding Julie and Alex. He won't wait forever. And as for these papers, it's only a matter of a few shares."

The Earl . . . Alex and Julie. It was monstrous. "Good God, at a time like this!"

"Uncle, the world hasn't stopped turning on account of your discovery." Such acid in the tone. "And the stock has to be liquidated."

Lawrence laid down the pen. "No, it doesn't," he said, eyeing Henry coldly. "And as for the marriage, it can wait forever. Or until Julie decides for herself. Go home and tell that to my good friend the Earl of Rutherford! And tell your father I will liquidate no further family stock. Now leave me alone."

Henry didn't move. He shifted the briefcase uneasily, his face tightening as he stared down at his uncle.

"Uncle, you don't realize—"

"Allow me to tell you what I *do* realize," Lawrence said, "that you have gambled away a king's ransom and that your father will go to any lengths to cover your debts. Even Cleopatra and her drunken lover Mark Antony could not have squandered the fortune that has slipped through your hands. And what does Julie need with the Rutherford title anyway? Alex needs the Stratford millions, that's the truth of it. Alex is a beggar with a title the same as Elliott. God forgive me. It's the truth."

"Uncle, Alex could buy any heiress in London with that title."

"Then why doesn't he?"

"One word from you and Julie would make up her mind—"

"And Elliott would show his gratitude to you for arranging things, is that it? And with my daughter's money he'd be very generous indeed."

Henry was white with anger.

"What the hell do you care about this marriage?" Lawrence asked bitterly. "You humiliate yourself because you need the money. . . ."

He thought he saw his nephew's lips move in a curse.

He turned back to the mummy, trying to shut it all out—the tentacles of the London life he'd left behind trying to reach him here.

Why, the whole figure looked fuller! And the ring, it was plainly visible now as if the finger, fleshing out, had burst the wrappings altogether. Lawrence fancied he could see the faint color of healthy flesh.

"You're losing your mind," he whispered to himself. And that sound, there it was again. He tried to listen for it; but his concentration only made him all the more conscious of the noise outside. He drew closer to the body in the coffin. Good Lord, was that hair he saw beneath the wrappings about the head?

"I feel so sorry for you, Henry," he whispered suddenly. "That you can't savour such a discovery. This ancient King, this mystery." Who said that he couldn't touch the remains? Just move perhaps an inch of the rotted linen?

He drew out his penknife and held it uncertainly. Twenty years ago he might have cut the thing open. There wouldn't have been any busybody officials to deal with. He might have seen for himself if under all that dust—

"I wouldn't do that if I were you, Uncle," Henry interrupted. "The museum people in London will raise the roof."

"I told you to get out."

He heard Henry pour a cup of coffee as if he had all the time in the world. The aroma filled the close little chamber.

Lawrence backed into the camp chair, and again pressed his folded handkerchief to his brow. Twenty-four hours now without sleep. Maybe he should rest.

"Drink your coffee, Uncle Lawrence," Henry said to him. "I poured it for you." And there it was, the full cup. "They're waiting for you out there. You're exhausted."

"You bloody fool," Lawrence whispered. "I wish you'd go away."

Henry set the cup before him, right by the notebook.

"Careful, that papyrus is priceless."

The coffee did look inviting, even if Henry was pushing it at him. He lifted the cup, took a deep swallow, and closed his eyes.

What had he just seen as he put down the cup? The mummy stirring in the sunlight? Impossible. Suddenly a burning sensation in his throat blotted out everything else. It was as if his throat were closing! He couldn't breathe or speak.

He tried to rise; he was staring at Henry; and suddenly he caught the smell coming from the cup still in his trembling hand. Bitter almonds. It was the poison. The cup was falling; dimly he heard it shatter as it hit the stone floor.

"For the love of God! You bastard!" He was falling; his hands out towards his nephew, who stood white-faced and grim, staring coldly at him as if this catastrophe were not happening; as if he were not dying.

His body convulsed. Violently, he turned away. The last thing he saw as he fell was the mummy in the dazzling sunlight; the last thing he felt was the sandy floor beneath his burning face.

For a long moment Henry Stratford did not move. He stared down at the body of his uncle as if he did not quite believe what he saw. Someone else had done this. Someone else had broken through the thick membrane of frustration and put this horrid plot into motion. Someone else had put the silver coffee spoon into the jar of ancient poison and slipped that poison into Lawrence's cup.

Nothing moved in the dusty sunlight. The tiniest particles seemed suspended in the hot air. Only a faint sound originated within the chamber; something like the beat of a heart.

Imaginings. It was imperative to follow through. It was imperative to stop his hand from shaking; to prevent the scream from ever leaving his lips. Because it was there all right—a scream which once released would never stop.

I killed him. I poisoned him.

And now that great hideous and immovable obstacle to my plan is no more.

Bend down; feel the vein. Yes, he's dead. Quite dead.

Henry straightened, fighting a sudden wave of nausea, and quickly took several papers from his briefcase. He dipped his uncle's pen and wrote the name Lawrence Stratford neatly and quickly, as he had done several times on less important papers in the past.

His hand shook badly, but so much the better. For his uncle had had just such a tremor. And the scribble looked all the better when it was done.

He put the pen back and stood with his eyes closed, trying to calm himself again, trying to think only, It is done.

The most curious thoughts were flooding him suddenly, that he could undo this! That it had been no more than an impulse; that he could roll back the minutes and his uncle would be alive again. This positively could not have happened! Poison . . . coffee . . . Lawrence dead.

And then a memory came to him, pure and quiet and certainly welcome, of the day twenty-one years ago when his cousin Julie had been born. His uncle and he sitting in the drawing room together. His uncle Lawrence, whom he loved more than his father.

"But I want you to know that you will always be my nephew, my beloved nephew. . . ."

Dear God, was he losing his mind? For a moment he did not even know where he was. He could have sworn someone else was in this room with him. Who was it?

That thing in the mummy case. Don't look at it. Like a witness. Get back to the business at hand.

The papers are signed; the stock can be sold; and now there is all the more reason for Julie to marry that stupid twit Alex Savarell. And all the more reason for Henry's father to take Stratford Shipping completely in hand.

Yes. Yes. But what to do at the moment? He looked at the desk again. Everything as it was. And those six glittering gold Cleopatra coins. Ah, yes, take one. Quickly, he slipped it into his pocket. A little flush warmed his face. Yes, the coin must be worth a fortune. And he could fit it into a cigarette case; simple to smuggle. All right.

Now get out of here immediately. No, he wasn't thinking. He couldn't still his heart. Shout for Samir, that was the appropriate action. Something horrible has happened to Lawrence. Stroke, heart attack, impossible to tell! And this cell is like a furnace. A doctor must come at once.

"Samir!" he cried out, staring forward like a matinee actor at the moment of shock. His gaze fell directly again on that grim, loathsome thing in the linen wrappings. Was it staring back at him? Were its eyes open beneath the bandages? Preposterous! Yet the illusion struck a deep shrill note of panic in him, which gave just the right edge to his next shout for help.

* * *

Furtively he read the latest edition of the *London Herald,* the pages folded and held carefully out of sight behind his darkly lacquered desk. The office was quiet now because of the board meeting, the only sound the distant clack of a typewriting machine from an adjoining room.

MUMMY'S CURSE KILLS
STRATFORD SHIPPING MAGNATE
"RAMSES THE DAMNED" STRIKES DOWN
THOSE WHO DISTURB HIS REST

How the tragedy had caught the public imagination. Impossible to walk a step without seeing a front-page story. And how the popular newspapers elaborated upon it, indulging in hastily drawn illustrations of pyramids and camels, of the mummy in his wooden coffin and poor Mr. Stratford lying dead at his feet.

Poor Mr. Stratford, who had been such a fine man to work for; remembered now for this lurid and sensational death.

Just when the furor had died down, it had been given another infusion of vitality:

HEIRESS DEFIES MUMMY'S CURSE
"RAMSES THE DAMNED" TO VISIT LONDON

Fiction

THE JEWEL OF SEVEN STARS

(Abridged)

Bram Stoker

Originally from Dublin, Bram Stoker in his own day was best known as the partner of Henry Irving in the running of the famous Lyceum Theatre in London from 1878 to 1905. Today, his name is synonymous with the world's most famous vampire—Count Dracula. Stoker's creation of this cult hero has proven to be an endless cornucopia for moviemakers, writers, and playwrights. It is now considered to be one of the all-time classics of horror literature. Unfortunately, Dracula (1897) has obscured his other works, some of which are equally deserving of attention. The Jewel of Seven Stars is an outstanding example of a work by Stoker that has fallen into unfortunate obscurity. Although I have abbreviated the novel in order to make it available to a wider audience, I guarantee that it still contains all the power and magic of the original.

"I knew you would come!"

The clasp of the hand can mean a great deal, even when it is not intended to mean anything especially. Following Miss Trelawny, I moved over to a dainty room which opened from the hall and looked out on the garden at the back of the house.

"I will thank you later for your goodness in coming to me in my trouble; but at present you can best help me when you know the facts."

"Go on," I said. "Tell me all you know." She went on at once:

"I was awakened by some sound; I do not know what. I only know that I found myself awake, with my heart beating wildly. My room is next to Father's, and I can often hear him moving about before I fall asleep. Last night I got up softly and stole to the door. There was not any noise of moving, and no kind of cry at all; but there was a queer kind of dragging sound, and a slow, heavy breathing. Oh! it was dreadful, waiting there in the dark and the silence, and fearing—fearing I did not know what!

"I pushed the door open all at once, switched on the electric light, and stepped into the room. I looked first at the bed. The sheets were all crumpled up, so that I knew Father had been in bed; but there was a great dark red patch in the center of the bed that made my heart stand still. As I was gazing at it the sound of the breathing came across the room, and my eyes followed to it. There was Father on his right side with the other arm under him. The track of blood went across the room up to the bed, and there was a pool all around him which looked terribly red and glittering as I bent over to examine him. The place where he lay was right in front of the big safe. He was in his pajamas. The left sleeve was torn, showing his bare arm, and stretched out toward the safe. It looked—oh! so terrible, patched all with blood, and with the flesh torn or cut all around a gold chain bangle on his wrist. I did not know he wore such a thing, and it seemed to give me a new shock of surprise."

She paused a moment; and as I wished to relieve her by a moment's divergence of thought, I said:

"Oh, that need not surprise you. You will see the most unlikely men wearing bangles. I have seen a judge condemn a man to death, and the wrist of the hand he held up had a gold bangle." She went on in a steadier voice:

"I did not lose a moment in summoning aid, for I feared he might bleed to death. We lifted father on a sofa; and the housekeeper, Mrs. Grant, tied a handkerchief round the cut. I sent off one man for the doctor and another for the police. When they had gone, I felt that, except for the servants, I was all alone in the house. Then I thought of you and, without waiting to think, I told the men to get a carriage ready at once, and I sent for to you."

She paused. I did not like to say just then anything of how I felt. I looked at her; I think she understood, for her eyes were raised to mine for a moment and then fell, leaving her cheeks as red as peony roses. With a manifest effort she went on with her story:

"Doctor Winchester was with us in an incredibly short time; then a policeman, Sergeant Daw, arrived; and then you came."

There was a long pause, and I ventured to take her hand for an instant.

We ascended to Mr. Trelawny's room, where we found everything exactly as she had described.

The Police Sergeant turned to Miss Trelawny and said:

"You say that you were outside the door when you heard the noise?"

"I was in my room when I heard the queer sound and I came out of my room at once. Father's door was shut, and I could see the whole landing and the upper slopes of the staircase. No one could have left by the door unknown to me, if that is what you mean!"

"That is just what I do mean, miss." He went to the windows.

"Were the shutters closed?" he asked Miss Trelawny in a casual way as though he expected the negative answer, which came.

"So far as I can see, the object was to bring that key to the lock of the safe. There seems to be some secret in the mechanism. It is a combination lock of seven letters; but there seems to be a way of locking even the combination." Then turning to the Doctor, he said:

"Have you anything you can tell me, Doctor?" Doctor Winchester answered at once:

"There is no wound on the head which could account for the state of stupor in which the patient continues. I must, therefore, take it that either he has been drugged or is under some hypnotic influence. So far as I can judge, he has not been drugged—at least by means of any drug of whose qualities I am aware."

The Detective began a systematic search of the writing-table in the room. In one of the drawers he found a letter sealed; this he brought at once across the room and handed to Miss Trelawny.

"A letter—directed to me—and in my Father's hand!" she said as she eagerly opened it. It said:

MY DEAR DAUGHTER,

I want you to take this letter as an instruction—absolute and imperative, and admitting of no deviation whatever—in case anything untoward or unexpected should happen to me. If I should be suddenly and mysteriously stricken down—either by sickness, accident or attack—you must follow these directions implicitly. If I am not already in my bedroom when you are made cognizant of my state, I am to be brought there as quickly as possible. Thenceforth, until I am conscious and able to give instructions on my own account I am never to be left alone—not for a single instant.

From nightfall to sunrise at least two persons must remain in the room, awake and exercising themselves to my purpose. I should advise you, my dear Daughter, seeing that you have no relative to apply to, to get some friend whom you can trust to remain within the house. Once more, my dear Margaret, let me impress on you the need for observation. If I am taken ill or injured, this will be no ordinary occasion; and I wish to warn you, so that your guarding may be complete.

Nothing in my room—I speak of the curios—must be removed or displaced in any way, or for any cause whatever. I have a special reason and a special purpose in the placing of each; so that any moving of them would thwart my plans.

ABEL TRELAWNY

That night we were not yet regularly organized for watching. Nurse Kennedy, who had been on duty all day, was lying down, as she had arranged to come on again by twelve o'clock. At nine o'clock Miss Trelawny and I went in to relieve the Doctor. He was bending over the bed as we came into the room.

"I am really and absolutely at my wits' end to find any fit cause for this stupor. And as to these wounds"—he laid his finger gently on the bandaged wrist which lay outside the coverlet as he spoke. "Have you any strange pets here in the house; anything of an exceptional kind, such as a tiger-cat or anything out of the common?" Miss Trelawny smiled a sad smile, as she made answer:

"Oh no! Father does not like animals about the house, unless they are dead and mummied. Even my poor kitten was only allowed in the house on sufferance; and though he is the dearest and best-conducted cat in the world, he is now on a sort of parole, and is not allowed into this room."

As she was speaking a faint rattling of the door handle was heard. Instantly Miss Trelawny's face brightened. She sprang up and went over to the door, saying as she went:

"There he is! That is my Silvio. He stands on his hind legs and rattles the door handle when he wants to come into a room." She opened the door, lifted the cat, and came back with him in her arms. He was certainly a magnificent animal. A chinchilla gray Persian with long silky hair; a really lordly animal with a haughty bearing, despite his gentleness; and with great paws which spread out as he placed them on the ground. Whilst she was fondling him, he suddenly gave a wriggle like an eel and slipped out of her arms. He ran across the room and stood opposite a low table on which stood the mummy of an animal, and began to mew and snarl. Miss Trelawny was after him in an instant and lifted him in her arms, kicking and struggling and wriggling to get away; but not biting or scratching, for evidently he loved his beautiful mistress. He ceased to make a noise the moment he was in her arms; in a whisper she admonished him:

"O you naughty Silvio! You have broken your parole. Now, say good-night to the gentlemen, and come away to mother's room!" As she was speaking she held out the cat's paw to me to shake. As I did so I could not but admire its size and beauty. "Why," said I, "his paw seems like a little boxing-glove full of claws." She smiled:

"So it ought to. Don't you notice that my Silvio has seven toes, see!" she opened the paw; and surely enough there were seven separate claws, each of them sheathed in a delicate, fine, shell-like case. As I gently stroked the foot the claws emerged and one of them accidentally—there was no anger now and the cat was purring—stuck into my hand. Instinctively I said as I drew back:

"Why, his claws are like razors!"

Doctor Winchester had come close to us and was bending over looking at the cat's claws. Whilst I was stroking the now quiescent cat, the Doctor went to the table and tore off a piece of blotting-paper from the writing-pad and came back. He laid the paper on his palm and, with a simple "pardon me!" to Miss Trelawny, placed the cat's paw on it and pressed it down with his other hand. The haughty cat seemed to resent somewhat the familiarity, and tried to draw its foot away. This was plainly what the Doctor wanted, for in the act the cat opened the sheaths of its claws and made several reefs in the soft paper. Then Miss Trelawny took her pet away. She returned in a couple of minutes; as she came in she said:

"It is most odd about that mummy! When Silvio came into the room first—indeed I took him in as a kitten to show to Father—he went on just the same way. He jumped up on the table, and tried to scratch and bite the mummy. That was what made Father so angry, and brought the decree of banishment on poor Silvio. Only his parole, given through me, kept him in the house."

Whilst she had been gone, Doctor Winchester had taken the bandage from her father's wrist. The wound was now quite clear, as the separate cuts showed out in fierce red lines. The Doctor held the blotting-paper down close to the wound. The cuts in the paper corresponded with the wounds in the wrist! No explanation was needed, as he said:

"It would have been better if master Silvio had not broken his parole!"

We were all silent for a little while. Suddenly Miss Trelawny said:

"But Silvio was not in here last night!"

"Are you sure? Could you prove that if necessary?" She hesitated before replying:

"I am certain of it; but I fear it would be difficult to prove. Silvio sleeps in a basket in my room. I certainly put him to bed last night; I remember distinctly laying his little blanket over him, and tucking him in. This morning I took him out of the basket myself. I certainly never noticed him in here; though, of course, that would not mean much, for I was too concerned about poor father, and too much occupied with him, to notice even Silvio."

The Doctor shook his head as he said with a certain sadness:

"Well, at any rate it is no use trying to prove anything now. Any cat in the world would have cleaned blood-marks—did any exist—from his paws in a hundredth part of the time that has elapsed."

Again we were all silent; and again the silence was broken by Miss Trelawny:

"But now that I think of it, it could not have been poor Silvio that injured Father. My door was shut when I first heard the sound; and Father's was shut when I listened at it. When I went in, the injury had been done; so that it must have been before Silvio could possibly have got in." This reasoning commended itself, especially to me as a barrister, for it was proof to satisfy a jury. It gave me a distinct pleasure to have Silvio acquitted of the crime—possibly because he was Miss Trelawny's cat and was loved by her. Silvio's mistress was manifestly pleased as I said:

"Verdict, 'not guilty!'" Doctor Winchester after a pause observed:

"My apologies to master Silvio on this occasion; but I am still puzzled to know why he is so keen against that mummy. Is he the same toward the other mummies in the house? There are, I suppose, a lot of them. I saw three in the hall as I came in."

"There are lots of them," she answered. "I sometimes don't know whether I am in a private house or the British Museum. But Silvio never concerns himself about any of them except that particular one. I suppose it must be because it is of an animal, not a man or a woman."

"Perhaps it is of a cat!" said the Doctor as he started up and went across the room to look at the mummy more closely. "Yes," he went on, "it is the mummy of a cat; and a very fine one, too. If it hadn't been a special favorite of some very special person it would never have received so much honor. See! A painted case and obsidian eyes—just like a human mummy. It is an extraordinary thing, that knowledge of kind to kind. Here is a dead cat—that is all; it is perhaps four or five thousand years old—and another cat of another breed, in what is practically another world, is ready to fly at it, just as it would if it were not dead. I should like to experiment a bit about that cat if you don't mind, Miss Trelawny." She hesitated before replying:

"Of course, do anything you may think necessary or wise; but I hope it will not be anything to hurt or worry my poor Silvio."

"Oh, Silvio will be all right. There are plenty of mummy cats to be had in Museum Street. I shall get one and place it here instead of that one. We shall then find out whether Silvio objects to all mummy cats, or only to this one in particular."

After a pause she went on: "But of course under the circumstances anything that is to be ultimately for his good must be done. I suppose there can't be anything very particular about the mummy of a cat."

Doctor Winchester said nothing. The room and all in it gave grounds for strange thoughts. There were so many mummies or mummy objects around which seemed to for ever be releasing the penetrating odors of bitumen, and spices and gums. In far corners of the room were shadows of uncanny shape. More than once as I thought, the multitudinous presence of the dead and the past took such hold on me that I caught myself looking round fearfully as though some strange personality or influence was present. It was with a distinct sense of relief that I saw a new personality in the room in the shape of Nurse Kennedy, allowing the doctor and Miss Trelawny to get some rest. There was no doubt that that business-like, self-reliant, capable young woman added an element of security to such wild imaginings as my own. The only thing which it could not altogether abrogate was the strange Egyptian smell. You may put a mummy in a glass case and hermetically seal it so that no corroding air can get within; but all the same it will exhale its odor. One might think that four or five thousand years would exhaust the olfactory qualities of anything; but experience teaches us that these smells remain, and that their secrets are unknown to us. Today they are as much mysteries as they were when the embalmers put the body in the bath of natron. . . .

All at once I sat up. I had become lost in an absorbing reverie. The Egyptian smell had seemed to get on my nerves—on my memory—on my very will. Without stating my intention, I went downstairs and out of the house. I soon found a chemist's shop, and came away with a respirator.

Though I really cannot remember being asleep or waking from it, I saw a vision—I dreamed a dream. I scarcely know which.

I was still in the room, seated in the chair. I had on my respirator and knew that I breathed freely. The Nurse sat in her chair with her back toward me. She sat quite still. The sick man lay as still as the dead. The light was very, very low; the reflection of it under the green-shaded lamp was a dim relief to the darkness, rather than light. The green silk fringe of the lamp had merely the color of an emerald seen in the moonlight. The room, for all its darkness, was full of shadows. It seemed in my whirling thoughts as though all the real things had become shadows—shadows which moved, for they passed the dim outline of the high windows. I even thought there was sound, a faint sound as of the mew of a cat—the rustle of drapery and a metallic clink as of metal faintly touching metal. I sat as one entranced. At last I felt, as in nightmare, that this was sleep, and that in the passing of its portals all my will had gone.

All at once my senses were full awake. A shriek rang in my ears. The room was filled suddenly with a blaze of light. There was the sound of pistol shots—one, two; and a haze of white smoke in the room. When my waking eyes regained their power, I could have shrieked with horror myself at what I saw before me.

The sight which met my eyes had the horror of a dream within a dream, with the certainty of reality added. The room was as I had seen it last; except that the shadowy look had gone in the glare of the many lights, and every article in it stood stark and solidly real.

By the empty bed sat Nurse Kennedy, as my eyes had last seen her, sitting bolt upright in the armchair beside the bed. She had placed a pillow behind her, so that her back might be erect; but her neck was fixed as that of one in a cataleptic trance. She was, to all intents and purposes, turned into stone. The bedclothes were disarranged, as though the patient had been drawn from under them without throwing them back. The corner of the upper sheet hung upon the floor; close by it lay one of the bandages with which the Doctor had dressed the wounded wrist. Another and another lay further along the floor, as though forming a clue to where the sick man now lay. This was almost exactly where he had been found on the previous night, under the great safe. Again, the left arm lay toward the safe. But there had been a new outrage, an attempt had been made to sever the arm close to the bangle which held the tiny key. A heavy "kukri" knife—one of the leaf-shaped knives which the Gurkhas and others of the hill tribes of India use with such effect—had been taken from its place on the wall, and with it the attempt had been made. It was manifest that just at the moment of striking, the blow had been arrested, for only the point of the knife and not the edge of the blade had struck the flesh. As it was, the outer side of the arm had been cut to the bone and the blood was pouring out. In addition, the former wound in front of the arm had been cut or torn about terribly; one of the cuts seemed to jet out blood as if with each pulsation of the heart. By the side of her father knelt Miss Trelawny, her white nightdress stained with the blood in which she knelt. In the middle of the room Sergeant Daw, in his shirt and trousers and stocking feet, was putting fresh cartridges into his revolver in a dazed mechanical kind of way. His eyes were red and heavy, and he seemed only half awake, and less than half conscious of what was going on around him. Several servants, bearing lights of various kinds, were clustered round the doorway.

As I rose from my chair and came forward, Miss Trelawny raised her eyes toward me. When she saw me she shrieked and started to her feet, pointing towards me. Never shall I forget the strange picture she made, with her white drapery all smeared with blood which, as she rose from the pool, ran in streaks toward her bare feet. I believe that I had only been asleep; that whatever influence had worked on Mr. Trelawny and Nurse Kennedy—and in less degree on Sergeant Daw—had not touched me. The respirator had been of some service, though it had not kept off the tragedy whose dire evidences were before me. I can understand now the fright which my appearance must have evoked. I had still on the respirator, which covered mouth and nose; my hair had been tossed in my sleep. Coming suddenly forward, thus enwrapped and disheveled, in that horrified crowd, I must have had, in the strange mixture of lights, an extraordinary and terrifying appearance. It was well that I recognized all this in time to avert another catastrophe; for the half-dazed, mechanically-acting Detective put in the cartridges and had raised his revolver to shoot at me when I succeeded in wrenching off the respirator and shouting to him to hold his hand.

Mrs. Grant took her mistress away and changed her clothes. She was back presently in a dressing-gown and slippers, and with the traces of blood removed from her hands. She was now much calmer, though she trembled sadly; and her face was ghastly white. It was so apparent to me that she did not know where to begin or whom to trust, so I said:

"Tell me what you remember!" The effort to recollect seemed to stimulate her; she became calmer as she spoke:

"I was asleep, and woke suddenly with the same horrible feeling on me that Father was in great and immediate danger. I jumped up and ran into his room. It was nearly pitch dark, but as I opened the door there was light enough to see Father's nightdress as he lay on the floor under the safe, just as on that first awful night. Then I think I must have gone mad for a moment." She stopped and shuddered. My eyes lit on Sergeant Daw, still fiddling in an aimless way with the revolver.

"Now tell us, Sergeant Daw, what did you fire at?" The policeman seemed to pull himself together with the habit of obedience.

"I went to sleep half-dressed—as I am now, with a revolver under my pillow. I thought I heard a scream; but I can't be sure, for I felt thick-headed as a man does when he is called too soon after an extra long stretch of work. Anyhow, my thoughts flew to the pistol. I took it out, and ran on to the landing. Then I heard a sort of scream, or rather a call for help, and ran into this room. The room was dark, for the lamp beside the Nurse was out, and the only light was that from the landing, coming through the open door. Miss Trelawny was kneeling on the floor beside her father, and was screaming. I thought I saw something move between me and the window; so, without thinking, and being half dazed and only half awake, I shot at it. It moved a little more to the right between the windows, and I shot again. Then you came up out of the big chair with all that muffling on your face. It seemed to me as if it had been you, being in the same direction as the thing I had fired at. And so I was about to fire again when you pulled off the wrap." Here I asked him—I was cross-examining now and felt at home:

"You say you thought I was the thing you fired at. What thing?" The man scratched his head, but made no reply.

"Come, sir," I said, "what thing; what was it like?" The answer came in a low voice:

"I don't know, sir. I thought there was something; but what it was I haven't the faintest notion."

When I went back to the sofa and took the tourniquet from Mrs. Grant, she went over and pulled up the blinds.

It would be hard to imagine anything more ghastly than the appearance of the room with the faint gray light of early morning coming in upon it. As the windows faced north, any light that came was a fixed gray light without any of the rosy possibility of dawn which comes in the eastern quarter of the heavens. The electric lights seemed dull and yet glaring; and every shadow was of a hard intensity. There was nothing of morning freshness; nothing of the softness of night. All was hard and cold, and inexpressibly dreary. The face of the senseless man on the sofa seemed of a ghastly yellow; and the Nurse's face had taken a suggestion of green from the shade of the lamp near her. Only Miss Trelawny's face looked white; and it was of a pallor which made my heart ache. It looked as if nothing on God's earth could ever again bring back to it the color of life and happiness.

Nurse Kennedy had slowly returned to her normal self late in the morning and Miss Trelawny slept into the afternoon. Before supper I was about to go out for a walk, when I noticed a man at the front door arguing with the butler. He claimed to be a colleague of Mr. Trelawny and insisted on seeing him. The butler refused to allow him in, saying Mr. Trelawny was too ill for visitors. I told the butler I would handle the matter. I took the man into the boudoir across the hall and sent for Margaret.

"I am a friend of Miss Trelawny's. My name is Ross."

"Thank you very much, Mr. Ross, for your kindness!" he said. "My name is Corbeck. I would give you my card, but they don't use cards where I've come from."

Miss Trelawny came very quickly and he began again:

"Good afternoon, Miss Trelawny. My name is Eugene Corbeck. I am a Master of Arts and Doctor of Laws and Master of Surgery of Cambridge; Doctor of Letters of Oxford; Doctor of Science and Doctor of Languages of London University; Doctor of Philosophy of Berlin; Doctor of Oriental Languages of Paris. I have some other degrees, honorary and otherwise, but I need not trouble you with them. Those I have named will show you that I am sufficiently feathered with diplomas to fly into even a sick-room. Early in life I fell in with Egyptology. I must have been bitten by some powerful scarab, for I took it bad. I went out tomb-hunting; and managed to get a living of a sort, and to learn some things that you can't get out of books. I was in pretty low water when I met your father, who was doing some explorations on his own account; and since then I haven't found that I have many unsatisfied wants. He is a real patron of the arts; no mad Egyptologist can ever hope for a better chief!

"I have been several times out on expeditions in Egypt for your father. Many of his treasures—and he has some rare ones he has procured through me, either by my exploration or by purchase—or—or—otherwise. Your father, Miss Trelawny, has a rare knowledge. He sometimes makes up his mind that he wants to find a particular thing, of whose existence—if it still exists—he has become aware; and he will follow it all over the world till he gets it. I've been on just such a chase now."

He paused, and an embarrassed look crept over his face. Suddenly he said:

"You are sure, Miss Trelawny, your father is not well enough to see me today?"

She stood up, saying in a tone in which dignity and graciousness were blended:

"Come and see for yourself!" She moved toward her father's room; he followed, and I brought up the rear.

Mr. Corbeck entered the sick-room as though he knew it. I watched him narrowly, for somehow I felt that on this man depended much of our enlightenment regarding the strange matter in which we were involved.

"Tell me all about it. How it began and when!" Miss Trelawny looked at me appealingly; and forthwith I told him all that I knew. He seemed to make no motion during the whole time; but insensibly the bronze face became steel.

"Good! Now I know where my duty lies!"

"What do you mean?" I asked.

"Trelawny knows what he is doing. He had some definite purpose in all that he did; and we must not thwart him. He evidently expected something to happen, and guarded himself at all points."

"Not at all points!" I said impulsively. "There must have been a weak spot somewhere, or he wouldn't be lying here like that!" Somehow his impassiveness surprised me. Something like a smile flickered over his swarthy face as he answered me:

"This is not the end! Trelawny did not guard himself to no purpose. Doubtless, he expected this too; or at any rate the possibility of it."

Margaret and I spent the rest of the afternoon looking over the curio treasures of Mr. Trelawny. From what I had heard from Mr. Corbeck I began to have some idea of the vastness of his enterprise in the world of Egyptian research; and with this light everything around me began to have a new interest. The house seemed to be a veritable storehouse of marvels of antique art. In addition to the curios, big and little, in Mr. Trelawny's own room—from the great sarcophagi down to the scarabs of all kinds in the cabinets—the great hall, the staircase landings, the study, and even the boudoir were full of antique pieces which would have made a collector's mouth water.

The most interesting of the sarcophagi were undoubtedly the three in Mr. Trelawny's room. Of these, two were of dark stone. These were wrought with some hieroglyphs. But the third was strikingly different. It was of some yellow-brown substance. Here and there were patches almost transparent—certainly translucent. The whole chest was wrought with hundreds of minute hieroglyphics, the deep blue of their coloring showing up fresh and sharply edged in the yellow stone. It was very long, nearly nine feet; and perhaps a yard wide. The sides undulated, so that there was no hard line. Even the corners took such excellent curves that they pleased the eye. Inside was a raised space, outlined like a human figure. "Truly," I said, "this must have been made for a giant!"

"Or for a giantess!" said Margaret.

Close beside the sarcophagus was a low table of green stone with red veins in it, like bloodstone. On it rested a strange and very beautiful coffer or casket of stone of a peculiar shape. It was something like a small coffin, except that it was an irregular septahedron, there being two planes on each of the two sides, one end and a top and bottom. The stone was of a full green, the color of emerald without its gleam. The surface was almost that of a jewel. It was quite unlike anything I had ever seen, and did not resemble any stone or gem that I knew. In length it was about two feet and a half; in breadth about half this, and was nearly a foot high. I tried to lift up the lid but it was securely fixed. It fitted so exactly that the whole coffer seemed like a single piece of stone mysteriously hollowed from within. On the sides and edges of the table, on which the coffer rested, were some odd-looking protuberances.

On the other side of the great sarcophagus, on a small table, stood a case of about a foot square. Within, on a cushion of cloth of gold as fine as silk rested a mummy hand, so perfect that it startled one to see it. A woman's hand, fine and long, with slim tapering fingers and nearly as perfect as when it was given to the embalmer thousands of years before. In the embalming it had lost nothing of its beautiful shape; even the wrist seemed to maintain its pliability as the gentle curve lay on the cushion. The great peculiarity of it, as a hand, was that it had in all seven fingers, there being two middle and two index fingers. The upper end of the wrist was jagged, as though it had been broken off, and was stained with a red-brown stain.

"That is another of Father's mysteries. When I asked him about it he said that it was perhaps the most valuable thing he had, except one. When I asked him what that one was, he refused to tell me. 'I will tell you,' he said, 'all about it in good time.'"

Shortly after supper, Doctor Winchester arrived. He had a large parcel with him, which, when unwrapped, proved to be the mummy of a cat. With Miss Trelawny's permission he placed this in the boudoir; and Silvio was brought close to it. To the surprise of us all, however, except perhaps Doctor Winchester, he did not manifest the least annoyance; he took no notice of it whatever. He stood on the table close beside it, purring loudly. Then, following out his plan, the Doctor brought him into Mr. Trelawny's room, we all following. Doctor Winchester was excited; Miss Trelawny anxious. I was more than interested myself, for I began to have a glimmering of the Doctor's idea. The Detective was calmly and coldly superior: but Mr. Corbeck, who was an enthusiast, was full of eager curiosity.

The moment Doctor Winchester got into the room, Silvio began to mew and wriggle; and, jumping out of his arms, ran over to the cat mummy and began to scratch angrily at it. Miss Trelawny had some difficulty in taking him away; but so soon as he was out of the room he became quiet. When she came back there was a clamor of comments:

"I thought so!" from the Doctor.

"What can it mean?" from Miss Trelawny.

"That's a very strange thing!" from Mr. Corbeck.

"Odd! but it doesn't prove anything!" from the Detective.

Doctor Winchester turned to Mr. Corbeck:

"I want you, if you will, to translate some hieroglyphic for me."

"Certainly, with the greatest pleasure, so far as I can."

"There are two," he answered, handing him the first mummy cat. The scholar took it; and, after a short examination, said:

"There is nothing especial in this. It is an appeal to Bast, the Lady of Bubastis, to give her good bread and milk in the Elysian Fields. There may be more inside; and if you will care to unroll it, I will do my best. I do not think, however, that there is anything special. From the method of wrapping I should say it is from Delta; and of a late period, when such mummy work was common and cheap. What is the other inscription you wish me to see?"

"The inscription on Mr. Trelawny's mummy cat."

Mr. Corbeck's face fell. "No!" he said, "I cannot do that! I am, for the present, not prepared to discuss any of the things in Mr. Trelawny's room." Then turning to me, he said, "Mr. Ross, I understand that you are to have a spell of watching in the sick-room tonight. I shall get you a book which will help to pass the time for you. It will be necessary, or at least helpful, to understand other things which I shall tell you later."

The book was by one Nicholas van Huyn of Hoorn. In the preface he told how, attracted by the work of John Greaves of Merton College, *Pyramidographia,* he himself visited Egypt, exploring the ruins of many temples and tombs.

The narrative went on to tell how, after passing for several days through the mountains to the east of Aswan, the explorer came to a certain place. Here I give his own words, simply putting the translation into modern English:

"Toward evening we came to the entrance of a narrow, deep valley, running east and west. I wished to proceed through this; for the sun, now nearly down on the horizon, showed a wide opening beyond the narrowing of the cliffs. But the fellaheen absolutely refused to enter the valley at such a time, alleging that they might be caught by the night before they could emerge from the other end. At first they would give no reason for their fear. They had hitherto gone anywhere I wished, and at any time, without demur. On being pressed, however, they said that the place was the Valley of the Sorcerer, where none might come in the night. On being asked to tell of the Sorcerer, they refused. The next morning, however, when the sun was up and shining down the valley, their fears had somewhat passed away. Then they told me that a great Sorcerer, in ancient days a King or a Queen, they could not say which, was buried there. They could not give the name, persisting to the last that there was no name; and that anyone who should name it would waste away in life so that at death nothing of him would remain to be raised again in the Other World. In passing through the valley they kept together in a cluster, hurrying on in front of me. None dared to remain behind. They gave, as their reason for so proceeding, that the arms of the Sorcerer were long, and that it was dangerous to be the last. The which was of little comfort to me who of this necessity took that honorable post. In the narrowest part of the valley, on the south side, was a great cliff of rock, rising sheer, of smooth and even surface. Hereon were graven certain cabalistic signs, and many figures of men and animals, fishes, reptiles and birds; suns and stars; and many quaint symbols. The cliff faced exactly north. There was something about it so strange, and so different from the other carved rocks which I had visited, that I called a halt and spent the day in examining the rock front as well as I could with my telescope. The Egyptians of my company were terribly afraid, and used every kind of persuasion to induce me to pass on. I stayed till late in the afternoon, by which time I had failed to make out aright the entry of any tomb. By this time the men were rebellious; and I had to leave the valley if I did not wish my whole retinue to desert. But I secretly made up my mind to discover the tomb, and explore it. To this end I went further into the mountains, where I met with an Arab Sheik who was willing to take service with me. The Arabs were not bound by the same superstitious fears as the Egyptians; Sheik Abu Soma and his following were willing to take a part in the explorations.

"Being baffled of winning the tomb from below, and being unprovided with ladders to scale the face of the rock, I found a way by much circuitous journeying to the top of the cliff. Thence I caused myself to be lowered by ropes. I found that there was an entrance, closed however by a great stone slab. This was cut in the rock more than a hundred feet up, being two-thirds the height of the cliff. The hieroglyphic and cabalistic symbols cut in the rock were so managed as to disguise it. I used much force, and by many heavy strokes won a way into the tomb. The stone door having fallen into the entrance, I passed over it into the tomb, noting as I went a long iron chain which hung coiled on a bracket close to the doorway.

"The tomb I found to be complete, after the manner of the finest Egyptian tombs, with chamber and shaft leading down to the corridor, ending in the Mummy Pit. All the walls of the chamber and the passage were carved with strange writings. We descended into the Mummy Pit. The huge sarcophagus in the deep pit was marvelously graven throughout with signs. The Arab chief and two others who ventured into the tomb with me, and who were evidently used to such grim explorations, managed to take the cover from the sarcophagus without breaking it.

"Within the sarcophagus was a body, manifestly of a woman, swathed with many wrappings of linen, as is usual with all mummies. Across the breast was one hand, unwrapped. Arm and hand were of dusky white, being of the hue of ivory that hath lain long in air. The skin and the nails were complete and whole, as though the body had been placed for burial over night. I touched the hand and moved it, the arm being something flexible as a live arm; though stiff with long disuse. There was, too, an added wonder that on this ancient hand were no less than seven fingers. Sooth to say, it made me shudder and my flesh creep to touch that hand that had lain there undisturbed for so many thousands of years, and yet was like unto living flesh. Underneath the hand, as though guarded by it, lay a huge jewel of ruby; a great stone of wondrous bigness, for the ruby is in the main a small jewel. This one was of wondrous color, being as of fine blood whereon the light shineth. But its wonder lay not in its size or color, but in that the light of it shone from seven stars as clearly as though the stars were in reality there imprisoned. Taking this rare jewel, together with certain amulets of strangeness and richness being wrought of jewel-stones, I made haste to depart. I would have remained longer but that I feared so to do. For it came to me all at once that I was in a desert place, with strange men who were with me because they were not over-scrupulous. That we were in a lone cavern of the dead, a hundred feet above the ground, where none could find me were ill done to me, nor would any ever seek. But in secret I determined that I would come again, though with more secure following, as I saw many things of strange import in that wondrous tomb; including a casket of eccentric shape made of some strange stone, which was in the great sarcophagus itself. There was in the tomb also another coffer which, though of rare proportion and adornment, was more simply shaped. The cover was lightly cemented down with what seemed gum and Paris plaster, as though to insure that no air could penetrate. Within, closely packed, stood four jars finely wrought and carved with various adornments. I had before known that such burial urns as these were used to contain the entrails and other organs of the mummied dead; but on opening these we found that they held but oil. I was warned of my danger by seeing in the eyes of the Arabs certain covetous glances. Whereon, in order to hasten their departure, I wrought upon those fears of superstition which even in these callous men were apparent. The chief of the Bedouins ascended from the Mummy Pit to give the signal to those above to raise us; and I, not caring to remain with the men whom I mistrusted, followed him immediately. The others did not come at once; from which I feared that they were rifling the tomb afresh on their own account. At last they came. One of them, who ascended first, in landing at the top of the cliff lost his foothold and fell below. He was instantly killed. Before coming away I pulled into its place again, as well as I could, the slab of stone that covered the entrance to the tomb.

"When we all stood on the hill above the cliff, the burning sun that was bright and full of glory was good to see after the darkness and strange mystery of the tomb. Even was I glad that the poor Arab who fell down the cliff and lay dead below, lay in the sunlight and not in that gloomy cavern. I would fain have gone with my companions to seek him and give him sepulture of some kind; but the Sheik made light of it, and sent two of his men to see to it whilst we went on our way.

"That night as we camped, one of the men only returned, saying that a lion of the desert had killed his companion after they had buried the dead man in very deep sand without the valley, and had covered the spot where he lay with many great rocks, so that jackals or other preying beasts might not dig him up again as is their wont.

"Later, in the light of the fire round which the men sat or lay, I saw him exhibit to his fellows something white which they seemed to regard with special awe and reverence. So I drew near silently, and saw that it was none other than the white hand of the mummy which had lain protecting the Jewel in the great sarcophagus. I heard the Bedouin tell how he had found it on the body of him who had fallen from the cliff. There was no mistaking it, for there were the seven fingers which I had noted before. This man must have wrenched it off the dead body whilst his chief and I were otherwise engaged; and from the awe of the others I doubted not that he had hoped to use it as an amulet, or charm. Whereas if powers it had, they were not for him who had taken it from the dead; since his death followed hard upon his theft. Already his amulet had had an awesome baptism; for the wrist of the dead hand was stained with red as though it had been dipped in recent blood.

"That night I was in certain fear lest there should be some violence done to me; for if the poor dead hand was so valued as a charm, what must be the worth in such wise of the rare Jewel which it had guarded.

"As I sank into the unconsciousness of sleep, I hid the graven Star Jewel in the hollow of my clenched hand.

"I waked out of sleep with the light of the morning sun on my face. I sat up and looked around me. The fire was out, and the camp was desolate; save for one figure which lay prone close to me. It was that of the Arab chief, who lay on his back, dead. His face was almost black; and his eyes were open, and staring horribly up at the sky, as though he saw there some dreadful vision. He had evidently been strangled; for on looking, I found on his throat the red marks where fingers had pressed. There seemed so many of these marks that I counted them. There were seven; and all parallel, except the thumb mark, as though made with one hand. This thrilled me as I thought of the mummy hand with the seven fingers.

"I paused not, but fled from the place. I journeyed on alone through the hot desert, till, by God's grace, I came upon an Arab tribe camping by a well, who gave me salt. With them I rested till they had set me on my way.

"I know not what became of the mummy hand. It doubtless is used as a charm of potence by some desert tribe."

Twice, whilst I had been reading this engrossing narrative, I had thought that I had seen across the page streaks of shade, which the weirdness of the subject had made to seem like the shadow of a hand. On the first of these occasions I found that the illusion came from the fringe of green silk around the lamp; but on the second I had looked up, and my eyes had lit on the mummy hand across the room on which the starlight was falling under the edge of the blind. I looked over at the bed; and it comforted me to think that the Nurse still sat there, calm and wakeful.

I sat looking at the book on the table before me; and so many strange thoughts crowded on me that my mind began to whirl. It was almost as if the light on the white fingers in front of me was beginning to have some hypnotic effect. All at once, all thoughts seemed to stop; and for an instant the world and time stood still.

There lay a real hand across the book! What was there to so overcome me, as was the case? I knew the hand that I saw on the book. Margaret Trelawny's hand was a joy to me to see; and yet at that moment, coming after other marvelous things, it had a strangely moving effect on me. It was but momentary, however, and had passed even before her voice had reached me.

"What disturbs you? What are you staring at the book for? I thought for an instant that you must have been overcome again!" I jumped up.

"I was reading," I said, "an old book from the library." As I spoke I closed it and put it under my arm. Nurse Kennedy was ready to go to bed; so Miss Trelawny watched with me in the room.

The next morning, Mr. Corbeck talked the whole matter over with me.

"I think you should know what followed Van Huyn's narrative. When Mr. Trelawny and I met, which we did through his seeking the assistance of other Egyptologists in his work, we talked over this as we did over many other things; and we determined to make a search for the mysterious valley. Whilst we were waiting to start on the travel, for many things were required which Mr. Trelawny undertook to see to himself, I went to Holland to try if I could by any traces verify Van Huyn's narrative. I set me to work to find what had become of his treasures; for that such a traveler must have had great treasures was apparent. At last, in the shop of an old watchmaker and jeweler at Hoorn, I found what he considered his chiefest treasure: a great ruby, carven like a scarab, with seven stars in the shape of the constellation of the Plough,[7] and engraven with hieroglyphics. The jewel was put in security in Mr. Trelawny's great safe; and we started out on our journey of exploration in full hope.

"We got together a band of Arabs whom one or other of us had known in former trips to the desert, and whom we could trust; that is, we did not distrust them as much as others. We were numerous enough to protect ourselves from chance marauding bands.

"Well, after much wandering and trying every winding in the interminable jumble of hills, we came at last at nightfall on just such a valley as Van Huyn had described.

"The following morning Mr. Trelawny and I went alone into the tomb. Within, we found a great sarcophagus of yellow stone. But that I need not describe: you have seen it in Mr. Trelawny's chamber. There must, however, be one sense of disappointment. I could not help feeling how different must have been the sight which met the Dutch traveler's eyes when he looked within and

---

[7] The Big Dipper.

found that white hand lying lifelike above the shrouding mummy cloths. It is true that a part of the arm was there, white and ivory like.

"I shall not trouble you with details of all we saw, or how we learned all we knew. Part of it was from knowledge common to scholars; part we read on the Stele in the tomb, and in the sculptures and hieroglyphic paintings on the walls.

"The tomb belonged to Queen Tera, who was of the Eleventh, or Theban, Dynasty of Egyptian Kings which held sway between the twenty-ninth and twenty-fifth centuries before Christ. She succeeded as the only child of her father, Antef. She must have been a girl of extraordinary character as well as ability, for she was but a young girl when her father died. Her youth and sex encouraged the ambitious priesthood, which had then achieved immense power. They were then secretly ready to make an effort to transfer the governing power from a Kingship to a Hierarchy. But King Antef had suspected some such movement, and had taken the precaution of securing to his daughter the allegiance of the army. He had also had her taught statecraft, and had even made her learned in the lore of the very priests themselves. He had used those of one cult against the other.

"But the King had gone to further lengths, and had had his daughter taught magic, by which she had power over Sleep and Will. This was real magic—'black' magic; not the magic of the temples, which, I may explain, was of the harmless or 'white' order, and was intended to impress rather than to effect. She had been an apt pupil; and had gone further than her teachers. She had won secrets from nature in strange ways; and had even gone to the lengths of going down into the tomb herself, having been swathed and coffined and left as dead for a whole month.

"Perhaps the most remarkable statement in the records, both on the Stele and in the mural writings, was that Queen Tera had power to compel the Gods. This, by the way, was not an isolated belief in Egyptian history; but was different in its cause. She had engraved on a ruby, carved like a scarab, and having seven stars of seven points, Master Words to compel all the Gods, both of the Upper and the Under Worlds.

"In the statement it was plainly set forth that the hatred of the priests was stored up for her, and that they would after her death try to suppress her name. This was a terrible revenge in Egyptian mythology; for without a name no one can after death be introduced to the Gods, or have prayers said for him. Therefore, she had intended her resurrection to be after a long time in a more northern land, under the constellation whose seven stars had ruled her birth. To this end, her hand was to be in the air—'unwrapped'—and in it the Jewel of Seven Stars, so that wherever was air she might move even as her Ka could move! This Mr. Trelawny and I agreed meant that her body could become astral at command, and so move, particle by particle, and become whole again when and where required.

"After extensive examinations of the tomb, we carefully removed all we could. With our heavy baggage, we set out on our laborious journey back to the Nile. The nights were an anxious time with us, for we feared attack from some marauding band. But more still we feared some of those with us. They were, after all, but predatory, unscrupulous men; and we had with us a considerable bulk of precious things. We had taken the mummy from the sarcophagus, and packed it for safety of travel in a separate case. During the first night two attempts were made to steal things from the cart; and two men were found dead in the morning.

"On the second night there came on a violent storm, one of those terrible simoons of the desert which make one feel his helplessness. We were overwhelmed with the drifting sand. Some of our Bedouins had fled before the storm, hoping to find shelter; the rest of us endured with what patience we could. In the morning, when the storm had passed, we recovered from under the piles of sand what we could of our impedimenta. We found the case in which the mummy had been packed all broken, but the mummy itself could nowhere be found. We searched everywhere around, and dug up the sand which had piled around us; but in vain. Mr. Trelawny finally said to me:

"'We must go back to the tomb in the Valley of the Sorcerer.'

"'All right!' I answered. 'But why shall we go there?' His answer seemed to thrill through me as though it had struck some chord ready tuned within:

"'We shall find the mummy there! I am sure of it!'

"The Arabs were surprised when we retraced our steps. There was a good deal of friction, and there were several desertions; so that it was with a diminished following that we took our way eastward again. Mr. Trelawny and I took ropes and torches, and again ascended to the tomb. It was evident that someone had been there in our absence, for the stone slab which protected the entrance to the tomb was lying flat inside, and a rope was dangling from the cliff summit. The first thing noticeable was the emptiness of the place.

"It was made more infinitely desolate still by the shrouded figure of the mummy of Queen Tera which lay on the floor where the great sarcophagus had stood! Beside it lay, in the strange contorted attitudes of violent death, three of the Arabs who had deserted from our party. Their faces were black, and their hands and necks were smeared with blood which had burst from mouth and nose and eyes.

"On the throat of each were the marks, now blackening, of a hand of seven fingers.

"Trelawny and I drew close, and clutched each other in awe and fear as we looked.

"For, most wonderful of all, across the breast of the mummied Queen lay a hand of seven fingers, ivory white, the wrist only showing a scar like a jagged red line, from which seemed to depend drops of blood.

"We got to Cairo all right, and from there to Alexandria. At Alexandria, Trelawny found waiting a cable stating that Mrs. Trelawny had died in giving birth to a daughter. Her stricken husband hurried off at once by the Orient Express; and I had to bring the treasures alone to the desolate house. Since he received that cable in the shipping office at Alexandria I have never seen a happy smile on his face.

"Work is the best thing in such a case; and to his work he devoted himself heart and soul. The strange tragedy of his loss and gain—for the child was born after the mother's death—took place during our second visit to the tomb of Queen Tera. He told me very little about his daughter; but I could see that he loved, almost idolized her. Yet he could never forget that her birth had cost her mother's life. She is unlike her mother; but in both feature and color she has a marvelous resemblance to the pictures of Queen Tera.

"Years later he sent for me early one morning. I was then studying in the British Museum, and had rooms in Hart Street. When I came, he was all on fire with excitement. The window blinds were down and the shutters closed. The ordinary lights in the room were not lit, but there were a lot of powerful electric lamps, fifty candle-power at least, arranged on one side of the room. The little bloodstone table on which the heptagonal coffer stands was drawn to the center of the room. The coffer looked exquisite in the glare of light which shone on it. It actually seemed to glow as if lit in some way from within.

"'What do you think of it?' he asked.

"'It is like a jewel,' I answered. 'You may well call it the "Sorcerer's Magic Coffer," if it often looks like that. It almost seems to be alive.'

"As I spoke he turned up the ordinary lights of the room and switched off the special ones. The effect on the stone box was surprising; in a second it lost all its glowing effect.

"'Do you notice anything in the arrangement of the lamps?' he asked.

"'No!'

"'They were in the shape of the stars in the Plough, as the stars are in the ruby!' I listened as Trelawny went on to explain:

"'For sixteen years I have never ceased to think of that adventure, or to try to find a clue to the mysteries which came before us; but never until last night did I seem to find a solution. It might be, I thought, that the light of the seven stars, shining in the right direction, might have some effect on the box, or something within it. I raised the blind and looked out. The Plough was high in the heavens, and both its stars and the Pole Star were straight opposite the window. I pulled the table with the coffer out into the light, and shifted it until the translucent patches were in the direction of the stars. Instantly the box began to glow, as you saw it under the lamps.

"'All at once it came to me that if light could have some effect there should be in the tomb some means of producing light; for there could not be starlight in the Mummy Pit in the cavern. Then the whole thing seemed to become clear. On the bloodstone table, which has a hollow carved in its top, into which the bottom of the coffer fits, I laid the Magic Coffer; and I at once saw that the odd protuberances so carefully wrought in the substance of the stone corresponded in a way to the stars in the constellation. These, then, were to hold lights. So all we want are the lamps. Where are the lamps? I shall tell you: In the tomb! Do you remember wondering, when we examined the tomb, at the lack of one thing which is usually found in such a tomb?'

"'Yes! There was no serdâb.'

"The Serdâb, I may perhaps explain," said Mr. Corbeck to me, "is a sort of niche built or hewn in the wall of a tomb. Those which have as yet been examined bear no inscriptions, and contain only effigies of the dead for whom the tomb was made." Then he went on with his narrative:

"Trelawny, when he saw that I had caught his meaning, went on speaking with something of his old enthusiasm:

"'I have come to the conclusion that there must be a serdâb—a secret one. I am going to ask you to go out to Egypt again; to seek the tomb; to find the serdâb; and to bring back the lamps!'

"I started the next week for Egypt; and never rested till I stood again in the tomb. There, in the very spot where I had expected to find it, was the opening of the serdâb. And the serdâb was empty.

"But the Chapel was not empty; for the dried-up body of a man in Arab dress lay close under the opening, as though he had been stricken down. I examined all round the walls to see if Trelawny's surmise was correct; and I found that in all the positions of the stars as given, the Pointers of the Plough indicated a spot to the left hand, or south side, of the opening of the serdâb, where was a single star in gold.

"I pressed this, and it gave way. The stone which had marked the front of the serdâb, and which lay back against the wall within, moved slightly. On further examining the other side of the opening, I found a similar spot, indicated by other representations of the constellation; but this was itself a figure of the seven stars, and each was wrought in burnished gold. I pressed each star in turn; but without result. Then it struck me that if the opening spring was on the left, this on the right might have been intended for the simultaneous pressure of all the stars by one hand of seven fingers. By using both my hands, I managed to effect this.

"With a loud click, a metal figure seemed to dart from close to the opening of the serdâb; the stone slowly swung back to its place, and shut with a click. The glimpse which I had of the descending figure appalled me for the moment. It was like that grim guardian which, according to the Arabian historian Ibn Abd Alhokin, the builder of the Pyramids, King Saurid Ibn Salhouk, placed in the Western Pyramid to defend its treasure: 'A marble figure, upright, with lance in hand; with on his head a serpent wreathed. When any approached, the serpent would bite him on one side, and twining about his throat and killing him, would return again to his place.'

"I knew well that such a figure was not wrought to pleasantry; and that to brave it was no child's play. The dead Arab at my feet was proof of what could be done! So I examined again along the wall; and found here and there chippings as if someone had been tapping with a heavy hammer. This then had been what happened: The grave-robber more expert at his work than we had been, and suspecting the presence of a hidden serdâb, had made essay to find it. He had struck the spring by chance; had released the avenging 'Treasurer,' as the Arabian writer designated him. The issue spoke for itself.

"Perhaps you do not know that the entrance to a serdâb is almost always very narrow; sometimes a hand can hardly be inserted. Two things I learned from this serdâb. The first was that the lamps, if lamps at all there had been, could not have been of large size; and secondly, that they would be in some way associated with Hathor, whose symbol, the hawk in a square with the right top corner forming a smaller square, was cut in relief on the wall within. Hathor is the goddess who in Egyptian mythology answers to Venus of the Greeks, in as far as she is the presiding deity of beauty and pleasure. In the Egyptian mythology, however, each God has many forms; and in some respects Hathor has to do with the idea of resurrection. There are seven forms or variants of the Goddess; why should not these correspond in some way to the seven lamps! That there had been such lamps, I was convinced. The first grave-robber had met his death; the second had found the contents of the serdâb.

"That was nearly three years ago; and for all that time I have been like the man in the Arabian Nights, seeking old lamps, not for new, but for cash. At last, not two months ago, I was shown by an old dealer in Mossul one lamp such as I had looked for. I wanted to see all his stock before buying; and one by one he produced, amongst masses of rubbish, seven different lamps. Each of them had a distinguishing mark; and each and all was some form of the symbol of Hathor. I got on as fast as it is possible to travel in such countries; and arrived in London with only the lamps and certain portable curios and papyri which I had picked up on my travels."

With all of this whirling through my mind, I resumed watch in Mr. Trelawny's room.

"Who are you? What are you doing here?"

Whatever ideas any of us had ever formed of his waking, I am quite sure that none of us expected to see him start up all awake and full master of himself. I was so surprised that I answered almost mechanically:

"Ross is my name. I have been watching by you! I am a Barrister. It is not, however, in that capacity I am here; but simply as a friend of your daughter. It was probably her knowledge of my being a lawyer which first determined her to ask me to come when she thought you had been murdered. Afterwards she was good enough to consider me to be a friend, and to allow me to remain in accordance with your expressed wish that someone should remain to watch."

"She thought I had been murdered! Was that last night?"

"No! Three nights ago."

"Tell me all about it! All you know! Every detail! Omit nothing! But stay; first lock the door! I want to know, before I see anyone, exactly how things stand."

Accordingly, I told him every detail, even of the slightest which I could remember, of what had happened from the moment of my arrival at the house.

I met Margaret in the hall. The moment she saw me her eyes brightened, and she looked at me keenly.

"You have some good news for me?" she said. "Is Father better?"

"He is! Why did you think so?"

"I saw it in your face. I must go to him at once." She was hurrying away when I stopped her.

"He said he would send for you the moment he was dressed."

She sat down on the nearest chair and began to cry. I felt overcome myself. The sight of her joy and emotion quite unmanned me. She saw my emotion, and seemed to understand. She put out her hand. I held it hard, and kissed it. Such moments as these, the opportunities of lovers, are gifts of the gods! Up to this instant, though I knew I loved her, and though I believed she returned my affection, I had had only hope. Now, however, the self-surrender manifest in her willingness to let me squeeze her hand, the ardor of her pressure in return, and the glorious flush of love in her beautiful, deep, dark eyes as she lifted them to mine, were all the eloquences which the most impatient or exacting lover could expect or demand.

Presently a bell rang from the room. Margaret slipped from me, and looked back with warning finger on lip. She went over to her father's door and knocked softly.

"Come in!" said the strong voice.

"It is I, Father!" The voice was tremulous with love and hope.

There was a quick step inside the room; the door was hurriedly thrown open, and in an instant Margaret, who had sprung forward, was clasped in her father's arms.

Here the father and daughter went into the room together, and the door closed.

When I told Mr. Corbeck that Mr. Trelawny had quite recovered, he began to dance about like a wild man. I then found Sergeant Daw and took him into the study, so that we should be alone when I told him the news. It surprised even his iron self-control when I told him the method of the waking. I was myself surprised in turn by his first words:

"And how did he explain the first attack? He was unconscious when the second was made."

Up to that moment the nature of the attack, which was the cause of my coming to the house, had never even crossed my mind, except when I had simply narrated the various occurrences in sequence to Mr. Trelawny.

"Do you know, it never occurred to me to ask him!" The Detective did not seem to think much of my answer:

"That is why so few cases are ever followed out," he said, "unless our people are in them. Your amateur detective never hunts down to the death. Well, Mr. Ross, I'm glad the case is over; for over it is, so far as I am concerned. I suppose that Mr. Trelawny knows his own business; and that now he is well again, he will take it up himself."

Soon after the Detective left, Mr. Trelawny called for me.

"Come in, Mr. Ross!" he said cordially, but with a certain formality which I dreaded.

"If things are as I fancy, we shall not have any secrets between us. Malcolm Ross knows so much of my affairs already, that I take it he must either let matters stop where they are and go away in silence, or else he must— know more. Margaret! Are you willing to let Mr. Ross see your wrist?"

She threw one swift look of appeal in his eyes; but even as she did so she seemed to make up her mind. Without a word she raised her right hand, so that the bracelet of spreading wings which covered the wrist fell back, leaving the flesh bare. Then an icy chill shot through me.

On her wrist was a thin red jagged line, from which seemed to hang red stains like drops of blood!

She stood there, a veritable figure of patient pride. As we stood thus for some seconds, the deep, grave voice of her father seemed to sound a challenge in my ears:

"What do you say now?"

My answer was not in words. I caught Margaret's right hand in mine as it fell, and, holding it tight, whilst with the other I pushed back the golden cincture, stooped and kissed the wrist.

We were interrupted by a knock at the door. In answer to an impatient "Come in!" from Mr. Trelawny, Mr. Corbeck entered. All the enthusiasm of his youth, of which Mr. Corbeck had told us, seemed to have come back to him in an instant.

"So you have got the lamps!" he almost shouted. "Come to the library, where we will be alone, and tell me all about it!"

The next evening after supper Mr. Trelawny took us into the study where Mr. Corbeck and Doctor Winchester were waiting, saying as he passed in:

"The experiment which is before us is to try whether or no there is any force, any reality, in the old Magic. That there is some such existing power I firmly believe. It might not be possible to create, or arrange, or organize such power in our own time; but I take it that if in Old Time such a power existed, it may have some exceptional survival. After all, the Bible is not a myth; if the Witch at Endor could call up to Saul the spirit of Samuel, why may not there have been others with equal powers; and why may not one among them survive? Indeed, we are told in the Book of Samuel that the Witch of Endor was only one of many, and her being consulted by Saul was a matter of chance. He only sought one among the many whom he had driven out of Israel; 'all those that had Familiar Spirits, and the Wizards.' This Egyptian Queen, Tera, who reigned nearly two thousand years before Saul, had a Familiar, and was a Wizard too. See how the priests of her time, and those after it tried to wipe out her name from the face of the earth. Ay, and they succeeded so well that even Manetho, the historian of the Egyptian Kings, writing in the tenth century before Christ, with all the lore of the priesthood for forty centuries behind him, and with possibility of access to every existing record, could not even find her name. Did it strike any of you, in thinking of the late events, who or what her Familiar was?" There was an interruption, for Doctor Winchester struck one hand loudly on the other as he ejaculated:

"The cat! The mummy cat! I knew it!" Mr. Trelawny smiled over at him.

"You are right! There is every indication that the Familiar of the Wizard Queen was that cat which was mummied when she was, and was not only placed in her tomb, but was laid in the sarcophagus with her. That was what bit into my wrist, what cut me with sharp claws." He paused. Margaret's comment was a purely girlish one:

"Then my poor Silvio is acquitted. I am glad!" Her father stroked her hair and went on:

"This woman seems to have had an extraordinary foresight. Foresight far, far beyond her age and the philosophy of her time. She seems to have seen through the weakness of her own religion, and even prepared for emergence into a different world. From the first, her eyes seem to have been attracted to the seven stars of the Plough from the fact, as recorded in the hieroglyphics in her tomb, that at her birth a great aerolite fell, from whose heart was finally extracted that Jewel of Seven Stars which she regarded as the talisman of her life. The Magic Coffer, so wondrously wrought with seven sides also came from the aerolite. Seven was to her a magic number; and no wonder. With seven fingers on one hand, and seven toes on one foot. She was born, we learn in the Stele of her tomb, in the seventh month of the year—the month in which the presiding Goddess was Hathor, the Goddess of her own house, of the Antefs of the Theban line—the Goddess who in various forms symbolizes beauty, and pleasure, and resurrection. Again in this seventh month—which, by later Egyptian astronomy began on October 28th, and ran to the 27th of our November—on the seventh day the Pointer of the Plough just rises above the horizon of the sky at Thebes.

"In a marvelously strange way, therefore, are grouped into this woman's life these various things. The number seven; the Pole Star, with the constellation of seven stars; the God of the month, Hathor, who was her own particular God, the God of her family, the Antefs of the Theban Dynasty, whose Kings' symbol it was, and whose seven forms ruled love and the delights of life and resurrection. If ever there was ground for magic; for the power of symbolism carried into mystic use, it is here.

"Remember, too, that this woman was skilled in all the science of her time. Her wise and cautious father took care of that, knowing that by her own wisdom she must ultimately combat the intrigues of the Hierarchy. Bear in mind that in old Egypt the science of Astronomy began and was developed to an extraordinary height; and that Astrology followed Astronomy in its progress. And it is possible that in the later developments of science with regard to light rays, we may yet find that Astrology is on a scientific basis. Bear in mind also that the Egyptians knew sciences, of which today, despite all our advantages, we are profoundly ignorant. That Magic Coffer of Queen Tera is probably a magic box in more ways than one. It may—possibly it does—contain forces that we wot not of. We cannot open it; it must be closed from within. How then was it closed? It is a coffer of solid stone, of amazing hardness, more like a jewel than an ordinary marble, with a lid equally solid; and yet all is so finely wrought that the finest tool made today cannot be inserted under the flange. How was it wrought to such perfection? How was the stone so chosen that those translucent patches match the relations of the seven stars of the constellation? How is it, or from what cause, that when the starlight shines on it, it glows from within—that when I fix the lamps in similar form the glow grows greater still; and yet the box is irresponsive to ordinary light however great? I tell you that that box hides some great mystery of science.

"In another way, too, there may be hidden in that box secrets which, for good or ill, may enlighten the world. We know from their records, and inferentially also, that the Egyptians studied the properties of herbs and minerals for magic purposes—white magic as well as black. We know that some of the wizards of old could induce from sleep dreams of any given kind. That this purpose was mainly effected by hypnotism, which was another art or science of Old Nile, I have little doubt. But still, they must have had a mastery of drugs that is far beyond anything we know. With our own pharmacopoeia we can, to a certain extent, induce dreams. But these old practitioners seemed to have been able to command at will any form or color of dreaming; could work round any given subject or thought in almost any way required. In that coffer, which you have seen, may rest a very armory of dreams. Indeed, some of the forces that lie within it may have been already used in my household.

"What I hold is, that the preparation of that box was made for a special occasion; as indeed were all the preparations of the tomb. Queen Tera did not trouble herself to guard against snakes and scorpions, in that rocky tomb cut in the sheer cliff face a hundred feet above the level of the valley, and fifty down from the summit. Her precautions were against the disturbances of human hands; against the jealousy and hatred of the priests, who, had they known of her real aims, would have tried to baffle them. I gather from the symbolic pictures in the tomb that she so far differed from the belief of her time that she looked for a resurrection in the flesh. It was doubtless this that intensified the hatred of the priesthood, and gave them an acceptable cause for obliterating the very existence, present and future, of one who had outraged their theories and blasphemed their gods. All that she might require in the accomplishment of the resurrection were contained in that almost hermetically sealed suite of chambers in the rock. In the great sarcophagus was the mummy of her Familiar, the cat, which from its great sire I take to be a sort of tiger-cat. In the tomb, also in a strong receptacle, were the canopic jars usually containing those internal organs which are separately embalmed, but which in this case had no such contents. So that, I take it, there was in her case a departure in embalming; and that the organs were restored to the body, each in its proper place—if, indeed, they had ever been removed. If this surmise be true, we shall find that the brain of the Queen either was never extracted in the usual way, or, if so taken out, that it was duly replaced, instead of being enclosed within the mummy wrappings. The jars, instead of containing the organs, contained oil; probably for the lamps. Finally, in the sarcophagus there was the Magic Coffer on which her feet rested. Mark also, the care taken in the preservance of her power to control the elements. According to her belief, the open hand outside the wrappings controlled the Air, and the strange Jewel Stone with the shining stars controlled Fire. The symbolism inscribed on the soles of her feet gave sway over Land and Water. Mark how she guarded her secret in case of grave-wrecking or intrusion. None could open her Magic Coffer without the lamps, for we know now that ordinary light will not be effective. The great lid of the sarcophagus was not sealed down as usual, because she wished to control the air. But she hid the lamps, which in structure belong to the Magic Coffer, in a place where none could find them, except by following the secret guidance which she had prepared for only the eyes of wisdom. And even here she had guarded against chance discovery, by preparing a bolt of death for the unwary discoverer. To do this she had applied the lesson of the tradition of the avenging guard of the treasures of the pyramid built by her great predecessor of the Fourth Dynasty of the throne of Egypt.

"You have noted, I suppose, how there were, in the case of her tomb, certain deviations from the usual rules. For instance, the shaft of the Mummy Pit, which is usually filled up solid with stones and rubbish, was left open. Why was this? I take it that she had made arrangements for leaving the tomb when, after her resurrection, she should be a new woman, with a different personality, and less inured to the hardships that in her first existence she had suffered. So far as we can judge of her intent, all things needful for her exit into the world had been thought of, even to the iron chain, described by Van Huyn, close to the door in the rock, by which she might be able to lower herself to the ground. That she expected a long period to elapse was shown in the choice of material. An ordinary rope would be rendered weaker or unsafe in process of time, but she imagined, and rightly, that the iron would endure.

"What her intentions were when once she trod the open earth afresh we do not know, and we never shall, unless her own dead lips can soften and speak.

"Now, as to the Star Jewel! This she manifestly regarded as the greatest of her treasures. In the old Egyptian belief it was held that there were words, which, if used properly—for the method of speaking them was as important as the words themselves—could command the Lords of the Upper and the Lower Worlds. The 'hekau,' or word of power, was all-important in certain rituals. On the Jewel of Seven Stars, which, as you know, is carved into the image of a scarab, are graven in hieroglyphic two such hekau, one above, the other underneath. But you will understand better when you see it! Wait here! Do not stir!"

As he spoke, he rose and left the room. In two or three minutes he returned. He held in his hand a little golden box. This, as he resumed his seat, he placed before him on the table. We all leaned forward as he opened it.

On a lining of white satin lay a wondrous ruby of immense size, almost as big as the top of Margaret's little finger. Shining through its wondrous "pigeon's blood" color were seven different stars, each of seven points, in such position that they reproduced exactly the figure of the Plough. There could be no possible mistake as to this in the mind of anyone who had ever noted the constellation. On it were some hieroglyphic figures, cut with the most exquisite precision, as I could see when it came to my turn to use the magnifying glass, which Mr. Trelawny took from his pocket and handed to us.

When we all had seen it fully, Mr. Trelawny turned it over so that it rested on its back in a cavity made to hold it in the upper half of the box.

The reverse was no less wonderful than the upper. It, too, had some hiero-glyphic figures cut on it. Mr. Trelawny resumed his lecture:

"As you see, there are two words. The symbols on the top represent a single word, composed of one syllable prolonged with its determinatives. You know, all of you, I suppose, that the Egyptian language was phonetic, and that the hieroglyphic symbol represented the sound. The first symbol here, the hoe, means 'mer,' and the two pointed ellipses the prolongation of the final r: mer-r-r. The sitting figure with the hand to its face is what we call the 'determinative' of 'thought'; and the roll of papyrus that of 'abstrac-tion.' Thus we get the word 'mer,' love, in its abstract, general, and fullest sense. This is the hekau which can command the Upper World.

"The symbolization of the word on the reverse is simpler, though the meaning is more abstruse. The first symbol means 'men,' 'abiding,' and the second, 'ab,' 'the heart.' So that we get 'abiding of heart,' or in our own lan-guage 'patience.' And this is the hekau to control the Lower World!"

He closed the box, and motioning us to remain as we were, he went back to his room to replace the Jewel in the safe. When he had returned and resumed his seat, he went on:

"That Jewel, with its mystic words, and which Queen Tera held under her hand in the sarcophagus, was to be an important factor—probably the most important—in the working out of the act of her resurrection. From the first I seemed by a sort of instinct to realize this. I kept the Jewel within my great safe, whence none could extract it; not even Queen Tera herself with her astral body."

"Her 'astral body'? What is that, Father?" There was keenness in Mar-garet's voice as she asked the question which surprised me a little; but Trelawny smiled as he spoke:

"The astral body, which is a part of Buddhist belief, long subsequent to the time I speak of, and which is an accepted fact of modern mysticism, had its rise in Ancient Egypt; at least, so far as we know. It is that the gifted in-dividual can at will, quick as thought itself, transfer his body whithersoever he chooses, by the dissolution and reincarnation of particles. In the ancient belief there were several parts of a human being.

"First there is the 'Ka,' or 'Double,' which, as Doctor Budge explains, may be defined as 'an abstract individuality of personality' which was im-bued with all the characteristic attributes of the individual it represented, and possessed an absolutely independent existence. It was free to move from place to place on earth at will; and it could enter into heaven and hold converse with the gods. Then there was the 'Ba,' or 'soul,' which dwelt in the 'Ka,' and had the power of becoming corporeal or incorporeal at will; 'it had both substance and form. . . . It had power to leave the tomb. . . . It could revisit the body in the tomb. . . . and could reincarnate it and hold converse with it.' Again there was the 'Khu,' the 'spiritual intelligence,' or spirit. It took the form of 'a shining, luminous, intangible shape of the body.' . . . Then, again, there was the 'Sekhem,' or 'power' of a man, his strength or vital force personified. These were the 'Khaibit,' or 'shadow,' the 'Ren,' or 'name,' the 'Khat,' or 'physical body,' and 'Ab,' the 'heart,' in which life was seated, went to the full making up of a man.

"Thus you will see, that if this division of functions, spiritual and bodily, ethereal and corporeal, ideal and actual, be accepted as exact, there are all the possibilities and capabilities of corporeal transference, guided always by an unimprisonable will or intelligence.

"Now comes the crown of my argument. The purpose of the attack on me was to get the safe open, so that the sacred Jewel of Seven Stars could be extracted. That immense door of the safe could not keep out her astral body, which could gather itself as well within as without the safe. And I doubt not that in the darkness of the night that mummied hand sought often the Talisman Jewel, and drew new inspiration from its touch. But despite all its power, the astral body could not remove the Jewel through the chinks of the safe. The Ruby is not astral; and it could only be moved in the ordinary way by the opening of the doors. To this end, the Queen used her astral body and the fierce force of her Familiar, to bring to the keyhole of the safe the master key which debarred her wish." He paused, and his daughter's voice came out sweet and clear, and full of intense feeling:

"Father, in the Egyptian belief, was the power of resurrection of a mummied body a general one, or was it limited? That is: could it achieve resurrection many times in the course of ages; or only once, and that one final?"

"There was but one resurrection," he answered. "In the common belief, the Spirit found joy in the Elysian Fields, where there was plenty of food and no fear of famine. Where there was moisture and deep-rooted reeds, and all the joys that are to be expected by the people of an arid land and burning clime."

Then Margaret spoke with an earnestness which showed the conviction of her inmost soul:

"To me, then, it is given to understand what was the dream of this great and far-thinking and high-souled lady of old; the dream that held her soul in patient waiting for its realization through the passing of all those tens of centuries. What were the lack of food or the plenitude of it; what were feast or famine to this woman, born in a palace, with the shadow of the Crown of the Two Egypts on her brows! What were reedy morasses or the tinkle of running water to her whose barges could sweep the great Nile from the mountains to the sea. What were petty joys and absence of petty fears to her, the raising of whose hand could hurl armies, or draw to the water-stairs of her palaces the commerce of the world! At whose word rose temples filled with all the artistic beauty of the Times of Old which it was her aim and pleasure to restore! Under whose guidance the solid rock yawned into the sepulcher that she designed!

"I can see her in her loneliness and in the silence of her mighty pride, dreaming her own dream of things far different from those around her. Of some other land, far, far away under the canopy of the silent night, lit by the cool, beautiful light of the stars. A land under that Northern star, whence blew the sweet winds that cooled the feverish desert air. A land of wholesome greenery, far, far away. Where were no scheming and malignant priesthood; whose ideas were to lead to power through gloomy temples and more gloomy caverns of the dead, through an endless ritual of death! A land where love was not base, but a divine possession of the soul! Where there might be some one kindred spirit which could speak to hers through mortal lips like her own; whose being could merge with hers in a sweet communion of soul to soul, even as their breaths could mingle in the ambient air! And in the realization of that dream she will surely be content to rest!"

Mr. Trelawny's face was full of delight. Holding his daughter's hand in his, he went on with his discourse:

"Now, as to the time at which Queen Tera intended her resurrection to take place! As you know, the stars shift their relative positions in the heavens. There can be no doubt whatever that astronomy was an exact science with the Egyptians at least a thousand years before the time of Queen Tera. Now, the stars that go to make up a constellation change in process of time their relative positions, and the Plough is a notable example. The changes in the position of stars in even forty centuries is so small as to be hardly noticeable by an eye not trained to minute observances, but they can by measured and verified. Did you, or any of you, notice how exactly the stars in the Ruby correspond to the position of the stars in the Plough; or how the same holds with regard to the translucent places in the Magic Coffer? And yet when Queen Tera was laid in her tomb, neither the stars in the Jewel nor the translucent places in the Coffer corresponded to the position of the stars in the Constellation as they then were. Thus it is that to us and our time is given the opportunity of this wondrous peep into the old world, such as has been the privilege of none other of our time; which may never be again.

"Imagine what it will be for the world of thought if there can come back to us out of the unknown past one who can yield to us the lore stored in the great Library of Alexandria, and lost in its consuming flames. Not only history can be set right, and the teachings of science made veritable from their beginnings; but we can be placed on the road to the knowledge of lost arts, lost learning, lost sciences, so that our feet may tread on the indicated path to their ultimate and complete restoration. Oh, what possibilities are there in the coming of such a being into our midst!"

Mr. Trelawny took up another theme:

"We have now to settle definitely the exact hour at which the Great Experiment is to be made. The logical time is the seventh hour after sunset. On each of the occasions when action was taken in my house, this was the time chosen. As the sun sets tonight at eight, our hour is to be three in the morning!" He spoke in a matter-of-fact way, though with great gravity; but there was nothing of mystery in his words or manner.

In a lofty frame of mind, and with less anxiety than I had felt for days, I went to my room and lay down on the sofa.

I was awakened by Corbeck calling to me, hurriedly:

"Come as quickly as you can. Mr. Trelawny wants to see us at once. Hurry!"

I jumped up and ran down to Mr. Trelawny's room. All were there except Margaret, who came immediately after me carrying Silvio in her arms. When the cat saw his old enemy he struggled to get down; but Margaret held him fast and soothed him. I looked at my watch. It was close to eight.

When Margaret was with us her father said directly, with a quiet insistence which was new to me:

"You believe, Margaret, that Queen Tera will not harm any of us in our attempt to assist in her resurrection?" After a pause Margaret answered in a low voice:

"Yes!"

In the pause her whole being, appearance, expression, voice, manner had changed. Even Silvio noticed it, and with a violent effort wriggled away from her arms; she did not seem to notice the act. I expected that the cat, when he had achieved his freedom, would have attacked the mummy; but on this occasion he did not. He seemed too cowed to approach it. He shrunk away, and with a piteous "miaou" came over and rubbed himself against my ankles. I took him up in my arms, and he nestled there content. Mr. Trelawny spoke again:

"You are sure of what you say! You believe it with all your soul?" Margaret's face had lost the abstracted look; it now seemed illuminated with the devotion of one to whom is given to speak of great things. She answered in a voice which, though quiet, vibrated with conviction:

"I know it! My knowledge is beyond belief!" Mr. Trelawny spoke again:

"Then you are so sure, that were you Queen Tera herself, you would be willing to prove it in any way that I might suggest?"

"Yes, any way!" the answer rang out fearlessly. He spoke again, in a voice in which was no note of doubt:

"Even in the abandonment of your Familiar to death—to annihilation?"

She paused, and I could see that she suffered—suffered horribly. There was in her eyes a hunted look, which no man can, unmoved see in the eyes of his beloved. Finally she answered:

"Even that!"

Then stepping over to where the mummy cat stood on the little table, she placed her hand on it. She had now left the sunlight, and the shadows looked dark and deep over her. In a clear voice she said:

"Were I Tera, I would say 'Take all I have! This night is for the Gods alone!'"

As she spoke the sun dipped, and the cold shadow suddenly fell on us. We all stood still for a while. Silvio jumped from my arms and ran over to his mistress, rearing himself up against her dress as if asking to be lifted. He took no notice whatever of the mummy now.

Margaret was glorious with all her wonted sweetness as she said sadly:

"The sun is down, Father! Shall any of us see it again? The night of nights is come!"

Mr. Trelawny asked us men to come with him. We presently managed to move an oak table, which had stood against the wall in the hall, into his room. This we placed under the strong cluster of electric lights. Margaret looked on for a while; then all at once her face blanched, and in an agitated voice she said:

"What are you going to do, Father?"

"To unroll the mummy of the cat! Queen Tera will not need her Familiar tonight. If she should want him, it might be dangerous to us: so we shall make him safe. You are not alarmed, dear?"

"Oh no!" she answered quickly. "But I was thinking of my Silvio, and how I should feel if he had been the mummy that was to be unswathed!"

Mr. Trelawny got knives and scissors ready, and placed the cat on the table. It was a grim beginning to our work; and it made my heart sink when I thought of what might happen in that lonely house in the mid-gloom of the night. The sense of loneliness and isolation from the world was increased by the moaning of the wind which had now risen ominously.

There was an incredible number of bandages; and the tearing sound— they being stuck fast to each other by bitumen and gums and spices—and the little cloud of red pungent dust that arose, pressed on the senses of all of us. As the last wrappings came away, we saw the animal seated before us. He was all hunkered up; his hair and teeth and claws were complete. The eyes were closed, but the eyelids had not the fierce look which I expected. The whiskers had been pressed down on the side of the face by the bandaging; but when the pressure was taken away they stood out, just as they would have done in life. He was a magnificent creature, a tiger-cat of great size. But as we looked at him, our first glance of admiration changed to one of fear, and a shudder ran through each one of us; for here was a confirmation of the fears which we had endured.

His mouth and his claws were smeared with the dry, red stains of recent blood!

"It is as I expected," Mr. Trelawny said. "This promises well for what is to follow."

By this time Doctor Winchester was looking at the red stained paws. "As I expected!" he said. "He has seven claws, too!" Opening his pocket-book, he took out the piece of blotting-paper marked by Silvio's claws, on which was also marked in pencil a diagram of the cuts made on Mr. Trelawny's wrist. He placed the paper under the mummy cat's paw. The marks fitted exactly.

When we had carefully examined the cat, finding, however, nothing strange about it but its wonderful preservation, Mr. Trelawny lifted it from the table. Margaret started forward, crying out:

"Take care, Father! Take care! He may injure you."

"Not now, my dear!" he answered as he moved towards the stairway. Her face fell. "Where are you going?" she asked in a faint voice.

"To the kitchen," he answered. "Fire will take away all danger for the future; even an astral body cannot materialize from ashes!" He signed to us to follow him. Margaret turned away with a sob. I went to her; but she motioned me back and whispered:

"No, no! Go with the others. Father may want you. Oh! it seems like murder! The poor Queen's pet . . . !" The tears were dropping from under the fingers that covered her eyes.

In the kitchen was a fire of wood ready laid. To this Mr. Trelawny applied a match; in a few seconds the kindling had caught and the flames leaped. When the fire was solidly ablaze, he threw the body of the cat into it. For a few seconds it lay a dark mass amidst the flames, and the room was rank with the smell of burning hair. Then the dry body caught fire too. The inflammable substances used in embalming became new fuel, and the flames roared. A few minutes of fierce conflagration; and then we breathed freely. Queen Tera's Familiar was no more!

When we went back to the room we found Margaret sitting in the dark. Though she had been crying, her eyes were now dry. Her father said to us in a grave tone:

"Now we had better prepare for our great work. It will not do to leave anything to the last!" Margaret must have had a suspicion of what was coming, for it was with a sinking voice that she asked:

"What are you going to do now?" Mr. Trelawny too must have had a suspicion of her feelings, for he answered in a low tone:

"To unroll the mummy of Queen Tera!" She came close to him and said pleadingly in a whisper:

"Father, you are not going to unswathe her! All you men . . . ! And in the glare of light!"

"But why not, my dear?"

"Just think, Father, a woman! All alone! In such a way! In such a place! Oh! It's cruel, cruel!" She was manifestly much overcome. Her cheeks were flaming red, and her eyes were full of indignant tears. Her father saw her distress; and, sympathizing with it, began to comfort her.

"Not a woman, dear; a mummy! She has been dead nearly five thousand years!"

"What does that matter? Sex is not a matter of years! A woman is a woman, if she had been dead five thousand centuries! And you expect her to arise out of that long sleep! It could not be real death, if she is to rise out of it! You have led me to believe that she will come alive when the Coffer is opened!"

"I did, my dear; and I believe it! But if it isn't death that has been the matter with her all these years, it is something uncommonly like it. Then again, just think; it was men who embalmed her. They didn't have woman's rights or lady doctors in ancient Egypt, my dear!"

By this time Mr. Trelawny, assisted by Mr. Corbeck and Doctor Winchester, had raised the lid of the ironstone sarcophagus which contained the mummy of the Queen. It was a large one; but it was none too big. The mummy was both long and broad and high; and was of such weight that it was no easy task, even for the four of us, to lift it out. Under Mr. Trelawny's direction we laid it out on the table prepared for it.

Then, and then only, did the full horror of the whole thing burst upon me! There in the full glare of the light, the whole material and sordid side of death seemed staringly real. The outer wrappings, torn and loosened by rude touch, and with the color either darkened by dust or worn light by friction, seemed creased as by rough treatment; the jagged edges of the wrapping-cloths looked fringed; the painting was patchy, and the varnish chipped. The coverings were evidently many, for the bulk was great. But through all, showed that unhidable human figure, which seems to look more horrible when partially concealed than at any other time. What was before us was Death, and nothing else. All the romance and sentiment of fancy had disappeared. The two older men, enthusiasts who had often done such work, were not disconcerted; and Doctor Winchester seemed to hold himself in a business-like attitude, as if before the operating-table. But I felt low-spirited, and miserable, and ashamed; and besides I was pained and alarmed by Margaret's ghastly pallor.

Then the work began. The cat had been embalmed with coarser materials; here, all, when once the outer coverings were removed, was more delicately done. It seemed as if only the finest gums and spices had been used in this embalming. As the unrolling went on, the wrappings became finer, and the smell less laden with bitumen, but more pungent. Now and again Mr. Trelawny or Mr. Corbeck would point out some special drawing before laying the bandage on the pile behind them.

At last we knew that the wrappings were coming to an end. Already the proportions were reduced to those of a normal figure of the manifest height of the Queen. And as the end drew nearer, so Margaret's pallor grew; and her heart beat more and more wildly, till her breast heaved in a way that frightened me.

The final wrapping was a wide piece the whole length of the body. It being removed, a profusely full robe of white linen appeared, covering the body from the throat to the feet.

And such linen! We all bent over to look at it.

It was as fine as the finest silk. But never was spun or woven silk which lay in such gracious folds, constrict though they were by the close wrappings of the mummy cloth, and fixed into hardness by the passing of thousands of years.

Round the neck it was delicately embroidered in pure gold with tiny sprays of sycamore; and round the feet, similarly worked, was an endless line of lotus plants of unequal height, and with all the graceful abandon of natural growth.

Across the body, but manifestly not surrounding it, was a girdle of jewels. A wondrous girdle, which shone and glowed with all the forms and phases and colors of the sky!

Margaret raised her hands in ecstasy. She bent over to examine more closely; but suddenly drew back and stood fully erect at her grand height. She seemed to speak with the conviction of absolute knowledge as she said:

"That is no cerement! It was not meant for the clothing of death! It is a marriage robe!"

Mr. Trelawny leaned over and touched the linen robe. He lifted a fold at the neck, and I knew from the quick intake of his breath that something had surprised him. He lifted yet a little more; and then he, too, stood back and pointed, saying:

"Margaret is right! That dress is not intended to be worn by the dead! See! Her figure is not robed in it. It is but laid upon her." He lifted the zone of jewels and handed it to Margaret. Then with both hands he raised the ample robe, and laid it across the arms which she extended in a natural impulse. Things of such beauty were too precious to be handled with any but the greatest care.

We all stood awed at the beauty of the figure which, save for the face cloth, now lay completely nude before us. Mr. Trelawny bent over, and with hands that trembled slightly, raised this linen cloth which was of the same fineness as the robe. As he stood back and the whole glorious beauty of the Queen was revealed, I felt a rush of shame sweep over me. It was not right that we should be there, gazing with irreverent eyes on such unclad beauty: It was indecent; it was almost sacrilegious! And yet the white wonder of that beautiful form was something to dream of. It was not like death at all; it was like a statue carven in ivory by the hand of a Praxteles. There was nothing of that horrible shrinkage which death seems to effect in a moment. There was none of the wrinkled toughness which seems to be a leading characteristic of most mummies. There was not the shrunken attenuation of a body dried in the sand, as I had seen before in museums. The flesh was full and round, as in a living person; and the skin was as smooth as satin. The color seemed extraordinary. It was like ivory, new ivory; except where the right arm, with shattered, bloodstained wrist and missing hand had lain bare to exposure in the sarcophagus for so many tens of centuries.

With a womanly impulse; with a mouth that drooped with pity, with eyes that flashed with anger, and cheeks that flamed, Margaret threw over the body the beautiful robe which lay across her arm. Only the face was then to be seen. This was more startling even than the body, for it seemed not dead, but alive. The eyelids were closed; but the long, black, curling lashes lay over on the cheeks. The full, red lips, though the mouth was not open, showed the tiniest white line of pearly teeth within. Her hair, glorious in quantity and glossy black as the raven's wing, was piled in great masses over the white forehead, on which a few curling tresses strayed like tendrils. This woman—I could not think of her as a mummy or a corpse—was the image of Margaret. She wore in her hair the "Disk and Plumes," which contained a glorious jewel; one noble pearl of moonlight luster, flanked by carven pieces of moonstone.

Mr. Trelawny was overcome as he looked. He quite broke down; and when Margaret flew to him and held him close in her arms and comforted him, I heard him murmur brokenly:

"It looks as if you were dead, my child!"

There was a long silence. I could hear without the roar of the wind, which was now risen to a tempest. Mr. Trelawny's voice broke the spell:

"Later on we must try and find out the process of embalming. It is not like any that I know. There does not seem to have been any opening cut for the withdrawing of the viscera and organs, which apparently remain intact within the body. Then, again, there is no moisture in the flesh; but its place is supplied with something else, as though wax or stearine had been conveyed into the veins by some subtle process. I wonder could it be possible that at that time they could have used paraffin. It might have been, by some process that we know not, pumped into the veins, where it hardened!"

As the appointed hour drew near, we went about our separate duties. We looked first to the windows to see that they were closed, and we got ready our respirators to put them on when the time should be close at hand.

Then, under Margaret's guidance we carried the mummied body of Queen Tera and laid it on a couch. He put the sheet lightly over it, so that if she should wake she could at once slip from under it. The severed hand was placed in its true position on her breast, and under it the Jewel of Seven Stars which Mr. Trelawny had taken from the great safe. It seemed to flash and blaze as he put it in its place.

Margaret beckoned me, and I went out with her to bring in Silvio. He came to her purring. She took him up into her arms, and pressing him close to her bosom where he purred loudly, we went back to the room. I closed the door carefully behind me, feeling as I did so a strange thrill as of finality. There was to be no going back now. Then we put on our respirators, and took our places as had been arranged. I was to stand by the taps of the electric lights beside the door, ready to turn them off or on as Mr. Trelawny should direct. Doctor Winchester was to stand behind the couch so that he should not be between the mummy and the sarcophagus; he was to watch carefully what should take place with regard to the Queen. Margaret was to be beside him; she held Silvio ready to place him upon the couch or beside it when she might think right. Mr. Trelawny and Mr. Corbeck were to attend to the lighting of the lamps. When the hands of the clock were close to the hour, they stood ready with their linstocks.

The striking of the silver bell of the clock seemed to smite on our hearts like a knell of doom. One! Two! Three!

Before the third stroke the wicks of the lamps had caught, and I had turned out the electric light. In the dimness of the struggling lamps, and after the bright glow of the electric light, the room and all within it took weird shape, and all seemed in an instant to change. We waited with our hearts beating. I know mine did, and I fancied I could hear the pulsation of the others.

The seconds seemed to pass with leaden wings. It were as though all the world were standing still. The figures of the others stood out dimly, Margaret's white dress alone showing clearly in the gloom. The thick respirators which we all wore added to the strange appearance. The thin light of the lamps showed Mr. Trelawny's square jaw and strong mouth and the brown shaven face of Mr. Corbeck. Their eyes seemed to glare in the light. Across the room Doctor Winchester's eyes twinkled like stars, and Margaret's blazed like black suns. Silvio's eyes were like emeralds.

Would the lamps never burn up!

It was only a few seconds in all till they did blaze up. A slow, steady light, growing more and more bright, and changing in color from blue to crystal white. So they stayed for a couple of minutes without change in the coffer; till at last there began to appear all over it a delicate glow. This grew and grew, till it became like a blazing jewel, and then like a living thing whose essence of life was light. We waited and waited, our hearts seeming to stand still.

All at once there was a sound like a tiny muffled explosion and the cover lifted right up on a level plane a few inches; there was no mistaking anything now, for the whole room was full of a blaze of light. Then the cover, staying fast at one side rose slowly up on the other, as though yielding to some pressure of balance. The coffer still continued to glow; from it began to steal a faint greenish smoke. I could not smell it fully on account of the respirator; but, even through that, I was conscious of a strange pungent odor. Then this smoke began to grow thicker, and to roll out in volumes of ever increasing density till the whole room began to get obscure. The coffer still continued to glow; but the lamps began to grow dim. At first I thought that their light was being overpowered by the thick black smoke; but presently I saw that they were, one by one, burning out. They must have burned quickly to produce such fierce and vivid flames.

I waited and waited expecting every instant to hear the command to turn up the light; but none came. I waited still, and looked with harrowing intensity at the rolling billows of smoke still pouring out of the glowing casket, whilst the lamps sank down and went out one by one.

Finally there was but one lamp alight, and that was dimly blue and flickering. The only effective light in the room was from the glowing casket. I kept my eyes fixed toward Margaret; it was for her now that all my anxiety was claimed. I could just see her white frock beyond the still white shrouded figure on the couch. Silvio was troubled; his piteous mewing was the only sound in the room. Deeper and denser grew the black mist and its pungency began to assail my nostrils as well as my eyes. Now the volume of smoke coming from the coffer seemed to lessen, and the smoke itself to be less dense. Across the room I saw something white move where the couch was. There were several movements. I could just catch the quick glint of white through the dense smoke in the fading light; for now the glow of the coffer began quickly to subside. I could still hear Silvio, but his mewing came from close under; a moment later I could feel him piteously crouching on my foot.

Then the last spark of light disappeared, and through the Egyptian darkness I could see the faint line of white around the window blinds. I felt that the time had come to speak; so I pulled off my respirator and called out:

"Shall I turn up the light?" There was no answer; so before the thick smoke choked me, I called again but more loudly:

"Mr. Trelawny, shall I turn up the light?" He did not answer; but from across the room I heard Margaret's voice, sounding as sweet and clear as a bell:

"Yes, Malcolm!" I turned the tap and the lamps flashed out. But they were only dim points of light in the midst of that murky ball of smoke. In that thick atmosphere there was little possibility of illumination. I ran across to Margaret, guided by her white dress, and caught hold of her and held her hand. She recognized my anxiety and said at once:

"I am all right."

"Thank God!" I said. "How are the others? Quick, let us open all the windows and get rid of this smoke!" To my surprise, she answered in a sleepy way:

"They will be all right. They won't get any harm." I did not stop to inquire how or on what ground she formed such an opinion, but threw up the lower sashes of all the windows, and pulled down the upper. Then I threw open the door.

A few seconds made a perceptible change as the thick, black smoke began to roll out of the windows. Then the lights began to grow into strength and I could see the room. All the men were overcome. Beside the couch Doctor Winchester lay on his back as though he had sunk down and rolled over; and on the farther side of the sarcophagus, where they had stood, lay Mr. Trelawny and Mr. Corbeck. It was a relief to me to see that, though they were unconscious, all three were breathing heavily as though in a stupor. Margaret still stood behind the couch. She seemed at first to be in a partially dazed condition; but every instant appeared to get more command of herself. She stepped forward and helped me to raise her father and drag him close to a window. Together we placed the others similarly, and she flew down to the dining-room and returned with a decanter of brandy. It was not many minutes after we had opened the windows when all three were struggling back to consciousness. I looked round the room to see what had been the effect of the experiment.

The great sarcophagus was just as it had been. The coffer was open, and in it, scattered through certain divisions or partitions wrought in its own substance, was a scattering of black ashes. Over all, sarcophagus, coffer and, indeed, all in the room, was a sort of black film of greasy soot. I went over to the couch. The white sheet still lay over part of it; but it had been thrown back, as might be when one is stepping out of bed.

But there was no sign of Queen Tera! I took Margaret by the hand and led her over. She reluctantly left her father to whom she was administering, but she came docilely enough. I whispered to her as I held her hand:

"What has become of the Queen? Tell me! You were close at hand, and must have seen if anything happened!" She answered me very softly:

"There was nothing that I could see. Until the smoke grew too dense I kept my eyes on the couch, but there was no change. Then, when all grew so dark that I could not see, I thought I heard a movement close to me. It might have been Doctor Winchester who had sunk down overcome; but I could not be sure. I thought that it might be the Queen waking, so I put down poor Silvio. I did not see what became of him; but I felt as if he had deserted me when I heard him mewing over by the door. I hope he is not offended with me!" As if in answer, Silvio came running into the room and reared himself against her dress, pulling it as though clamoring to be taken up. She stooped down and took him up and began to pet and comfort him.

We examined the couch and all around it most carefully. But all we could find was a sort of ridge of impalpable dust, which gave out a strange dead odor. On the couch lay the jewel of the disk and plumes which the Queen had worn in her hair, and the Star Jewel which had words to command the Gods.

In the autumn Margaret and I were married. On the occasion she wore the jewel which Queen Tera had worn in her hair. On her breast, set in a ring of gold made like a twisted lotus stalk, she wore the strange Jewel of Seven Stars which held words to command the Gods of all the worlds. At the marriage the sunlight streaming through the chancel windows fell on it, and it seemed to glow like a living thing.

The graven words may have been of efficacy; for Margaret holds to them, and there is no other life in all the world so happy as my own.

We often think of the great Queen, and we talk of her freely. Once, when I said with a sigh that I was sorry she could not have waked into a new life in a new world, my wife, putting both her hands in mine and looking into my eyes with that faraway eloquent dreamy look which sometimes comes into her own, said lovingly:

"Do not grieve for her! Who knows, but she may have found the joy she sought? Love and patience are all that make for happiness in this world; or in the world of the past or of the future; of the living or the dead. She dreamed her dream; and that is all that any of us can ask!"

ACKNOWLEDGMENTS

Alcott, Louisa May. "Lost in a Pyramid, or The Mummy's Curse," *The New World,* vol. 1, no. 1, January 16, 1869.

An Ancient Egyptian Priest. "The Demon-Possessed Princess" (written c. 300 B.C.). James Henry Breasted, *Ancient Records of Egypt,* vol. 5, Chicago, 1906–1907.

Belzoni, Giovanni Battista. "Raiding Mummies' Tombs," *Narrative Operations and Recent Researches {or Discoveries?} in Egypt and Nubia,* 1820.

Bradbury, Ray. "Colonel Stonesteel's Genuine Home-Made Truly Egyptian Mummy," *Omni* magazine, May 1981. Reprinted by permission of Don Congdon Associates, Inc. Copyright © 1981 by Ray Bradbury.

Carter, Howard, and A. C. Mace. "Opening King Tutankhamen's Tomb," *The Tomb of Tut-Ankh-Amen,* 1923.

Christie, Agatha. "The Adventure of the Egyptian Tomb." Reprinted by permission of Harold Ober Associates Incorporated. From *Poirot Investigates,* Berkley Books. Copyrighted © 1924 by Agatha Christie.

Davis, Theodore. "Raiding Mummies' Tombs," *The Tomb of Iouiya and Touiyou,* 1907.

Doyle, Sir Arthur Conan Doyle. "Lot No. 249," *Harper's,* September 1892.

Edwards, Amelia. "Raiding Mummies' Tombs," *A Thousand Miles Up the Nile,* 1891.

Haggard, Sir H. Rider. "Smith and the Pharoahs," *The Strand,* December 1912.

Kipling, Rudyard. Excerpt from "Dead Kings," a chapter of "Egypt of the Magicians," *The Idler,* 1914.

Lovecraft, H. P. "Under the Pyramids." Copyright © 1924. Reprinted by permission of Arkham House Publishers Inc. and JABberwocky Literary Agency, PO Box 4558, Sunnyside, New York 11104-0558.

Peters, Elizabeth (Barbara Mertz). "The Locked Tomb Mystery." Copyright © 1989 by Elizabeth Peters.

Poe, Edgar Allan. "Some Words with a Mummy," *American Whig Review,* April 1845.

Rice, Anne. Excerpt from *The Mummy or Ramses the Damned* by Anne Rice. Copyright © 1989 by Anne Rice. Reprinted by permission of Ballantine Books, a Division of Random House Inc.

Rohmer, Sax (Arthur Sarsfield Ward). "The Death-Ring of Sneferu," *Tales of Secret Egypt,* 1918.

Stoker, Bram. *The Jewel of Seven Stars* (abridged), 1902.

Twain, Mark. "The Majestic Sphinx," *The Innocents Abroad,* 1869.

Weigall, Arthur. "The Malevolence of Ancient Egyptian Spirits," *Tutankhamen and Other Essays,* 1924.

Williams, Tennessee. "The Vengeance of Nitocris," from *The Collected Stories of Tennessee Williams.* Copyright © 1948 by Tennessee Williams. Reprinted by permission of New Directions Publishing Corp.